T'HUG

Steve Hanson vs The Children of Kali

MATT ANDRUS

Book 2 of The Unexplained, Explained

For my daughter, Maggie,
With Love

Steve Hanson vs The Children of Kali

Book 2 of The Unexplained, Explained

After their labor was over, they offered to return to the Goddess the handkerchiefs with which they had done their work, but she desired them to keep them as the instruments of a trade by which their posterity were to earn their subsistence and to strangle men with these *rumals*, as they had strangled the demons, and live by the plunder they acquired; and having been the means of enabling the world to get provided with men by the destruction of the demons, their posterity would be entitled to take a few for their own use.

William H. Sleeman, from the *Ramaseeana*, 1837

Prologue

India, 1841, south of Cattuck, the town of Gurnah

The corpses of a thousand dead surrounded us.

Captain William Cresswell rubbed his eyes and looked up from his finished report, still finding it difficult to believe, even though it was an account of what he had personally experienced the previous day.

A garish idol of Kali, both beautiful and terrible, presided over the bloody altar.

The t'hug came at me with his tulwar. I parried his cut with my saber, our curved blades an equal match.

Cresswell stood up from the desk and stretched. Outside the window of the small fortress he was in, he could see clouds illuminated by the first hint of dawn. He had been writing all night.

At a little over six feet tall, he towered over most men. Thirty-two years of age, he had dark brown hair and a thick beard. He was still wearing his bright red uniform with white breeches and polished black boots. The breeches had blood stains on them from when he had cut down t'hugs back at the charnel grounds.

It should have been a simple mission. T'huggee was all but

destroyed. Thousands of t'hugs had been imprisoned overseas. Hundreds more had hung from Company gallows. For the past two years, no one had found mutilated bodies of t'hug victims in wells or shallow graves.

But there were rumors of one last group in the frontier region between the East India Company's presidencies of Madras and Bengal.

William Sleeman, founder and Superintendent of the T'huggee Suppression Department out of Jubbalpore, had dispatched Cresswell and Lt. Malcolm to investigate. With them, they had a small detachment of twelve Indian soldiers–sepoys–and Chidoo, the group's approver.

Cresswell looked back out the window. He could see another glow illuminating the darkness— the remains of the t'hugs' temple smoldering from the fire that had destroyed it.

Jackals barked in the distance. With the charnel grounds nearby, the area was thick with them. Cresswell recalled a phrase from the t'hugs secret language, *Ramasee.*

Baean geedee sona leedee. A jackal crossing from right to left brings gold.

The surviving t'hugs would be emboldened when witnessing such an omen, maybe even enough to attack the fort.

Jubbalpore needed to be informed. His report had to get out in case he didn't survive the next few days. But t'hugs watched the fort and roads for Company men. He needed a messenger they wouldn't suspect, someone invisible to even the most astute scouts the enemy had.

He had the perfect man in mind.

Cresswell brought out a long, leather-bound case. He peeled back the velvet interior and hid his report and the page he had torn out of the t'hug's bible underneath it. Restoring the lining, he placed his saber, its blade notched from his earlier duel, inside and shut the case.

A knock came at his door, and the fort's commander strode in. His blue uniform was a stark contrast to Cresswell's red. Captain Jacob Chancellor of the Madras 54th was also shorter than Cresswell, and he kept a few feet between them so he wouldn't have to crane his neck.

Chancellor frowned as he looked over his Bengal counterpart. "My God, did you get any sleep last night?"

"Some," Cresswell lied. The less anyone knew what he planned, the better. "What is the situation outside?"

"The whole town is in an uproar. Many of Gurnah's men are dead back at the *shmashana*. You should hear the women—"

"Two of my sepoys are dead also," Cresswell interrupted. "Those men we killed were t'hugs. Do you know much about t'huggee?"

Chancellor shook his head.

Cresswell wasn't surprised. T'huggee was mostly a Bengal phenomenon.

"Killing is in their blood, and it runs in their families. If the father is a murderous t'hug, then so is the son. This whole town must be infested with them." Cresswell pronounced the word as *toog*.

"What do we do next?" Chancellor asked. His eyes were wide as he looked back over his shoulder as if he were expecting t'hugs to jump out of the room's shadows and start strangling him.

"Those reinforcements you mentioned earlier should be here mid-morning. When they arrive, we will search the town. I have an approver with me, a former t'hug, who, for a lighter sentence, will identify any t'hug at large."

"What about the local's basic rights, the law—"

"The laws have changed. Approver testimony alone is enough now. And if the local leader, the town's *zamindar*—" Cresswell looked questioningly at Chancellor.

"Vankatesan," Chancellor filled in.

"Is proven to be harboring t'hugs, then his property is forfeited."

"What are your plans with the t'hugs that you capture?"

Cresswell looked grim. "Their horrid profession is irresistible to them, Chancellor—their taste for blood indelible and will never be eradicated while life exists."

Chancellor nodded his understanding as he made his leave. Cresswell followed him out, his sword case in hand. Chancellor had duties to attend to, and the two men parted ways in the fort's courtyard. Cresswell headed for the stable, informing the sentry posted there that he was checking on his horse. Once inside, though, he went to where Debun was sleeping.

Cresswell had just met the man yesterday when he rescued him from t'hugs, an act that had started the previous day's nightmarish events.

Cresswell bent over the small Indian. The man was a *chamar*, a low-caste leatherworker. A person no one would normally touch or let alone notice.

Perfect.

Cresswell shook him awake.

Debun's hands went up to his neck, where a red welt now encircled.

"Debun, it's just me," Cresswell explained in Hindustani.

"Captain?"

"I need your help, Debun."

"Anything, I am in your debt."

Cresswell handed him the sword case and a coin purse. Debun's eyes widened when he felt the purse's weight.

"My sword was damaged, and I wish to send it back to my home in Calcutta for repair," Cresswell said. "Can you carry it for me?"

"Yes, Captain." The *chamar* looked pleased that he could do something so crucial for Cresswell.

"Keep it hidden in the leathers you are carrying. When you reach my home, hand the case to my valet. Tell him this message: 'Look under the velvet.'"

Cresswell said the phrase in English. Debun didn't need to understand what he was truly carrying. He had Debun repeat the message several times.

"Your life depends on secrecy," Cresswell added.

"When do you wish me to leave?"

"Today."

* * *

Chancellor's reinforcements arrived as scheduled. To Cresswell's relief, they were all British regulars. Outside of his sepoys, Cresswell didn't trust anyone with Indian blood running through their veins.

Chancellor didn't give his men time to rest but instead prepared them to search the town. Helping Chancellor with this was his sixteen-year-old son, Alex, a "pension boy" learning to be a soldier by his father's side.

Cresswell had his men up also. His small support train of three wagons, along with the Indians and *bishti* water carriers that accompanied it, stayed behind in the fort. With his ten sepoys and Lt. Malcolm, the search party numbered more than sixty men, all armed with Brown Bess muskets.

More than enough.

As they took to the streets, Cresswell noticed with satisfaction that though men watched them from every doorway, no one paid attention to Debun as he left town.

The sepoys rounded up the men of Gurnah. They made each villager stand in front of a one-eyed Indian with iron fetters on his legs. Each time, though, Chidoo would shake his head.

Cresswell frowned. "Chidoo doesn't recognize any of them."

His ranking sepoy, a tall Indian with a thoughtful face, spoke up. "I am not surprised, Captain," Dhuuna said. "We came here looking for Goulah t'hugs. What we faced yesterday was not low-caste cattle thieves."

The sun rose higher as the search progressed. Cresswell was considering calling for a break to let the men rest from the heat when Dhuuna approached him.

"Captain, Lt. Malcolm has found their hiding place."

* * *

Dhuuna led Cresswell to a building that looked like a warehouse. It had a gated courtyard large enough to park several wagons. Chancellor was stationing men around it.

Cresswell strode inside, taking a moment for his eyes to adjust to the dark. He was expecting t'hugs hiding in some hay or piles of fabric stolen from some merchant. He wasn't prepared for what he saw.

Treasure.

It was as the cavern from *Ali Baba and the Forty Thieves*. The warehouse was stacked with open crates that exposed what was inside them.

Countless gold coins, plates, and vases. Strands of pearls hung over the edges of some of the crates. Others held statues made of ivory, trimmed with gold and encrusted with gems.

Lt. Malcolm turned to him.

"They resisted, but we forced our way. We couldn't believe what we saw when we opened the crates," Malcolm said.

Cresswell ran a hand through the gold, feeling its weight.

"There's more, Captain," Malcolm added.

He led Cresswell to more crates toward the back. They held spheres that looked to be made from some sort of dark beeswax. They were wrapped in leaves for transport.

Opium.

The East India Company (EIC) had a massive opium operation in India, accounting for about 20 percent of Company revenue, mostly from trade with China. Chests like these were in high demand and belonged in a Calcutta warehouse, not out here on the frontier.

Someone was making a lot of money.

There was shouting outside. A hostile crowd was forming beyond the courtyard wall.

"Lieutenant, get back out there and shut the doors behind you. Make sure the perimeter is secure. If those men are going to make a move, it's going to be soon."

Malcolm saluted and left, the room darkening as the doors were closed. Cresswell turned back to the few men that remained. Chancellor and his son, along with three Madras British soldiers, were ogling the treasure.

"Chancellor, have your men seal all of this back up. Let's try to find out where it was going."

Chancellor gave orders to his men, and they moved to the crates in the back of the room. Cresswell turned to his sepoy.

"Dhuuna, see if there's another way out of here."

The sepoy moved toward a large door, sliding it to the side. It revealed a small storeroom—and the thing hidden there.

Kali.

The wooden idol stood ten feet tall. Her skin was painted a dark blue, and her carved face held a visage of rage. The eyes were blazing red, as were her lips and the long tongue that hung out between ivory fangs. A round ruby glittered on her forehead. Her hair was black and hung down to her waist unbridled. Her chest was bare, and a tiger skin girdled her waist.

She had four arms, and each bore a weapon. The upper pair held tulwars, curved swords like his saber. Their tips almost touched each other above her head. Her lower right hand held a khadga, a smaller straight blade with a crescent wedge on its end. The lower left hand held a pale-yellow loop of cloth. It was a *rumal,* the weapon of the t'hugs.

One other feature stood out. Hanging from the elbows of the upper arms were two diamonds, each about the size of a dove's egg, and they sparkled even in the room's dim lantern light. Tear-drop shaped, they looked as if they could slide off her arms like beads of water at any moment.

The diamonds confirmed it for Cresswell. It was the same statue he had seen during yesterday's encounter. The t'hugs had rescued their idol from the burning temple and brought it here. Cresswell smiled to himself. More proof to show Jubbalpore of the t'hugs' ungodly ways.

After opening the door, Dhuuna had stumbled back in fear and turned toward Cresswell. The look of fear on Dhuuna's face turned to one of confusion as he gazed at his commander.

The Indian reached for his rifle slung over his shoulder. He raised it and aimed at Cresswell's head. Cresswell barely had time to utter one last word in shock at what was happening.

"Dhuuna—" Cresswell said, his voice laced with disappointment.

The sepoy fired. The rifle's report was deafening inside the room, so Cresswell felt, rather than heard, the slug pass inches by his right cheek.

Dhunna had missed. He was now dropping his rifle and drawing his saber.

Nearby, Chancellor drew his pistol and fired. Dhuuna collapsed to the ground.

Cresswell was going for his pistol also, but when he saw the Madras officer shoot his traitorous sepoy, he instead nodded his appreciation. Cresswell turned and looked over his right shoulder to see if Dhuuna's bullet had hit anything.

One of Chancellor's men was on the ground, as Dhuuna had shot him in the middle of his forehead. But another detail dominated Cresswell's attention.

The soldier had a length of cloth in his hands.

A *rumal*.

Cresswell spun back toward Chancellor. He and his son were standing nearby with broad smiles. Cresswell went for his pistol again.

Hands grabbed him from behind. The remaining two Madras soldiers had come up back from his left. Each held a wrist and placed a hand on his shoulder. Twisting his arms behind him, they forced him down. With a grunt of pain, Cresswell fell to his knees.

Chancellor came forward and relieved Cresswell of his pistol. His son moved past Kali to a back door in the building and opened it.

A half-dozen Chinese men entered; their faces hidden by wide-brim straw hats. They moved to the stored opium.

A tall Indian dressed in a delicate white robe, his black hair cut short, strode in behind them. A firm jawline, piercing dark eyes, and high cheekbones lent him a noble appearance. Cresswell had seen him before.

The t'hug who had made the sacrifice back at the temple, and most likely, the region's *zamindar*.

Vankatesan.

He was carrying the religious tome that had been at the temple, along with another large book. After bowing to Kali, he placed both on a table.

Cresswell looked at them, surprised that the second book was one that he knew well.

A copy of the *Ramaseeana*, Sleeman's treatise on t'hugs and their secret language.

"I understand you've been searching for me," Vankatesan said.

"My men are outside, t'hug," Cresswell growled. "And they heard the gunshot. There is no escape this time."

Vankatesan didn't look worried. Instead, he pointed toward the large front doors. Alex opened them.

Cresswell's jaw dropped as his face took on an expression of disbelief and despair.

All his men lay dead. Three of Chancellor's men were gathered around each one, one man on the prone victim's back, his *rumal* tight around the neck, while another man held the wrists. The third was behind, holding the ankles.

Cresswell stared, unable to comprehend that it wasn't Indians who had strangled his men but British soldiers. Thinking allies surrounded them, Cresswell's men never had a chance.

Even Chidoo wasn't spared. Cresswell could see the approver lying amongst his men, a surprised look on his face.

Cresswell turned toward Chancellor.

"Chancellor! In God's name, why?"

In answer, Chancellor strolled over to one of the crates. He dipped his hand into it and scooped up a handful of gold coins. He let them fall through his fingers.

"When I signed up back in England to fight for God, Queen and country, they paid me twenty shillings," Chancellor answered as he let the tinkle of each falling coin accentuate his response. "Here, in India, Vankatesan has shown me a better way."

The last gold coin fell into the crate.

"I follow a new god now, Captain."

Cresswell looked back outside. The soldiers were turning the bodies over and bringing out daggers. They were preparing to gouge out the eyes of the corpses. It was the t'hugs way of making sure all were indeed dead.

"Stop, we need their clothing unstained," Vankatesan shouted. "Remove their uniforms. After that, you may dispose of them."

The Madras soldiers put away their daggers and continued their task of stripping Cresswell's men.

Cresswell watched, outrage consuming him.

"What do you need their uniforms for?"

Vankatesan gestured to the crates and Kali.

"All of us, and this wealth, are sailing to England. Here in India, people will witness men of the T'huggee Department boarding the *Deptford*. Unfortunately, *Deptford* will never reach Calcutta. She, along with the men of the T'huggee Department, will be reported missing at sea. Meanwhile, *Deptford* will be rechristened *Plymouth* and arrive in England three months from now."

While Chancellor was talking, a tall and handsome teenaged boy walked into the room. He was dressed in a flowing white robe and had a yellow sash around his waist. He joined Vankatesan.

"My son, Sheodeen," Vankatesan announced proudly.

Cresswell could see the resemblance. "You, your son, and your fellow Indians are going to have a hard time being accepted in England," he said.

"Trust me, Captain, all men are the same. This gold will overcome all prejudices."

"Is that how you got all of these men to forsake God?"

Vankatesan knelt close to Cresswell, eye to eye. He switched languages. "Do you speak Hindustani?"

Puzzled, Cresswell nodded.

"That is refreshing," Vankatesan continued in his native language. He briefly looked at the men holding Cresswell. "These days, most Europeans can't be bothered, so I can safely answer your question. Everyone here believes that I am a prophet."

"How?"

"My family has always been a powerful one. Our wealth rose from the opium smuggling we did out of the nearby port and the tribute our t'hugs brought to us from the roads. We Vankatesans even rubbed shoulders with the Mughal emperors of the Peacock Throne. For centuries we have been looked to for leadership in politics and religion."

Vankatesan paused as if remembering past days of glory. He looked back at Cresswell.

"Then the Company arrived. With that came change. Soon, it wasn't Mohammedans but Christians I was paying to look the other way. That's how I met Chancellor here."

Cresswell grimaced at that. Such graft was common amongst Company men.

"But Sleeman and his Suppression Department were closing in on my family's operations. To save their own necks, t'hugs were confessing everything. I knew it was only a matter of time before Sleeman found me.

"I asked Chancellor what more we could do. But he was also frightened, for the net was tightening on him and his men also since they were neck-deep in my opium smuggling operation." Vankatesan glanced toward the Chinese men busy securing the drug-filled crates.

"He told me he could do nothing, for the men of the Company believed that they were in the right and that their powerful, wrathful God gave them purpose. I believed him, and I reasoned that if I were to continue in my ways, my t'hugs, and all who worked with me, would need a wrathful god of their own to follow."

Vankatesan looked over at the copy of the *Ramaseeana*.

"And I found one."

"What in bloody hell are you talking about?" Cresswell growled. "Kali has always been the driving force behind t'huggee."

"It's never been about religion, Cresswell; it's been about wealth," Vankatesan replied. "Something you and your superiors have never been able to grasp. However, I felt that the change to worshipping Kali would be an easy one if I made a few concessions." Vankatesan now looked at his bible.

"A blend of Eastern and Western ideologies, made more palatable with gold for those who follow me—Kali's one, true prophet!"

"A prophet of death! I've seen your temple, Vankatesan," Cresswell replied as he glanced at the statue over Vankatesan's shoulder. "So I witnessed how you were trying to appease your dark god—"

The t'hug leaned forward, his teeth bared and his eyes flashing with rage.

"Really? Then tell me, Captain, when they hung some t'hugs a few years back and then cut off their heads and shipped their skulls back to England, what god were you trying to appease?"

Cresswell was taken aback. "That wasn't God. That was science."

"Ah yes, science," the t'hug said as he backed off, his face serene again. "Your belief that we Indians are born to murder. That it is passed on from father to son, like the shape of our faces."

"It's been proven," Cresswell replied. "You t'hugs have a natural inclination for the work of death."

Vankatesan shrugged. "Believe what you will; I subscribe to a different theory—that we are all are born to a clean slate."

Vankatesan stood up and paced about the room. He stopped near his son and put his hand on the boy's shoulder, who was looking at Cresswell with anticipation. Vankatesan switched back to English.

"I believe that a man is not born to kill but that he must be taught."

Both Indians were staring at Cresswell. Then the t'hug leader turned toward Chancellor.

"Captain, how old is your son?" Vankatesan asked.

"He is sixteen."

"And how is his training coming along?"

"He has been observing since he was twelve, and he has been a handler twice this past year," Chancellor answered proudly.

"Then it is time, Captain, time for him to take up the office of *bhurtote*."

Cresswell could see the disappointment in Sheodeen's face, and he watched grimly as young Chancellor unraveled his blue cummerbund from around his waist and approached him. Cresswell knew what was to happen next, for he was familiar with the term.

Bhurtote. Strangler.

The boy appeared nervous as he circled behind. Cresswell turned toward Chancellor.

"Chancellor, he's your son, for God's sake! Stop this!" Cresswell shouted.

Chancellor didn't answer. Vankatesan spoke up instead.

"We will do it the traditional way. Alex, wait for my signal."

Cresswell could hear the boy twisting his *rumal* to make it more rope-like.

Vankatesan was making exaggerated movements in front of him like he was performing on a stage. He turned his back on Cresswell.

Cresswell, on his knees already, did the only thing he had left.

He prayed.

He first prayed for forgiveness. He had killed men for his Queen and country. He hoped God didn't hold that against him.

Vankatesan, seeing everyone was in position out of the corner of his eye, patted his robe. He produced a pipe as he turned around. He uttered the *jhirnee*, the t'hug signal phrase to strike.

"Bring the tobacco."

The *rumal* passed in front of Cresswell's face and settled around his neck. It tightened painfully.

Unable to breathe, Cresswell spent the next moment praying for his wife and son. He asked God to watch over them in his absence.

Then he prayed for Debun.

A part of his mind was aware of how strange it was to not focus his last thoughts on his beloved son and beautiful and devoted wife of ten years and instead direct them to a man he had just met the previous day. A man who was considered the lowest of the low. Untouchable.

Cresswell's blood was now roaring in his ears, and darkness crowded the edge of vision. He glanced up. Kali looked like she was mocking his prayers as her face leered over Vankatesan's shoulder. Behind him, the boy put a foot on his back so that he could pull with more vigor, like he was tying up a bundle of straw.

Helpless anger consumed Cresswell, but he focused on his praying —silently begging God that somewhere, somehow, his final message would find its way into the right hands.

And then the darkness at the edge of his eyesight filled his whole vision, and Cresswell's world ended.

Part One

BELE

Chapter 1

Present day

Clackamas County, Oregon, Saturday, 10:11 a.m.

The cow was in bad shape.

Hanson wasn't surprised. It was why he had been summoned here.

The animal was lying on its side in the dry grass, its head bent toward its back, the legs unnaturally askew. Entrails were spilled out in a wet mass from a long slit in its underbelly. Hanson circled the black-and-white Holstein and found its eyes gouged out. On the backside, its udder and genitalia were intact. Large black flies hovered lazily over the carcass warming up under the September morning sun.

"A real cattle mutilation, and so close by—" Hanson began, unable to contain his excitement. He looked over at the dairy farmer standing near him. Ben Tully looked like he didn't share his enthusiasm.

"I mean, I'm sorry for your loss," Hanson added. That didn't sound right either. "Your financial loss, that is," he finished lamely.

"Going to be a hassle to replace," Tully replied as he nudged one of the cow's back legs with the toe of his boot. The broken limb fell into a more normal-looking position. The dairyman looked up, his gaze studying Hanson as if he were appraising him one more time.

Both men were in their early fifties stood a little less than six feet tall. The similarities ended there. The stocky dairy farmer's face looked like creased leather, while white hair peeked out from underneath a worn baseball cap with a cattle feed supplier's logo.

Hanson had a slimmer physique. His dark hair was still thick and full, though it had a touch of gray. Bright green eyes, a clean-cut face, and a boyish grin made Hanson look ten years younger than Tully.

"Have you seen anything like this before?" Gary asked.

Hanson glanced at Tully's son, who had accompanied them on the quarter-mile hike up the hill rising above the dairy farm. Blond, tall, and lanky, the teen looked like a younger version of his father. Gary had his cell phone out, and he was taking selfies with the cow in the background.

"Only in photographs and television specials," Hanson answered as he circled the cow again. He snapped off his own pictures with his phone's camera, and he knelt to get some close-ups.

"You do this for a living?" the teen asked.

"It's a hobby," Hanson replied as he looked up from the cow's pile of organs. "I follow unusual events for my blog, *The Unexplained, Explained*. It's how your dad found me."

"I looked up cattle mutilations right after I called the sheriff. Your website had an article detailing the recent increase in mutilations in eastern Oregon. Your bio said you lived in the Portland area," Tully senior said.

Hanson grunted in acknowledgment as he stood back up. An alert had chimed on his phone when Tully had reached out through his blog's email earlier that morning.

"I looked up mutilations too. Some people think aliens do this. Do you believe that?" Gary asked.

The kid hadn't read his blog though. "No, I'm more of a skeptic. I try to look for a more rational reason when something unusual happens."

"So, what's the deal with cattle mutilations?"

"Back in the seventies, ranchers in the Midwest began reporting a spike in cattle dying unnaturally."

"The seventies? That's like ancient history."

Both men frowned at the teenager as Hanson continued. "It was the long slit in the underbelly that had everyone excited."

Gary had his camera pointed at the wet mass of entrails. "It looks like it was done with a scalpel," he observed.

"That's what most people thought," Hanson replied. "Surgical precision. No marauding animal could make a wound like that. Only organ-hunting aliens, satanic cults, or government agents in black suits and riding black helicopters could be responsible."

"If it wasn't them doing it, then how?"

"Have you ever ripped a sheet in half?"

"Yeah."

"Sheets tear in a straight line when you apply an opposing force on it. It's the same here, only it's the stress of bloating that causes the tear. Ranchers back in the seventies thought their livestock were being dissected. They didn't realize the cows were just bursting open because of natural forces."

"Other websites also talk about the cows missing their eyes, organs, and even the anus." Gary challenged, though he was smiling when he said the last part.

"Scavengers don't tear through a cow's tough hide for the filet mignon. They go for areas of easier access," Hanson replied.

Gary was looking at the cow's back end. "No way, that's too gross."

"Don't believe me? Look up the 'hyena eating elephant' video."

Gary's thumbs flew on his phone. The kid exclaimed in dismay as he watched the video.

"That hyena stuck his whole head in there, up to his shoulders! That's not right."

"The unexplained, explained," Hanson said with a grin.

Ben Tully was at the cow's head, rocking it back and forth. The neck had been broken.

Hanson's amused smile disappeared when he saw that. He knelt by one of the cow's legs and shifted it around also. It moved easily back and forth. It, too, had been broken at the joint.

"Ever seen anything like that on television?" Tully asked.

"A few times in the more unusual cases," Hanson answered. "And the bloating thing happens when the animal is found after a few days. You told me this happened last night."

Tully was silent, his face grim.

"Someone attacked your cow," Hanson finished, and he could guess what was on the rancher's mind.

A man with a knife was on the property last night.

"I thought so too. I just wanted a second opinion from someone who's studied this shit before," Tully replied.

Both men stood up from the animal. Hanson looked around. They were on top of a hill of dry pasture. The ranch itself was a quarter-mile north. A paved highway could be seen winding below a few hundred yards to the south.

"Do you mind if I walk down to the road?" Hanson asked.

Tully, on the phone with his vet, nodded absently. Hanson started down the hill and kept an eye out for signs of the cow killer. In some spots, where the earth was softer, human footprints going in both directions could be seen.

The sun was higher in the sky now, and Hanson unzipped his gray hoodie. As he walked, he kept the tracks to his left. The last thing he wanted was a sheriff's deputy in his face acting upset about ruined evidence.

A gully was forming on his right. It developed into a deep cut that ended at a culvert passing beneath the highway. The fence angled a bit up the gully, its wires crossing the ditch where it wasn't as pronounced.

The V shape in the fence caught Hanson's attention. It created a space where a car could drive off the highway and tuck in amongst some trees.

He glanced at the highway shoulder. Someone had pulled off the road. The vehicle's tires had left parallel lines that led into a gap between the tree trunks.

Hanson aimed his phone's camera lens, feeling a bit let down as he took photos of the car tracks. He had told the Tullys that he was a skeptic, but the truth was, a part of him still wanted to believe. Hanson had come out here hoping for cows with missing hearts and scorched circles where alien spacecraft had landed. Instead, he had the tire tracks of some crazy dude who didn't like cattle. *Had a beef with cows.* Hanson spent a few moments updating his blog from his phone.

With his photos uploaded, Hanson turned to leave but stopped when something on the other side of the fence caught his eye. There was a splash of blue amongst the dried brush in the gully. He couldn't tell what the source was from his side of the fence, though it felt out of place. Curious, he spread the strands of barbed wire and carefully squeezed through the gap. Closer, and at a better angle, he could see that it was a pair of blue denim pants.

That had the shirtless body of a man still in them.

Hanson reeled back in horror.

The man was in worse shape than the cow.

Chapter 2

The man was on his side, his abdomen cut open. Internal organs, more recognizable than the cow's, had spilled out onto the dry weeds. Limbs rested at unnatural angles, and ruined eyes stared sightlessly as large flies gathered on the corpse.

Unlike the cow, though, deep cuts were all over the pale chest and arms, as if some maniac had rushed the man with a large knife, stabbing while the victim put up his hands in defense. Hanson couldn't tell if the stab wounds included the neck. The victim had a thick, dark beard. Dried blood caked the earth under the body.

Lightheaded, Hanson stumbled back to the fence and pushed through it recklessly. He could feel the barbs tug at his clothes and scratch his skin. Like the last guy getting out of the water in a sea full of sharks, Hanson panicked a bit. He fell out the other side, scooting backward while still on the ground, panting in fear.

A feeling of déjà vu rolled over him, as if he had experienced the scenario before. The sensation surprised him, and he focused on it as he stood back up. As a kid, he used to consider déjà vu a superpower. Seeing the future. Precognition. As an adult, he had studied the phenomena for his blog.

The word itself was French, meaning "already seen." Science was still unsure what caused it, with theories ranging from microsecond differences in brain hemispheres communicating with one another to the mind picking up on familiar stimuli.

Hanson passed it off to his recent viewing of the cow, and as he did when he was younger, he made a prediction as to what would happen next.

A white truck will come around the corner on the highway.

No vehicles at all approached. Realizing he had to report what he had found, Hanson gave up on seeing the future and started back up the hill.

Tully was still there when Hanson arrived out of breath. The kid was gone, already halfway down the homestead side of the hill and passing a sheriff's deputy who was walking their way. Both men could see Gary pause long enough to show the deputy some images on his phone.

Tully frowned. "Going to be a circus around here," he said.

"It's worse than you think," Hanson added shakily.

* * *

By noon, the highway below was crowded with police cars and large mobile crime scene trucks. White news vans with satellite dishes mounted on them added to the congestion. Hanson turned back to the mutilated cow. Yellow police tape marked off a thirty-foot-diameter circle around what was now a major crime scene. One lone deputy stood guard. Tully was at the road below being interviewed by the authorities.

Hanson thought about his own interview an hour earlier with grim-faced county deputies who wanted to know everything about him.

He had rambled as his anxiety level spiked. The entire morning had been difficult for him since his usual routine was to stay secluded in the safety of his own home. Even meeting the Tullys had been a challenge, the anxiety he felt was akin to the heart-racing moment of waiting for one's turn during roll call. Talking to the authorities was like making a speech in front of a thousand people.

Hanson gave his life story, explaining that he had grown up in Astoria. After high school, he joined the Marines, as his father had before him. Discharged with honor and enrolled at Portland State University, which led to a job as IT support at a Cosgrove's supermarket.

He would have gone on about his ex-wife and daughter, but the deputies had steered him to his blog. What did he know about cattle mutilations?

Hanson gave the same story he gave the Tullys, showing them his call logs, the email that had brought him out here, and his latest blog entree. It included an image of the cow he had posted only hours earlier. They asked him to take it down, not post any details or photos about the crime, and wait while they corroborated his story.

It didn't take long. Tully must have told them the same thing, and Hanson heard the deputy on guard duty receive the go-ahead on his radio to let him leave.

Hanson turned away, eager to go. He was feeling drained and needed to get home to recharge. He took a few steps but stopped short.

A woman, already halfway up the hill, was approaching.

Even at that distance, he could see that she was beautiful. She was tall and had long, straight blonde hair pulled back in a ponytail. She looked to be in her mid-forties. She was striding up the hill, picking her way through the pasture with confidence. Her attire was tan leather boots, jeans, and a blue button-up shirt with the sleeves rolled up.

Hanson postponed his departure and reached for his phone. He wanted to avoid the awkwardness of two people closing in on each other over a long distance. Do you look at them or pretend to stare at something interesting in the distance? Smile? Nod your head? Say something? Or keep on walking in silence? It was always an agonizing ten to twenty seconds.

He held his phone up to his face and pretended he was texting.

The woman was now skirting around the police tape toward him. Though he looked busy on his phone, Hanson was using the time to think of something clever to say, discarding opening lines as soon as he thought of them. She was now close enough for him to see that she had clear blue eyes. She was looking straight at him, so he opened his mouth to say something.

"What are you doing here?" the deputy asked as he stepped between Hanson and the woman.

Though she at first appeared surprised by the intrusion, the woman quickly adapted. "Hello, Officer," she said with a bright smile. "My name is Samantha Ramsell. I'm a reporter. I had heard of some livestock being attacked. Can you tell me anything of what happened here last night?"

"You shouldn't be up here; there was a homicide at the road below. This whole area is a major crime scene."

"Are you saying the crimes are related?" she asked.

"That's all I can say, ma'am."

Hanson, watching them talk, realized that at the moment, he was forgotten. He tried to work up some righteous indignation at the deputy for screwing up his opportunity to dazzle the blonde but could only muster a faint sense of gratitude. This moment would now be one that he could look back on and wonder "what if," rather than cringe at what would inevitably have been an epic failure.

He took advantage that no one was no paying attention to him and turned to leave. The reporter's and deputy's conversation became indistinct as he circled to the far side of the cow. He thought he heard the deputy's radio crackle as he started down the hill.

The woman's voice rang out behind him.

"Excuse me!"

Though he thought it unlikely that she was talking to him, he turned. The deputy was gone, having been called away. The woman was still there, her beauty incongruous next to the carcass at her feet. Her blue eyes were looking straight at him again.

"Is your name Steve Hanson?"

Chapter 3

Hanson froze for a moment, trying to think of how this reporter knew his name. She did look familiar.

Christ, did I forget her name?

How could I?

Defeated, he answered. "Yes. But I'm sorry, have we met?"

She was strolling around the police tape's perimeter. "No, but I do get that a lot. I used to anchor the news on one of the local TV stations."

That jogged his memory. She had been a popular television presence. "I thought you transferred away."

"I stayed in the area; I just gave up broadcast," she answered. She was still walking.

Hanson realized then that he had also been walking, subconsciously keeping the eviscerated cow between the two of them. His usual nervousness around new people manifesting a defense. He forced himself to stop and do an about-face so that he would approach her.

"Do you work for a paper?"

Samantha shook her head. "I freelance now. I contribute to that national news blog, *Left Unsaid.*"

Hanson was impressed. She most likely had a considerable following.

He looked down the hill toward the news organizations kept at bay by the police.

"How did you know to come up the back way? And find me, for that matter?"

"I have a police scanner app on my phone," she answered, holding up her cell to emphasize the point. "I heard the county sheriff's code for a body found just off the highway."

"But there was something else," she added as she glanced at the cow. "A bit earlier, the same sheriff's office had a call about someone killing and mutilating a cow at Triangle T Ranch. An online map showed the ranch bordering the highway. That let me know to come up this way. But I didn't know much about cattle mutilations."

"So, you explored further online and found what I posted this morning on my blog," Hanson guessed.

"*The Unexplained, Explained*," she affirmed, with just the barest hint of a smile. Hanson wondered at the visual cue. Did it mean she liked it or that she was amused at his little blog?

"You're lucky you caught my post. The sheriff already had me pull it down."

"Really? They wouldn't ask that unless there was some sort of connection with the murder case."

"Well...um—"

"I have a few friends on the road below. The police are saying that someone local, driving home late last night, was most likely slain after pulling up behind someone else already stopped on the roadside."

Hanson shifted from foot to foot, not looking her in the eye. He was wondering how angry the police would be if they knew he was talking to a reporter.

She noticed his discomfort.

"You're the one who found the body."

"Yes."

"And you feel the two events here are related."

"Yes." *Damn*. He was still shuffling around. He forced himself to stand still and look up at her so that he could meet her gaze.

Too late. She was staring at the bull's gouged eyes instead.

"But it's more than just proximity that ties the two together," she said as she turned back to him and studied his face. "The police aren't saying what happened to the victim."

Hanson didn't say anything, but his eyes must have darted toward the internal organs on display nearby.

"The murder victim is mutilated like the cow, isn't he?"

The defeated expression on Hanson's face told her all. She was dancing mental circles around him.

She smiled again. "Relax; a reporter never reveals her sources."

She looked at cow's broken limbs and made another guess.

"It must have been terrible to find the body."

Hanson, giving in, answered. "It was."

"Any idea as to how they were killed?"

"The dairy farmer had a vet out here for an initial necropsy, but he won't know for sure for a while. My guess is that the bull was somehow tranquilized and then killed with a knife."

"How about the man?"

"That's easier. The victim had defensive wounds on his arms," Hanson answered, thinking about all of the cop shows he watched on TV. "I think the psycho attacked him with the same knife."

Samantha was busy typing in the information as fast as Hanson provided it. When she finished, she switched to another screen. She frowned as she read what was there.

"My competition below has discovered that the dairy farmer has a son with a Twitter account. They know about the cow. They are also jumping on the kid's tweets that the cow was ritualistically cut up by a satanic cult."

Hanson shook his head. He'd thought he convinced Gary that wasn't the case.

"Do you think it was devil worshippers?"

She looked downcast now. He guessed it was because now everyone knew about the cow, and she had just lost her edge on the story.

"I wouldn't go with that angle."

"Why not?"

"Because Satanism isn't as widespread as everyone thinks," Hanson replied. "You look like you were a little young to remember the satanic moral panic of the eighties."

"Moral panic? You mean like the UFO crisis last year?"

Hanson kept the alarm he was now feeling off his face. He had been in the middle of that fiasco. He had also been commanded by the president herself to not reveal his involvement. He needed to steer Samantha back to the case at hand.

"No, this is different. A moral panic is the masses worked up about some hidden danger. Like the witch-hunts in Europe and Salem, Massachusetts."

"That was a long time ago, and people back then were a superstitious lot."

"It still happens. Accusations were made against a daycare center several decades ago. Children were saying that they were being ritually abused by Satanists. People went bananas. Soon, hundreds of kids all over the country were telling tales of being molested and raped in dark basements with pentagrams and sacrificed animals on nearby altars. Adults under hypnosis spoke of repressed memories of the same thing."

"People believed all that?"

"Yes, and it got even crazier. Churches and media guessed that the number of practicing devil worshippers in the states was over a million. At the panic's peak, some were talking about a worldwide conspiracy, with the powerful brainwashing our kids, preparing them to take over the planet in the name of Satan."

Her eyebrows were raised. "How did it end?"

Hanson gestured to the dried manure around him.

"It was all bullshit. People took a hard look at the social workers interviewing the children and realized that they were asking leading questions and guiding them to give false answers with anatomically correct dolls. They were making up a threat that wasn't there."

Samantha was still frowning and didn't look convinced.

"Look, before you print your story, all I am saying is that thirty years ago people went to extraordinary efforts to find devil worshippers up to no good. They didn't find any. You should at least consider that."

The frown was gone, and now she was looking straight at him. "I will," she replied.

Hanson noticed that the deputy was returning. Time to go. He debated if he should offer his number, maybe under the pretense of helping her out with her story in the future.

She beat him to the punch. "Let's exchange phone numbers," she suggested as she brushed aside a lock of blonde hair that had worked free from her ponytail. "Just in case I have any more questions."

They leaned in close together with their phones. Hanson could smell the barest hint of her perfume. He was expecting her phone's wallpaper to have an image of a boyfriend, but instead, it contained a picture of an older couple. Her parents? His cell phone had his two cats side by side on a fence. He could see her faint smile again out of the corner of his eye as they tapped in each other's digits.

She turned away to face the officer approaching. "Thanks again," she said, over her shoulder.

"No problem," Hanson replied as he started down the hill, his mind not on the mystery of a mutilated cow and gruesome murder, but instead on how he should have said something better than "no problem."

Chapter 4

Suburbs of Washington DC, Saturday, 10:22 p.m. EDT

Arthur was about to text Marcia back when he saw two men walking up the sidewalk toward him. For time's sake, he decided to do the one thing that all men hated to do.

Ask for directions.

Based in Atlanta, he was in DC for a realtor convention. Mostly. He was also here to cheat on his wife. He had hooked up with Marcia on a website designed for extra-marital affairs, trading photos and messages with her. At thirty-five years of age and a full head of blond hair, Arthur still felt he had what it takes to play the field.

But the same technology that made it easy to find Marcia also made it difficult to hide his infidelity. Phones, Ubers, and credit card statements could be tracked. This was why Arthur found himself in the parking lot of a DC Applebee's with a crappy off-brand burner phone that couldn't find the tavern that Marcia had decided would be a better meeting place.

The two men were nearby. They were clean-cut-looking guys in white collared shirts with silk ties and dark fall jackets to ward off the night's chill. Both appeared to be in their early thirties. One was tall, his hair longish and blond. The other was slightly smaller, looked Indian, and had short, dark hair.

Swallowing his pride, Arthur approached them. "Excuse me; I'm looking for a bar. Could any of you tell me where *The Bard* is?"

Though he looked a bit surprised at being approached by a stranger, the shorter man smiled back and pointed vaguely behind Arthur. "The new place? It's about twelve blocks that way."

"Wrong," the blond guy replied as he rolled his eyes. He pointed in a different direction. "I think it's more to the east."

"I was close," the Indian grinned. "Look, we're both heading that general direction ourselves, and I'm sure that between us, we can find it. Do you want to walk over with us?"

It was late, and Arthur was in a dark, unfamiliar city. Having some locals guide him along the way seemed like a good idea. He studied both a bit more closely. Nothing seemed off with the two men.

"That would be great."

Introductions were made. The Indian's name was Sanjay. He explained that he and his friend Todd had just left the retirement party of another coworker and were looking to continue their night out.

Sanjay and Todd kept up their good-natured argument on the tavern's location, though the topic soon shifted to Todd and his effort of buying his first home.

Arthur, feeling more at ease since he could contribute to the conversation, lent some home-purchasing advice now and then.

The three men turned right onto a side street, following Sanjay's lead. Arthur saw that it was dark and deserted.

"I think I've led us astray," Sanjay muttered, his head turning back and forth in confusion.

Todd pulled out his phone and fell back a bit as he focused on it. "Don't worry, I'll look it up," he said.

Ahead of them, a man rounded the corner and approached them. Arthur's group had stopped near an alley, dark since the streetlight was broken. The guy's clothes were worn and tattered, and Arthur felt reassured that he had let these two men accompany him.

Sanjay stepped forward. A few feet away, the man stopped, wary.

"Hey, sorry to bother you, we're lost. Do you know where *The Bard* is?" Sanjay asked.

The stranger's stance relaxed, and his expression softened. Arthur wasn't sure, but he seemed to be of Indian descent, like Sanjay.

"Go back up the street and cross the main drag," the man answered, pointing back behind them. "It's in the other direction."

"Thanks," Sanjay replied as he turned to smile at Arthur. "I guess Todd was right all along."

"I can see how someone could get lost," the other man continued, glancing upward, "It's so dark around here you can even see the stars tonight." He patted his pockets and pulled out a lighter.

"Can I bum any of you guys for a cigarette?"

Arthur, who had reflexively looked up, opened his mouth to reply, but his answer was cut short when he felt something wrap around this neck and tighten. His hands clawed briefly at the noose. Silk. Todd's tie.

He couldn't breathe. He tried to get his fingers under the material, but Sanjay, his smile gone, rushed forward and grabbed both of his hands. Arthur's eyes darted to the stranger, looking for salvation there.

None was to be found. He moved on him also, and the three men dragged Arthur into the alley. Once shrouded in even deeper shadows, the stranger kicked out Arthur's feet.

Arthur fell to the ground with a bone-jarring impact. Sanjay knelt in front of him, an iron-like grip on his wrists. Todd sat on his back and pulled the noose even tighter. Arthur tried to kick, but the cigarette guy had grabbed his ankles.

He was helpless.

He tried to call out, but no sound escaped his constricted throat. He looked up pleading, searching for Sanjay's eyes in the dark.

"Don't take it personally, Arthur," Sanjay said, his voice cold, dispassionate. "You were fated to die this day, for Kali must be fed."

Arthur died wondering at those words.

The three thugs kept their positions with the still form for a few moments more to ensure that life had left their victim.

Ravi, the man known to Arthur as Sanjay, looked over at the blond man standing up from the corpse on the ground.

"*Soosal Purna*, Jason," Ravi told him, using his friend's real name and the thug's ancient code language, Ramasee, to let him know that he had tossed his *rumal* expertly around the victim's neck.

Jason nodded as he casually put his tie back on.

Ravi turned to the third man.

"Shekhar, *bykuree kurna*," he commanded.

Shekhar strode to the alley's mouth to stand guard. The two remaining thugs bent over the body.

"Guess he won't be meeting Marcia tonight," Jason said as he fished out Arthur's phone.

"True that," Ravi replied. The thugs had hacked the dating site years ago. It was them that Arthur had been corresponding with.

Searching the body produced a wallet and a Patek Philippe watch. Ravi gave the timepiece to Jason.

"*Bhurtotee beegha*," Ravi said, essentially: as the strangler, your share of the spoils. The cash in the wallet the three would share equally.

Ravi's phone vibrated. He looked at the screen.

"It's Vankatesan and the *Sath Zut*. Something's happened," he said, looking about. His phone was giving off a noticeable glow. "I need to read the full message. How secure is this place?"

The alley was Jason's *bele*, or place for murder. All thugs had their personal *beles*, locations carefully scouted for killing unnoticed. This was the fifth time the blond man had strangled someone in this alley.

"The buildings nearby are unoccupied," Jason answered. Both men picked up the limp body, the head and limbs hanging down like a rag doll's as they carried it deeper into the alley. Ravi turned back to his phone, opening the encrypted files that had been sent to him.

"There's a problem in Oregon," Ravi read aloud, "Gabrial and Neeraj were out there. Gabe was practicing his role as *kuthowa*."

Kuthowa, the man who cuts up and disposes of the bodies.

"Someone stumbled on them, and they had to kill him," Ravi frowned. "*Kanthuna Kucha*," he finished.

There had been no time to bury the body.

Discovery.

"Is it that bad?" Jason asked. "There have been close calls before."

"It's not what happened, it's who discovered it," Ravi said. He opened another file. It contained an article posted earlier in the day from a blog called *The Unexplained, Explained.*

Jason was now reading over Ravi's shoulder.

"See, it's all about cattle mutilations," Jason said assuredly.

Ravi opened the following file. It was a lengthy story from the same blog, posted several years earlier. Both men read it silently, their eyebrows knitting in concern.

"The same guy who found the body wrote this?" Jason asked, alarmed.

Ravi nodded while opening another file.

"Yes, and the *Sath Zut* has determined that the author," he looked closer, "a guy named Steve Hanson is now *tikhur.*"

A man dangerous to thugs.

"Do we know what he looks like?"

"Apparently, he values his privacy. He doesn't have a Facebook or LinkedIn account," Ravi answered as he read further. "However, Kali found an image on his daughter's Tumblr account."

There was a JPEG file, a photo of a man sitting in a recliner with two cats. The cats looked angry at being forced to pose. One was clawing at the man's leg, the other twisting in his arms, its mouth wide open, ears back. The man looked surprised at the cats' reactions. The photo had a label.

"Because of all the dads in the world, my dad is you. Love, El."

Jason snorted. "This guy is *tikhur?*"

Shekhar approached them with keys in his hands.

"It's clear out there. Should I bring the van around?" Shekhar asked.

"There's been a change," Ravi replied. He explained the situation.

"Oregon," Shekhar exclaimed. "I have to be back to work by Monday."

"I know. Jason and I were to be the ones to drive the body back home," Ravi answered. "Instead, we are going to fly out and meet up with Gabrial and Neeraj in Portland. Jingsheng and Remington are driving up from the temple."

"Six of us for one man?" Jason asked.

"Someone else has caught Kali's attention," Ravi replied. "Most of the news from Portland is following a satanic cult angle. However, one woman's news blog seems to parallel Hanson's web page. The *Sath Zut* thinks there is a connection."

Ravi typed a name into his phone's search engine. Dozens of thumbnail images appeared for the woman.

"Samantha Ramsell," Jason read aloud. "So, what now?"

"First, instead of taking Arthur's body back home with us, it stays here," Ravi said. Shekar grunted in acknowledgment. As the group's *kuthowa,* it was his duty to prepare and bury the body for emergencies such as this. He strode over to Arthur's still form, pulling out a knife as he reached for the face. The other two moved back to the front of the alley to keep watch.

"The *Sath Zut* wants us to make both of them disappear," Ravi said.

"Hanson is nothing, but Ramsell is a high-profile target," Jason said worriedly. "She even has her own Wikipedia page. This whole thing could get out of hand."

"Unlikely," Ravi said, "We will use the focus on devil worshippers to our advantage."

The street was still deserted. Behind them, both could hear the faint noise of Shekhar cutting into the corpse's joints. Ravi turned to his phone one more time.

"Anyway, the *Sath Zut* says it must be done, for Kali wills it," Ravi continued as he studied the photos of Hanson and Ramsell side by side. He shifted his attention to their faces. "We have no choice. Their fate is already written."

Chapter 5

Portland, Sunday 4:02 p.m. PDT

"Should I be afraid?" FBI Agent Dan Fisher asked as he took a few steps back.

"Relax, man, I'm good with these things," Hanson answered as he held up a pair of throwing axes.

The two men were standing in Hanson's backyard. It was another warm day, and the sun was lowering in a clear blue sky. A tall cedar fence, accompanied by neatly trimmed laurel bushes, gave the yard some privacy. A tree trunk about three feet in diameter and cut two feet thick was placed in a makeshift rack to make a target.

Fisher, holding two bottles of beer in his hands, kept his distance as Hanson threw.

The ax bounced off the chunk of wood as its backside hit the target.

"Looks like you need more practice."

"I need some luck," Hanson replied. He pushed up his shirt's sleeve on his right shoulder, exposing a tattoo of a blue-colored twenty-sided polyhedron with the number 20 front and center. Hanson rubbed the tattoo with his left hand. He then threw the second ax, hitting the target dead center.

"Natural twenty always succeeds," Hanson said, grinning.

Fisher knew that the image the tattoo was based on came from Hanson's gaming hobby. Slaying dragons on paper. A good luck charm that the skeptic, though still superstitious, blogger believed in.

"Maybe you should stick to something safer, like foils. Don't you fence also?" Fisher asked.

"I used to," Hanson answered. "Back when I could move fast on my feet."

Though a few years younger than Hanson, Fisher was also feeling his age and could sympathize. The FBI agent was also carrying more weight since he was a bit taller and much more muscular. Since he had just finished his workday, he was still wearing a dark gray suit and tie. It was a stark contrast to Hanson, who had on a bright blue shirt with a yellow lion's head printed on it. The phrase "For the Alliance" was printed below.

Hanson threw several more times, and the axes found their target. He then spiced up his throwing routine by putting himself on a timer. Hanson had an app named Bot-timer that simulated a spaceship's computer counting down for a self-destruct or launch scenario. Hanson set it for ten seconds. As the app counted down, Hanson threw four axes in rapid sequence.

"3...2...1...we have lift off!" a robotic voice intoned from the phone's speaker as the last ax hit the target dead center.

"I rule!" Hanson yelled as he threw up his hands.

"Yeah, um, just leave some women for the rest of us," Fisher replied as he shook his head.

His hands now empty of weapons, Hanson reached for one of the beers Fisher was holding. He took a long drink from it. "So, what brings you out here from your office? Are you on the case I called you about?"

"No, the sheriff department has that investigation well in hand. I swung by to see how you're doing after finding that body."

That was an excuse. The truth was, Fisher had been concerned about Hanson's well-being for a while now. The guy was a recluse. It was nearly impossible to get him to go out and do anything social unless it had to do with the weird and unusual.

The two men had met last year during the Bigfoot murder case on Mount St. Helens. Since then, their friendship had grown, and now Fisher was naturally worried about Hanson's avoidance of the outside world. In his opinion, it wasn't healthy.

"I'm fine," Hanson answered, though his eyes had a slightly haunted look about them.

Fisher noticed the expression, and he felt he needed to keep Hanson talking and get it all out. He shifted the conversation to yesterday's events. Hanson brought out his phone to show off his gallery of dead cow photos. He also expressed curiosity as to who the victim was. Fisher knew that answer, and he informed Hanson that the man's name had been Don Rasmussen. A local farmer who had been at the wrong place, at the wrong time.

"The news is saying it's a satanic cult. That sounds like right up your alley," Fisher added.

Hanson shook his head. "Unlikely. As I was telling Samantha—"

Fisher reached out and thumped Hanson on his chest, where the lion symbol was.

"Samantha?"

"Samantha Ramsell. A news reporter," Hanson answered. "She used to be on TV."

The name meant nothing to Fisher, and his face remained blank.

"Here, I'll show you," Hanson said. Both men walked through the back door and into the living room. Mismatched modern furniture filled it. Hanson's sizeable flat-screen television was on and running, though it was muted. It showed the actor Martin Landau wearing a futuristic uniform with one black sleeve standing in front of a window looking out onto the moonscape.

Large photographic prints depicting different landmarks of the Astoria area were hung on the staircase wall. Two cats, a tabby and a Russian blue, lounged on carpeted cat stands.

Hanson turned on a laptop on his coffee table. He called up a web page with multiple images of an attractive blonde woman sitting at a news desk, or holding a microphone while outside on a news story.

"You met her?" Fisher asked, skepticism in his voice.

"She was there covering the story for a blog," Hanson answered as he opened a new page. A website named *Left Unsaid* popped up. Underneath the masthead, the headline *Cattle Mutilator Graduates to Murder* was front and center.

Fisher read the attached article. It had the same facts as last night's news broadcasts, though it didn't have any speculation on satanic involvement. Instead, it focused on the concept of moral panics.

"I talked to her. I was her source," Hanson added.

I talked to her. To Fisher, that was huge. The primary reason Hanson had been moping around his home all year was that a volcanologist he had feelings for, Dr. Makani Bateman, had left for Sumatra after Mount St. Helens had settled down from its eruption. Hanson moving on and talking to another woman was a significant step in the right direction.

"So, you met this beautiful woman yesterday, and all you have in your phone's gallery is a dead cow."

"She knew my name. We exchanged phone numbers," Hanson said defensively as he pulled up a short contact list on his phone. He held up the phone to Fisher's face.

"All I see is ten digits."

"It's her."

"Prove it. Call her right now."

"And say what?"

"Something like, 'hello'? Come on, Steve. Ever since Makani left last year, it's been nearly impossible to get you out of your house."

A pained look crossed Hanson's face, and he turned back to the laptop.

"I'll show you I'm not completely helpless around women."

Hanson moved the cursor to a new tab on the blog's site.

"I've already contacted her. I gave her my address and wrote that she can reach out to me anytime she wants if she needs more information."

Fisher saw that Hanson was indeed on Samantha Ramsell's official *Left Unsaid* message page. He straightened up and looked thoughtfully out a side window. A grin spread on his face.

"That was a good move."

Hanson's eyes narrowed in suspicion. "What do you mean?"

"She's here."

Hanson stood up and looked out. Samantha was getting out of a newer model blue Mustang. She removed her sunglasses as she shut the door.

"Jesus Christ," Hanson exclaimed, turning toward Fisher. "Stall her!"

Hanson ran down the hall, pulling off his shirt as he did so.

Chapter 6

Samantha walked toward the Craftsman-style house. It was two stories and had a porch that spanned the entire front. The home's dark earth tones complemented the well-manicured lawn and low rhododendron bushes. A silver van was parked in the driveway.

A tall black man came out the front door. His hair was neatly trimmed, and he was wearing a well-cut suit. Samantha recognized him.

Dan Fisher.

He was the FBI agent who was at the center of the Mount St. Helens case last year, an event that was infamous due to the paranormal events associated with it.

And now he was stepping out of the home of Steve Hanson, a debunker of the paranormal.

Interesting.

He approached, and his gaze was intense as he studied her. Then a smile spread across his face, and he held out his hand to shake hers.

"Samantha Ramsell? I'm Special Agent Dan Fisher. It's nice to meet you."

He knew her name. That meant that Hanson was already sharing details about the murder with Agent Fisher. That confirmed it for her. There was a professional relationship between the skeptic and the FBI.

"Agent Fisher, I—"

A stern frown chased away his smile as he guessed what was on her mind. "I can't talk about Hanson's role in last year's crisis."

"So, he was involved—"

Fisher held up a hand. "As I said, I can't talk about it. And I'm comfortable with that," the FBI agent said. "However, Hanson can't keep a secret worth a damn if someone is asking him direct questions."

"And you don't want me to ask those questions."

"I know it's natural for you to be curious and that I can't stop you. All I can do is let you know is that Hanson would find himself in a difficult situation if he were to elaborate on anything that happened last year."

Samantha could tell that Fisher wasn't telling her to back off because he was a bureaucratic jerk. He cared about Hanson's wellbeing.

"Then I guess I'll focus on the case at hand. Are you helping him with the mutilation case?"

"That I can answer. At the moment, no."

She glanced at the van. It had decals on the back window of a stick figure family: a father and daughter, both holding lightsabers. Two cats were also depicted. Everyone had big cartoon smiles.

But no wife.

"Divorced?"

"Yes. His daughter lives mostly with her mother," Fisher answered. "After the split he purchased the van. It's a midlife crisis thing for him."

She glanced at her Mustang.

"I know, not your typical sports car. Hanson chose it because it's futuristic looking and has powered sliding doors and a large video screen for navigation. The doors open on voice commands, like a little space shuttle."

Behind her, out of her field of vision, Hanson's hand poked through the curtain and gave a thumbs-up sign.

"Now, if you'll excuse me," Fisher said as he looked at his watch and slowly turned to leave. "It's time for me to go home."

* * *

Inside, Hanson peeked through the curtains and watched Fisher get into his truck. He turned to the two cats.

"Behave."

He heard the beginnings of a knock. He whipped open the door so fast that her hand was still up in the air.

"Samantha, hey, what brings you here?" he asked as he nonchalantly leaned against the wall.

"I'm sorry to show up like this unannounced, but I was hoping to get a little more from you for a follow-up story."

"Sure, come in."

She was wearing jeans and a yellow T-shirt that she kept tucked in. Her hair was still in a ponytail. Hanson thought about how her presence brightened up his living room.

He was in jeans also, along with a button-up shirt with the sleeves rolled up. A casual look, he hoped. His *World of Warcraft* shirt was tossed into the bottom of his closet. She didn't need to know how much of a nerd he really was.

She was kneeling and petting the cats at her feet.

"The Russian blue is Bingo. The tabby is Sebastian," Hanson said, glad for their distraction as he reached for the television remote. In his haste he had forgotten to turn it off.

The cats didn't hold her attention long enough. She stood up and turned to the screen. "What show is that?"

Christ.

"*Space:1999,*" he answered.

She looked blank.

"It was a mid-70s show from England starring Martin Landau and Barbara Bain. The moon gets blasted out of orbit, and their moon base hurtles through space for weekly adventures."

"Like *Star Trek?*"

He almost launched into a lecture on the differences between the two shows. But he remembered that he was trying to tamp down his nerdiness.

"Yes, something like that."

"I'm sure it's interesting. However, binge-watching British sci-fi isn't why I'm here. Did you find anything more on cattle mutilations?" she asked.

"I did," Hanson answered, grateful for the change of subjects. "On my blog, I wrote that mutilations had been a thing since the seventies. That isn't true. Charles Fort, a researcher into unusual phenomena at the turn of the twentieth century, had noted that cattle mutilations occurred in England in the middle and late nineteenth century."

"That's almost two hundred years ago," Samantha said. "Even with just the smallest fraction of livestock deaths being human related, doesn't that suggest a cult of some sort?"

Hanson paused. He couldn't deny that. But he still felt it wasn't satanic ritual crap.

"I'm not sure now," he admitted.

"I'm sure you'll figure it out," she said confidently. "But in the meantime, there's another reason I'm here. My editor liked my story, but she thinks the article needs a face, someone to relate to."

"You wish me to be identified in the story?" Hanson asked. Butterflies were forming in his stomach.

"But in a good way," she smiled.

He thought about it a moment. It couldn't be that bad.

"Sure, if it will help," he said. "Follow me."

He led her down a hall to a back room.

"The command center of *The Unexplained, Explained*," he announced.

It was a spare bedroom made into an office. A desk with a computer was set in the corner, next to a small bookshelf dominated by a huge *Ripley's Believe it or Not* book. The rest of the shelves were brimming with titles starting with the words *Mysterious* or *Unknown*. The wall behind the computer was covered with 3x5 note cards, each one carefully tacked to the wall, forming a grid pattern. Each card had an image with a label underneath. Most cards also had big red Xs on them. Others, like the card for UFOs, had question marks.

Samantha moved closer to the wall. Many of the images were recognizable, such as the Loch Ness Monster or large-eyed aliens. Others were more obscure. She turned to look back at him.

"It's my way of tracking the world's mysteries as they fall one by one," he said.

"You sound sad about it," she said.

"I think everyone is a little sad when a bit of the magic of the world disappears."

Hanson sat down at the computer and called up a page.

"My research into satanic ritual abuse I did a few years back," he said. "If you want, I can set you up a link to it for your story."

"Thanks," she replied as she leaned in to look at the page.

That close, he could smell her perfume again, and he wondered at her showing up at his place. Was she interested in him, or was it all work related? Should he ask her out? Just thinking about that released a flood of memories of embarrassing attempts of asking women out. He brought his mind back to the present.

"Any word on yesterday's victim?"

"There's a name now, and the family's been notified. But no official cause of death yet," she said.

"You have a way of finding out?"

"I have some sources," she answered. "I should know by the end of the week." She looked at his desk.

"May I take your photograph while you're sitting there? A picture says a thousand words," she explained. "This one says there's someon looking for the truth."

Hanson liked that. He ran his fingers through his hair and sat up straighter in his chair as she took a few photos.

"I think that's all I need for now."

He walked her to his door as the cats watched from their perches.

She turned toward him. "Thanks again, Steve. If you remember anything else, don't hesitate to call."

Hanson grinned. "If I figure this out, I promise, I'll give you the exclusive."

He opened the door for her, wondering if he should ask her out at that very moment. What's the worst that could happen? Even if she didn't say yes, no harm done. He took a breath and opened his mouth to speak...

Later that night, as he took off his reading glasses and put away his book on alien abductions, he looked at his two cats lying at the foot of his bed.

"I'll ask her next time I see her," he promised them as he reached for the light.

As usual, if the cats understood him, they gave no indication.

Chapter 7

Pearl District, Three Sirens Tavern, Thursday, 1:45 p.m. PDT

"*B*husmee bele. *Gurtha pucka kurna,*" Ravi said into his phone, switching to *Ramasee* as Candace dropped off his fish and chips. She was smiling at him as she did so. The thug grinned back at his server, enjoying the fleeting moment of flirtation, glad that she didn't understand what he had just told Vankatesan.

The earth is soft at the killing grounds. The bodies shall be buried deep.

"Excellent," Vankatesan replied. "How are the other preparations coming along?"

"Jason is scouting the second tavern as we speak," Ravi answered, keeping an eye on the waitress as she took an order four tables away. "The others are locating any cameras on our path. We will disable what we can tonight."

"*Dautun?* Police?" Vankatesan asked. Though he was secure in his home, he too was bouncing back and forth between English and *Ramasee*. Old habits.

"*Bajeed.* Safe from danger," Ravi answered. "We are in the northwest fringe of downtown: warehouses and light industrial. The area is watched mostly by private security firms. We noted their patrol patterns last night."

"This needs to work, Ravi," Vankatesan said. The thug could detect the stress in his leader's voice. "Ramsell published another news story with her online newspaper site."

Ravi understood as he had read the blog also. A mild hysteria was building on most media outlets, focusing on the possibility of satanic cults spreading. That was good for the thugs. However, Ramsell was still following a different path, her headline reading: *The Devil Is Not in the Details.* And now she had Hanson named as a source and that he was working on finding the truth. There was even a picture of him, looking apprehensive in front of his computer. He didn't photograph very well.

"*Bote hona*, he will fall into our snares," Ravi said. "Though it would help if our *bykureeas* could find out what he does on a Friday night besides signing in on his Xbox Live account and playing *World of Warcraft*."

"Kali's will has been bent toward him the past few days. What you know is all we have."

Ravi frowned. They usually had more to go on when inveigling a victim and luring him out. Hanson's online footprint was minuscule. Conspiracy nut-off-the-grid minuscule. Which didn't make sense. From what Ravi understood from the blog, *The Unexplained, Explained*, Hanson didn't believe in conspiracies.

He thought about the photograph again, Hanson's awkward pose, and the look in his eyes. The truth hit Ravi out of the blue.

Not a conspiracy nut.

Introvert.

"It's enough, Vankatesan. I will call you after it's done," Ravi said with excitement in his voice.

"Good," Vankatesan replied. He gave his young thug a short blessing. "Kali be with you."

"And with you."

Outside the tavern's window, a crow landed on the sill to the right. Ravi stared at it for a moment.

A good omen.

Ravi switched back to Ramsell's news article. Hanson's image filled his screen.

Ravi studied his eyes.

Thugs were divided up into specialists, each with their own jobs. *Kuthowas* cut up the corpses. *Lughas* dug the graves.

And the *sothas* conned the unwary victims.

Ravi was a *sotha*. An extrovert, he was comfortable in any social situation. He could read people. Make them feel comfortable to discover their weaknesses or desires.

He could see it in Hanson's eyes. What he desired was on the other side of that camera.

Ramsell.

With Hanson, they had little to go on. But Samantha was an open book, her life laid bare on Facebook, Instagram, Twitter, and Wikipedia. The thugs realized a few years back that Big Brother wasn't spying on people's lives; people were ramming their lives down Big Brother's throat.

Luring Ramsell in would be simple. Ravi knew what motivated her.

And then she would be the bait to bring in Hanson.

A smile was back on his face as he finished his lunch. Candace swung around and picked up his plate.

"I see you liked our fish and chips," she said. "Our regulars say they're the best in the city."

"True that," Ravi replied. "I'll have to come back to this place next time I'm in town."

"Just remember, I work the lunch shift," she said as she locked eyes with him for a fraction of a second longer than she needed to before turning away to get his bill.

Ravi got the hint. In all honesty, he wished he could linger and follow through with Candace, but the thug just didn't have the time. Kali was a harsh mistress, and she demanded blood. Ravi looked at Hanson's image again.

And by tomorrow evening, she will have it.

Chapter 8

Sherwood, Oregon, Friday, 5:25 p.m. PDT

"Five...four...three...two...one...destruct!" Bot-timer announced from Hanson's phone.

"Bean dip is done!" Hanson shouted toward the kitchen as he turned off the timer app on his phone.

It was *Dungeons and Dragons* night. Hanson had driven south to the home of his friend Robert Tolmany, a doctor who role-played as a cleric. Andrew Stedman, the group's mage, was also there. The rest of the party had yet to arrive.

They were an old adventuring group, having been at it for three decades. Hanson always looked forward to their monthly gatherings.

The three were in costume. Andrew and Robert wore spellcasting robes. Hanson, dressed as a paladin, had on chain armor and a red cape. His sword leaned against the dining room wall.

Tolmany walked in with the bean dip.

"Elf needs food, badly," Stedman said as he dipped a chip.

In the next room, the television was on. Network news anchor Doug Morgan, looking stately in a suit and tie, was going through a rapid-fire preview of the night's stories; storms were pounding the East Coast.

Covid was still lurking in underdeveloped countries where it had been challenging to deliver vaccines. Fighting raged in the Middle East. National news correspondent Jennifer Steel was positioned to interview a congressman railing against Muslim immigrants trying to flee the violence.

As usual, Tolmany turned his television off with his remote shaped like a Harry Potter wand.

"Magic," he said with a flourish as he walked back into the dining room. He grabbed Hanson's sword. "Much more powerful than a simple blade."

Hanson backed up a bit. "Careful. That sword's the real deal. It will take off limbs."

Tolmany gently put it back. Stedman went to the kitchen and returned with three beers. He knocked over a saltshaker as he placed them on the table. Hanson took a pinch and tossed it over his shoulder.

Stedman laughed at that. "A self-proclaimed skeptic, and yet you still throw salt."

Hanson shrugged. "I blame my mother. She was superstitious. I think those old habits will be the last things I let go of."

The table was surrounded by hard, wooden chairs and one soft office chair from Tolmany's den.

"Let's roll for the chair," Andrew said.

All three snatched up twenty-sided dice. Hanson rubbed his right shoulder.

"Speaking of superstitions," Tolmany said, as he rolled up a five on his die.

"Yeah, no fair, you only use that for emergencies, like Total Party Kill situations," Stedman added. His die clattered on the table, coming up with twelve.

Hanson eyed the comfy chair. "I'm an old man; this is important."

He tossed the die. All of them watched as it came up with a seventeen.

"Every time," Stedman groaned as he pulled out a wooden chair. They had some time to kill before the others arrived. Typically, the conversation at this point would be catching up on each other's work and family. But for once, Hanson had something interesting to offer. He related his past week with the others. Both of his friends took notice at the mention of Samantha visiting his home.

"She was checking you out. Did you ask her on a date?" Tolmany asked.

"Haven't thought about it," Hanson answered. He took a long drink on his beer, hoping to signal that that topic was over.

The others weren't letting up. "Jeez, man, it's been…what, over a year since Makani left," Stedman said. "How do you get by?"

"I know," Tolmany said, a sly grin crossing his face, "I think Steve taps that tattoo on his right shoulder before he goes to bed."

Stedman, getting the innuendo, nodded.

"I've always wondered how Hanson has lasted all of this time," Stedman said.

"With that natural twenty, his right hand never fails," Tolmany added.

"The unexplained—," they both said.

"Save it," Hanson said, glaring at them.

Laughter filled the room. The men began talking about the upcoming game.

Hanson's phone trilled. The other men shook their heads at him.

"No phones," Tolmany said, reminding him of the house rule.

Hanson guiltily reached for his cell. He was going to turn his phone off, but it was Samantha's number. He didn't let it ring a second time.

"Samantha, hi," Hanson answered.

"Steve, I hope I'm not catching you at a bad time."

"Of course not, I'm just doing some…stuff with old friends," Hanson replied.

"What sort of stuff?"

"Um…cards, we're playing a game of cards," Hanson said as he used his left hand to do the rolling, "go with it" motion.

The others stared for a moment but then got the idea.

"Ante up!"

"I'll take two cards!"

"Fold!"

"Show me the River!"

With a look of disgust on his face, Hanson left the room.

"So, what's up? Do you have more questions for your next article?"

"Actually, I'm heading over to a bar near the Pearl District. I was hoping you could join me."

Hanson was so surprised it took him a moment to answer.

"Sure. I would love to come over."

"There are several bars to choose from in that area. I'm told there's a good, central parking lot to use."

She gave him the cross streets. Hanson mapped it out and told her he would be there in about an hour. He rejoined his friends.

"I think I have a date," Hanson said. He felt some guilt. It was rare for him to bail on a night out with his friends. "I hope you don't mind."

Tolmany and Stedman stood up and smoothed out their robes before answering.

"Go, Steve," Stedman said. "We all think this is good for you."

"But not looking like that," Tolmany added as he eyed Hanson's costume. "You're about my size; let me look to see if I have something that fits."

A moment later, he came back in with a tan-colored button-up shirt. Hanson rolled up the sleeves. Tolmany finished the outfit with a dark-blue fall jacket.

Stedman looked it over. "Presentable."

Hanson picked up his sword.

"I promise I'll hang around longer next time."

"Just text the details," Tolmany replied with a grin. He and Stedman were back at the table, rolling for the office chair again. Hanson could hear yells and groans as he closed the door.

It was threatening rain, a weather pattern that looked like it would follow him as he headed back north to Portland. Hanson zipped up the jacket as he headed to the van.

"Computer, open door."

The passenger side door slid open. Hanson laid the long sword on the back seat and covered it with his red cape.

Hanson headed back into Portland on I-5. A short while later, he took the exit for the Pearl District north of downtown.

He looked at the navigation screen on his dash. Samantha had directed him to a spot a little north and west of the Pearl. It was more of a working-class area. Hanson figured there must be some up-and-coming edgy brewpubs that people liked to discover.

Due to the thickening clouds and late time, it was getting dark when he rolled into the almost empty parking lot. He saw Samantha's blue Mustang under a lamppost. She was standing next to it with two men.

Hanson's heart sank. He didn't know this was going to be a group affair. He swung his van to the left and parked a bit away so that he wouldn't be right on top of the others.

Giving the men a short nod, Hanson smiled at her as he locked his van.

"Steve, I'm so glad you could make it," Samantha said. "I have some new acquaintances who flew in from back East." She turned toward the two men with her. "They're journalists who are interested in my story. When I told them about you, they insisted on meeting you."

So, it was more of a business meeting than a date. And he being here was not her idea. Hanson kept the disappointment from showing on his face as he looked the two guys over. One guy was tall, with Nordic features. The other was shorter, with black hair and a dark complexion. He offered his hand to Hanson.

"Hello, I'm Sanjay," the guy said with a smile.

Chapter 9

Since he now found himself in a social situation with strangers, Hanson withdrew and barely said a word as the others chatted around him, which worked out because Sanjay liked to talk. The other man's name was Todd. From what he overheard, the two men worked for one of the national network news stations back in New York, where the dairy farm murder was starting to get some notice.

Samantha and Todd paired up and walked on ahead, deep in conversation. That didn't stop Sanjay from attempting to break down Hanson's barriers.

"Samantha says you don't believe it's a satanic cult," Sanjay said.

Hanson, his eyes on Samantha in front of him, answered distractedly.

"True. I mean, I think it's unlikely, that is."

Sanjay was studying Hanson's face thoughtfully. "You two just met, right?"

"Yeah, out in that pasture last week."

"And I'm guessing you thought it was just going to be Samantha waiting for you here."

Jesus, thought Hanson, was he that obvious?

"We asked her to call you to meet us out here."

Hanson shrugged as he tried to appear nonchalant. "She's hot on a story. I can tell it's all business with her."

"I don't know about that," Sanjay said. "We've been corresponding with her. She can't stop talking about you."

Hanson stood a bit straighter. He was both surprised and pleased to hear that.

"She may not have told you, but Samantha used to be a big deal back East. But her producer boyfriend dumped her for a younger woman for both professional and personal reasons. The guy thought he could take the other woman further up the news network ladder."

"I didn't know," Hanson said.

"It devastated Samantha. She left New York and moved out here to the West Coast. But people back East still remember how talented she was. That's why Todd and I are here. We might be able to get a segment on the national news and maybe convince her to get her network career started again."

Hanson was now listening intently. This sounded important.

"What can I do?"

"Your presence here is a great help. Todd and I are hoping to get some more of your insights," Sanjay said. "And maybe we can help you out also."

"What do you mean?"

"We'll get you a real date with Samantha," Sanjay said with a grin. "Have you ever had a wingman before?"

"No. I don't get out that often," Hanson confessed.

"No problem. I was able to hook up Todd here with his now-wife," Sanjay said. "If I could pull that off, getting you and Samantha another date will be easy."

Todd, hearing his name, turned and looked back. Sanjay just waved at him, grinning. Todd grinned back cluelessly.

"Todd and I will both be your wingmen," Sanjay continued as he brought out his phone and typed out a text.

Ahead of them, Todd reached for and read his phone while still talking with Samantha.

"Todd is going to text me info about her," Sanjay explained. "So that we can discover some common ground. Tell me about yourself."

Flattered that someone was interested in his life story, Hanson gave Sanjay a quick rundown on his personal history. He included the more exciting stuff, such as playing football in high school, throwing the javelin in track, and elk hunting when he was a teenager. He also mentioned that he had joined the Marines, as his father had before him. After that, he went to college here in Portland. Hanson pointed out that he started his *Unexplained, Explained* blog around five years ago.

"Do you have any other hobbies?" Sanjay asked.

Hanson hesitated a little. "Roleplaying and comic book conventions," he answered.

"We're leaving that part out," Sanjay said, grinning again. "Trust me, I'm good with people. Just let me guide the conversation."

They reached a place called The Three Sirens. It looked like an older place: wood painted brown with white rock girdling its lower half.

It was dark and crowded in the main room. Todd, though, found them a booth near the back. Sanjay maneuvered Hanson and Samantha to one side of the table while Todd went for some beers.

Samantha leaned over to Hanson.

"Steve, thanks again for meeting us out here."

"Anytime," Hanson answered, enjoying her closeness.

"So, tell me how you two met," Sanjay asked.

Samantha talked about finding Hanson by the mutilated cow. Hanson added that he was impressed that she figured out how to approach the crime scene from the back way.

Sanjay listened intently, though he sometimes broke up the conversation by asking pointed questions. Hanson answered most of them. He soon caught on that Sanjay was directing the conversation so that Hanson would dominate it.

Todd came back with the beers and asked what he had missed. Sanjay filled him in by focusing on what Hanson had talked about.

"Is all of your blog about paranormal stuff?" Todd asked.

Hanson felt all their eyes on him.

"Not all of it," Hanson answered. "I also follow urban legends, hoaxes, and general misconceptions that we all have about everyday life." He shrugged. "I think the weird and paranormal are more interesting, but I look into the mundane also."

"What would be a mundane misconception?" Todd asked.

"You don't have to drink eight glasses of water a day," Hanson answered as he took a sip from his beer. "You can get your fluid intake from other sources."

Sanjay and Todd looked at each other and then clinked their glasses together.

"I'll drink to that," they said in unison.

Samantha smiled and touched her glass to Hanson's.

"What else have we got wrong?" Sanjay asked.

"You're not swallowing six spiders a year in your sleep," Hanson continued.

Everyone else at the table looked relieved.

"And vitamin C doesn't stop colds," Hanson finished.

"I always load up right before a flight," Sanjay groaned.

"Don't get me wrong, it's good for your health, and it stops scurvy," Hanson said with a grin.

"Well, if it was good for my health, at least it helped me in track and field back in high school," Sanjay said.

"I took track also, hurdles," Samantha said.

"Same here," Hanson added, "I threw the javelin."

The conversation shifted to that for a while. Hanson realized that the others could have interjected, but Sanjay left them alone by holding up his phone to Todd as if something important had come up. Both were intent on it.

These guys take their wingmen job seriously.

Todd fetched more beers. While they drank their second rounds, the conversation drifted back to the story Samantha was working on, though Sanjay frequently asked for Hanson's input.

They finished their drinks, and Todd suggested they walk to another bar. As they stood up to leave, Hanson was satisfied to note that their passing was unnoticed by the other patrons' intents on their phones. He thought about going out more often, just to have a quiet drink alone.

Outside, Todd and Sanjay paired up, leaving Hanson with Samantha. It was dark out, but fortunately, not raining.

Other people were out and about on the street, drifting by like shadows. Though they weren't threatening, Hanson and Samantha instinctively walked a bit faster so that they could catch up with the others, giving them the comfort of safety in numbers.

She looked over at him and took a step closer. "So, Steve, with all this talk of dead cows and cults, I've never really had the chance to talk about anything personal with you. Do you have any family in your life?"

"I was married, divorced now," Hanson answered, thrilled that she was interested. "We have a daughter, Elanor; she's in high school." Hanson brought up his phone and showed her the image of a teenager with long, brunette hair.

"She's beautiful."

"Yeah, about the only thing I got right in that marriage."

"My mother is still in Astoria," Hanson continued. "Dad passed away when I was six."

"I'm sorry."

"Thanks," Hanson quickly answered, wanting to move on from that. Though it had happened long ago, his father's death still resonated with him. "How about you? Ever get married?"

"No, too busy with my career. I was close to someone once. It didn't work out."

Hanson noticed a pained expression cross her face. Sanjay was right; this other guy must have done a real number on her. He changed tack with his small talk.

"Did you choose the next place we're going to?" he asked.

"No. I'm more of a wine tasting and charcuterie board sort of gal," she answered. "These local microbrew pubs were Sanjay's idea."

It wasn't that long of a walk, but it was taking them away from their vehicles. Returning home was going to take a while.

They reached the second bar, the *Bunco Kelly*, an updated tavern. Hanson could see the stainless-steel vats in the back half of the building for the pub's own microbrews. A notice on the door advertised that a local band, the *Dirty Mopheads*, were to perform this evening. The parking lot was small and packed. The street also was crowded with cars. Hanson figured that all this walking did save them some hassle.

They went inside, and two other men joined their group.

Chapter 10

It happened quickly.

It was darker and louder at Kelly's than it had been at the Sirens. There was also only one table left, but it seemed unusable because two men at a nearby table were crowding it.

For Hanson, that would have been it, time to move on to somewhere else.

Not for Sanjay. He looked the room over, and his eyes rested on the two men. He strode over to them.

"Jeez, what's he doing?" Hanson asked, alarmed at Sanjay's forwardness.

Todd smiled. "Give him a minute."

Sanjay talked to the two men. They glanced over Hanson's way and shifted around their table a bit. Sanjay waved his group over.

Though uneasy about intruding, Hanson followed the others. Samantha seemed okay with it.

The two men at the table stood up to shake hands. Both looked to be in their thirties. The first guy was short, with dark curly hair and a mustache. The other was Asian, about Hanson's height, and had close-cropped straight hair. Both were wearing buttoned-up shirts and had their light jackets and scarves hung on the backs of their chairs.

Mustache was named Bryce, the other Kim. Both explained that they worked back East for a sporting wear company and had been in town for the past week on business.

Sanjay made introductions for his group as everyone sat down. Once again, he made sure that Hanson was placed next to Samantha. Todd offered to show their appreciation to the two men by buying everyone drinks.

A New York Yankees hat rested on the table. Sanjay gestured to it.

"I told Bryce here that Todd and I are from New York also."

"Everyone around here is hung up on the local soccer team, the Portland Timbers," Bryce said. "No offense, but I miss talking about a real American sport."

Hanson smiled back. "None taken, but just don't say that around the Portland Timber's Army; those guys take football seriously."

"True that," Sanjay said.

Everyone laughed. Sanjay's demeanor made everyone feel included, and Kim and Bryce turned their chairs a bit to face everyone.

"What business are you guys in?" Kim asked.

Hanson, trying to keep it simple by explaining that he was IT support at a nearby supermarket. Samantha told them she was a freelance reporter.

Sanjay didn't let it go at that. He told the others about their roles in the recent murder case.

"The satanic cult thing," Kim said. Hanson frowned to himself but let that misconception pass.

Todd came back with the drinks. All of them raised their glasses to each other.

"To the Timbers," Bryce said as he looked over his shoulder to make sure no one heard his earlier comments.

Déjà vu rolled over Hanson again.

This was all familiar to him as if he had experienced it before.

But he hadn't. Sitting in a tavern with a woman and four strangers? Nothing like this had ever happened in his life.

Precog superpower? As usual, he made a prediction. A brunette would walk in through the front door.

It didn't happen. Hanson sighed to himself in disappointment.

"What do you do for recreation around there?"

Hanson looked up. Sanjay was talking to him. Hanson thought about his answer. Lately, he was more of a stay inside guy. And Sanjay had suggested he shouldn't mention the roleplaying.

"I used to hunt."

Samantha spoke up. "So did I."

Sanjay looked at her. "That's surprising."

"My dad was a hunter," she continued. "And it was a tradition in our family, so he took me out deer hunting on several occasions."

"For me, it was my uncle who took me out," Hanson said, looking at the others. "Any of you hunt before?"

The four men shook their heads.

"Honestly, I've never hunted wild game," Sanjay said.

Hanson wasn't sure, but there was the barest hint of something in Sanjay's expression. He shrugged it off. Most likely, Sanjay was opposed to hunting but was just being polite for the conversation.

"But I gave it up," Hanson continued, "too—"

"Messy," Samantha finished. "All of that field dressing."

"Field dressing?" Kim asked.

"You have to gut the animal. It cools it down faster and slows down bacteria growth," Hanson answered.

He paused, thinking about the man and cow he had found earlier. He had thought that the evisceration was somehow ceremonial. What if there was a practical reason?

A memory tickled at his consciousness, barely out of reach. He shrugged it off.

"And it helps lighten the load," Hanson continued.

"Is a deer heavy?" asked Kim.

"You bet," Hanson said. The drinks were catching up to him a little, and he decided to be a little more daring with the group. "I remember one time I was all alone. The carcass was so heavy that I had to drag it by grabbing it by its back legs and pulling it toward my truck."

"That must have taken forever," Todd said.

"It did," Hanson said. "My uncle, who was across the canyon, radioed me, wondering why it was taking so long. I told him what I was doing and that I was half a mile away. He radioed, 'You idiot, the antlers are digging into the ground. Grab them instead, and it will slide along smoother.'"

"Did that work?" Todd asked.

"Yeah, it went faster," Hanson said, grinning. "But an hour later, I found myself a mile from my truck."

It took them all a moment to get it, but they all burst out laughing. Todd went for more beer.

"So, you write a blog," Bryce said.

"The Unexplained," Hanson answered as he took a drink. Even the beer was tasting better tonight.

"I had an aunt who used to tell stories of aliens floating her out of her bedroom to do experiments. I always thought she was lying," Bryce continued.

"She wasn't," Hanson said.

They all looked at him like he was crazy.

"I mean, though she wasn't being abducted by aliens, she truly believed she was."

"How's that possible?"

"It's called Old Hag Syndrome," Hanson explained. "Back in the day, people would wake with a hard time breathing, like there was a pressure on their chests. When they looked up, it was into the baleful face of this demonic hag astride them, trying to steal their souls.

"Victims found themselves paralyzed under her magic. They couldn't escape. Then the hag would cast another spell, and they would find themselves floating, being carried to hell itself. Only at the last moment could they wrench themselves from the paralysis and throw off the creature."

"What was happening?" asked Samantha. Hanson noticed that she was leaning in, intent on his story. In fact, everyone was intent on him. It gave Hanson pause. Usually, he shrank into the background as he listened to others talk. Tonight, though, he was the center of attention. The life of the party.

He liked it.

"When you're dreaming about playing a game of tennis, what is it that keeps you from crashing into your bedroom wall?"

"During REM sleep, your body paralyzes itself," Bryce answered.

"Right. Unfortunately, some people can wake up still paralyzed in a semi-REM state. The mind is hallucinating, and the partial paralysis can translate to the constricted chest feeling. Another side effect is that most people feel there is an unwelcome presence in the room with them, and they dream up their worst nightmare, a demon on their chest."

"How does that explain my aunt's aliens?"

"Hags are a thing of the past. Aliens are now foremost in our minds. So now we imagine glowing tractor beams paralyzing and constricting us as we float out of our bed with alien surgeons standing by.

"So, though your aunt truly believed, she was just the victim of a sleeping disorder."

The whole table stared at him. Then Sanjay whispered,

"The Unexplained—"

"Explained," everyone at the table finished as they raised their drinks and laughed.

Samantha's phone lit up. She called up the text message and read it intently. She looked around at the others, then at him. She gave him an "I will tell you later" look.

"Anything else we all have wrong in your blog?" Kim asked.

"Rub-a-dub-dub, three men in a tub is not what you think it is," Hanson answered. "And there's a debate about the color pink not existing at all."

The rest of the night continued like that. Everyone around him peppered him with questions, and Hanson held reign. The next few hours, thanks to Sanjay's orchestrations, were a pleasant blur of socializing. The music was also good as the *Dirty Mopheads,* with each band member sporting a different colored swath of thick hair, performed. The time flew by.

Sanjay looked at his watch.

"Hey, I know it's not that late, but for Todd and myself, it feels like three in the morning. I don't know about you guys, but we're ready to head on out."

"We Ubered over here," Kim said. He and Bryce stood up and put on their jackets and scarves.

"We can drive you," Todd replied.

Hanson wanted to stay and have some alone time with Samantha, but he thought about the situation. It was a long, dark trek back to the cars.

"We should all walk together," he said as he reached for his coat.

Outside, it was starting to drizzle, the beginnings of Portland rain. Hanson wondered if they would make their vehicles before the real downpour.

There were still plenty of cars in the lot, and the street was busy. However, all it took was a short walk and the turning of a corner to find themselves on a long, quiet road, empty of vehicles.

The other men were striding ahead; Hanson guessed more manipulation by Sanjay.

Hanson was still feeling great, but now he wondered about what he should say next. Samantha was walking close to him, intent on her phone.

"There's no signal out here," she said.

Hanson brought out his phone. No bars. He looked around him.

"It must be these warehouses. It's like a canyon out here."

She shrugged and put away her phone. Hanson felt her eyes on him. "I had a good time tonight."

"So did I," Hanson answered, thinking his reply was the understatement of the year.

They all walked on, drifting in and out of light and darkness between streetlamps. Hanson realized they were moving up an alley, a shortcut to the parking lot. Sanjay glanced back, a satisfied look on his face. Hanson could guess what he was thinking.

My work here is done.

Hanson began rehearsing in his mind what he was going to say to Samantha next.

The two of us should get together again.

He hoped she would answer yes. Or better yet, say that she didn't want the night to end.

They were coming up on the last corner. Hanson had to make his move now. He leaned in closer to her. She turned to him, expectation on her face as if she had been waiting all this time for him to say something.

"Maybe we should—"

"Hey, I think someone's hanging out around our cars," Todd said.

Hanson looked up. The rain was coming down a bit harder now. Of the three lampposts that reared above the lot, only one worked, so it was difficult to see two dark figures near Samantha's car.

Including Hanson's van, four cars remained on the lot. Hanson guessed the third was Sanjay's rental. The fourth maybe belonged to the mysterious lurkers.

"Are they thieves?" Kim asked.

"I don't know, but maybe we should let Sanjay do all of the talking," Todd suggested.

"True that," Sanjay replied. "The rest of you hang back a bit."

Kim and Bryce moved to the opposite side of Hanson and Samantha as if to shield her from danger from behind.

As a group, they moved closer. Hanson pulled out his phone. Still no bars.

"Too bad we can't call for the police," he said.

"I think we'll be okay. There's six of us and only two of them," she replied. "But while I have a chance, I should tell you about my earlier message. It was from my guy at the police station. I know how Rasmussen was killed."

Hanson only half-listened as he watched Sanjay split off from their group and close in on the strangers. The two men looked menacing the near dark, but that quickly changed after a few moments of talking to Sanjay. Their postures relaxed, and smiles spread across their faces. Sanjay had a grin of his own as he walked back. Relieved, Hanson turned back to Samantha.

"How did he die?"

"He was strangled from behind, with a garrote. All of the knife wounds were done postmortem."

Sanjay, with the two strangers walking behind him, rejoined the group.

"It's okay, their car broke down, and they're waiting for a tow. However, they've run out of smokes, and they're hoping we can help with that."

Sanjay's grin broadened.

"So, does anyone have a cigarette?"

Chapter 11

Hanson made a prediction.

Where Kim's jaw would be.

When Samantha told him how Rasmussen had died, vague déjà vu became sharp reality. In a fraction of a second, he understood everything that had transpired the previous week.

And the danger they were in now.

Hanson spun around, his left hand tapping his lucky tattoo as he blindly threw a straight right.

He connected. As he had guessed, Kim was directly behind him, his scarf stretched out in both hands. As Hanson's fist slammed into Kim's face, his fears were confirmed.

Thugs.

Impossible.

Kim's head snapped back as he collapsed to the ground.

One down.

In his peripheral vision, he saw Bryce springing toward Samantha's back, his scarf held up high also.

Not a scarf.

A rumal.

Jesus Christ.

Hanson grabbed the *rumal* in the middle and yanked it down. Bryce turned to him, surprise on his face. Hanson slugged him near his right eye, and his hand ached from the impact. Staggered, Bryce fell into a puddle, moaning.

Two.

Nearby Sanjay, Todd, and the two strangers stood in the rain, frozen for just a moment.

"Samantha, follow me! They're a bunch of thugs! Run!" Hanson yelled. He sprinted for his van. He got past Todd before the guy could move.

Stunned, Samantha paused, but then she moved also. However, she was a few steps behind Hanson, and Todd, now reacting, took a few steps out to block her.

She changed direction and went for her car. Her hand plunged into her coat pocket as she reached for her keys.

* * *

Hanson, not aware of what she was doing, kept running. His van was forty feet away. He could hear the splashing feet of multiple pursuers behind him.

He needed a weapon. His sword was in the van.

"Computer, open doors!" he shouted.

His van remained dark and silent.

Hanson swore to himself. Was it the sound of the pounding rain interfering?

He was twenty feet away now, and he wasn't planning on stopping. If that door didn't open, he was crashing into it.

"Computer, open doors!" he yelled with desperation in his voice.

A pause, then LED lights outlining the van's windows lit up like a Christmas tree, and the doors slid open.

Hanson dove in headfirst.

He was moving so fast that his forward momentum carried him clean out the door on the other side, and he tumbled back out onto the wet pavement.

But, while he was inside, his hand had searched out and wrapped around the cape and sword on the rear seat. He carried them out with him.

On the ground, Hanson fumbled with the cape.

"He's on the other side of the van," Todd yelled nearby. "Gabe, swing around the front."

Hanson heard splashes coming around from both front and back. They were going to be on him soon.

His hand closed on the hilt of his long sword.

The car alarm from the Mustang started blaring.

Damn it. Samantha hadn't followed him. Though she must have hit the panic button on her key fob, which was a good thing. He hoped it would keep the thugs at bay.

Hanson brandished the sword. He was still kneeling when the thug named Gabe, a tall, dark-haired man with a unibrow, came charging around the front of the van.

The thug was holding a knife, not a *rumal*. This guy was a *kuthowa*, making him the thug responsible for the horrific postmortem damage done to the man and the cow down south. Hanson saw a hard glint in the man's eyes. The *kuthowa* meant to do the same to him.

The thug rushed him; his knife held up for a downward stroke. Still low to the ground, Hanson swept his blade out in front of him with all his strength and cut his opponent's left leg off immediately below the knee.

With no leg to support him, the thug went down hard, shrieking in pain. He dropped his knife as he threw out his hands to break his fall. When he hit the ground, he curled up a bit so that he could wrap both hands around the stump of his leg.

Three down.

The *kuthowa's* blood loss was remarkable. The thug moaned in agony as he gripped his leg.

Hanson had no time to dwell on the gruesome scene. He spun around to see Todd rushing up on him, appearing as if he would tackle him.

Hanson sprung up and used a classic fencing move, stepping forward with his right leg as he lunged. He drove the point of his blade through Todd's right shoulder.

Todd gasped in pain and surprise. Pulling out the blade, Hanson sidestepped so that the hulking blond sailed by him and tripped over the other thug on the ground. Todd crashed down to the asphalt; his one good arm flung outward to break his fall.

He tried to stand back up, but Hanson came up behind him and smacked him on the back of the head with the broad side of the blade. It was like hitting the thug with a metal bat. Todd sagged back down with a groan. The *kuthowa,* still in a fetal position, appeared to be unconscious also.

Four.

The alarm on the Mustang stopped, and Hanson looked over. He couldn't see anyone else. That meant everyone was on the other side of the vehicle.

On her.

Hanson leaped through his doors again. Setting off car alarms was a good idea, but if he triggered his, it might alert them that he was coming, and they might kill her that much quicker.

"Computer, one-minute delay, red alert, and engine start."

Hanson jumped out the van's opposite door, praying that he wasn't too late.

* * *

Samantha couldn't believe what was happening.

The evening had been a pleasant one. The thought of going back to New York had excited her, and she had looked forward to seeing Hanson again. She found him attractive, though she wasn't sure if the feeling was mutual. He hadn't reacted to her hints back at his home. So tonight, when he looked like he would ask her out, she was pleased that her doubts were dispelled.

But only for a moment. He had then turned her world upside down by throwing punches and shouting at her to run.

She couldn't believe it, but she trusted him, so now she was running for her life.

Todd had cut her off, so Samantha turned back toward her Mustang. She could see one of the newcomers pull a knife and start running for Hanson's van.

Sanjay made a grab for her, but she stiff-armed him and knocked him to the ground. She ran for the driver's side door.

The other parking lot lurker, an Indian like Sanjay, was nearby. He grabbed at her also, but the heavy rain was in his eyes, and it threw off his aim. He clutched her purse instead. She let it slip off her shoulders.

Her thumb found the panic button on her key fob.

Her car alarm went off, a loud and piercing blast that filled the parking lot. She hoped the noise would dismay her pursuers as she put her hand on her car door handle.

It didn't. They were on her in an instant. Sanjay grabbed hold of her hands, his grip like a vise. The other Indian came up behind her and kicked her feet out from under her.

Sanjay, still holding her hands, knelt as he guided her to the ground. She fell hard, landing flat on her stomach onto the pavement. She gasped as the wind was knocked out of her.

Hands grabbed her ankles before she could stand back up. Sanjay continued to kneel slowly so that his face was close to hers.

The ground was cold, and sharp gravel was pressing into her. It was raining so hard now that she was lying in a half-inch of oily parking lot water. Her hair was plastered to her face, which held a grimace of pain and fear.

She looked up. Sanjay's face was cold and expressionless.

"Sanjay?" she whimpered as she struggled to get the next word out. "Why?"

"Kali must be fed Miss Ramsell, and she will delight in your blood," Sanjay answered, his eyes piercing. "And if it makes you feel any better, realize that your sacrifice is helping save the world."

What the hell? Even in her moment of panic, she couldn't help but wonder at her attacker's words. To her side, she could see the feet of another man approaching. They stopped near her keys on the ground.

Hands reached down and thumbed a button on the fob. The car alarm ceased.

Bryce.

It was eerily quiet after the alarm's cessation, and there was no sign of Hanson. Sanjay didn't look worried. Despair clutched at her. Hanson must be dead.

Bryce stepped over her. His weight settled on her lower back.

"Couldn't we have picked a night when it's not raining?" he growled from behind her.

"It's Portland. I hear it always rains," the Indian at her feet answered.

"A pity we couldn't do this at the temple, in front of Her holy presence," Sanjay said, reverence in his voice. "We would be dry there."

"Hanson knocked Jingsheng out cold and gave me a black eye," Bryce said. "What happened, Ravi?"

Ravi? Samantha was still looking at Sanjay. He reacted to Bryce's question.

"*Chuk ho jana,* he must have figured it out in the end," he answered. "Though, too late, really."

"Well, Vankatesan will be glad to hear that this loose end is tied up," Bryce said.

A length of cloth slowly wrapped around Samantha's neck.

"Tied up, get it," Bryce chuckled behind her.

Sanjay still had a grip on her wrists. Bryce had called him Ravi. His real name? She decided to switch to it.

"Ravi? Please, don't do this," she sobbed. Mucous was running from her nose into her mouth, a salty taste mixing with the rain.

"Do not beg to me, Miss Ramsell," Ravi replied as he knelt lower. He looked slightly above her eyes. "We can see on your brow that you are marked for death by Kali. We are but her instruments."

"We are killing two of them tonight. Does that double our shares?" Bryce asked.

"It does," Ravi said, the rainwater dripping off his chin. "Though it doesn't change the normal weekly schedule."

Bryce grunted with satisfaction at that. The cloth tightened.

Samantha gasped, her body writhing as she tried to twist away. It was no use. The three men held her down.

No sound could escape her lips, and the ground was so cold and hard. But that feeling was growing distant, fading as her senses shut down.

She stopped struggling and felt her body relax. The glow from the streetlight became dimmer.

Then she faintly heard a sound, unlike anything she had ever heard before. A heavy, cutting noise. It was followed by a scream.

The noose around her neck loosened, and Samantha sucked in a deep breath with a loud gasp. Her lungs filled with air, and her vision cleared. She felt the rocks on the ground again pressing painfully into her. But the pressure on her neck was gone. Bryce must have let go of the scarf he was holding.

Something fell to the ground next to her. She glanced at it.

Bryce hadn't let go of the scarf; his hand was still gripping it.

It just was that his hand and arm were no longer attached to his body.

Before she could really register that, she saw a foot sweep by and connect with Ravi's face. Ravi's head snapped back, and he let go of her wrists as he toppled over.

Bryce fell away also, howling in pain as he scrambled away, the stump of his left arm clutched in his right hand.

She looked up. Hanson was standing over her, holding, of all things, a sword. He moved toward the man at her feet. She could hear the blade swishing through the air as the other Indian screamed. Her feet were released.

Hanson grabbed her arm with his free hand and hauled her up. She felt unsteady, but he put his left arm around her and supported her. He felt warm after the cold ground. She leaned into him as she pulled a long, thin scarf from her neck.

"Samantha, can you breathe? Did they damage your windpipe?" he asked wildly.

She could breathe, but it was painful. She nodded that she was okay.

A voice shouted out behind them. Ravi, though he sounded different. Both turned toward him.

Ravi's face was in ruin. Blood gushed from a broken nose, and he was missing a front tooth. The damage made him sound a little more nasal. He had a feral look in his eyes as he rose from the ground, a different man than the one she had just met earlier in the evening.

"Kali has marked her, Hanson," Ravi screamed. "She belongs to us now."

Hanson held his sword out and pointed it at Ravi.

"If you want her, you're going to have to go through me and three feet of sharpened steel," Hanson shouted back. He gestured to the hand on the ground. "And we both know how that's going for you."

Samantha saw movement out of the corner of her eye. The other Indian, who had a cut across his cheek, was rushing them with a pickaxe in his hands.

A pickaxe?

"Steve, behind you!" she shouted hoarsely.

Hanson let her go and spun around. The Indian was aiming for Hanson's chest. He parried the attack, and his blade cut through the weapon's wooden handle. The tapered metal end of the weapon flew away as Hanson swept his sword back and sliced off a few of the attacker's fingers.

The man yelled in pain and clutched his hand.

Hanson spun back on Ravi, who was stepping forward.

"Guess that guy wanted some more," Hanson said, keeping the blade between him and Ravi. "Do you?"

Ravi looked like he was going to say something else, but noise from somewhere else drowned him out.

It was a sound Samantha hadn't heard since her childhood, from when she watched those old *Star Trek* episodes with her dad.

The *Enterprise's* red alert klaxon.

It was coming from Hanson's van, which was also flashing red lights. Hanson put his arm around her waist again and began moving. The men around them were confused and enraged as Hanson half carried her away to his vehicle.

They made it to the van. Their attackers tried to follow, but they were all seriously wounded and could barely move. Samantha climbed into the passenger's seat as the van's klaxon blared. Hanson ran for the other side of the van, and when he opened the driver's door, she could see Todd rolling on the ground while holding his head. Hanson tossed his sword onto the back seat as he jumped behind the steering wheel.

The engine was already running. Hanson slammed the vehicle into gear as he yelled out a command. "Computer, cancel red alert and close all doors."

Behind her, the rear doors hissed shut as the van sped out of the parking lot.

Chapter 12

"Did you lose them?" Samantha yelled as she looked behind her. The move pained her, and she lifted a hand to her neck to rub it.

"No one's behind us," Hanson answered. Cold drops of water ran down his back. She was also soaked, and the front of her shirt was a black, oily mess. Hanson turned up the heaters in the van.

His answer chased away the fear that was on her face, replacing it with an expression of relief. She began patting her waist as she explored her pockets.

"We need to call the police," she said. "Damn it, they have my purse, my phone, and my keys. They have everything." She turned back toward him. "Steve, let me use your phone," she demanded. "The police may be able to track my cell."

Hanson ignored her outstretched hand. "Samantha, they're already gone. And your phone is most likely destroyed, or they're still jamming it."

"Jamming?"

"Our phones weren't working back there. One of them must have had a jamming device in their coat pockets."

"They're not jamming us now. And they must have my car. The police need to know."

"I agree, but we can't use my phone. The police might trace it back to me."

"Why does that matter?"

"Because in the back of my van is a sword with the blood of four different men on its blade," Hanson answered. "While we're giving statements about the attack and your stolen car, the police will be wondering how we got away. They will be looking through my van's windows and may notice my bloody back seat. Questions will be raised. Shit, I might have killed one of those men."

"It was self-defense."

"Self-defense is a complicated issue, and all they have is our word. The police will concentrate on the tangible evidence that they do have; the blood in my van."

Hanson spotted a payphone near a gas station. He pulled his van on the street behind the building and took a moment to check for cameras.

"I agree that we do need to let the police know that dangerous men are out there. But not with my cell."

Hanson hiked his jacket over his head as he ran over to the payphone.

He dialed 911 and kept the call short. Police might vector in on the phone's location. Hanson told the operator that men were firing guns at each other at a nearby parking lot and to send multiple police units. He also advised sending police to nearby hospitals, just in case men with serious wounds showed up.

Hanson hung up while the operator was still asking questions.

He wiped the handset with his shirt and made his way back to the van. He handed his cell phone to Samantha as he pulled away.

"If there is anyone close to you, call them. Warn them about strangers," he instructed her.

She called her parents back in Boston. She kept it brief as she explained that she was okay but to be wary themselves. It was the only call she made.

Hanson pulled into the lot of a twenty-four hour convenience store. He took the phone back and made his own call.

She answered on the fourth ring with a sleepy but worried tone.

"Who is this?" A pause, maybe to look at her screen, then his ex-wife's voice changed to one of annoyance. "Steve, it's one o'clock in the morning."

"Grace, I need you to check on Elanor," Hanson said.

That got her attention. He could hear her getting out of bed. The sound of her husband stirring also reached his ear.

"Grace, who is that?" Jeff asked.

"It's Steve. He said I need to check on El."

"Why? El's here, isn't she?"

Jeff Hamilton's voice receded. Grace had met him at a social gathering while Hanson, as usual, had made excuses to stay at home. Jeff, a tall, successful lawyer with graying temples and steely blue eyes, was an outgoing guy who knew how to have a good time. Grace, a beautiful, petite blonde who was starving for a good time, fell for him quickly.

Their divorce was no surprise. For Hanson, it was inevitable. Every woman he was ever close with soon grew weary of his self-imposed seclusion. He was surprised that she had stuck around for as long as she did, though he realized later that it mainly had to do with keeping a stable home for their daughter.

He heard a door open and a young woman's voice.

"Mom!"

"She's here, she's okay. El's on the phone with her friends. God, Steve, you made it sound like she snuck out and was in an accident," Grace said.

"Grace, listen, I was attacked a little while ago."

"My God, Steve! Are you okay?"

"I'm fine. I was able to get—"

Her concern was fleeting, and it was replaced with disapproval. "Does this have to do with that satanic thing? El said she had a message last week that you were there at that farm."

"Yes, it has to do with that," Hanson said, "Grace, look, I know El isn't going to like it, but she has to stay in. Don't let her out of your sight."

"Steve, what the hell!?"

"Grace, please. Don't even let her go to school till I figure this out. She stays home. And have Jeff check your security system."

"No school? Steve, she's missed so much school already due to COVID a while back. What's going on?"

"It's a cult," Hanson answered. He glanced over at Samantha, who was staring at him. Hanson's face reddened a bit as he used the same line that Samantha had used on her parents. "I'm part of an expose' on them. There's been some pushback, and they might target you. Everyone new in your life is now suspect, no matter how pleasant they are. Make sure both Jeff and El know that."

"You're worrying me."

"It'll be okay, Grace. Just don't trust strangers. I'll call later with updates."

Hanson hung up and slumped back in his seat, drained.

"Ex-wife?"

"Yeah, we divorced five years ago."

"She didn't sound happy to hear from you."

"During the last few years of our marriage, she wasn't happy with me at all."

"It must be difficult dealing with her since you share a daughter," Samantha added.

"Actually, she's not half bad as far as exes go, and her husband treats my daughter well," Hanson admitted, "it's just the…"

Looks of pity that they give me every time they see me.

"What?" she asked, wondering at his pause.

"Never mind," Hanson answered. He turned to his phone again and sent out a quick group email, alerting everyone he knew to watch out for strangers. He then phoned his mother back in Astoria and spent some time convincing her to visit her brother for a while.

"What now?" she asked after he hung up.

"Both of our places are unsafe," Hanson answered. Images of Bingo and Sebastian waiting by empty food dishes flashed across his mind. "But I need to check on my cats. Do you have a friend that you could stay with?"

"Connie lives nearby, right across the Willamette, on the east side of town."

"Good, we'll get some disposable phones from this store, and then I will take you there. After I check out my place, we will figure out what to do about this tomorrow."

"Okay, but before we do, at least tell me what they are. You acted as if you knew."

"Oh, I thought you heard me when I shouted it out back there."

"You only yelled that we were surrounded by a bunch of thugs. What are they, Steve?"

He realized then that she hadn't grasped that he was using the word *thug* in its original meaning. In the heat of the moment, he had forgotten that over the past centuries, the term had evolved. Long ago, it was a Hindi word used for the murderous deceivers who roamed India's highways. Now, it was more of a generic label for brutish men seeking to do physical violence on a person or property. It must have been easy for her to misconstrue what he had yelled out in desperation.

So, this time he said it slowly. Carefully. As if one word explained everything.

"They're thugs."

Chapter 13

FBI campus near Portland Airport, Saturday, 2:50 p.m. PDT

Samantha eased the red Honda Civic into the FBI visitor parking lot. The car was borrowed from her friend, as were the slacks and dark blouse she was wearing. Her hair was up, and a colorful silk scarf was tied loosely around her neck.

Hanson had called her in the morning to tell her that he had informed Agent Fisher what had happened, and they had been granted a three o'clock appointment at the FBI field office near the Portland Airport.

Hanson pulled up as she got out of the car, his van splashing through the puddles left from last night's rain. The weather was still cool and cloudy, so Hanson was wearing a brown sweater over a white collared shirt. His eyes were red from lack of sleep, and he hadn't shaved for over twenty-four hours.

"Everything okay at your place?" she asked.

"Yeah, the cats are fine, and no vases were knocked over due to hungry rages," he answered with a small smile. He glanced at her scarf. "How do you feel?"

"It hurts," she admitted as she raised her hand to her neck. "But it's not bad now."

"That's good to hear," Hanson said. He gestured toward the four-story brick building on the other side of the wrought iron fence.

"Fisher is waiting for us inside."

Hanson and Samantha checked in at the small gatehouse, where they were expected. Once their identification was confirmed, they were given visitor badges. Upon entering the main building, they were shown to what looked to be a small conference room. Samantha could see passenger jets approaching Portland Airport through its windows.

Agent Fisher strode into the room. Samantha turned from the windows and glanced at Hanson. His face lit up for a moment at the sight of his friend, but that quickly disappeared as he tried to act nonchalant about the two of them knowing each other.

"Special Agent Dan Fisher, thank you for seeing us," Hanson said as he nervously tugged and straightened out his sweater about his body.

Fisher rolled his eyes. "Relax, Hanson. Samantha understands we know each other from the Mount St. Helens incident and that for now that's all she needs to know." Fisher fixed her with a glare as he said the last part.

Though curious about the two men's relationship, Samantha put those questions on the back burner. Agent Fisher sat down and placed a laptop and thick manilla folder he was carrying on the table.

That meant Hanson's idea had paid off. He had told her that he would ask Fisher to look for any records that the FBI had on thugs. It appeared that they had a lot, and she hoped it was informative. She had spent most of her morning reporting her stolen car to the police. She had been careful not to cloud the matter by mentioning thugs and the wounds that Hanson had inflicted on them. Thus, she had only a little free time looking up thuggee and getting some basic information about them.

Fisher was powering up the computer, and soon the dark blue background of the FBI website filled the screen. He looked back up at her.

"Now, what Hanson told me sounded rather incredible, so I would like to hear from you, Samantha. What do you think is happening here?" Fisher asked.

His question surprised her. Hanson was convinced that they were dealing with thugs, and she had expected Agent Fisher to be on the same page. That didn't appear to be the case. The FBI agent was sternly staring at her as he slowly tapped his pen on the table.

She thought about her answer. She didn't want to sound like a wild conspiracist. "We have reason to believe that there's a religious criminal enterprise operating undetected here in the United States."

His eyes narrowed, and the frequency of his pen tapping increased a bit.

"So, a secret cult."

"Yes."

He opened the folder. "I've looked up the blog you contribute to and read your stories about what happened last week up at that dairy farm. You seemed to think it wasn't a cult."

"That's not accurate. I didn't think it was a satanic cult."

"And now you think a group devoted to the Hindu Goddess of Death is more plausible," Fisher said with a trace of sarcasm.

This wasn't going well. Her eyes darted toward Hanson. "Yes."

Fisher looked in that direction also.

"You're awfully quiet over there, Hanson, as usual. You're the skeptic in this room, and I could detect your hand behind Miss Ramsell's reporting. How did you make the jump to,"—Fisher pushed his pile of folders forward—"this?"

Hanson cleared his throat. "I think it all ties in with something I found earlier in the week."

Fisher fished out a photograph from the top folder and looked at it. Gruesome entrails and broken legs dominated it. "The dead cow. And because of that, you believe an ancient Hindu cult is still alive and well?" He asked incredulously.

Samantha could see a pained expression on Hanson's face.

"There was more," he answered.

"The body," Fisher acknowledged. "I've read the police report. The man was strangled. And because of that, and a dead cow, you made the jump to *Phansigars?*"

Hanson's eyebrows shot up.

"Yes, I know a little about the subject. I've had a few hours to read up on it," Fisher continued as he pulled a few pages out of the folder and laid them in front of him.

"*Phansigars*, that was the other name for them, right? The Hindi word for stranglers. Thug meant deceivers," Fisher said. He then began reading from his papers.

"They were members of a well-organized confederacy of professional assassins who traveled in gangs throughout India for centuries. About one-third was Muslim, the rest Hindu. Thuggee was hereditary, being passed on from father to son. They would join travelers on the road, and when the time was right, they would throw a noose around their victim's neck. This would be done after observing certain omens and practicing religious rituals to Kali, the Hindu Goddess of Destruction, who they served. They could speak a secret language, which they used to hide their intent from their victims. The entire country was infested with them, and they are thought to be responsible for over a million deaths." Fisher looked up from his reading. "Does that sound about right?"

"Where did all of this come from? We're not the first to mention thugs to the FBI, are we?" Samantha asked.

"You're not. As Hanson suggested, I did a computer search through our files. It turned out that twenty years ago, a man named Henry Cresswell down in Los Angeles thought as you two do now and claimed there were thugs still at large. He brought it to the Bureau's attention. The agent who caught that case had spent some time researching the subject."

Fisher leaned back in his chair and gestured at the paperwork in front of him.

"A lot of this information came from libraries. The agent had looked through encyclopedias, history books on India, and religious texts. He made photocopies of what he found. These were later scanned into our system. I printed them up today."

"So most everything you know comes from twenty years ago?" Hanson asked.

"Yes."

"Then there's something I need to explain to you right off the bat," he added.

Fisher's eyes narrowed again.

"And what's that?"

"The reason why I know so much about thuggee," Hanson continued as an apologetic look crossed his face. "I did an article about them a while back for my blog—"

Fisher was already shaking his head in exasperation, appearing as if he knew what Hanson was going to say next. For her, after the few articles she had read online, what Hanson revealed came as a shock.

"All of that paperwork, all of that history, is a lie," Hanson continued. "There was no such thing as thuggee."

Chapter 14

Fisher appeared angry. Samantha looked like she wanted to hit him.

"Let me clarify," Hanson hastily said as he held up his hands and scooted away from her in his chair a bit. "Thuggee did exist, but not as we know it."

"What does that mean?" Samantha asked. She was rubbing her neck as if it pained her.

Hanson gestured for the laptop. Fisher pushed it toward him. Hanson called up his website and entered "thug" into his blog's search bar. A sepia-toned photograph of grim-looking men wearing turbans, sitting cross-legged on a rug, popped up. Above was the article's title.

Was Thuggee Just Imagined?

"Let's start with the basics. We've been pronouncing it wrong. It's *toog*. It's the Hindi word *t'hag*, for swindler, or deceiver. Con men."

"When did the British first come aware of the *toogs*...thugs?" Samantha asked. Hanson understood her struggle. Pronouncing it as thugs was easier.

"The Company became aware of them in the early nineteenth century."

"Company?" Fisher asked.

"It wasn't the British Empire that fought the thugs; it was a corporation," Hanson answered. "The East India Company."

"What could a corporation do?" Samantha asked.

"The EIC was more than just a business by then. They were the governing force of most of India. They had their own locally recruited and trained army, the sepoys, who used superior British weapons and military tactics. The EIC controlled a country whose population numbered in the hundreds of millions from a London boardroom."

"That doesn't sound like a good idea," Fisher observed.

"It wasn't," Hanson said. "And India suffered for it. But the problem we will focus on was banditry. It was rampant, and the EIC spent a lot of effort fighting highway robbers in all forms. And while doing this, they discovered something more sinister.

"Near the town of Etawah, they began finding dozens of horribly mutilated bodies in wells. They weren't locals, so it was deduced that the victims were travelers from distant regions.

"For the next several years, except for the accumulation of more corpses, no headway could be made on the murders. The Company offered a reward. That worked. Arrests were made, and one guy started talking. He confirmed a term that until then had been only whispered and hinted at for the British authorities. Thug. And when he went on in detail, the British realized that they had on their hands a criminal enterprise that was unique."

"What made them different?" Fisher asked.

"Their *modus operandi*," Hanson explained. "Bandits, or *dacoits* as they were known in India, robbed and plundered through the threat of open violence, so victims had a chance to survive. On the other hand, thugs quietly murdered everyone they were going to rob."

"Everyone? How?" Samantha asked.

"During the cold season, pilgrims and travelers would take to the roads, mostly in small caravans for security. Thugs latched onto them by using their con men specialists, the *sothas*. *Sotha*, and other thug terms, came from the thug's secret slang language, *Ramasee*. Intelligent and handsome, *sothas* could pass as upper-caste Brahmins or traveling sepoys. They would infiltrate a group to discover their destination and how much wealth they possessed. Afterward, they would outnumber their victims and isolate them."

"That was in this paperwork," Fisher said. "Thugs would join the main host in small groups at a time."

"Victims feared dacoit attack. As they traveled, they would come across other men on the road with the same concern. The *sothas*, already ingratiated in the party, would recommend that everyone should band together for safety."

"And the original caravan didn't realize that all of the newcomers knew each other," Samantha guessed.

"Correct. They would arrive at a pleasant campsite. Trees provided shade, and wells were nearby for water. The caravan leader would call for a halt, not realizing where they were stopping at a place of the thug's own choosing, what they called a *bele*, a place for murder."

"That's the part I find most difficult to believe. Can it be that easy?" Fisher interjected as he shook his head. "You're in unfamiliar territory, and survival instincts are on high alert. I can't imagine anyone trusting a group of strangers enough to let themselves be outnumbered at night."

Both Hanson and Samantha were still for a moment, distant looks in their eyes.

"They're good at it," Samantha said quietly.

Fisher's eyebrows furrowed a bit in puzzlement at Samantha's input. Hanson resumed his narrative.

"Camp would be made, the newcomers would prove to be good company, and the pilgrims would all soon be relaxed. At that moment, a thug would utter the *jhirnee*, the code phrase that signaled the attack.

"*Bring the tobacco.*

"In concert, the thugs would strike. The *chumoseea* would grab the victim's wrists. Another would kick out the feet. The *bhurtote* would wrap a *rumal* around the victim's neck."

"Three men to one?" Fisher asked.

Hanson called up an image on the laptop, a watercolor painting showing three thugs attacking a fourth man. The picture was labeled.

Thugs Strangling a Traveler.

Samantha's face paled. Hanson hastily minimized the picture.

"When the traveling season was over, the thugs would return to their villages, which were far away from where they practiced their dark trade, so as not to implicate their home. There, they would give their local leader, the *zamindar*, his cut. A tax for providing the thugs a haven. Secure, thugs would return to their normal occupations, like farming or maintaining shops."

"What you just explained doesn't jibe with what I have," Fisher said as he pushed all the paperwork away from him in disgust. "Reading omens or eating a special sugar called '*goor*'? Magic pickaxes? And what about their blood-soaked Goddess, Kali? Thugs took all their cues and directions from her priests. They murdered in her name, killing for the sake of killing. Millions of Indians died on the road. It's in these notes. Where did all of these details come from?"

"William H. Sleeman," Hanson answered.

"Who was he?" Samantha asked.

"A Company civil servant in his early forties who could speak several languages, knew the local culture, and wrote volumes on various subjects. Stationed in the Jubbulpore District, he sought and secured the leadership position for taking on the thugs by writing an anonymous letter to the *Calcutta Literary Gazette*. Sleeman was right about one thing: the thugs were a problem. But he embellished in what they were and their scope. Alarmed, the Company leadership organized the Thuggee Suppression Department. Sleeman then stepped forward to run it."

"He created his own job," Fisher said in disbelief.

"EIC management felt something had to be done. The opium trade was taking off, and incredible amounts of cash transfers traveling overland weren't making it to their banks. Sepoys on leave were also disappearing. Sleeman had a plan to put an end to the thug problem. He used approvers, former thugs now informants that confirmed suspected thugs, thus 'approving' their arrest. Sleeman also had his men catalog everything the approvers said, noting names, family affiliations, home bases, victims, and what was plundered. *Bele* locations were mapped out."

"Weren't the high courts a problem?" Samantha asked. "Most of what the Suppression Department had was hearsay."

"The Company simply changed the laws, and Sleeman used a frontier judge and court sympathetic to his causes," Hanson answered.

"It must have been easy after all of that," Fisher commented.

"It was, and Sleeman had one more ace up his sleeve. Early in the campaign, he had captured the most notorious thug of them all, Feringeea. This man was a charismatic, intelligent leader who had been at it for years. He gave up a tremendous amount of information to Sleeman.

"With all of this in place, the Thuggee Department rounded up and convicted nearly four thousand thugs by 1840, hanging five hundred *bhurtotes*, and deporting the others to far off penal colonies. Sleeman smashed thuggee in a decade."

Hanson paused, looking at the paperwork on the table.

"But he wasn't done with the thugs just yet," he said.

"Kali," Samantha guessed.

"The British back then felt like they were surrounded by idol-worshipping heathens. Kali was a threat, and they wanted reasons to get rid of her. This prejudice colored Sleeman's questions during interviews. He hammered his prisoners on how Kali fit into thuggee.

"Now look at the interrogation from the thug's view. They're trying to save their necks from the hangman's noose. The word back in the holding cells is that the better the story, the better your chances. What's a thug to do?"

"You tell your captors what they want to hear," Fisher replied.

"And 'imagined thuggee' was born," Hanson said. "The thugs talked, and a vocal minority said some rather fantastic things. It's these cherry-picked confessions that survive to this day.

"Sleeman wrote a book that included the transcripts from these interviews. He called it the *Ramaseeana*, for one chapter was 'a vocabulary of the peculiar language used by the thugs', *Ramasee*. Paton, who worked with Sleeman, had his notes transcribed also. A third man, Dr. Sherwood, who lived in the Madras area, published his interviews with some captured *pharsingers*.

"So really, everything that we have considered fact for the past two hundred years comes from a handful of men. Men who inserted their own prejudices and beliefs into their reports."

Samantha and Agent Fisher looked at the papers, which, by now, were scattered all over the table.

"How did the change of opinions on thuggee come about?" Samantha asked.

"Historians have been giving thuggee a second look for some time," Hanson answered. "Several of them published the idea that it never existed at all. That it was all in the fearful British's imagination. A 'Colonial Construct.' Cynics also claimed the British invented thuggee to create fear and push through draconian laws to control the population. Other historians have taken up the issue, searching through Company records to find proof that a watered-down form of 'real thuggee' existed. Their conclusion was that it did. Not a cult of a bloody Goddess that sacrificed millions, but a group of desperately poor bandits that murdered tens of thousands."

"Interesting presentation," Fisher said. "But in your effort to convince me that an ancient murderous secret cult is in the here and now, you've left out the one important fact that I'm sure all of your historians agree upon."

Fisher picked up the paper that he had read off earlier.

"One hundred and eighty years ago, the British wiped them out. Thuggee is no more."

Samantha reached up behind her neck to undo the knot on her scarf. She carefully removed the scarf, as if its touch hurt her. She held up her chin slightly. Hanson could see Fisher's eyes widen.

"What if they didn't," Hanson said.

The scarf had been concealing a wound, a glaring red ring, slightly swollen, around Samantha's entire neck. Fisher stared at it as Hanson continued talking.

"What if the British, instead of wiping out a group of ruthless bandits, created a monster?"

Chapter 15

"What happened to your neck?" Fisher asked with concern in his voice.

"The thugs tried to strangle me last night," Samantha answered.

"Strangle?" Now the tone was disbelief, and he rocked back in his chair. "And where was this again?"

"At their *bele*—" Hanson began.

"A parking lot," Samantha clarified.

"Hanson had told me that you were attacked, but he didn't tell me everything," Fisher said. "Maybe you two better do so now."

Hanson described the night. When he reached the parking lot fight, he toned it down a bit, and left out the sections where he cut off arms and legs. He wasn't sure if all the thugs survived his attack, and he was worried that Fisher would be obligated to report that to the local authorities.

Fisher stared at him when he finished. Hanson squirmed in his chair, unsure if the FBI agent believed his version of the fight.

"Do you always carry a sword in your van?"

"Only on game night," Hanson answered, his face reddening a bit.

"Please don't tell me that you also dress up for game night," Fisher pressed. Hanson didn't answer. Fisher shook his head and turned to Samantha.

"Hanson noted that you called him. So that means that they reached out to you initially."

"About midweek, I received an email through my blog account. A man named Sanjay had sent me a message, saying that my stories were getting traction back East. He wanted to set up a meeting."

Hanson listened. This was all new information for him.

"You must have checked him out," Fisher guessed.

"I did," Samantha said. "He had sent an attachment in the email. It had background information on him and links to access his social accounts. I looked up all of them. They appeared legitimate."

"Whoever these guys were, they must have backstopped themselves so that they would pass some level of scrutiny," Fisher mused. "But you must still have connections with old work colleagues. Did you call them to further verify these strangers reaching out to you?"

"No. In his email, Sanjay...Ravi...made it sound like they were trying to get an exclusive with me, and he didn't want any potential rivals to get wind of it."

"And you bought all of that?"

"I did. But you need to understand, going back East, with a big story in hand, it's what I've wanted for a long time. He mentioned all the right people, all the right organizations. He just..."

"Pushed all the right buttons," Hanson finished.

"Steve, I'm so sorry." She looked away with guilt. "I was blinded by something I wanted so much. I led us both into a trap."

Hanson smiled at her. "It's okay. You were dealing with a *sotha*. They used to spy on potential victims in Indian villages. Now, they must be using social accounts to data-mine, learning all they need to know to ensnare whoever they want."

"Did they reach out to you also?" she asked.

Hanson thought about his staying home alone every weekend.

"No. I don't have much for them to work with."

She turned back to Fisher. "He called me later to set up our meeting and asked me to bring Steve along."

Fisher glanced at Hanson. "Sounds like your thugs weren't as careful as history leads us to believe." Fisher had brought his hands up to make the air quote hand gesture when he said the word *thugs*.

"I don't follow," Hanson said. He was feeling a touch of resentment toward his friend. After all they had been through together, he had thought Fisher would accept his story at face value.

"Let's assume that they succeeded," Fisher continued. "Where would the police start the investigation?"

"My computer," Samantha answered.

"And your phone," Fisher added. "They would use those to find the bars you were at, and then they would have video, witnesses, and the URLs of this Sanjay guy."

"I don't think so," Hanson interrupted.

"And why not?" Fisher asked.

Hanson pushed the laptop toward Samantha.

"Call up your blog account," he said.

She tapped away at the keyboard. Her page appeared on the screen.

"The emails from Ravi, they're gone," she said. She looked at Hanson. "You knew."

"As IT support at work, our nightmares are email attachments. There was a virus hidden in the one you received. It's loose in your employer's system, and it's clearing your recent history and erasing any correspondence with the thugs."

"Suspects," Fisher said.

"Thugs," Hanson shot back in a mocking voice while doing air quotes himself and making a face. He then shook his head and pointed at the screen. "What's that email you haven't opened yet?"

The message in question did not have a header. She clicked on it. The email was only a short sentence in large red letters.

"YOU SHOULD HAVE TAKEN US SERIOUSLY"

A detailed image of a pentagram finished the email.

"What the hell?" Fisher exclaimed.

"Not hell. It's a misdirect. The thugs wanted to point you toward devil worshippers and send you on a wild goose chase," Hanson said.

"We still have her phone."

"Which only has untraceable calls."

"Witnesses at the bar."

"Again, nothing. Everyone was focused on the *Dirty Mopheads* and not us. And even if they were, everyone knows that eyewitness descriptions are unreliable. And if someone did give you a description of the men we were with last night, after reading that email, police would be assuming that they were followers of..."

Hanson sat up straight and did an impersonation of the Church Lady from *Saturday Night Live*. "Satan!"

Frowning, Fisher changed his tack of questioning.

"You said that the British created a monster. What makes you think that?"

Hanson looked at Samantha. "Tell him what they were saying when they were attacking you."

"Ravi stated that I was marked, and Kali must be fed, that she will delight in my blood," she said quietly. Her hand moved up to her neck, and she absently rubbed the welt there as she continued. "That my death would save the world."

"From what I have read, things a thug would say," Fisher said.

"An 'imagined' thug," Hanson corrected. "I spent most of the night thinking about this. Since many details were invented by Sleeman and lying thug prisoners, these concepts shouldn't carry on with surviving 'true' thugs. The fact that Samantha overheard this suggests that at some point in history, someone read Sleeman's *Ramaseeana* and thought it was a damn good idea for a new religion."

"When do you think that happened?" Samantha asked.

"When true thuggee fell, around the mid-nineteenth century."

"What are you basing that guess on?" Fisher asked.

"Cows. We know there's some sort of relationship between the recent murder and mutilated cows, which have been going on for 170 years." Hanson reached for the computer again and began typing.

"Here, in the United States?" asked Fisher.

"No, it started out in England. It made the jump to the US in the seventies."

"Okay, cows in England were dying in the 1850s. That's still very slim. I'd be more interested if you told me people were getting strangled."

A web page flashed up on the screen. It had a banner sized header.

The Garroters of London.

Hanson scrolled down the page. A drawing of two dapper-looking men mugging a third man by grabbing him from behind and choking him was now on the screen.

"In London, back in the 1850s, there was a rash of attacks in which thieves would first strangle victims with garrotes. The press sensationalized it and created a moral panic."

"How bad did it get?" Samantha asked.

Hanson scrolled down some more. He stopped on a photograph of what looked like a small gun mounted on a belt buckle.

"Some guy invented an 'Anti Garrotter Belt Pistol,'" Hanson answered. "This device was attached to the belt at your back. If someone came up behind you, the victim could fire the weapon by pulling on a string."

"If the attacker was tall enough, his balls would get blown off," Samantha said as she stared at the image. "Useful."

Both men shifted uncomfortably in their chairs.

"Last night's attack brought me back to this," Hanson continued. "Before, I had thought little of it, for it shows English blokes choking English blokes. And thugs are—"

"Indians," Samantha finished. "But last night, only two of the men were Indian. Three were Caucasian. One was Asian. Chinese, I think."

"Which makes me think that the English garrotters could have been thugs, clumsily practicing a new religion. But when people started wearing ball buster belts, this garroting thing died down. Then the cattle mutilations started up."

"So, practice body disposal with the cows, graduate to humans later?" Samantha asked.

"Yes," said Hanson.

"Do you think what's happening now is a local thing?" Fisher asked.

"No. I think it's nationwide," Hanson answered.

"What makes you think that?"

"Two things," Hanson answered. "I've been tracking cattle mutilations for years. Their locations create a large arc across the West and Midwest over a length of time. More than one man."

"What's the second?" Fisher prodded.

"The thugs mentioned a schedule, as if their murders happened weekly," Samantha answered.

For a while, it had appeared that they had Fisher's interest. But now, he looked annoyed again.

"So, you think that these guys have been killing someone once a week for the past fifty years?" He grabbed the computer and called back the FBI website. He then hit a tab marked "Serial Killers."

"And right under our very noses?" Fisher said, anger now in his voice. "Fifty-two murders a year, for five decades? We track things like this. Do you think we're a bunch of idiots over here?"

"You have been tracking them," Hanson answered. He snatched the computer back and moved the cursor to a different tab from the FBI's dropdown list. A new page cycled up, and it displayed photographs of American citizens. Everyone in the room focused on the page's header.

Missing Persons.

Chapter 16

"Thugs made the bodies disappear," Hanson continued.

"By putting them down wells?" Samantha asked.

"That, and by whatever method was available for them," Hanson said. "Most of the time, they used the terrain, like dragging them into thick vegetation or throwing them into gullies.

"But in well-traveled areas, thugs had a few more specialists on hand. Their grave diggers were called *lughae*. Their main tool was not a shovel, but a pickaxe."

"One of the men came at you with a pickaxe last night," Samantha said.

"The British made a big deal about thugs worshipping pickaxes," Fisher added.

"Another British misconception?" Samantha asked.

"No, this one was true. However, what the British didn't consider was that most Indians venerated their tools of the trade."

"So, just a simple, common superstition of the times," Fisher noted.

"Right. But to truly remain undetected, it took more than just a hole in the ground," Hanson continued. "Disposing of the bodies fell to the *kuthowas*.

"Bloating corpses tended to cause cracks in the soil above. The smell of decay escaped, and in no time, animal scavengers had the graves dug up.

"Thugs had an answer for that. The *kuthowa* cut open the bellies to prevent bloating. Wounds were made between the ribs. This aided in the body's rapid dissolution."

"What about the joints being cut and broken?" Fisher asked.

"If the ground was hard and rocky, the *lughae* would dig small round graves. The victim's legs and arms were folded back on the body and stuffed into the holes."

"So, you're saying that they have been burying bodies that way for the past forty years? That's over two thousand people. And no one has found them yet? That's impossible."

Hanson remained quiet.

"And how many thugs do you think there are?" Fisher continued. "And they're all serial killers? Do you know what it takes to become a serial killer?"

"I do. That was something that Sleeman investigated. The whole nature versus nurture thing. The British believed that the desire to murder was in the Indian's blood or due to the shape of their skull. That it was inherited. Nowadays, we think that sociopaths are made, not born."

"And only 4 percent of the population are sociopaths," Fisher said. "Making it unlikely that an entire group can be exclusively sociopaths."

"I don't think our current thugs are sociopaths," Hanson said. "I think they're fanatics who are following a religion invented by the British."

"How does that lead them to kill?" Fisher asked.

"Their religion explains a lot about their actions. The British were fixated on this whole Kali relationship with thuggee," Hanson answered. "Through their interviews, they learned of the thug's origin myth. A thug's version of their own Genesis."

"Was this myth completely made up by the thugs?" asked Samantha.

"No, it's based on the *Devi Mahatmya*, a Hindu religious text focusing on the power of the Goddess. Some of the chapters tell of the Goddess's battle with the asuaras, or demons, that were plaguing mankind.

"One of these asuras was named Raktabija, the Blood Seed. Raktabija was so tall that the ocean only came to his waist as he stood in it. His size allowed him to stride all over the world with ease. He was also destroying mankind as fast as they were being created, drawing infants' souls to himself as they were born."

"Wait a minute, is this some sort of Hindu bible story?" Fisher asked.

"Yes, and a popular one, like our Adam and Eve, or the Flood," Hanson said, his brows furrowed in annoyance at being interrupted.

"Anyway, terrified Indians prayed to their Gods for help. The Gods responded by calling upon their ten-armed warrior Goddess, Durga, to put him down…

"As tall as a mountain herself, Durga descended from the heavens onto the earth, where she found the demon striding up a valley, searching for more victims.

"Raktabija was in the form of a hairless, wicked-looking man, wearing only a dhoti and wielding a great sword in both hands. Durga, always with a calm and serene expression on her face, was dressed in a red sari and bore a weapon in each of her ten hands. Each of these magically enhanced weapons were boons, or gifts, from the other Gods. In her mind, there was only one outcome to this battle.

"Though seemingly outmatched, Raktabija rushed her, the earth shaking under him as he swung his massive sword. Durga responded by parrying with a few of her weapons and using the rest to cut him down, his blood raining on the earth from his wounds.

"Raktabija roared in agony as he backed away from her onslaught. But he also had a smile on his face. It was then that Durga understood why he was named the Blood Seed.

"As each drop of blood touched the ground, a human-sized version of Raktabija would spring up. Durga hadn't really hurt him. She had created a vast army that was intent on destroying her.

"They rushed her, and they used their claws to grip her skin and climb up her legs. They pierced her with their swords, stinging her like a swarm of fire ants.

"Now it was her turn to cry out in pain. Durga stamped on them. This only caused more blood to spill and the demon army to grow. Meanwhile, Raktabija pressed his attacks, swinging his massive sword.

"As Durga parried his blows, she realized she was only making things worse.

With a frown, she backed away a bit, her long strides taking her away from the mass of demons at her feet. Mountains crumbled and canyons formed as Raktabija howled in triumph, thinking that she was retreating from the battle.

"But she wasn't. She only wanted a moment to summon assistance. With her brow knitted in concentration, a ray of light blazed from her forehead as she called out for help.

"And Kali answered.

"Raktabija watched as a form materialized in front of Durga. He was familiar with the Hindu pantheon, populated with serene, noble gods, such as Shiva, Lakshmi, or Vishnu. But when Kali turned and faced him, he realized that this one was different.

"Her skin was a dark blue, almost black. Her long, dark hair laid unbridled about her, partially covering her naked breasts. She had four arms, the top two holding long, curved tulwars.

"A long tongue hung and writhed out of her snarling, fanged mouth. Her eyes blazed red, and Raktabija couldn't help but notice that they gazed upon him not with fear…

"But with hunger.

"With a scream that shook the heavens, Kali sprang forward. Raktabija, his army a carpet around his feet, let her approach as he raised his blade. When she closed with him, his minions swarmed up her, stinging, while he brought down his sword.

"She brought up her two tulwars to parry the blow. He half expected her to cut at him with her other two hands, but he soon realized she was using them to scoop up the demons on her body and toss them into her gaping maw. The demons fell in, shrieking in despair as she consumed them whole.

"Without spilling a drop of blood.

"They dueled that way, with Kali occasionally cutting at the demon. He would let it happen, hoping that some of his blood would drip off the blade. But Kali's tongue would always get there first, lashing out and catching the drops and drawing them into her.

"Her onslaught was overwhelming, and Raktabija thought about fleeing. He looked to the ground to see how much of his army remained to cover his escape. To his dismay, he saw that they were all gone. He looked back up.

"Too late. With a feral cry, Kali was on him. She cast aside her swords as she

used three of her arms to pin his. The fourth tilted his head to the side, and her fanged mouth clamped on his exposed neck.

"And Kali drained Raktabija, the Blood Seed, dry.

"The earth quaked as she let his husk drop to the ground. It should have ended there, but Kali was drunk from the blood of the demon. She flew into a rage and started a crazed, stamping dance that rocked the earth and destroyed all near her. The other Hindu Gods realized they had traded one problem for another. They sent her husband, Shiva, to stop her.

"Shiva arrived, and he tried to calm the rampaging Kali, but she wasn't listening. With the whole world falling apart around them, Shiva, the Destroyer, did the only thing he could.

"He laid himself at her feet.

"Not realizing it, she stepped on him in her mad dance. When she did look down and saw him lying there under her feet, she instantly calmed down, her tongue hanging out in shame and regret. She knelt and picked up her beloved, and they quit the battlefield. The world, and its people, was safe once more."

Samantha had a series of images of Kali up on the monitor.

"So is that why almost every picture of Kali shows her standing on Shiva," she asked. "He was trying to stop her from destroying the world?"

"Yes," Hanson answered. "Stepping on your husband was against all social convention and propriety. Such a *faux pas* was enough to prevent Armageddon."

"How does this relate to the thugs?" Fisher asked.

"I wanted to tell you the orthodox version first," Hanson answered. "For the thugs tell this story differently. You see, in their version…"

"Kali was losing.

"There were simply too many Raktabija minions on her. She bled from each sting, and her blood flowed away from her as rivers. She stumbled, crushing demons underfoot and creating dozens more. Her defenses were weakening, and Raktabija's raining blows were beating her down.

"Kali was drenched in perspiration from her exertions, her hair clinging to her shoulders in ringlets. Beads of sweat were dripping off her.

"Raktabija strode forward and brought his blade crashing down in an overhead blow. She barely parried it by raising her tulwars above her.

"But unnoticed by him, she also crossed her lower arms. She raised her weapon-less hands to her upper elbows, using her fingers to capture some of the sweat beading there. These drops she slung downward, and they crashed into the earth.

"And from the sweat of Kali rose two men.

"They were paragons of manhood, perfect in every way. Both were bare-chested, clothed only in white dhotis and yellow turbans. Held in their outstretched arms were yellow rumals.

"They were born knowing what to do.

"They fell on Raktabija's army from behind, sneaking upon the stragglers, wrapping their rumals around the demons' necks.

"Killing them without spilling a drop of blood.

"They continued their dark trade while the battle between the Gods raged as a thunderstorm above them, never deviating from their task.

"Seeing her creations at work, Kali strengthened her defenses by summoning blades to her lower hands so that she could use four blades to parry his blows. Unaware of what was happening below, Raktabija smiled to himself. If she couldn't take time to consume his army, this battle would be his. He would be anni-hilating a Goddess this day.

"But she didn't weaken as he expected. She seemed to be getting stronger. Confused, he looked down to see what his minions were doing. Confusion turned to fear as he saw countless bodies lying dead at his feet, his army somehow destroyed.

"When he looked back up, she was already on him.

"Things went on as before. She went mad. Shiva calmed her. But this time, as they both were quitting the battlefield, she glanced back.

"The two men she had created were still there, on their knees, their heads bowed down.

"She went to them, and when they looked up, they saw that the towering titan-sized demon destroyer was gone. In its place was a beautiful, blue-skinned woman with a benevolent smile on her face.

"With her four arms, she bade them to rise. They offered to return the rumals to her, but she gestured to them to keep them instead.

"She told them that they were her children. And since they helped destroy the demon and thus enabled the world to be populated with men once again, she would allow them to take a few men of their own and prosper from the wealth plundered from them. And though murder was a sin, she would forgive them if the killing *were made in her name. From the battle they just witnessed, the men realized that blood was her food, and if she were not fed, disease, death, and the destruction of the entire world would follow. The men pledged themselves to her and continued killing in her name, leaving the bodies for her. Since rumals were their weapons, they learned to kill with deception, honing the skill to a fine art. In Hindi, there is a word for such deceivers…*

"T'hug."

Chapter 17

"Do you think he believed us?" Samantha asked.

They were sitting in a booth at a restaurant near the FBI office. Hanson was watching jets approaching the airport as he picked at his calamari appetizer.

"This isn't the first time Fisher and I have dealt with the...um... incredible," Hanson answered. "So, I'm sure he does. But we have some things working against us. He told us the FBI dismissed the Cresswell case twenty years ago because the evidence Cresswell had promised didn't hold up. I guess we have less official FBI support than I had hoped."

Samantha's mouth was full of calamari, so she grunted her acknowledgment as she turned to Hanson's laptop computer on the table. She busied herself by scrolling through *The Unexplained, Explained* website while she chewed.

After a moment, she looked up at him and smiled. "There's a lot of interesting articles in here."

"Thanks," Hanson said, enjoying the compliment and alone time with her. It felt like they were on a date.

"How do we find these guys," she asked as she helped herself to some more of the calamari.

"We gave Agent Fisher that name you overheard, Vankatesan, before we left," he answered. "Though I don't think he can work on this case in a formal capacity, he may be able to look into some things on his own. We should let him handle it."

"Steve, I don't think that is going to be enough," she said. "There's only so much that Agent Fisher can do alone."

Hanson shifted in his seat. A large part of his anxiety dealt with not crossing anyone in authority, such as Fisher's managers in the FBI. But he also didn't want to spend the rest of his life looking over his shoulder. Self-preservation won out.

"We need to find this Vankatesan guy," he said.

"I've been thinking about that," she replied with a relieved smile. "They've been in my computer. Can we follow him that way?"

He shook his head. "No. They're covering their tracks. I noticed it as I looked over my website this morning. An unusual amount of IP addresses are being blocked by the people perusing my website. I think it's thugs using TOR and reading up on me."

"TOR?"

"Acronym for 'The Onion Router.' It's software that uses relays all around the world to mask your location and identity. Even the NSA admits it can't crack it."

"Show me."

He called up his tracking software on the laptop. Graphs and colorful pie charts filled the screen.

"Okay, here's where it all started, with Tully reaching out and finding my article on cattle mutilations."

He pointed at the screen and moved two entries down.

"That's you."

His fingers continued downward to point out the more recent emails, but she stopped him with a question.

"I was third?"

"Yes."

"Who was second?"

It was starting to sound like an Abbot and Costello routine. He almost said, "I don't know," but instead looked closely at the screen to refresh his memory.

"It was from the campus server at Reynolds University, in New York," he answered.

"What if that was them?"

"Thugs? They seem to be careful at covering their tracks."

"Yes, but this whole thing started with a mistake on their part. Maybe the thugs were sloppy and didn't follow their computer protocols in their panic."

"Possible. But it's still a big campus. Where do we start?" Hanson asked.

"Here," she said, as she called up a search engine and typed in: Vankatesan, Reynolds University.

A list of choices came up, all in blue font. She selected the first one.

"I don't think that's going—" he began.

A Reynolds University bio page for one of its professors cycled up. Vankatesan.

A handsome Indian in his early forties dominated the screen. His face was clean-shaven, and his thick, curly hair was cut short. He had an easy-going smile. His eyes were clear and bright with intelligence.

"Huh," Samantha said. "I was sort of expecting someone with a mustache to twirl."

Hanson read the text.

Professor Tanvir Vankatesan, PhD. in Indian history and British imperialism.

"He's kind of handsome," she continued.

Hanson looked back and forth between her and the computer. It was as if the image itself was inveigling her.

"He's a thug," he said emphatically. "That's a thug if I ever saw one."

She snapped out of the photograph's spell.

"You're right," she said, rubbing her neck. "It's too much of a coincidence."

"Now we go back to the FBI," he said.

"Not so fast," Samantha said. "What we have is still flimsy at best, and with the Cresswell case dropped, we don't have anything to back up what we are saying. We should go over there and check him out ourselves."

We. He thought about flying over to New York with her. The idea had merit. Hanson started thinking about taking an indefinite leave of absence from work. Explain it as a medical issue. As in, if he didn't figure this out, he would be dead.

"Okay, I'm in," he said. "I just need to make some arrangements back here at home."

Hanson dialed a number and put his phone on the table

"Any luck at the FBI?" Tolmany asked as he picked up the call.

"Not really," Hanson answered. "But Samantha and I think we have a lead on one of the thugs. We're going out of town. I need a couple of favors."

"Sure, name it," Tolmany said.

"Keep an eye on my ex's house."

"Easy. Next favor." He sounded apprehensive about this one.

"Feed my cats."

"I will, but I'm not singing to them as you do. You're going have to do your cat song right now while I record it so that I can play it for them."

Hanson sighed and picked up his phone. As his face turned a deep shade of red, Hanson sang while Samantha watched.

"And kitties have stormy eyes, that glow at the smell of fries..."

Part Two

KHOMUSNA

Chapter 18

The bele, Tuesday 1:35 p.m. PDT

Fisher pulled his red Jeep Renegade into the last remaining space in the parking lot. The sky above was thick with gray clouds, so he powered up his window in case it rained.

His stomach growled, and he frowned at the vehicles parked around him. He was skipping lunch to look this place over on his own time, as Hanson's story was too fantastic to bring to his superiors.

When Hanson had called him in the middle of the night last weekend with his wild story of thugs assaulting him, Fisher had only half believed him. He knew Hanson well enough to realize that his friend wouldn't make up an attack.

But blaming it on a secret murderous cult thought long dead by every published history book in existence was another matter.

Another theory had instantly sprung to Fisher's mind as he sat up in bed while Hanson babbled about his encounter. Social media made it easy for people to form camps of differing opinions, and people didn't like it when others challenged their ideas. A mild anti-satanism hysteria was growing in the nation. Fisher could picture a group of devout Christians taking it upon themselves to teach reporter Samantha Ramsell and her source, skeptic Steve Hanson, a lesson on the insidious nature of the devil.

He had also come up with a reason for Hanson's motivations. Hanson's judgment was clouded by the presence of Samantha Ramsell. Fisher could sympathize that his lonely friend had wanted to impress the beautiful reporter with a theory of an outlandish threat. A threat that was right up the skeptic's alley of the weird and unusual.

These thoughts had set the tone for last Sunday's meeting. Fisher did feel something was going on and that there was some danger. But after reading the file the FBI had on thugs, he was confident that they weren't the source of Hanson's attack.

Until he saw the wound on Samantha's neck.

It was unlike anything he had seen before, and it was enough to introduce a shade of doubt in his thinking and to start looking into some things on his own.

Fisher stepped out of his rig and stood to the side. The area had some light traffic as local workers returned from their breaks. Fisher envied them as he watched several people toss fast-food bags into a nearby garbage bin. His stomach rumbled again, and he thought about what he had learned so far.

During yesterday's lunch break, he had gone over some Portland Police reports. Two complaints from this area had been filed last week. Kelly's and the Sirens had been hit by thieves breaking back windows and trying to crack the two bars' safes. Both attempts had failed, and instead, the thieves had wrecked the surveillance systems.

Leaving both taverns that Hanson had visited without working security cameras.

There was another report, this one written out by officers responding to a 911 call. Gunshots were reported in a parking lot. The officers had responded quickly, but no one was to be found.

Fisher had listened to the call itself. It sounded like Hanson, though it wasn't wild, incoherent shouting like most calls. He was being careful with what he was saying. And what he told the police was different from what he had told him. It was apparent Hanson was trying to force a strong police response, but he was also trying to hide something.

Fisher explored the area, recalling the word Hanson had used for the parking lot.

Bele.

A thug's murder site. As Fisher searched, he tried to imagine Hanson and Samantha finding themselves outnumbered three to one in this location at night.

Near the edge of the lot, he discovered a large, brown stain. He knelt by it.

Blood.

The rain had washed it out somewhat, but there was no mistaking it. Someone had lost a lot of blood here.

The reason for Hanson's evasiveness was becoming apparent. Hanson was a former Marine, and Fisher knew that his friend could handle himself in a fight. And the lengths he would go to avoid dealing with anyone with authority.

His frown deepening, Fisher strode over to one of the several lamp posts rising above the vehicles.

He could see they were outfitted with new LEDs. Hanson had described the encounter as happening in the near dark. The area should have been as lit up like a football field on Friday night.

He looked lower down the post. Near the bottom was an access plate. Fisher selected the screwdriver from his Leatherman multi-tool he carried at his belt and removed the two screws.

Inside, wires ran up the hollow core. One of them had been cut.

What the hell?

He replaced the cover and stood back up, his eyes searching. He located another sizeable bloodstain on the pavement. Hanson hadn't chased off his attackers by flashing his sword, as he had said. He had cut at least two of them, maybe even critically. Fisher's shoulders sagged a bit as he exhaled deeply, his theory of angry churchgoers fleeing his mind with his breath. He rolled Hanson's theory through his mind.

Thugs.

Was it possible? Though he hadn't let on to Hanson, last weekend, and the movie *Indiana Jones and the Temple of Doom*, wasn't his first exposure to the lore of thuggee.

He had been studying serial killers back at Quantico. Naturally, that led to the morbid curiosity on who were the most prolific killers in history. He had looked it up on the web.

Near the top of the list had been a man simply called Thug Behram. The king of the thugs and responsible for 931 deaths. The article noted that other thugs used simple *rumals* to kill. Behram had a twist. A large coin, called the Canova Medallion, was sown into the cloth, which he disguised as his cumberbund. Behram was known to "expertly" cast the *rumal* around the victim's neck so the medallion would press against the Adam's Apple and apply more crushing pressure.

That entry had stuck in Fisher's mind. Nearly a thousand men, dead by one hand. He had looked up Behram again last night. Hanson had been right that thuggee was going through revision. Behram no longer held a top spot. His count had been reduced to 125 victims.

Still, a lot of people.

Could a group of men be killing at that level now?

Fisher stepped off the lot and onto the grounds surrounding it. Shrubbery grew thick in the soft soil. He moved slowly, scanning the environment, kicking aside any littler that was in his way.

Though he was half expecting it, he almost fell into a hole. Pulling back a branch, he studied it.

It was round, three-and-a-half-feet deep, and about the same in diameter. Dirt was piled nearby.

Not the rectangular dimensions and depth of a grave. But if some killers took the time to gut and break joints on their victims, two corpses could fit in there. Fisher shuddered, momentarily imagining Hanson and Samantha, backs broken so that they could be folded to fit into the hole and their eyeless faces staring up at him.

He took a few photos with his phone and then walked back to his vehicle, pondering his next move. He would have to let his ASAC know something was going on and make this an official investigation. But how to explain thuggee to his boss? He was still struggling with that thought when his phone vibrated. It was a text message.

Don't be mad. Samantha and I have a lead on Vankatesan. Don't tell anyone. I am not sure of the thug's reach with local law enforcement. And by local, I mean I ♥NY.

"Goddamit!" Fisher shouted. The heads of several passerby's turned his way in alarm, and he ducked into his jeep to avoid their stares. Hanson and Samantha had given him a name earlier, Vankatesan. It would appear that they had tracked him to New York. Fisher hoped that they would be careful. The website from his Quantico days didn't just have Behram listed as a prolific killer. There were at least three other thugs with over five hundred murders to their names. If this Vankatesan was a thug, all Fisher could think about was that this guy could be a homicidal maniac, doing only God knows what at this very moment.

Chapter 19

West Village, New York, 4:50 p.m. EDT

Tanvir Vankatesan kissed his wife goodbye, hoping to chase away the worried look on her face.

"He's not doing as well in math as I had hoped," she explained.

Vankatesan looked fondly at Samaira. Though their marriage had been arranged, he still thought of his wife as the most beautiful woman he had ever met.

"I'm sure it's just a phase," he reassured her. "You've done well with his homeschooling."

"But Jayesh is fourteen now, and our plan was for him to go to public school when he reached twelve. COVID ruined that, and I just don't want him to be behind the other children," she said, her dark eyes filled with worry. "Maybe we can bend the rules about the internet a bit and let him use the Khan Academy online math program for more practice."

He ran a hand through his thick, black hair. Even though he was forty-three years old, he showed no signs of gray. And unlike a few of his comrade professors, his body was still slim and athletic from his intense physical workouts at the university's gyms.

As usual, he had a difficult time resisting her gaze, but he put up a feeble resistance.

"Sweetheart, you should see the kids now at school. Their noses buried in their phones and computers while I give lectures their parents spend thousands of dollars for. I'm telling you, once our son starts down that slippery slope—"

"We'll manage him," she interjected with a smile. "Even with all of the internet's downfalls, it can still be a help to him."

"Okay," he said, "We'll give it a try. But right now, I must take care of a few things at work. Let's talk about it a bit more when I get back."

He left his West Village home, the skies clear and the air warm. His car and driver were waiting for him outside. Both the car service and the house were more than he could afford on his university salary. This had been pointed out by envious colleagues. He always explained the discrepancy by revealing that he had come into a large inheritance. He was teaching because he enjoyed it.

That, and his love for his family, was true.

He slid into the car, his smile disappearing as the vehicle pulled away.

It was just most everything else about his life was a lie.

It was something he had noted in his own reading of the *Ramaseeana.* Sleeman and the men of the Thuggee Department had struggled with the duality they observed with the thugs' lives. The British had thought they were chasing ruthless monsters, only to be surprised that they had captured men who cared for wives and children back home. Feringeea himself, the cleverest thug of all times, had been ensnared due to his affection for his family. The British had detained his wife and child, and though Feringeea had the chance to flee beyond the department's reach, he had stayed close, for he could not forsake them. That had allowed his pursuers to track him. In the end, even he was captured.

Vankatesan's ancestor almost two centuries ago had also noted this in the Thuggee Department's reports. He realized that since families could be exploited, secrecy was paramount. So now, the marriages of the thugs were prearranged. All the wives came from the daughters of other thug families. Each girl was carefully homeschooled throughout her entire education, carefully controlling what they learned and teaching them how to obey their husbands. Though like mob wives, some suspected that the source of their husband's wealth came from illicit means, none knew the true extent of what their husbands were.

Sleeman had touched on that during his interviews, asking the thugs if their wives would ever reproach them if they knew what they did. The thugs acknowledged that some would but also bragged that the fidelity of the wives of thugs was proverbial throughout India. Sleeman had asked if what was for fear of the *rumal*.

That was part of it, the thugs had answered.

His wife, unaware of what he was, had no *rumal* to fear. Though, in the past, some wives had come dangerously close to figuring it out. Kali had marked them then, and they were taken care of. Their grieving husbands understood the sacrifice.

Kali had willed it.

But now, another danger to secrecy was the internet. Like the daughters, the sons went through a strict indoctrination process of their own, learning from an early age that secrets must be kept from even their own mothers. After that, the boys were taught that they had a special calling and that great rewards came from their endeavors.

But kids shared everything now online. His wife thought his reluctance to let their boy use computers or smartphones had to do with keeping him from developing bad habits. It was really a policy adopted by the thugs years ago to make sure the boys didn't foolishly reveal too much.

Guess what! My dad says I'm a thug! ;)

As if he needed more problems now. Things were spiraling out of control on the West Coast. Gabrial, Jacobson's boy, was dead due to blood loss from his leg being cut off by a sword.

And now the rest of the team was limping back home. The wounded had made their way to a thug who practiced medicine in Idaho. Dr. Lee had sent him a report just this morning. An arm was missing, and deep cuts on the others. Jason and Ravi had concussions. Chang a broken jaw. Lee said he had never seen such carnage.

Hanson was proving to be a more significant problem than anyone had anticipated.

The car pulled up to his building on the Reynold's campus. It was near and affiliated with Columbia University. He liked the location. Central Park and the Hudson were nearby. The hotel right across the street had a nice restaurant.

No cafeteria food for him. The life of a strangler was the life of wealth and pleasure. Kali provided, and he could easily afford what the restaurant offered. COVID had put a temporary halt to dining out a few years back, but fortunately, his wife's cooking was excellent. She had been brought up well, and she knew her role in life.

He turned to the driver. "Dasgupta and Blackbourne are at their usual hotels downtown. Pick them up and bring them here," Vankatesan ordered.

Vankatesan strode into the building, taking the stairs for exercise. His classroom and office had a receptionist area. Since he had no more classes this day, Debbie wasn't there this afternoon. He unlocked the door and went inside.

It was like stepping into another world.

The room was large, measuring forty by ninety feet, the door located in the northeast corner. Nine windows covered the west wall, stretching up to the room's twenty-foot-high ceiling. They were flanked by yellow and white drapes. Chandeliers lit the room, and twenty-four desks were arranged on a large rug.

Paintings of historical India adorned the walls. In between those exotic weapons were mounted. Small statues of Indian Gods filled more shelves. A few diplomas covered the wall behind his desk.

Students always gravitated to the statues when they walked into the room, asking him if he worshiped the strange, multi-armed idols.

It would always be his first lesson for them. He would patiently explain that the West's views of Hindu statues were their largest misconception of India. That they were not "idols", but *murtis*, representations and conduits of the Divine, and not Divine themselves. Hindus did not worship idols.

It was not a standard classroom, and the reason for it, as his lifestyle, was money. His father, before he passed away, had left a large endowment with the university. That, and Vankatesan's *sotha* skills, had allowed him to work in comfortable conditions, setting his classroom and schedule as he saw fit. His popular class on India and British Colonialism was in such demand that students only got in through a lottery.

He sat down at his desk, once again regretting that he was in the building for a weekend event eleven days ago. Bad news had reached him through his phone, and he had turned to his nearby but unprotected school computer to monitor the extent of the damage. That mistake had further compounded the situation. Things seemed so grave that the thugs had prayed to Kali and beseeched her aid, and she had bent her will toward Hanson. The omens were favorable, and plans were put in motion to end the Hanson threat and appease their ravenous Goddess.

They failed.

Ravi reported that Hanson and Ramsell had survived the thugs' attempt on their lives, and worse, Vankatesan's name had been uttered.

Now the situation was a catastrophe.

Several thugs held high positions in law enforcement in major cities. They were instructed to use their resources to track Hanson. Earlier in the day, Vankatesan had received a distressing update.

Hanson and Ramsell were on a plane heading to New York.

Alarmed, Vankatesan had next informed thugs employed in banks to monitor Hanson's and Ramsell's credit cards. He needed to know where they were staying and, if possible, disrupt their accounts. All thugs in the area had received a call also. They were to gather at the university. If the *tikhurs* did show up here, they were in for a surprise.

He leaned back in his chair and rubbed his eyes.

How could it get any worse?

Someone opened his door without knocking. Vankatesan turned toward it, realizing then that his unforgiving God had just given him the answer to his questioning prayer.

A man and woman walked into the room. The woman had her cell phone out in front of her. The man was offering his hand as he introduced himself.

"Professor Vankatesan? My name is Steve Hanson. This is Samantha Ramsell. We have some questions for you."

Chapter 20

Samantha lowered her phone but kept it in front of her. She had a translation app running. Hanson had told her to configure it to Hindi in case Vankatesan tried to send out a message they couldn't understand while they were in the room with him.

She was hoping Vankatesan would have panicked when they walked in. Instead, he had a broad smile on his face as he reached out and shook Hanson's hand.

The two men were a study in contrasts. Vankatesan was wearing a tailored shirt, and he looked like he had just stepped out of a photo spread in a fashion magazine. His silk tie sported a ruby tie-clasp that matched his cufflinks, and his bespoke pants fit him perfectly. His bright smile was wide and his gaze steady as he looked over herself and Hanson.

On the other hand, Hanson appeared like he was stuck in the past with the dark red turtleneck and old jeans that he was wearing. Awkward and unsure of himself, he never seemed to focus on the person in front of him. Instead, he cast his gaze about to study the room.

She glanced over the place herself. She was expecting a sterile classroom. It felt more like a museum. Statues of Indian Gods were arrayed on shelves, and they stared back at her. Samantha tried to pick out Kali.

She finally settled a benign-looking female form with light bluish skin and four arms.

"I'm sorry, have we met?" Vankatesan asked as he gestured to Hanson and herself to sit in one of the front desks. They both took a seat as he leaned on the edge of his desk, looming over them.

"We haven't met personally," she said.

"Let me guess. Your child is a student of mine, and you're here to talk about his or her grades."

"We don't have a kid in your class," Hanson said as he finally straightened up and looked at Vankatesan.

"I'm sorry, I just thought you were a couple," Vankatesan said.

Hanson didn't reply, but his face reddened a bit.

Seeing that Hanson was tongue-tied, Samantha spoke up. "We're not, and we think you know who we are."

Vankatesan's smile was shrinking, but he kept his gaze steady.

"And who are you?"

"We're the ones who got away back in Oregon," Hanson answered. "From your thugs."

Vankatesan stared at them like a professor letting a student's stupid remark sink in with the rest of the class. It caused Hanson to fidget a bit more.

"Is this a joke?"

"No joke. I'm sure you know what a thug is," Hanson shot back.

"I do," Vankatesan said. "I teach British Colonial history in India. I spend several afternoons each semester discussing the concept of thuggee."

"So, you believe thuggee existed?" Samantha asked. Though Vankatesan didn't act threatening, she was still comforted that the rest of the building teemed with students right outside the door.

"I do," Vankatesan said. "Though I have always thought of them as bandits and not the bloodthirsty religion that for a while was listed in the *Guinness Book of World Records* for the most murders by a cult."

"They were listed in *Guinness*?" she asked.

"The theory decades ago was that they were responsible for over a million murders, Miss Ramsell."

"We're concerned with the here and now," Hanson interjected. "We have evidence that a current murder leads straight back to you."

"Though I should throw you out for such slander, I'd like to hear why you think that," Vankatesan said calmly, though his eyes narrowed.

"Someone from this campus looked at my blog," Hanson revealed.

"Yes...and?" Vankatesan replied, an amused smile on his face.

"And the men who tried to kill me said your name," Samantha finished.

"It's a common name, and there are many computers associated with this university," Vankatesan said. "Anything else?"

Samantha remained silent. She noticed that Hanson didn't say anything either. He was looking back down at the rug as if it fascinated him.

"Maybe you can tell the police thuggee is in my blood," Vankatesan continued. "Or due to the shape of my skull. That's another thing the British believed back then. That all Indians were naturally disposed to evil and murder. They even sent the heads of thugs to England to see what made an Indian a killer." Vankatesan was tapping his own head to make his point.

Frustrated, Samantha said nothing. This meeting had been Hanson's idea. He had wanted to blitz Vankatesan by showing up in his office as fast as possible before their target could gather his wits. It wasn't working, and so far, Hanson, her thug expert, was no help.

Vankatesan's phone trilled on the desk behind him. He politely held up a hand as he circled to the back of the desk to answer it.

She pushed her phone forward a bit. The call could be from a fellow thug. She made sure the app was still tuned into Hindi.

Vankatesan was staring at her phone while he answered his. Did he suspect?

He kept the conversation short as he talked rapidly in a foreign language. He hung up the phone and looked up at his guests, a predatory smile on his face.

"I'm sorry; I know that was a bit rude not using English," he explained. "That was my father. He's coming to my place tonight and was wondering what was for dinner."

Samantha looked down at her phone. The program had recorded what was said, but it gave her a notification that the translation had failed.

At her side, Hanson spoke up.

"You're lying."

Vankatesan turned toward Hanson and regarded him coolly.

"Really, I didn't know you understood Hindi, Mr. Hanson."

"I don't," Hanson said. Samantha could see that he now had his own smile as he stood up and faced Vankatesan. "But I do understand *Ramasee*."

Chapter 21

"What did you say?" Vankatesan asked, his mouth slack with confusion.

"*Ramasee*, Vankatesan," Hanson continued. "Or, as Sleeman put it: the peculiar dialect of the thugs, in which he was satisfied that there was no term he was not acquainted with."

"I know what it is," Vankatesan growled. "I'm just surprised you know it."

"It wasn't that difficult," Hanson replied. He was moving closer to a nearby mounted spear just in case the thug went for something in his desk. "The history books describe ramasee as an entirely different language. It isn't. *Ramasee* is just cant. Argot. Slang."

"And I heard the thugs back in Oregon using it," Samantha added as she stood by Hanson's side.

"We figured all of you were. *The Ramaseeana* is scanned and posted online," Hanson said. "Though it's huge at seven hundred pages, Sleeman's list of thug terms makes up only a couple dozen of those."

"On the flight over, we decided to focus on a few keywords," Samantha said. "As when traveling in a foreign country. 'Where is the restroom? Where is the bus stop?' Travelers teach themselves just enough to get around."

"Except, in this case, we went with thug warning phrases," Hanson put in.

Vankatesan remained behind the desk, his glare deepening.

"Your side of the conversation was *saur, bhitree gote hona, a ho to ghyree chulo,*" Hanson continued.

"Which means someone who has escaped our clutches in the past has fallen into our snares again," Samantha translated. "So, if you are coming, pray descend."

"Which won't be soon enough for you, prof," Hanson said. He was pleased with himself. There was no way Vankatesan could have anticipated their arrival. The thug may have just called for help, but it would take a while for his backup to arrive in New York traffic.

Vankatesan stalked around his desk toward them.

Samantha backed up and moved slightly behind Hanson. She put a hand on his left shoulder.

Her touch sent a thrill through his entire body. But Hanson couldn't dwell on her closeness. He inched toward the spear.

Vankatesan stopped at the desk Samantha had been sitting at. He reached down to her phone that was still there and turned off the translation program that was also voice recording.

He looked up, his face serene.

"Kali is a shield around me, my glory. She will protect me and sustain me," Vankatesan said.

Samantha's eye's widened slightly in shock.

"You don't deny it," she said.

"There's no point now," he replied. "Besides, Hanson here seemed convinced as soon as he saw me. I guess after studying thuggee, all Indians must now be suspect in his eyes."

Hanson shook his head. "I did know, Vankatesan. But it's not the fact that you're Indian. It's your rug that sealed the deal."

Samantha looked down as she tried to pick out what he had seen at their feet.

Hanson continued. "Sleeman's beliefs that thuggee was hereditary caused an unexpected problem. What to do with the sons left behind when the fathers were imprisoned or hung. He came up with the 'School of Industry' in Jubbalpore. A prison for the approvers and a reformatory for their sons. Inside, both were taught the trade of putting together tents and weaving carpets. Thugs soon had a reputation of being the finest carpet weavers in India."

Hanson held out his arms and gestured downward all around him.

"We're standing on a genuine thug rug."

Vankatesan said nothing, but Hanson could tell he had guessed right.

"Is there anything you don't know," Vankatesan sneered.

"Yes, how many have you murdered, Professor? Does Berham's record still stand?"

In his pocket, Hanson's phone chimed. Keeping an eye on the thug in front of him, Hanson reached for it.

"Thugs do not commit murder, Hanson," Vankatesan said softly. "It is the Goddess who kills. We are but her instruments."

"These quotes you and your thugs keep using," Samantha said, "Hanson said they were things said by desperate prisoners trying to save their own skins. How are they your gospel now?"

Vankatesan's eyes flicked at the wall behind his desk to an old Oxford diploma hanging there.

"An ancestor of mine, Pravnev Vankatesan, was a prophet, Miss Ramsell. He realized that Kali was speaking to him through the thugs held prisoner by the Christians. As they suffered in the crucible of Company 'justice,' they let it be known that Kali was now furious and that if we weren't allowed to follow her way, the end for the world would come. These visions let us appreciate our relationship with Kali and define our role in protecting all humankind."

"Keep telling yourself that while you rot in prison," Hanson said as he glanced at his phone's screen.

It was a text from his bank, alerting him that his credit cards had been reported stolen. New cards were already in the mail, and the old cards were frozen for his protection.

What the hell? His cards were in his wallet.

"What do you plan to do? Have me arrested? You don't have anything on me except vague theories," Vankatesan said.

"We've been to the FBI," Samantha answered. "We may not have solid evidence, but we have enough for them to turn their attention toward you. And though you've been careful, we're betting that even you will not survive their scrutiny."

Hanson was only half listening. How could his bank cards be reported stolen?

He remembered what he had told Fisher earlier. That thugs weren't thugs full time. They had other professions. And if thug bank employees had access to his cards—

Hanson grabbed Samantha's hand. "Come on, we're leaving," he said urgently.

She looked surprised. "Why? What's wrong?"

"They knew we were coming," Hanson answered as he took a few steps toward the door.

He was too late. Out in the hall, the building's fire alarms sounded off.

ise="text-align:center"># Chapter 22

"Yelling won't help, Hanson," Vankatesan said, a hard glint in his eye as he pulled out a pale-yellow scarf from his desk drawer. "The building is old, and all of the rooms are soundproof."

The door burst open, and two men strode in. Both had gray and thinning hair and were dressed in tailored suits with ties. The first one was tall and Caucasian. The second man was an even taller Indian, and he was struggling to attach a suppressor to a Glock as he walked in.

"Blackbourne, shut the door," Vankatesan barked over the sound of the fire alarms outside.

The first old thug closed the door, and the wailing klaxon in the hall was muffled. The Indian, satisfied with the state of his gun, swiftly brought his Glock up.

A spear slammed into the gunman's shoulder, and with a scream, he dropped his pistol. The Glock clattered to the floor.

Hanson hadn't hesitated when the two thugs had entered the room. He snatched the nearby spear off the wall and heaved it with all his strength. It struck with so much force that it pinned the thug to the wall behind him.

Though his arm ached from the strain from his previous throw, Hanson grabbed another spear and slung it toward Vankatesan, who ducked behind his desk. The second spear missed Vankatesan's head by inches and stuck into the plaster behind him.

"Stay right there, asshole," Hanson growled as he cast about for another weapon on the wall.

"Steve!" Samantha yelled behind him.

Hanson glanced back. She was bent over one of the student desks and was pushing it forward. Guessing at what she was doing, he joined her. With his help, it moved forward and bumped up against the desk in the second row.

Ahead of them, the former gunman was howling in pain as he pulled at the spear with his left hand. The man named Blackbourne was bent over as he searched for the gun. Vankatesan looked ready to lunge for the weapon also.

Hanson's and Samantha's train picked up the desk in the first row, the whole pile gathering speed as they pushed forward. Blackbourne, hearing the furniture scoot across the floor, looked up.

Too late.

The desks smashed into him and knocked him back into the wall, the gun now lost in a jumble of desk legs. The speared thug screamed some more as he was forced to change his position. Vankatesan retreated to his corner.

Samantha's phone was still resting on its desk. She grabbed it. Blackbourne, giving up on the gun, went for a knife sheathed at his belt.

Kuthowa, thought Hanson.

Hanson thought about going to the wall for a kukri he had spotted, but Samantha dragged him out the door and slammed it shut.

They found themselves in Vankatesan's outer receptionist area, a small room with several enormous filing cabinets and a desk for an office specialist. It must have been the secretary's day off, for the two of them had yet to see anyone stationed in the room.

The alarm was deafening out here. The door had a lock but no key. Hanson leaned into it. The door heaved as someone on the other side pushed on it.

"I won't be able to hold it when all three of them are on it," Hanson shouted.

"Maybe this will hold them," Samantha yelled back. She moved to a tall file cabinet and tilted it over. It crashed into the door.

"We have them trapped. Should we call the police?" Samantha asked.

"There may be more coming," Hanson answered. "We're out of here!"

They fled out into the hall, both hoping that some stragglers were left in the building to help them out.

The halls were empty, and the floor's other classroom doors were closed and secured.

They ran to the main staircase. Hanson looked down the stairwell.

Two levels down, he spotted a half dozen men running up it. One of them looked up and pointed.

"Not that way," Hanson yelled. They both fled down the hallway, taking several turns. At the end of it, Hanson saw the glowing sign he was hoping for.

EXIT

They opened the door. The emergency stairwell. It was empty.

"Run!" Hanson shouted.

They both pounded down the stairs. It was quieter in here. Four stories down, Hanson could see a door on a different wall than the others. Most likely it opened directly to the outside. They were halfway down the flight when the door they had used opened above them.

"*Buhupna!*" someone cried out.

"What does that mean?" Samantha asked, panting.

"The victims are escaping," he answered grimly.

They flew down the remaining three levels. Above them, they could hear the pounding of numerous feet as the thugs gave chase.

They reached the bottom with their lead intact. The exit door beckoned, and Hanson pushed on it.

Home free!

It barely budged.

It was barred. Hanson could open it a little bit, but something was jammed through the handles on the outside.

He looked around them. They were in a ten-by-ten room with walls of cement.

"We're trapped," Samantha said.

"Get behind me," Hanson said as he craned his neck to look up. The thugs were two flights up. He was sure these guys had more than *rumals* for weapons.

"*Aule bhae ram ram,*" a voice said on the other side of the door.

A thug was posted outside the door. He had just yelled out a *Ramasee* phrase, but Hanson couldn't quite place it.

Samantha stepped forward.

"Peace to thee, friend," she replied, her voice several octaves lower.

Hanson remembered it then. An old thug passcode and recognition phrase from *Ramaseeana.* He heard something slide on the other side of the door, and it cracked open. An Indian peeked in.

"What's—"

Hanson didn't let him finish. He threw his weight at the door and smashed it into the thug guarding it. It crashed into the man's face and drove him back.

Hanson and Samantha leaped through the doorway. The thug, a beefy-looking guy with long dark hair and a short beard, was trying to stand back up. Hanson punched him across the jaw. The man went down, and his head smacked into the pavement. He didn't get back up.

Behind him, Samantha was locking up the exit by sliding a metal-handled broom through the door handles.

Just in time. The doors heaved a bit as if several men were pushing on it. The broom handle held.

"Come on!" Hanson shouted. They both sprinted around the corner and found themselves on the sidewalk and amongst a crowd. They slowed down to blend in. Firetrucks with sirens blaring were pulling up. College students were holding up their phones, recording what was happening. Hanson and Samantha kept on walking, zigzagging through the throng.

"Steve, shouldn't we be heading back to the hotel to retrieve our luggage?"

"We can't. They're already there," Hanson answered as he glanced over his shoulder.

She grabbed his arm and stopped him on the sidewalk.

"How do you know that?" she demanded.

Hanson pulled out his phone and held it up so that she could see the message sent from his bank.

"They've frozen my account," he answered. "And if they can do that, then they know where we've used them. They know about our rooms at the hotel."

They had booked separate rooms. Hanson had wondered the entire flight if that would change and that sometime in the night, there would be a knock on his hotel door.

Samantha was looking at her phone. "My banks have reported my cards stolen also. I can't use them," she said. "Steve, how did they do this?"

His shoulders slumped a little as he made his confession. "I underestimated them and their reach. Over the decades, they must have ingratiated themselves into key positions throughout the states," he answered. He scanned the people walking around them. "There must be more than I imagined. Any one of these men around here could be a thug."

She looked pissed at that revelation, and Hanson felt the chance of a midnight knock on his door becoming less and less probable. She began digging through her purse.

"How much cash do you have on you?" she asked.

"A little over fifty dollars," he said as he opened his wallet.

"I have one hundred ten. That's barely enough for fast-food burgers and cabs around here."

It was getting darker out, and the temperature was dropping. Hanson was beginning to wish he had his jacket, but that was back in his room. He had worn the turtleneck just to annoy Vankatesan. He and Samantha walked away from the crowd. Hanson kept a lookout for anyone following them.

"And we have nothing but the clothes on our back, and we still have to make it to our flight tomorrow morning," she said.

They already had tickets for the second leg of their trip, a flight to Los Angeles to look up the man who had filed a report with the FBI two decades ago, Cresswell.

They just had to survive the night here in New York.

Samantha was still talking. "Maybe my parents can wire us some money, or I could call up some old friends."

"Don't," Hanson replied as he shook his head. "Assume that through the internet they know everything about us. That the phones of everyone we know are being monitored, and that every financial trick we come up with will be blocked."

Samantha came to a stop, and she looked upward. Hanson followed her gaze. She was staring at a cluster of impossibly slender skyscrapers. The tall, thin buildings were catching the ruddy glow of the setting sun. It was a beautiful sight, but her eyes had a distant look to them, and her lips downturned in a frown.

"Shit," she sighed.

"What?"

"You told me back in Portland that the thugs researched me. Well then, I know a person and place the thugs would never dream about keeping tabs on," Samantha answered. She hailed a cab, and they both got in. The cab driver had on a mask, one of the small percentage of holdouts that would most likely never give up masks in public, no matter how well the vaccines performed against COVID. Samantha gave the cabbie an address from memory.

As the cab pulled into traffic, she entered a phone number into her cell and began texting.

"Don't worry, I'm sure the thugs aren't monitoring this number," she said as her glance met his worried stare. Her fingers continued to fly across the screen. "But I have to give this person a heads up."

Whoever she was communicating with responded quickly, and for the moment, Samantha was focused on her phone. Hanson looked out his window. They were traveling down Central Park West. To his right, more expensive high-rises loomed above them. Hanson gaped at them like a gawking tourist.

They pulled up to one of the glittering towers. It rose into the sky like a needle. Samantha put away her phone as they got out. Hanson paid the cab driver, wincing at how expensive it was.

The apartment building had its own doorman, an older man with bushy eyebrows and a red uniform. His face lit up when he saw Samantha as if seeing a long-lost daughter.

"Sam, a sight for sore eyes," he said.

She gave him a hug.

"It's good to see you, Roger," she replied.

"Now I know why he was hanging around down here," the doorman said as he jerked his head back a bit and looked over his shoulder.

Hanson's gaze followed Roger's gesture, and he spotted a man waving at them.

He was movie-star handsome. He had thick, wavy blond hair and piercing blue-gray eyes, and his tanned skin and white teeth were flawless. He was dressed in a tailored suit, appearing as if he had just returned from a night at the opera. Samantha gave a curt nod back at him.

"Who is this guy?" Hanson asked.

"His name is David Carbonaux," she said without any enthusiasm as the man strode forward to meet them. Hanson realized he must have still looked confused, for she explained further.

"He's my ex."

Chapter 23

Carbonaux gave Samantha a hug, a grin spread across his face. Hanson couldn't see her expression.

Carbonaux extended a hand toward him.

"You must be the Steve Hanson in her recent news stories," he said.

Hanson shook his hand, both men squeezing a bit harder than they needed to.

"And you're Carbonaux. I've heard a lot about you," Hanson replied, which prompted Samantha to furrow her eyebrows as she searched her memory.

Hanson realized his mistake. Samantha hadn't told him a single thing about her ex-boyfriend. Everything he knew had come from the thugs.

Carbonaux seemed too excited to care.

"Come on inside," he said as he led them into the building's marbled lobby to a bank of elevators. Hanson marveled at how polished every-thing looked. Carbonaux pressed the button for the thirtieth floor.

It was quiet the first few seconds. Hanson could have cut the tension with a knife. He desperately tried to think of something to say, but elevator rides with strangers ranked right up there with approaching someone from a distance.

Fortunately, Samantha and Carbonaux started up some small talk, mostly about national news anchor Doug Morgan being close to retirement. From what Hanson could gather, Carbonaux worked closely with the guy.

The elevator opened into an opulent hallway of exotic wood paneling and a thick, dark gray carpet. Polished brass fixtures illuminated the area.

Carbonaux opened his door and then stood aside, waving his hands with a flourish, as if he were leading them into something grand, like the Taj Mahal.

It wasn't far from it.

It was the windows that stood out. They stretched twelve feet from floor to ceiling and served as the exterior wall for the entire apartment. Large columns set thirty feet apart were the only things breaking apart the view, which showcased New York's dramatic skyline, a blaze of red backlighting it from the recent sunset.

The place was huge. To the left were the living and dining room. To the right, a hall and the bedrooms. Hanson noticed a cat dart into a doorway beyond the dining room.

Carbonaux turned around and made a show of adjusting his tie.

"Now, I hate to get down to business so soon, but I have a dinner reservation to catch. What exactly is the favor you need of me, Samantha?" he asked.

Samantha hesitated a moment. "Steve and I need a place to stay tonight. I was hoping to borrow the keys to the apartment."

Carbonaux had a stunned look on his face, appearing as if Samantha had just told him she had concrete proof that aliens existed. Then a smirk slowly crossed his face.

"Hanson, could you give us a moment alone?" he asked.

Hanson looked between them, not getting what was happening. Samantha gave a slight nod.

"Sure, I'll be in the next room," Hanson answered. The cat seemed to know where it was going, so Hanson followed it.

He found himself in the kitchen. The room was deep in shadow since its lights were off. Hanson helped himself to bottled water from the fridge.

The cat was under the table. Hanson located some cat food in a cupboard. He dished out the meaty bits and gravy, already feeling better in the cat's presence.

The ruddy sunset provided some illumination. Hanson sat down in the gloom and brought out his new phone to check his messages.

He had one from Tolmany, who was using a burner phone also, so the call had been untraceable by the thugs. His report stated that his ex-wife and daughter were okay, as were Sebastian and Bingo.

Hanson looked down at Carbonaux's cat.

"You would like them," Hanson said.

His friend had information from Hanson's mother also. She was at her brother's ranch, watching her favorite show, reruns of *The A-Team*, while surrounded by her nephews. Country boys who were wary of strangers. No smooth-talking *sothas* were going to get near her.

Satisfied with that, Hanson switched off his voicemail and pulled out a blue business card from his wallet.

It was one of Fisher's. After he had sent a text to alert his FBI friend what he was up to, he had ditched that phone. He didn't want Fisher tracking him and sending other agents to stop him. Hanson punched in the number on the card. Fisher answered before the first ring finished, and as usual, he got right to the point.

"That was stupid going dark," Fisher said. "Are you both all right?"

"We're fine," Hanson said, surprised at Fisher's worried tone. He had expected more anger. "But why the concern?"

"I checked up on your story," Fisher answered. "I went to your...*bele* and found a hole dug in the ground."

Hanson's blood chilled a bit. A *gobbah*, the circular graves dug up by *lughas*. It had been meant for him and Samantha.

"You believe us now?"

"I believe enough to know you're screwing around with real danger. What's happening over there?"

Hanson told him everything.

"You have him recorded speaking *Ramasee*?"

"Yes."

"I'm glad you're both alright," Fisher added. "Are you sure you don't want any agents sent your way?"

"Positive. The thugs knew we were coming. I'm not sure of their reach. They could have people in the Bureau."

"Understood. What's your next move?"

"Samantha is securing a place for us to spend the night," Hanson answered. "Then we're taking Avian Airlines to see that Cresswell guy in California. Our flight, Avian 951, lands in L.A. at 5:50 p.m."

"I want to meet him also. I'll rendezvous with you at LAX. I will also start digging into the background of this Vankatesan guy."

"Good, I'll see you tomorrow."

Hanson hung up, elated. Now, they were getting somewhere.

Hanson looked down. The cat had finished eating and was now winding between his legs. *Bunjaree.* That's what thugs called cats. Their appearances on expeditions were considered omens.

Hanson reached down and petted it. He glanced at the doorway to the living room, where Samantha was talking to her ex-boyfriend.

The cat was purring. Hanson took that as a good omen.

* * *

"You have a lot of nerve showing up here asking for help," Carbonaux snarled, turning on her when Hanson left the room.

"Please, David, we're—" Samantha faltered a bit. She couldn't reveal the true reason. "I'm a bit short on money at the moment."

"I'm not surprised," Carbonaux continued. "That blog you work for must not pay very much."

She didn't say anything. Instead, she turned away to look out the window. She still couldn't escape him. His gloating reflection mocked her.

"But what surprises me is you coming back. I remember another night here," he said. "When you said a lot of things in anger. That I wouldn't make it on my own. That I would fail. That you were the driving force of our success."

He was right. She had said those things. Their relationship had started out with so much promise. He was intelligent and driven, eager for success. So was she, and for a while, things were great. More than great. But then she learned of a darker side. He was willing to get the story no matter what the cost, even influencing things himself if it would jazz the news segment up and get him higher ratings.

They had fought much over that, finding themselves at an impasse. So, Carbonaux had found someone who shared his vision.

"You weren't lying. She really is here," a new voice said behind Samantha.

Samantha turned toward the woman who just entered the room.

A tall, slender, and beautiful brunette wearing a long, dark dress stood in the bedroom hall. Pearls encircled her neck, and a large diamond flashed on an engagement ring. Samantha knew her.

National news correspondent Jennifer Steel, the woman who now shared Carbonaux's bed and his vision of how the news should be delivered.

"What does Miss High and Mighty want?" Steel asked.

"The key to the apartment," Carbonaux answered.

Steel looked amused at that. "Really? I knew she had fallen since we parted. But I didn't realize how low."

"I don't know where my key is. Do you still have yours?" Carbonaux asked.

"I do. It's in my purse back in the bedroom. Samantha, follow me while I retrieve it, then you may go. I don't want to be late for our dinner function."

"The network is throwing Jennifer a little party," Carbonaux explained, his tone telling her that he was relishing the moment. "Doug Morgan is retiring soon. Jen is to be his replacement as the national news anchor."

Samantha felt the color drain from her face.

National news anchor.

That was supposed to be her.

Samantha glumly followed Jennifer into the master bedroom, feeling shabby in her jeans and floral print blouse and matching scarf. Meanwhile, Jennifer talked about how everything was great in her life.

Samantha wanted to be anywhere but here, where these two had betrayed her both professionally and personally. But on the streets below, thugs prowled as they searched for her and Hanson.

So, while Jennifer bragged, she stood there and took it.

* * *

Hanson stood up as Carbonaux strode into the kitchen. The guy looked relaxed, happy even. Hanson felt a sense of relief. Things must have gone well with Samantha.

Bunjaree scampered away. Hanson held up the water bottle.

"I hope you don't mind. It's been a long day."

Carbonaux waved it off. "Go ahead." He joined Hanson with his own bottle of water. "What do you think of the view?"

Hanson turned back to the windows. "It's impressive. This whole place is. Though it's more than I thought—"

"Someone in my position could afford," Carbonaux finished.

"I can't," he continued as he looked outward. "My family was originally in shipping." He gestured around him. "This is a result of my inheritance."

"Why broadcast journalism?"

"Controlling information is where it is all at now, Hanson," Carbonaux replied. "I let my brother run the shipping business. I still have my share of all future profits coming my way."

"Your father passed away?"

"When I was thirty. But before he died, he told me to follow my dreams. Take what I want. Don't let anyone stop me. Passing on wisdom, it's what all successful men do with their sons."

Hanson continued to stare out the window, a memory coming to him.

Carbonaux took a drink from his water bottle. Though Hanson didn't see it, a look of contempt was on the other man's face.

"And what of your father, Hanson? What words of wisdom did he pass on to you?"

Still staring out the window, Hanson didn't immediately answer.

Carbonaux opened his mouth to repeat the question, but Hanson finally responded.

"Be good."

"What was that?" Carbonaux said, unsure of what he just heard.

"My dad said, 'be good,'" Hanson repeated.

"That's it?"

"He was dying...cancer," Hanson answered. It was a subject he rarely talked about, something he kept bottled up. But now it came all tumbling out. Maybe it was his own recent brushes with death that gave him the desire to confess. "It came on fast. I was six. At first, the after-school visits to the hospital were mostly watching my dad talking with relatives. Grown-up stuff. But on the last day—"

Hanson, his gaze focused on the last patch of color fading from the sky, paused as he remembered.

"I was pulled out of class. As usual, Dad was lying on the hospital bed, but he was barely able to talk. Mom was there, and she told me that he wanted to hear how my day in school went. I think I blabbed on for most of the hour as he lay there, listening. Then all the devices hooked up to him started setting off alarms, and the doctors moved to take me away. But right before they did, he managed to look at me and say those two words."

"That's all you got out of him?" Carbonaux asked, incredulous. If he had any sympathy for the situation, he wasn't showing it.

Hanson didn't answer, his mind still dwelling on his childhood. To him, it hadn't seemed like advice.

It had felt like a commandment.

Be good.

"It would appear you got the short end of the stick there, Hanson," Carbonaux continued. "Be good. That's not much to work with."

Hanson turned to respond, but a beautiful woman walked into the room. Jennifer Steel. Hanson's jaw dropped a little. She was an actual celebrity. Then he noticed Samantha standing quietly behind her.

Everything the thugs had revealed about Samantha flashed through Hanson's mind.

Steel had been the other woman.

And now these two were lording it over her.

He had to do something to help Samantha out.

"Well, I guess it's time for us to go. We have a big story to work on," Hanson said as he moved toward the door. He hoped that would keep Carbonaux and Steel second-guessing themselves.

Across the room, he noticed Samantha quietly shaking her head, a horrified look on her face.

"Let me guess, more dead cows?" Carbonaux asked, barely able to hide a smile.

"Maybe next time you're in town, you could *explain* it to us," Steel added with her own grin.

They were let out into the hall, and the door was closed behind them. Hanson thought he detected some laughter through it.

On the ride down the elevator, Samantha handed him a key. She informed him that she had secured a place for them to stay.

They grabbed a quick and cheap meal at a nearby diner and then took a cab to Carbonaux's second place. Samantha further explained that he now kept it for when family was in town to visit him. After that, she was quiet for the rest of the ride as she stared out the window.

Hanson, for his part, was thinking of the night ahead. Did this place have two bedrooms? His mind raced as he thought of what he should say once they got there.

The second place was not as nice as the high-rise. A few bricked steps led up a brass panel with buzzer buttons for several dozen apartments. The key got them through the locked front door.

The same key unlocked an apartment on the third floor. Again, not the high-rise, but still more richly appointed than his home back in Portland.

And it had only one bedroom. Samantha went straight to it. Hanson remained in the main room, rehearsing one last time what he had carefully refined in his mind for this moment.

She walked back out with a pillow and some bedding and plopped them on the couch.

"I hope you don't mind, but I'm going straight to bed. We have a big day tomorrow," she said, not looking him in the eye. She went back into the bedroom and shut the door behind her.

Stunned, Hanson stared at the closed door. Had he read all the signs wrong? She had seemed pleased spending time with him on the flight over.

Maybe he did something wrong. With a sigh, he explored the place a bit. The fridge was empty. He tosses the key into a bowl on the counter.

Gold lettering on the key's leather fob caught his eye.

J.S.

Jennifer Steel.

The keys were hers. Hanson frowned. Samantha had said that Carbonaux now kept the place for when his family showed up. Why did Steel have her own set?

Again, his mind rolled over what Samantha had said.

Now kept the place.

Which implied, at some other point, it was used for something else.

Hanson looked around him.

This was where Carbonaux and Steel had met to cheat on Samantha.

He looked back at the bedroom door, finally realizing how painful it was for her to stay here so that they would both be safe as the thugs hunted for them.

Hanson spent a few minutes making up the couch, then peeled off his clothes down to his boxers and crawled into his makeshift bed. In his mind, he replayed his interactions with Carbonaux, coming up with retorts and rebuttals he wished he had used earlier.

Though armed with hindsight, Hanson still lost all the imagined arguments playing out in his head. Samantha's ex-boyfriend held too many advantages, and Hanson fell asleep with Carbonaux's mocking laughter echoing in his mind.

Chapter 24

Lower Manhattan, New York, 9:35 p.m. EDT

They called themselves the *Sath Zut*.

The seven original clans. Lore had it that seven great thug families were expelled from twelfth-century Delhi. They had spread, and they settled into every corner of India, practicing thuggee wherever they went. A ruling class of thugs going back centuries.

Sleeman and others had seized on these stories of high lineage, using them to reinforce their Western preconceptions of oriental evil and mystique. Vankatesan's ancestor, Pranev, in the process of building an opium smuggling empire, had read Sleeman's reports and had adopted the organizational concept.

He was forming a triad. At one point, Indians, who controlled the network funneling stolen opium to waiting ships, which was handled by the English, as their steam-powered vessels controlled the oceans. They delivered to the final point of the triad, Chinese ports, where local smugglers distributed the drug to the masses.

A vast criminal enterprise managed by Pranav's new *Sath Zut*. Seven ruling families, three of which were Indians, two English, and two Chinese.

But Pravnev had been more than a rich drug lord. That distinction was a boon, a gift from Kali for doing her bidding. He was also her prophet, and he had had visions. Visions that took the old, flawed ways of thuggee and made them something new. Something that could withstand the onslaught of the men of the East India Company. Thugs that had a divine purpose and now indeed followed Kali.

And killed in her name.

Tanvir Vankatesan turned away from the window and faced his current *Sath Zut*.

Blackbourne, Dasgupta, and Liang were in the room with him. Dasgupta's arm was in a sling. A thug doctor had tended to his wound, and potent painkillers kept his pain in check, though not his rage.

Liang was a tall, handsome man in his fifties. He kept his black hair cut short and his face clean-shaven. His *bele* was in Philadelphia.

The others, who were spread across the states and couldn't make it on such short notice, were present electronically, their faces displayed on monitors on the room's back wall. The communication system had been installed a few years back when the pandemic had raged across the world. The plague was a clear sign of Kali's displeasure. The thugs had adapted by using the latest conference technology to rapidly respond to the crisis. They had also increased the number of sacrifices to two victims a week instead of one.

Their plan had worked, and COVID was now under control. The sacrifices per week were eased back to normal levels, but the online meetings had remained.

Zhang, tall like Liang but with a rounder face, was depicted on the left-most screen. He transmitted from his base of operations in Los Angeles.

Another screen had Mukherjee's image. Of the seven, he was the youngest, his father having passed away of heart failure recently. At twenty-nine years of age, he still had a boyish look about him when he flashed an easy smile. His home was Chicago.

The third screen held the image of a man wearing a cowboy hat. Wrinkles creased his weather-beaten face. Chancellor. He was located near the thug's temple.

The room they were in was forty floors up in an office high-rise. It was a simple arrangement consisting of a front receptionist area and a lavish board room, paneled in dark, exotic woods. Gold plated sconce light fixtures illuminated the space. A proper, thug-woven carpet from Jubbalpore covered the floor. A twenty-foot-long ebony table was set in the middle of the room. Four expensive chairs were placed on the table's east side and faced west. Three other chairs were pushed up against a far wall.

A small, red placemat with gold braid edges was set at the center of the table. Resting on it were four small gold plates and four gold chalices. A silver decanter and a dome-covered silver serving platter stood off to the side. The thug's bible, a large book inset with gems on the cover, rested nearby.

Blackbourne, Liang, and Dasgupta moved to the table and stood in front of their chairs. Vankatesan approached the table.

It was time for the *tuponee*, the ritual of the thugs.

Once observed after the murder had been committed, it was now used to sanction any formal gathering of thugs.

Vankatesan drew forth a small, silver coin. It was over two hundred years old, a Mughal issue from Murshidabad, not an East India Company copy from Calcutta. He placed the coin on the red cloth on the table.

"The *Roop Dursun*," he intoned. The silver offering.

He poured water that had been blessed by Kali from the decanter into the four gold cups. On the screens on the east wall, he could see that Chancellor, Zhang, and Mukherjee had similar cups already in front of them.

Then he took the lid off the serving platter, revealing five small communal-like wafers.

Goor.

Unrefined sugar. The sacrificial food of the thugs. As Feringeea had told Sleeman, to taste the fatal goor was to be a thug forever. Even if a man possessed all that he desired, he would still return to thuggee.

Vankatesan set down four of the wafers onto the gold plates. The fifth he left on the tray.

He placed the settings in front of each man and in front of his chair. He circled the table so that he stood with the other men. They and the thugs electronically present on the screens behind them were all facing west.

"Great Goddess! As you have vouchsafed us in the past, so we pray to thee, fulfill our desires," Vankatesan prayed aloud.

Mukherjee, on his right, spoke the *Jhirnee*, using an old but common phrase uttered by thugs of old.

"*Tombako kha lo,*" he intoned.

The other six men present repeated the prayer, and then all carefully consumed their goor, careful not to let a crumb spill to the ground. They washed it down with the holy water.

The four men at the table sat down and turned their chairs to face the other men's images. They were now on a video chat conference, carefully secured by their own expensive systems and the Tor network.

Chancellor got right to the matter at hand.

"How bad is it?"

"Dire," Vankatesan answered. "We have been discovered, and Hanson and Ramsell have threatened that they are going directly to the FBI."

"You believe them?" Zhang asked.

"I do," Vankatesan answered. "So far, they have proven to be as relentless as Sleeman himself."

"You've been reckless," Zhang accused. "All of this could have been avoided."

"No," Vankatesan said as he stood up. "All of this was inevitable."

"We all knew this day was coming," Vankatesan continued, his hands making a sweeping gesture at all the equipment mounted on the wall in front of him. "And the reason is staring us in the face."

"Computers, and the internet, have made our work so much easier," Blackbourne protested. "Everyone's life posted for Kali to sift through. Never has it been so easy to choose and inveigle someone or to plunder what we want."

"Progress is a two-edged sword," Vankatesan said. "The police have cameras on every corner. Our victims carry cell phones that are GPS enabled, beacons giving the authorities their last locations before they disappeared. We have already triggered thirteen Ashanti Alerts ever since that new law passed recently. And every day, I struggle to keep my boy from the internet, lest he brags about being a chosen of Kali."

"Thuggee will prevail," Liang said.

"No," Vankatesan said quietly. "Thuggee, as we know it, is over."

Shocked silence filled the room.

"Our scouts that work with Kali know that Hanson is on his way to Los Angeles tomorrow," Vankatesan continued.

Zhang's face wrinkled in disgust. "Cresswell."

"No one believes that old man," Chancellor added.

"They will now," Vankatesan said. "And once Hanson reaches there, I figure we will then have only a few days before he, and the FBI, finds all of us."

"Days!" Dasgupta said in alarm.

"How do we stop him?" Chancellor asked.

"*Khomusna*," Vankatesan replied, letting the word hang in the air for a moment.

Murder, without ceremony.

"The protocols?" Mukherjee asked. "Those are drastic measures—"

"They are. You will notice I did not crush the extra wafer in offering to Kali," Vankatesan interjected. He glanced at the silver platter on the table, where the last wafer remained. "We are fighting for our lives now. Sometimes, we must kill just to save ourselves, and not the world."

"We need to do this to buy us some more time," Vankatesan continued. "To bring thuggee to a temporary end, we must bring all thugs together one last time for the final *chutaw*, the division of our wealth. And like our forefathers did when they left India, we must prepare a blood sacrifice to appease Kali for a decade. Then, when the world isn't looking for thuggee anymore, we shall arise once again, as we have always done."

"Which of the protocols are we enacting?" Blackbourne asked. "The nuclear plant meltdown?"

"The Wall Street crash scenario is better. We've infected their programs from the inside a few years back," Liang offered. "After the *chutaw*, we will all have extra money to invest in a ruined market and cryptocurrency."

"We are going with the airline protocol," Vankatesan announced, his voice firm.

"That will get the FBI, and everyone else for that matter, off our backs for sure," Mukherjee said. "But of the three, it is the most difficult to enact."

"Still, we are going with it," Vankatesan said, his tone making it sound final.

Liang looked like he wanted to argue about it, but Dasgupta changed the subject.

"How much money are we talking about?"

"As you know, all thugs share in the wealth we bring in yearly. Even the lower castes live well," Vankatesan answered. "But, as Blackbourne noted, the past few years have been good to us, and we have been adding to our secret accounts overseas."

"How much?" Blackbourne and Zhang asked in unison.

"Over ten billion dollars."

"Even with five hundred of us thugs—" Liang began.

"We're all rich," Blackbourne finished. His eyes were lit up in anticipation.

"So that's it, after the *chutaw* and the sacrifice, we all just walk away from each other for the next decade?" Chancellor said, his voice dampening the elation they were all feeling.

No one replied. They all knew where he was going with this.

"Actively practicing thuggee is what bound us all together, kept us all safe," Chancellor continued. "A few years down the line, what's to stop the lowest paid of us from deciding that their share wasn't enough? What's to stop them from threatening to become modern-day approvers unless we bend to their blackmail demands?"

Vankatesan felt all eyes on him. All seven of them knew the answer. They just wanted him to articulate it.

"*Bhans lena,*" he said.

"*Bhans lena,*" Chancellor echoed.

"*Bhans lena,*" the others repeated.

Vankatesan could see the greed in their eyes.

"Kali will gather them all in her embrace," Vankatesan added.

The others seemed comforted by this, though Vankatesan could see that the mention of ten billion dollars played a more significant role in assuaging their feelings of guilt.

The men all stood. Vankatesan walked over to the table and picked up the silver coin, returning it to his pocket.

"How does this happen?" Dasgupta asked.

"Within in the hour, Chancellor will send out the message to all thugs that they are to gather at the temple in a few days. Then, as put forth by Pravnev," Vankatesan opened the bible to a page marked by a ribbon, "we will make the blood sacrifice to Kali."

"What of the protocol?"

"All the computer programs necessary for switching in our man are in place at three different airlines of our choosing. I have a specific target. Hanson and Ramsell are flying west on Avian 951. Our pilot will take that plane over."

"Now I understand why you wanted the airline protocol," Dasgupta said, his eyes smoldering. He wanted revenge against Hanson also. "But what of the original pilot? Isn't there a chance he will start asking questions when he's replaced for no reason?"

Chancellor's voice came over his speaker.

"We're taking care of that."

Chapter 25

Atlanta, Wednesday, 3:54 a.m. EDT

Tom Sanford's phone vibrated and chirped on the hotel room's nightstand.

Being an airline pilot, he couldn't ignore it. With a groan, he reached over to his nightstand and answered it on its fourth ring.

"Yeah?" he mumbled with his eyes still closed.

Silence.

"Hello?" he said, his tone more irate than sleepy now.

Whoever was on the other end hung up. Most likely a wrong number. Annoyed, Sanford looked at the time on his phone. It was close to 4:00 a.m. His flight was slated for the early afternoon. He laid his head back on his pillow, hoping sweet oblivion would find him quickly.

There was a soft knock on his door.

"Housekeeping," an accented voice said.

Sanford didn't react, hoping that whoever was out there would go away, but the knocking persisted.

"Housekeeping," the voice repeated.

Now truly angry, Sanford leaped out of bed. He whipped open the door, not caring to put on anything over his boxer shorts.

"What do you want," he snarled.

An Asian man was standing in front of him, his eyes downcast. The guy was dressed in simple blue jeans and a white undershirt. He was holding out a bundle of carefully folded sheets in front of him. Right behind him was another Asian with a similar bundle. A third one was wiping down the floor's ice machine with a towel down the hall.

"The sheets you ordered," the man in front of him said.

"I didn't order any sheets," Sanford snapped back.

The man held them up again.

"Sheets," he said.

Sanford frowned. The man barely understood English. He held up his hand, palm outward while shaking his head. The universal gesture for "I don't want it". He then proceeded to shut the door, but the little Asian guy darted under his arms and into his darkened room.

"Sheets for room 412," the houseman said as he pointed at the bed.

"Look, you idiot," Sanford replied as he turned to face the guy and strode toward him. "This is room 312."

The guy looked confused. "412? Upstairs?" The houseman looked and pointed up.

"Yes, upstairs," Sanford answered as he glanced up also.

Something wrapped around his neck.

It was cool and wet. It took him a moment to realize it was the towel that the guy down the hall had been using on the ice machine. The thin fabric of the towel was now twisted, almost cordlike.

The other sheet-carrying man rushed in also, carefully shutting the door behind him as he threw down green glow sticks on the bed and floor.

Sanford reached for the garrote, but the first guy grabbed his hands. He felt all three men guide him to the bed. They laid him out on his stomach.

The guy holding his hands sat on the floor and braced his feet against the side of the bed. Sanford tried to kick at the guy on his back, but someone grabbed his ankles.

He tried to scream, but the noose was too tight, and it dug painfully into his neck. But the pain didn't last long.

Oblivion soon found him.

* * *

The three thugs held their positions for an extra minute to make sure all life had left their victim. Then they wrapped the body in the plastic sheet they had with them. Lifting the mattress up, they placed the corpse within the box frame. Sanford's luggage and personal belongings, except for his phone, were placed in there as well.

"This seems familiar," the foot holder said.

"Because it is," the *bhurtote* replied. "It's an urban legend. The body under the bed. A couple has their honeymoon spoiled by the smell of a hidden corpse."

The leader of the group, Chu, pulled out his phone and looked it up. "You're right," he said, his earlier accent now gone. "Only listen to this. Bodies have been found before. It's one of those urban legends that have actually proved to be true."

The three men scooped up the light sticks and stuffed them into their pockets. They then wiped everything down. Chu put the pilot's phone in a padded envelope.

"Formal sacrifice in a few days, can you believe it," the foot holder said. "I never thought I would see it in my lifetime."

"It's a long way to the temple. Are you flying?" the *bhurtote* asked.

"Driving," Chu answered. "After tomorrow, no one is flying."

The three men took folded baseball caps out of their back pockets and put them on. After making certain no one else was in the hall, the three thugs made their way out through separate exit doors, turning their faces away from cameras. Chu swung around to the front parking lot, where there was a blue mailbox. He dropped the padded envelope inside.

When the FBI began tracking the missing pilot's phone, it would look like Sanford took an erratic trip through town. When they finally figured out that the phone was somewhere in the mail, they wouldn't be able to get their hands on it until it reached its destination.

Alaska.

Chu left the lot and vanished into the night.

Chapter 26

Atlanta, Hartsfield-Jackson International Airport, 1:14 p.m. EDT

Richard Ganesh strode into the terminal.

His blue jacket had a bald eagle image stitched onto it, his epaulets three gold stripes, marking him as a copilot for Avian airlines.

The *rumal* in his jacket's pocket marked him as a thug.

Other pilots and flight attendants were also moving across the concourse, their wheeled luggage trailing behind them. Ganesh only had a backpack, appearing as if his workday would be a short one, and he would be able to make it back home that night.

He wasn't.

The backpack held a bomb hidden in a laptop. Ganesh wasn't planning to come home ever again.

Khomusna was in effect.

Only he could save thuggee, or the world, for that matter, now.

He was going to his death with pride. A part of him felt for his wife and three-year-old son. They would suffer in the short term when authorities descended on his house, finding the secret room with its decoy Koran and prayer rug and a laptop filled with Islamic extremist websites. A ruse years in the making. But his share of the *chutaw* was now to increase tenfold, and that would make its way to his family when the dust settled. And when his son became a thug in the next decade, he would learn that his father's name was honored in the same breath as Feringeea, Rumzan, and Thug Berham himself.

Bolstered by that thought, Ganesh turned toward the security checkpoints.

Four more thugs fell in beside him.

Ganesh kept his eyes straight ahead, not reacting to them, knowing that every moment of him on the ground would be studied. The authorities would be looking to see if anyone were aiding him.

Two of the men moved ahead of him. He sensed two others take up positions directly behind.

All these thugs were *sothas*, men who could talk their way through any situation.

They joined the crowd at the security checkpoints. Ganesh kept his eyes open for any bomb-sniffing dogs. If any were seen, one of the men behind him, his pockets filled with jerky, would move to distract the dog team.

None were encountered. The thugs faded over to the right, toward the TSA PreCheck lines.

PreCheck was a program that allowed paying customers to go through security at a faster pace. Unlike the other security lines, members could keep on their shoes, belts, and light jackets. Laptops could be kept in bags for their trip through the x-ray machine.

Ganesh fell in line and observed the TSA employees at work. Hartsfield-Jackson was the world's busiest passenger airport. When it came to security, all the newest security programs and equipment came here first. The men and women staffing this security area were all professionals, veterans with years, even decades of experience.

Unfortunately for them, thugs had been honing and practicing their dark trade for centuries.

Ganesh studied the man running the x-ray scanner. He appeared to be well over fifty, with brown hair graying at the temples and a little extra weight around the middle. He continuously pushed up his wire-rim glasses as he peered at his monitor. His name tag announced him as Leon Krafton.

Another TSA agent was manning the metal detector. He was a younger man with curly blonde hair. He held a metal-detecting wand in his hand, and he seemed to be working with the zealousness of someone new to the job. Ganesh wondered if he was going to be a problem.

PreCheck had two lines. The thugs in front of him went for the left. Ganesh fell in behind a heavyset woman going through the right.

The *sothas* breezed through their metal detector and were waved onto the other side of their x-ray machine. They made a show of carrying on an animated conversation as they gathered their belongings from their bins.

Ganesh placed his backpack in his bin.

The thug behind him placed a similar pack in his bin and pushed the whole thing forward so that the two containers were touching. The third thug did the same, forming a train of three identical bins.

The woman in front of him stepped through the metal detector, but alarms sounded off. Wand guy waved her over.

Ganesh watched his bomb enter the x-ray machine, picturing its image now on the TSA agent's screen.

He knew it wouldn't pass scrutiny.

To the practiced eye, several things would stand out. The laptop was an older, larger model. Inside of it were two large capacitors, cylinders placed where they had no right to be. They were there so that no errant charge made its way to the detonation caps. The C-4 was packed into the slots where the laptop's two batteries normally would be. Being of different densities, they would appear as a lighter shade of gray. To power everything, the battery was in the DVD slot. That alone would grab any TSA agent's notice.

If he was paying attention.

The *sotha's* voices carried over even to Ganesh.

"How was she in bed?" one of them, a tall bald man, asked.

"Like a tiger," the younger one replied. He had thick, dark hair, and his face was tan and handsome. "Her old man just wasn't doing it for her anymore."

"What's her name?" the bald thug asked.

"Jill Krafton."

Ganesh observed the TSA agent give a start. Even in the noise of a crowded room, the guy had picked out his last name.

"How long have you been seeing her?" the bald thug pressed.

Ganesh guessed that Jill Krafton was the name of the TSA agent's wife. And instead of taking this moment to study the image in front of him, the man did what any husband would do when he overheard someone bragging about having sex with his wife.

He turned around and faced the other man.

For a moment, it looked like a brawl was going to happen then and there. But handsome thug threw out his next line.

"A year now, she lives down in the Jonesboro area."

Ganesh watched Krafton, halfway out of his chair, slowly sink back into it. The thug's script was playing out. Krafton didn't live in the Jonesboro area, so he wasn't being cheated on. It was just a weird case of coincidence for the TSA agent. He slowly spun his chair back to his screen.

The image of the bomb was gone.

The thugs in Ganesh's line had not been idle. When Krafton turned away, the middle thug pushed the last of the three tubs forward, scooting the bomb-laden bin out of the x-ray machine.

The thug behind Ganesh made a show of moving forward and leaning in as he spoke up.

"Is that x-ray machine going to melt my Zeroid robot?"

The middle thug's bin was now showing up on the scanner. Something within it had a distinct shape.

"No, it's safe," Krafton said. Ganesh could hear some excitement in the x-ray tech's voice. "Those little toy robots are so hard to find. Which Zeroid is it?"

"The silver one," the thug answered with a hint of pride. "Zintar."

Krafton's other weak spot, Ganesh guessed. When *Khomusna* went into effect, the thugs had bent Kali's will toward anyone they could exploit. Krafton had been singled out. His life laid bare before the Goddess. He, like the pilgrims the thugs had met and befriended on the roads of India centuries ago, never had a chance.

The TSA agent with the wand was finishing up with the woman, who looked a little peeved that the extra money she spent hadn't paid off. He waved Ganesh through.

Ganesh stepped through the metal detector, leaving Krafton to discuss the finer details of toy collecting the thug leaning over the x-ray machine.

The metal detector's alarms sounded off. The overzealous kid waved him over.

Ganesh frowned as he tried to think of what he had forgotten that would set off the alarms. He held his arms out as the guy waved the wand around him.

It beeped over his lower jacket pocket.

"Empty the pocket, please," the TSA agent said grimly.

Ganesh complied, his hand settling on his key ring. He pulled it out and displayed it to the unsmiling TSA agent.

"Everything," the agent ordered as he pointed at the pocket.

There was a noticeable bulge there. Feeling like he was caught red-handed, Ganesh pulled out what he had stuffed into his pocket.

His *rumal*.

Ganesh was going to his death. He was taking his most prized possession with him.

The TSA agent snatched the yellow scarf out of his hand and studied it, turning it over as if it had something to hide. Ganesh started to sweat a little.

In his lifetime, he had killed four of Kali's chosen victims with it.

Ganesh could sense eyes turning his way. The line was backing up, and tension filled the air. His fellow thugs were moving away. If things went wrong at this phase, the contingency was to blow the bomb here and now. He began reaching for his backpack.

"For God's sake, Tyler, give the man back his scarf," Krafton scolded. "It's not like he's going to murder anyone with it."

Chastened, the younger TSA agent handed the *rumal* back to Ganesh. Around them, everyone laughed at the tension-breaking joke.

With his *rumal* back in hand, Ganesh laughed with them.

Chapter 27

Wednesday, 1:45 p.m., Hartsfield-Jackson International Airport

"Check out the tail wing," Hanson said as he turned around with a smile back on his face. Samantha was glad for his change in attitude. He had been quiet and withdrawn, even by his standards, for the entire morning.

They had left the apartment early to catch their morning flight out of New York. Hanson had already been awake and showered when she got up, and she had found him intent on his laptop computer in the living room. He had told her he was looking up Hindu Temples in the United States, as he felt that the thugs might be hiding in one of them.

She could tell the real reason he was pretending to be busy. He was hurt and confused by her seeming rebuff last night, and he was trying his best to conceal it.

She felt terrible about what had happened. The truth was she had wanted him more than anything at that moment, but not right after her confrontation with her ex-boyfriend, and certainly not in that apartment. It would have felt like they slept together for all the wrong reasons.

She wished she could have explained it, but she wasn't sure how without exposing her own profoundly personal pain. So, both had been quiet on the short hop to Atlanta, and back on the ground, they walked the entire length of the concourse in silence. It was only now that he had finally spoken up. Following his suggestion, she looked out the window.

Their next plane was noticeably larger, a Kessler wide-body airliner. Several cargo doors on its flank were open. Airport employees were loading large pallets covered with yellow netting onto it. She looked up at the tail. Like all of Kessler's Avian Airline planes, it had the image of a bird painted on its tail wing.

Their last plane had had a bald eagle on it. This one had a great horned owl.

"A bad omen for thugs," Hanson revealed as he sat down with his back against the glass. She joined him. She was wearing the same clothes as yesterday. Hanson wasn't. She had made him ditch the turtle-neck and purchase a cheap souvenir T-shirt at the airport. It was blue and had *My Parents Went to New York and All I Got Was This Lousy T-Shirt* printed on its front.

"Why did thugs make such a big deal with these omens?" she asked.

"Most Indians did back then," he answered. "War, disease, famine, and the weather. Everyone looked for signs to help them avoid the dangers they faced every day. Thugs were no different, and they had an added dimension to worry about. The law. If a thug read his omens wrong, he could be caught and hung, or worse, strapped in front of a canon and have it set off."

"That sounds awful," she said as she winced at the thought.

"It was considered a spectator event," Hanson said. "Blood and body parts flew everywhere. You know, like that comedian that splattered watermelons—"

"I get the picture," she said.

"Thugs had their own gurus whose job was to report on these portents. Entire expeditions could be canceled if something as innocuous a rabbit was heard crying out nearby."

"Rabbits?"

"Yeah, rabbits, partridges, and owls. Those drove thugs crazy. But some omens could be favorable, and their murdering expeditions would carry on."

"And Sleeman figured this out."

"Dr. Sherwood beat him to it by a decade. He interviewed the captured men in the Madras district who called themselves *phansigars*, the stranglers. He made an interesting point, stating that 'as ridiculous as their superstitions must appear, they are not devoid of effect. They serve to the important purposes of cementing the union of the gang, of kindling courage and confidence.'"

"So, observing favorable omens helped instill confidence?"

"Like an athlete wearing his lucky socks to a big game," Hanson answered. Samantha noticed his left hand reaching for his right shoulder. She had seen him do that several times since they had met. He must have realized she was watching, for he let his hand drop back down.

"Sleeman built on this through his own interviews. But he and others were sidetracked by the idea that thugs also took their cues from the priests of Kali. Historians agree now that formal Kali worship by thugs at major temples was not happening. But back then, Sleeman believed it was."

"So that's why you've been studying Hindu temples all morning?"

"Yes. I think our thugs are based on how the British imagined them. That they have a central location somewhere, dedicated to Kali. We need to find it."

"Any luck?"

"No," he answered with a frown. "They can't have their own place out in the open. They're hiding within an existing place of religious significance. Somewhere important to Kali."

"Maybe this Cresswell can help us out."

"I hope so," he said as he looked to his right. The flight crew was entering the passageway to the plane. It was almost time to board.

When it was their turn, they made their way through the line. Samantha kept looking over her shoulder, as did Hanson. No one appeared to be following them.

Once onboard, Hanson pointed toward an overhead storage bin.

"On some of the larger versions of these Kessler Ospreys, the crew sleeps in a room above business class," he said. "Their emergency exit is a secret door in one of those bins. Can you imagine someone tumbling out of one of these?"

She only grunted in acknowledgment of Hanson's nerd chatter as she focused on how comfortable the business class recliner seats looked. They continued down the aisle toward their economy class section.

At least it was a wide-body plane. Rare for domestic flights, but this hop to Los Angeles was just the first leg of an extended flight to Hong Kong for the jet.

She looked the cabin over. Avian resulted from a recent merger, and the plane, like the airline itself, was new. Billionaire Wayne Kessler was expanding his empire.

Hanson was still talking as they passed by the jet's third set of exit doors.

"And here's the trapdoor to the cargo area," he said as he pointed downward.

Their seats were just a short way farther in the central rows.

"How do you know so much about planes," she asked as they settled in.

"I don't, but I do know secret doors," he answered. He fastened his seatbelt. "You know, castles and whatnot."

Other passengers filed on by. Samantha entertained the possibility that they might have the center four seats to themselves. The plane seemed lightly booked. Even though the threat of COVID had lessened over the years, some airlines were still trying to reach pre-pandemic occupancy levels.

A family of four sat right behind them. The children looked young. She hoped they weren't seat kickers.

They took to the air. Hanson leaned forward and adjusted the small screen in front of him to display the map that showed the plane's location. He glanced over at her.

"How are you doing after last night?" he asked. "Was it difficult seeing your ex?"

"We kept it civil," she lied. She changed the subject. "One thing I've wondered about. Why the *rumal*?" She pointed at her own scarf. "Why scarves?"

"Several theories about that. There was a legal loophole with the Mughals. If one killed by strangulation, they weren't put to death when caught."

"Life imprisonment then if no bloodshed?"

"That, or the Mughals simply cut the nose off the guy and let him go."

"They were harsh back then."

"Different times," Hanson said. "Another reason was the caste system. Getting the blood of someone who was lower caste on you was a serious problem. It required extensive purifying rituals. *Rumals* solved that."

"Why not rope?"

"They started out with ropes. They used to lasso their victims or snare them with a hoop on the end of a stick. It just got to the point that anyone with rope, or any weapon for that matter, was treated with suspicion. In the end, thugs switched to the ultimate stealth weapon, their clothing."

"But we don't have caste or legal loopholes for murder. Why stick with the *rumal*?"

"Now we're dealing with imagined thugs. The whole 'blood seed' origin. For our thugs, *rumals* are a gift from Kali. A divine weapon."

"And when they use it, she protects them?"

"Yes."

The Osprey jetliner reached cruising altitude. Hanson powered up his laptop. Samantha could see that he was again reviewing Hindu temples across the United States.

She turned to her phone to look up thuggee. It amazed her that while some sites were turning to the modern way of thinking of thuggee, many others still had them as bloodthirsty assassins killing only in the name of Kali. She jotted down notes on a yellow notepad.

Hours passed, and she rubbed her tired eyes. Hanson glanced over at the notes she was taking.

"Find anything interesting?" he asked.

"Yes, it's like you said. There is a lot of disagreement on what thuggee was," she answered. "And another thing bothers me. How did thugs reconcile murder? How does one deal with killing?"

"Religion helped. Though it's a mistake to think of thugs as ritual assassins, killing for the sake of killing, some still had a belief that Kali forgave them of the sin of murder if they followed the omens correctly."

"Faith was part of it."

"Sure, like it is for all religions. Do it in the name of heaven, justify it in the end."

"Poetic."

"Old song," Hanson replied. "Another excuse is that many of them were former soldiers and still saw themselves as such. A specialized military branch that treated people on the road not as travelers, but as the enemy to be killed and plundered."

"That helps?"

"Yes. It's something they teach you in the military. Don't think of the opposing force as human. Think of them as simply the enemy," he answered as his eyes took a distant look.

"It helps," he finished quietly.

She had done some digging, so she knew that Hanson was a former Marine and that he had seen some action during Desert Storm. The thug attack the other night was not his first fight.

"And then there's what Ravi said back at the *bele*," Hanson continued. He frowned at the use of the thug's real name.

"That my fate was written on my forehead. That I belonged to Kali?"

"A Hindu belief is that our destinies are written on our foreheads. Thugs comforted themselves by claiming that they were religiously attuned enough to read this destiny. This absolved them of murder since Kali fated her victims to die. They were just her instruments."

She reflexively rubbed her forehead to feel for anything there. Nothing. She smiled and looked forward. Hanson's flight map had them south of Las Vegas. Agent Fisher was meeting them at the airport, and he even had some cash to loan them while they sorted out their banking problem.

One thing they hadn't decided on was where they were going to stay. Even with Fisher's help, money was still an issue.

A good excuse to share a room. But after last night, she wondered if Hanson would even broach the subject. Most likely, he wouldn't. She would have to take the initiative.

"Where do you think we should stay tonight?" she asked.

"I've been thinking about that," he answered. He was trying to sound casual. "With our funds tight, maybe we should think about—"

He didn't finish the sentence. The plane's copilot, pushing a food cart ahead of him, arrived in their section. He parked it against the wall that divided the economy class cabin from the rest of the plane. He then reached over his shoulder and pulled a laptop from his backpack and placed it on the cart. The copilot opened the computer and it powered on. Its screen displayed a computerized version of a jet's instrument panel.

A flight attendant approached him.

"Richard?" she asked. Samantha could detect puzzlement and concern in her voice.

"Do not call me by that name anymore," the copilot replied as he turned so that he could address everyone in the immediate area. "My true name is Ali Pershad." He held up a cell phone in his right hand, his thumb pressing a red button glowing on the screen. He gestured to the laptop with his left.

"And this is a bomb."

Chapter 28

"Stay in your seats," the copilot instructed.

Hanson, and everyone else, froze in place. A few cell phones rose to record what the man ahead of them was doing.

Samantha leaned in close.

"Steve, this can't be a coincidence," she whispered.

"It's not," Hanson replied. "Pershad was a Feringeea alias. This guy's a thug."

"And he's blowing up a plane?" she asked. "What happened to *rumals?*"

"It looks like we're past *rumals* now," Hanson answered.

He leaned over a bit so that he could look down the aisle. The terrorist...thug...was only five rows down, as was the computer. While "Ali" gave instructions to the attendant, Hanson studied the laptop.

It was an older model, its case thick and bulky. The monitor was displaying a basic airplane instrument panel in blue. The jet's airspeed, altitude, and direction were discernable from where he was sitting. One segment of the screen showed an outline of the plane. The exit doors, and some windows, were highlighted in yellow. The top right corner displayed a countdown timer. It read fifty-five minutes.

Ali's voice boomed louder. The attendant had handed him the headset that was used for announcing safety measures. More cell phones were popping up, though some passengers had them pointed at themselves. The few people who had masks on were taking them off, and Hanson could see tears in people's eyes as they started recording their last messages.

"Delgado, do you hear me?" Ali asked.

The voice of the airliner's captain came over the PA system.

"I hear you, Ganesh," Delgado answered angrily. "What the hell is going on?"

"My name is Ali; you will address me as such," the copilot replied. "I am fighting for the rights of Muslims in the Indian subcontinent, and I have a bomb to further that end, Delgado. The first thing I want you to realize that if you radio the situation to anyone, I will destroy the plane. I am sending Robin forward to confirm that I have the ability to know everything you do in the cockpit."

Hanson watched for a moment as the thug beckoned the attendant forward. He had her bring out her phone so that she could take photographs of the laptop. She then moved toward the front of the plane with her pictures of the computer.

"Why is this thug trying to pass himself as a Muslim terrorist?" Samantha asked.

Hanson thought about it. Deception was right up the thug's alley, but why all of this? And if thugs could get a bomb on the plane, why did one of them stay on board?

"I don't know. But don't yell out that he's a thug. I think he will set off the bomb if we do that."

The pilot's voice came back on. "Okay, Ali, I see it."

"Do you remember the laptop bomb on the Somali jet a few years back, the one that blew a hole in the side of the plane?"

"Yes."

"My bomb makes that one look like a firecracker," Ali continued. "Do you understand?"

"Yes."

"Good, and just in case anyone here has any ideas, let me explain how it works."

Around him, Hanson noticed a few men and women on the plane quietly unfastening their seatbelts, tensing up as if ready to rush the bomber.

"The button my thumb is on is a switch. It will broadcast a signal via Bluetooth if it is not depressed, and the bomb will explode. That connection is password protected, so none of you will be able to hack into the system. It is the same with the keyboard buttons. Touching them, or the power switch, will set off the bomb."

Hanson noticed that while the thug was talking, his eyes were scanning the cabin. He was looking for something.

"I have a Bluetooth device plugged into the plane's black box," the thug continued. "The black box records flight data in real time. I am receiving this information on the laptop. That means I know everything you are doing in the cockpit, Delgado."

"I understand."

"Good. The program displayed is my fail-safe if anyone here overcomes me. No matter what, it goes off in an hour. Should the landing gear be deployed, the bomb goes off. If any of the exit doors are disarmed or opened, the bomb goes off. If you belly-land this plane so that airspeed drops to zero—"

"The bomb goes off," Delgado finished.

The people who looked like they were going to rush the copilot settled back into their seats.

"What do you want me to do?" Delgado asked.

"Switch off the plane's transponder. Turn north and take us low. Use the mountains to evade radar. When we are far enough off course, we will turn back to L.A. and approach from the north. I wish to fly over the Hollywood Hills."

Delgado's voice. "Why?"

"It will be a demonstration to those on the ground of my ability to control this plane's flight path. Once over L.A. airspace, I will broadcast my demands. There are more like me, Delgado, and we are taking to the skies these next few days. The West will soon learn to leave the Indian subcontinent alone."

The plane's cabin was filled with a general murmur of voices, and practically everyone had their phones out. Hanson turned to Samantha.

"Hollywood Hills?"

"He's lying about sending a message once over L.A. I think he means to destroy the plane while it's above the Hollywood sign," she answered.

Hanson saw her reasoning. "There's almost always has a tourist's camera pointed at it. It would be the perfect showcase for a terrorist bombing," Hanson finished grimly. He looked back up.

The thug's eyes locked on his.

Now Hanson understood what the thug had been looking for. Him. The copilot held Hanson's gaze for a moment, a pleased look crossing his face. Then he turned away as he launched into an ideological rant.

"This is my fault," Hanson said quietly.

"Steve—"

"I shouldn't have pushed Vankatesan. You, these people, are all going to die because of me."

"Steve, there was no way knowing he was capable of doing this."

She was right about that. *How did Vankatesan pull this off?*

The Osprey banked hard to the right as it adjusted its path north. Hanson gripped his armrests and glanced to his side to view the desert landscape outside the windows.

A blinking indicator on the laptop switched off—the transponder. Ali had a look of satisfaction when he noted it.

The plane began making a steep descent.

Hanson turned back to his screen in front of him. The little jet icon was pointed north, just west of the Nevada-California border.

I know this place.

"Steve," Samantha said, reaching out to hold his hand, "I just want to say—"

"We're going to make it," he finished.

"Steve, it's a bomb with a hair-trigger in the hands of a madman."

"We just have to turn off the computer, just for a moment, and get his phone away from him."

"How? That computer is programmed for every contingency. Touching any key or button—"

"I know, but I'm betting they didn't think of what I have in mind."

He grabbed her notepad and pen and began sketching out a rough map. He labeled a few key landmarks.

Satisfied with the map, Hanson tore out the page, folded it several times over, and wrote a brief message on the small square remaining. He then reached for his wallet and pulled out a blue business card.

"Steve, what are you doing?"

He quietly told her his plan.

"What? That's insane. That can't possibly work."

"There's a chance, there's precedence," he whispered unconvincingly. She still looked skeptical.

"Wave over that flight attendant on your left and make it look like she's helping you out," he added.

The whole time, the attendants had been moving up and down the aisle as they calmed people down. The thug allowed it, confident in his control of the situation. Hanson kept an eye on him as Samantha dropped her phone on the aisle to her left. The attendant bent over to pick it up and hand it back to her. Samantha passed the note and card to her at the same time. The attendant, not missing a beat, continued calming people for a few more moments and then walked out of their section and into the next. To Hanson's relief Ali ignored her and continued with his manifesto.

"Do you really think it will work?" Samantha asked.

"That depends on Captain Delgado."

* * *

Captain Luis Casa-Delgado, intent on the upcoming landscape as he made his descent, was startled by the knock at the door.

"Check to see who it is," he ordered.

Laura Stricklan, the flight attendant that had taken his copilot's place when he had announced he was getting up to use the lavatory, was sitting behind Delgado in the first observer's chair. She stood up and went to the back of the cabin.

Soon Delgado heard another attendant on the speaker. "Laura? I know it's against protocol, but I need you to open the door. There's an FBI agent out here."

Delgado, an imposing-looking fifty-year-old man with a thick mustache, frowned. It was against protocol to open the cockpit door.

But protocol was no help when the other guy had a bomb. And, at the moment, Delgado wasn't concerned about reprimands. He had already made up his mind when the terrorist had laid out his demands.

Before he reached a populated area, he was bringing the plane down.

"Let her in."

Laura opened the reinforced door. She slammed it shut after Sheila rushed in.

"Captain, an FBI agent passed me his card and a note. His name is Daniel Fisher, and his note illustrates a way to get the bomb off the plane!" Sheila gasped out, nearly out of breath in her excitement. She held out a piece of yellow legal pad paper toward him.

Delgado read it.

"Holy Mother of Jesus," Delgado said. "This is the most loco idea I have ever read!"

"He even drew a map," Sheila added.

Delgado glanced at it. It was peppered with landmarks he didn't recognize, except for the name for the region itself. He looked to the right of the map. He could make out one other recognizable feature.

Furnace Creek Airport.

Due to the bomb, he couldn't land there. But it had a VORTAC beacon. He could navigate the area shown on the crude map.

Shelia was putting away the paper.

"Keep that out."

"Captain."

"We're doing this. Laura, get in the copilot's chair. I'm going to need your help. Sheila, let that Fisher guy know this is going to happen."

Sheila left, and Delgado turned his gaze back to the desert landscape filling his view. He adjusted a bit to the west to put the airliner in the area the agent had on his map.

It was a loco idea. But it was better than sure death.

* * *

The brunette attendant returned into their section. She made brief eye contact with Hanson and gave the slightest of nods.

Hanson glanced out the window. The Osprey was at a thousand feet. Low desert mountains could be seen in the distance.

He looked over at Samantha.

"Get ready—"

"We have to stop him," someone shouted behind them.

Hanson, and dozens of cameras, turned.

A huge, sun-bleached blond man had stood up at the rear of the plane. Hanson guessed he was over 6'3" and two hundred fifty pounds.

"I'm tired of listening to your Muslim bullshit, ragtop," the man shouted as he pointed at Ali. "If you think you're going to blow us up over L.A.—"

The thug looked unimpressed. "I suggest you sit back down."

"Or what?" the large man yelled as he advanced a few feet. "Let your thumb off that button? Better now than later. I say we take this guy down. Who's with me?"

No one budged.

"Fucking cowards," the man yelled, his face red. "I'll do it myself."

He charged forward.

Hanson leaped up, his shoulder low, to block him. The big guy smashed into him, and for a moment, Hanson held his ground. Then Hanson's feet slid on the aisle's carpet as the large man quickly pushed him back.

Others jumped up to help Hanson. They all grappled the guy, and they formed a struggling mass that surged forward. People cleared the front seats next to the bomber, and Hanson and the others wrestled the large man down onto the vacated row. Ali, who was only a few feet away, looked as if he was going to release the button.

"Don't do that. It's okay, it's handled," Hanson said desperately as he turned to the thug with his hands up.

Ali looked back in forth between Hanson and the struggling group near him. Two men had the guy's arms. A woman had him in a chokehold.

"We can talk about this. No one needs to die," Hanson continued.

The thug's gaze settled on Hanson.

"Yes, we can talk," Ali said. "What is your name?"

Hanson realized then that he and the thug were the only two left standing. And that every passenger, and every camera, in the cabin was focused on him. One of his worst nightmares come to pass.

Jesus Christ.

"Steve Hanson," he answered.

"Hanson," the thug repeated, relishing Hanson's apparent discomfort. "How does it feel knowing that the lives of all of these people rest on you?"

Hanson paused as he measured his words. He couldn't mention Kali, as that could force the thug to set off the bomb prematurely.

"But their lives are not on me, Ali. They're on you. Are you sure that your…God will forgive you for these deaths today?"

Outside, Hanson could see the ground rushing up. Delgado was going for it.

"My God—Allah—will forgive me, Steve Hanson," Ali answered. "Paradise awaits me."

"Traitor!" the big man yelled as he strained against his captors. "Don't talk to this terrorist! Hanson, is that your name? For God's sake, for your country, take this guy out now! Don't let him kill thousands more!"

Hanson wavered. Too many cameras. He felt like a deer caught in headlights. The big guy was right. When the NTSB recovered the cameras from the wreckage, history would remember him as the man who put his life first, at the risk to potential victims on the ground.

The plane was at five hundred feet.

Hanson made his choice. His left hand was still up, palm open, a gesture to the thug that he meant no harm. But his right hand he held low, and near his hip. It was hidden slightly behind his body, and he slowly clenched it into a fist.

His plan had to work.

The woman applied pressure to the man's throat, and he calmed down. In the sudden silence, Hanson could hear the two kids that had been sitting behind him whimper.

Ali gestured toward them. "What are they doing?"

Hanson looked back over his shoulder. The mother was sitting between her two children, her arms wrapped around them. Their heads were bowed as they whispered together.

Hanson turned back around. "They're just praying, man."

Ali smiled. "Prayer. That is good. I also pray, Steve Hanson. I pray that after today, all of you infidels will finally see the wisdom of Allah. And if not, I pray that my brothers will have the strength to strike more unbelievers down." The thug paused as if something new occurred to him. "And what of you? What do you pray for, Steve Hanson?"

Three hundred feet. The jet was starting to shake as if it were coming in for a landing. Some of the passengers looked out the window, alarmed at how close the ground was. Most of them kept their cameras on Hanson.

Cornered, Hanson answered. "Honestly, I'm praying for a miracle. I'm praying that somehow, your laptop bomb over there will turn itself off, and then I will have a chance to punch that smug smile off your face. Then I will hand you over to the big guy over here so that he can go all patriotic on you."

The thug's smile broadened. "Then I guess we shall see who has the more powerful God."

Hanson shook his head. "Wrong, Ali. We all worship the same God. The real question is…" Hanson nodded toward the laptop. "Which one of us is God listening to."

The thug's eyes followed Hanson's.

So both men were staring at the computer when it turned itself off.

Chapter 29

The thug took his thumb off the cell phone's screen.

The laptop didn't explode.

Confused, Ali turned and faced Hanson, a question on his lips.

Whatever that question was, he didn't get it off. Hanson was already moving, his fist inches from the thug's face.

He connected with a bone jarring blow, and the copilot's head snapped back. Hanson continued his forward motion and slammed Ali into the wall. With a groan, the thug dropped the phone.

Hanson looked over his shoulder. "Let him go!"

Stunned, the three captors of the blond man released their holds. Hanson shoved the thug into the big guy's lap.

"He's all yours," Hanson said.

The blond man's face lit up as he wrapped his arms around the copilot.

"Someone grab me some duct tape!" he roared.

No one volunteered. The plane was shaking, and it was nearly impossible to stand. Passengers remained in their seats as they screamed in fear. It felt as if they were coming in for a crash landing as the pilot skimmed the ground.

Hanson dove for the phone. He picked it up and placed his thumb on the pulsing button depicted its face.

Just in time. The computer cycled back on, and the cockpit display filled the screen. Hanson noticed that the bomb's timer didn't reset. The instrument panel remained for a few moments, and then the screen went dark again.

"Samantha!" Hanson yelled. "The trapdoor!"

Samantha leaped out of her seat, grabbing Sheila's arm as she did so. The flight attendant threw aside a rug to reveal a hatch.

The two women struggled with the trapdoor as the plane shook around them. Half of the passengers were still screaming in terror. The other half were holding their breath as they filmed Hanson closing the laptop. He took care while doing so. He didn't want to apply too much pressure and depress any buttons on the keyboard.

Samantha hauled the hatch open. Hanson moved over and looked in.

It was a tight fit. Boxes secured with yellow netting were just a few feet below the surface of the floor. A lucky break there. If Avian had been using cargo containers, the clearance would have been only inches. This whole plan would have been over before it started.

He handed the laptop gingerly to Samantha.

Then he laid down on his stomach and began to worm his way into the hold, his right thumb pressed on the bomb switch. The storage area was dark and cramped, but he could see a path to the back of the hold.

Samantha handed him the laptop. When he had that in hand, he risked a glance at the copilot. The big guy had Ali in a bear hug. Satisfied, Hanson turned to the flight attendant. "The computer can't handle the black box's input while we're at this altitude, so it's crashing and going through hard reboots. Tell the captain to keep us low for as long as possible."

She looked out the window, where the ground could be seen rushing by. "What is our altitude?"

"We're at periscope depth," Hanson answered as he inched forward and out of sight, so he barely heard Sheila's next question.

"Periscope depth? Where the hell are we?"

* * *

Marvin DeSoot parked his SUV in the empty lot. Outside, the sight of a weird desert wasteland greeted him, a salt-encrusted hexagon pattern covered the area instead of sand dunes.

"I thought parks had trees," Monica, his sixteen-year-old daughter, said from the back seat.

"Honey, how hot is it out there?" his wife Lori asked.

"It's early October. The temperature is only 102 outside," Marvin answered. He put on a hat to protect his balding head.

They stepped out into the heat. A platform had been built off the parking lot, and they all walked over to it.

Marvin breathed in the thick air, enjoying the alien nature of the place.

"It's quiet," his daughter said at his side.

He smiled at her. That was another bonus to the area—no cell phone service. For once, he had her attention.

He pointed at a brown sign nearby. "Let's take a picture next to that."

He marched them over. His wife and daughter posed on each side of the sign as he called up his camera app.

A roaring sound filled his ears. He looked to the south, stunned at what he saw.

A large passenger jet was coming in for a landing.

It was about a half-mile west of the parking lot, and it looked to be only fifty feet off the ground. Its landing gear was not down.

"My God, Marvin, are they coming in for a crash landing?" Lori asked.

"I don't know, but I'm going to switch to video for posting online. Stay next to the sign," Marvin commanded.

He began recording as the jet, an Avian Airliner, judging by the owl on its tail, swept by. It didn't crash but instead continued on. As it faded into the distance, he hit the playback button on his phone. He had always thought it would be thrilling to visit Death Valley, but he hadn't expected this. His family crowded around him as he reviewed the scene.

He froze it on the money shot—the plane in the background and right over the sign his wife and daughter were standing next to.

BADWATER BASIN
282 Feet/85.5 Meters
BELOW SEA LEVEL

* * *

Delgado struggled as he fought against the turbulence caused by ground effect. They were too close to the surface for the wind vortices off the wingtips to form correctly.

Avian 951 was shaking itself apart.

"Seventy feet," Laura called out.

He had her watching the ground proximity warning system. The safety component had its own audio alerts, which he had turned off. He didn't need to listen to the plane repeatedly tell him "Terrain ahead." All he needed to know was how far he was off the ground.

And since he didn't dare glance away from the window, Laura was his new copilot.

"Captain, altimeter has us 150 feet below sea level."

That made sense. The FBI agent's map had this region at two hundred fifty feet below sea level.

The vibrations through the chair increased a bit. He guessed at Laura would say next.

"Fifty feet."

He nudged up a bit and considered going higher, but Sheila's voice came at him from behind.

"Captain, it worked. We have Richard. The FBI agent is making his way for the aft cargo bay door," she said. "He says if we maintain this altitude, the laptop will stay off."

"Laura, radio ahead. Let LAX know of our situation," Delgado said. "And ask about Tom Sanford. He should have been my copilot today."

"Do you need any more help, Captain?" Sheila asked worriedly from behind him. "Should I read off anything else on the instrument panel?"

"No," Delgado said through gritted teeth as he felt the vibrations change again through his chair. "Instruments aren't of any use. I'm flying this thing by the seat of my pants."

* * *

Hanson made his way toward the back of the plane.

It was slow going. He couldn't even crawl properly. His right hand was clutching the phone, his thumb aching as he held down the button. The laptop was balanced on the palm of his left hand. He had to wriggle his body without the use of his arms.

And the whole plane shaking violently didn't help either. It was as if he was in the starship *Enterprise* while caught in an alien ship's tractor beam.

He was almost at the end of the pallets when the plane suddenly bucked. He floated to the top of the cargo bay and his back pressed against the ceiling. The cargo followed him, and for a panicky moment, Hanson thought he was going to be crushed.

The netting held, restraining the bulky packages below him, and Hanson drifted back down on top of them as the cargo settled.

"Sweet Jesus," he muttered as he wormed forward the last few feet.

* * *

Samantha and everyone else not belted into their seat in the Osprey's cabins sailed up into the ceiling.

She hit hard, bouncing off it and back down to the deck. She came to a rest near the trapdoor.

Samantha groaned in pain. That was drowned out by passengers screaming in fear again. A dozen phones had flown from their owner's hands and were now scattered around her. She looked over to where the thug was being held.

He, and the others involved in the scuffle, were lying on the floor also. All were holding their heads; the plane's surge having taken them by surprise. The big man was out cold.

The thug stood up.

He appeared unhurt. Stepping over his captors, he made his way to the hatch.

Her shoulder was throbbing from its impact on the ceiling, but Samantha ignored that as she jumped up and took a swing at the copilot. She connected, and he grunted as he stumbled back. She took a step forward to continue her attack but slipped on a phone on the carpet and stumbled to her knees. He took advantage of that to grab her and cast her aside. He then dove into the hold. Being closest to him, only she heard what he said next.

"Kali provides."

He slammed the door shut. Samantha crawled over and struggled to open it, but the thug must have locked it from the other side.

She stood up and moved about twenty feet farther back on the plane, trying to guess where Steve would be. She started shouting and stomping on the floor.

"Steve! Behind you!"

Sheila joined her.

"What happened?" she asked as she tried to maintain her balance while the plane shook.

"The copilot is down below; he's locked the door!" Samantha answered. She turned away to shout toward the floor again. "Steve, for God's sake, behind you."

Sheila started down the aisle to inform the captain, but then she paused and turned back.

"Who's Steve?"

* * *

Hanson slid onto the floor of the cargo bay.

He was at the room's center point. The bay was only half full, the area right behind the nine-foot-wide outer door being devoid of any pallets. It left about a ten-foot by ten-foot space. It was dimly lit, and he could see the glow of a control panel just left of the door.

The shaking was much more pronounced down here. Hanson couldn't even stand without one hand gripping the netting near him.

The unevenly stacked boxes near him formed a shelf. He slid the laptop onto it and secured it behind the netting. Once again, the indicator lights winked.

He stood up and bumped his head on the padded ceiling. Clearance was only five and a half feet down here. Bent over, his left hand gripping the netting, he made his way slowly to the Osprey's starboard wall. A switch was there. Hanson braced himself and pressed the button to open it.

The shock almost overwhelmed him. The dim and cool cargo hold changed to desert brightness and heat instantly, the room's temperature jumping forty degrees upward.

The wind and noise were a surprise also. The plane's screaming jet engines were less than fifty feet away. It stunned Hanson. Only his grip on the netting kept him from being swept out by the swirling wind.

He stumbled back to gather his wits. The ground was rushing by impossibly fast. Knees shaking, he looked back at the computer. He had to time this next part precisely. He could see the indicator lights. He watched them switch on for a few moments and then switch off.

His window of opportunity. He moved his thumb off the screen and threw the cell phone out the door.

The cell phone broadcasted its detonation code to the inert laptop. But a few moments later, it didn't matter anymore. Though it was possible it would continue to broadcast on the desert floor, it was now out of range. Hanson breathed a sigh of relief. Without the detonator switch in his hand, getting rid of the bomb would be much simpler. He began making his way back toward it.

Ganesh spent a few extra moments making sure the trapdoor would remain secure. He didn't need Ramsell interfering with him.

Satisfied with that, he reached back for a side pocket on his backpack. His second cell phone detonator was there. All he needed to do was power it on and hit the switch loaded on the home screen.

Light, heat, and the roar of the jet's engines filled the room. Hanson had opened the cargo door. Rage consumed Ganesh.

He was too late.

The bomb was already off the plane.

Failure.

Realizing he had trapped himself in the cargo hold, the thug despaired for a moment. Then his hand, still in the backpack's pocket, felt the softness of his *rumal*. He pulled it out and began twisting it. Plan A had failed. A smile returned to Ganesh's face as he started crawling.

Plan B.

Hanson pulled himself back to the laptop and kneeled next to it, pleased that his plan worked. And when the plane landed, Fisher could show his superiors at the FBI that someone was trying to kill him and Samantha. And then maybe the FBI could convince the thug to confess. Ali, or whatever his name was, would become the first approver in over 150 years.

Thinking of that brought a look of satisfaction to Hanson's face. He was about to free up the computer from its make-shift shelf when something reached his ears above the roar of the jets. Thumping on the ceiling above him, and he thought he could just detect his name.

He glanced up.

A *rumal* wrapped around his neck.

The vibrating floor must have thrown the thug off, for the *rumal* was imperfectly cast, and it caught on Hanson's right ear.

That gave Hanson a moment to jam a few fingers from his right hand under the noose. He brought up his left hand and worked a few of those fingers under the cloth also.

The thug tightened the *rumal*, a twisting motion that brought his knuckles together.

"Where's your God now, Hanson?" the thug screamed.

Hanson tried standing up, but he only succeeded in crashing his head against the ceiling. The thug seized the moment and started giving Hanson the bum's rush as he pushed him toward the open door.

Hanson's scrambling feet couldn't get any traction, and they were almost at the edge when he finally brought up his left leg and braced it against the wall. He pushed off.

That sent both men flying through the air along the edge of the cargo bay, spinning in the vortex created by the rushing wind. They slammed into the aft wall of the hold, and both groaned in pain from the impact.

They were close to the edge as they struggled. Hanson lurched forward to roll back into the cargo bay. The thug rolled with him, and both men wound up in the center of the hold, the thug still at Hanson's back. Grunting in pain, Hanson felt the pitch of the floor change. The airliner was rising and turning.

"Do you fear death, Hanson?" the thug hissed, his mouth close to Hanson's ear. "I do not. We thugs are truly the chosen, the children of Kali, created of her sweat. I look forward to being welcomed back to the Mother's embrace."

Hanson couldn't answer, the thug's noose was too tight. His grip on the cloth prevented him from passing out due to blood loss to the brain, but he was in danger of asphyxia. Fighting with the noose around his neck was like struggling underwater. His muscles were screaming for oxygen. He could feel himself weakening, and the *rumal* was pressing deeper into his neck. The thug had him, and Hanson realized it was only a matter of time now.

* * *

"Five hundred feet," Laura said.

Delgado grunted in acknowledgment. They had run out of subsea level floor, and ahead, the valley was narrowing, the mountains on both sides crowding in. And just a few moments ago, Sheila had informed them that Ganesh had locked himself in the hold with the FBI agent.

The indicator light showed that the aft cargo door was still open. The FBI agent's note had stated that the lower deck doors were not part of the laptop's monitoring program. They wouldn't set off the bomb when used.

"What now?" Laura asked.

"The agent had said keep it below sea level," Delgado answered. "I'm turning back for another run. Right or left?"

Laura looked at the map. "Left, there's a canyon stretching back south."

Keeping to a canyon would help. Their altitude was increasing as the ground elevation rose. That created another problem; the pressure difference in the cabin and the cargo hold would place undue stress on the floor that divided them. Fortunately, the FBI agent's map showed them how to avoid the mountains as much as possible. For some reason, this Fisher guy knew Death Valley like the back of his hand.

Delgado banked left hard, the engines shuddering under the strain. The maneuver sent the plane south down a canyon.

Still too high though. His eyes searched forward, looking for lower ground. Up ahead, Delgado could see an unusual bright patch of terrain. It looked flat, so he angled for it. He needed to hug the floor again and relieve the pressure difference.

"What's that ahead?" he asked Laura, nodding to the bright patch of ground rapidly approaching.

She consulted the map. "He has it labeled. It's called Racetrack Playa."

Delgado frowned. He recognized the word *playa*. It meant a dry lakebed. But why was it called Racetrack?

* * *

Floyd Wheeler turned on the GoPro strapped to his forehead to record the vista around him. Though he was off-screen, his voice added narration as he panned the camera.

"Finally, I have arrived at Racetrack Playa," he said dramatically for the video. "An adventure long in coming."

The camera pointed down. That revealed a hard desert floor cracked in a hexagonal pattern.

His coworkers had scoffed at him when he told him of his trip to this mysterious area. He ignored them as he ignored the naysayers on the web. For him, this place was a pilgrimage, and his GoPro panned over to the reason he was here.

The Sailing Stones.

Several rocks, some the size of bowling balls, were close by. Behind them, grooves were gouged into the ground, serpentine furrows that had formed when the stones had plowed their way across the desert floor.

"As you can see, the stones moved on their own accord," Wheeler continued. "Some say the wind pushes them, but how is that possible? Some of these stones weigh over a hundred pounds."

The camera panned around again. The desert floor was shimmering, the heat creating a mirage that made it look like he was surrounded by water. The lower part of the mountains nearby couldn't be seen.

"It's as if I am all alone, separated from all mankind," Wheeler narrated as he turned back to the stones. He pointed his camera at the patterns etched across Racetrack Playa's surface.

Weeping could be heard off-camera.

"Nature is trying to communicate with me, but I don't understand," Wheeler said, sniffling. "What does it mean?"

More crying could be heard as the camera focused on a stone.

"I don't understand," he continued. "Won't someone send me a sign?"

The ground trembled, and the video image shook with it. The GoPro showed the rock he was focused on vibrating slightly, and dust fell away from it.

Then the camera's microphone picked up a new sound—a dull roar. The camera angle changed quickly, moving back and forth as Wheeler scanned the area to the north. Less than a quarter-mile away, a huge jet, only fifty feet off the ground, burst out of the mirage's veil.

It was headed straight at Wheeler, and its bulk filled the screen. It seemed to react to him, dipping up and down quickly as it passed overhead. Wheeler's screams of fear could be heard as the jet roared by, kicking up dust as it did so. Flailing arms and legs were briefly visible as Wheeler rolled along the ground, pushed by the jet's backdraft.

And then, as quickly as it had arrived, it was gone.

The camera's view gyrated as Wheeler stood back up.

"What was…?"

The narration cut off as the camera stopped its roving and focused on one spot on the desert floor.

The Sailing Stones were gone, as were the tracks in a thirty-foot radius. The jet's backwash had obliterated the immediate area. It was as if God himself had reached down with a finger and rubbed it all away.

A geological miracle, years in the making.

Gone in an instant.

The camera's view dropped lower as Wheeler fell to his knees. His sobbing could be heard in the background.

"I don't understand…I don't understand…."

* * *

The thug and Hanson's limp form were cast upward as the plane bucked.

They crashed into the padded ceiling. The thug, focused on Hanson, was surprised when they went airborne, and he smacked his mouth and nose into the back of Hanson's head when they came to a sudden stop. Stunned, he let go of the *rumal* with a groan.

For Hanson, the pain of the impact was like a slap to the face. His eyes snapped back open, and he gasped a deep breath of air. His eyes darted around as he tried to figure out where he was.

He was on the ceiling, and the thug's mass was pressing on him from below. Hanson wasn't sure what force was fighting gravity to keep them there, but an old phrase came to mind.

What goes up…

He moved his hands from his neck pushed off from the ceiling with everything he had.

They both hurtled toward the floor of the cargo bay, the thug's arms flailing. They smashed into it, and a spray of blood and teeth blew by

Hanson's left cheek as the thug explosively exhaled. The thug groaned with pain as Hanson sat up and pulled the *rumal* off his neck.

The wounded thug tried to crawl away. Hanson leaped on his back and wrapped the yellow scarf around his neck. The guy got both hands under it and desperately tried to pull it off.

"How does that feel?" Hanson yelled hoarsely above the roar of the jet engines. "I guess the *rumal* is on the other neck now!"

The thug got his legs under him and pushed. Both flew backward and into the left fuselage wall.

They crashed into it. The thug began throwing back his head in an attempt to smash Hanson's face.

It didn't work. The guy still had on his pack, and it kept them far enough apart so that the thug's head couldn't reach him. Hanson pulled the *rumal* even tighter, twisting so that his knuckles pressed against the man's neck.

The copilot freed up a hand and groped back over his shoulder and searched for Hanson's eyes. That also couldn't reach. For a moment, Hanson thought he had the thug right where he wanted him when the thug changed tactics and reached forward and to his left. Hanson glanced over.

They were sitting next to the bomb, its indicator lights holding steady. Realizing that the bomb was still on the plane, the thug was now stretching for it, and he succeeded in wedging his fingers partway in, feeling for the mouse pad.

Hanson pulled him back, and the lid snapped shut. Frustrated, the thug struggled more violently to reach his weapon of mass destruction.

He had to get that computer off the plane. Gripping the *rumal* in his right hand, Hanson lunged for the computer with his left and got a hold of it. He tugged it free and held it up and above his head.

Just one toss, and this was over.

The thug redoubled his efforts, letting go of the *rumal* around his neck and slamming an elbow into Hanson's gut. Hanson gasped in pain and dropped the computer.

It fell between them. Not wanting the thug's wild struggles to set off the bomb, Hanson let go of the *rumal* and pushed him away. He then scrambled up into a hunched-over standing position, ready for the thug to turn back around and attack him. The thug surprised him, though, by rushing for the forward edge of the open cargo bay door. Relieved, Hanson used the moment and looked for the computer at his feet.

It was gone.

He glanced up. The thug had now turned and was facing him as he stood near the cargo door panel, the wind whipping at his clothes and the *rumal* around his neck. He had something in his hands.

Another cell phone. With a sinking feeling, Hanson realized that the thug had a second detonator.

The cargo bay tilted drastically. The plane was climbing, and the shaking subsided. The engines roared louder as power to them increased. The thug had a look of wild triumph on his bloody face as he turned on the cell.

"You only pray to your God, Hanson. I've killed for mine. Let me show you what true devotion looks like!"

Bent low, Hanson charged, but he knew he was too late. He was only halfway to the thug when he held up his phone.

"*Kali Ke Jae!*" the thug shrieked as he thumbed and then released the glowing red button on the screen.

Even above the roar of the jet engines, both men heard the high-pitched whine of capacitors charging.

From the thug's backpack.

Surprised by where the sound was coming from, the thug reflexively turned and reached back over his shoulder.

Hanson kept charging, and he hit the thug square in the chest with his right shoulder, knocking him out of the plane. Hanson would have followed, but he made a desperate reach for the doorway's frame and grasped it. He held on for dear life.

The bomb exploded the barest fraction of a second later a few hundred feet behind the tail wing, close enough to cause the jet to pivot a few degrees clockwise. Hanson looked over his shoulder. It was a massive explosion, and it would have ripped the Osprey clean in half had it detonated inside the plane.

The jet corrected, swinging back counterclockwise as it was climbing and outrunning the explosion blooming below it. The air was quickly getting colder. Though he wasn't technically outside the plane, the wind shear was still strong enough to keep him parallel to the cargo bay floor.

And the pressure difference was now causing air to flow from the plane, pushing him outward. Hanson knew he couldn't hold on in the full force of the jet stream. He let go with his left hand and took a moment to slap his right shoulder.

He pulled himself forward, his left hand stretching for the panel, feeling for the bottom button. He pressed it.

The door started to slowly shut. Hanson prayed for it to close faster as his grip weakened.

* * *

Everyone on the plane felt the bomb go off. Samantha, the only passenger left standing in the aisle, held onto a seat as Avian 951 spun sideways a bit. Passengers screamed. Others were dictating their last words into their phones, sure that the end was near.

After a few impossibly long seconds, the jet straightened out. It was still steeply climbing though.

Delgado's voice came over the speakers. "We're okay. I'm not feeling the loss of any systems. Everyone, please return to your seats. Sheila, the cargo bay doors are closed. Has anyone come out of there yet?"

Up front, the flight attendant was shaking her head as she spoke into the handset.

The airliner leveled out. Samantha, and dozens of cell phones, focused on the trapdoor.

For several long moments, nothing happened. Then, the sound of a lock being undone could be heard. The big guy, who was now conscious, moved over and leaned over the hatch.

It opened, and everyone held their breath for a moment as the man gazed downward. Then he reached down and hauled Hanson out of the hold.

The cabin erupted into yells and clapping. Hanson, whose hair was standing on end as if he had been in a wind tunnel, leaned against the big guy shakily. Hearing the applause, he looked up in surprise and turned several shades of red.

Now the passengers were turned 180 degrees in their seats, trying to include themselves in the recordings they were taking of Hanson, talking as they did so. Samantha smiled to herself. As a journalist, she could understand. They were all feeling as if they were a part of history, and they wanted to share it with the world.

As she started walking forward, the man standing next to Hanson held out his hand. "Hey, dude, no hard feelings?"

Hanson grinned. "Fine by me, man."

The boy from the row behind Samantha darted forward to stand in front of Hanson. "Where's the other guy?" the kid asked.

A tough question, and Samantha noticed that Hanson paused before answering. She guessed that he was struggling with how to explain death to a child.

"He left. He told me he wanted to go and meet his maker," Hanson finally said.

Before Samantha could reach him, the boy's mother rushed forward and gave Hanson a hug.

Chapter 30

Edwards Airforce Base, 7:45 p.m. PST

Hanson gave up on the chopsticks and switched to a spoon to eat his Chinese food.

"Hungry?" Samantha asked.

"Starving," he replied as he shoveled fried rice into his mouth. With their funds low, they hadn't eaten much in the past twenty-four hours. And after his exertions on the plane, he felt like he could eat a horse.

The two of them were sitting in a small conference room. Avian 951 had been diverted to Edwards Airforce Base, and F-22 Raptors had escorted them in. Once on the ground, all electronic equipment capable of recording had been confiscated. Passengers were led away to different areas to be debriefed.

Though they weren't free to explore the base, they were treated as guests, not prisoners. Their room even had a flat-screen television and its own bathroom.

The debriefing itself had been short. Just enough to establish who they were and what they had witnessed. Hanson had a feeling that the actual interviews were yet to come.

"Does it hurt to swallow?" Samantha asked, concern on her face as she reached out across the table towards Hanson's neck.

"Nah, it's not bad—" Hanson began.

The door to their room opened, and Fisher strode in. Hanson choked a bit on his sweet and sour chicken.

"We can explain," he said.

Fisher held up a hand as he closed the door. "You don't need to. I get it. You flashed my card so that what you said next would carry some more weight. Just do me a favor. When other agents question you, make it clear that it was all your own idea."

Hanson grinned. "Will do."

"Now, I do have another concern."

"He was a thug," Samantha answered.

Fisher frowned as he sat down. "Tell me everything."

They did, and Fisher's face took on a look of amazement as they finished their story.

"How in the hell did you know that their computer would be affected?" Fisher asked. "I've seen the map you drew and your note. You wrote something about flying below sea-level altitude would make the computer crash."

Hanson shrugged his shoulders a bit and hung his head in embarrassment. "It's an urban legend," he quickly mumbled.

"What?"

"It's an urban legend," Hanson repeated.

"I don't understand," Fisher said.

"There's an urban legend about sophisticated jets malfunctioning because of unique geographical features. The primary example being Israeli F-16s losing their computer systems while flying low over the Dead Sea. Some versions of the story have the F-16s flipping upside down. Upon investigation, the pilots realize the problem was flying below sea level."

"I thought urban legends weren't true," Samantha said.

"Most aren't, and so was this one. However, there is some real precedent out there. F-22 Raptors had their own problems. Their computers crashed when they crossed the International Date Line.

They had to limp back to Hawaii by following a tanker like a flock of geese."

"And you thought it would work today?" Fisher asked.

"I thought there was a reasonable chance," Hanson replied. "Remember, I work in the IT department at my supermarket. That program the copilot was running looked like a custom job. Programmers like to keep it simple, and one shortcut is to design the program to deal with only positive integers as input."

"Like airspeed and altitude," Fisher said.

"Correct. The possibility of negative altitude numbers from the black box didn't cross the mind of whoever programmed that laptop."

"I'm just glad it worked," Samantha said. "But how do you know so much about Death Valley? I saw you whip out that map."

"The Sailing Stones of Racetrack Playa. You know, those large rocks that move on their own and leave trails in the desert. I've been fascinated by them for years," Hanson explained. "Everyone back in the day thought some sort of cosmic forces were at work.

"I thought it was freakish storms due to the region's altitude variations pushing the rocks around. I studied topographical maps until I could navigate Death Valley with my eyes closed."

"That explains the map," Samantha said. "But now I'm curious about the rocks."

"Scientists finally witnessed it happening a few years ago. During winter, on rare occasions, that desert can be an inch's deep lake that freezes over. Those rocks get locked in the ice. Then the sun comes up, and the ice starts breaking up into large sheets. When the wind kicks in, these sheets act like sails. They move across the ground—"

"And drag the boulders with them," Fisher finished.

"Yes, sometimes for hundreds of yards. The ground is soft, so tracks are left behind."

"And in the summer, when everything evaporates, the incriminating evidence of how it happened is gone," Samantha guessed.

"The unexplained—" Hanson began, his arms spread out wide.

"Yeah, yeah, we get it," Fisher interjected. "Next question. You said the last thing the thug yelled was, *'Kali Ke Jae.'* What's that?"

"Glory to Kali," Hanson answered.

"A suicidal thug's final words?" Samantha asked.

"Yes, but don't think of it as suicide. Thugs see it as part of their struggles against us. When it came to hanging or death, Sleeman noted that four out of five thugs chose to place the noose around their own necks and step off the platform on their own because the rest of us are lower caste. We're not worthy to kill them."

Samantha and Fisher spent a few moments thinking that over. She spoke up first.

"What happens next? How is the Bureau going to move against the thugs?" Samantha asked.

"You two have been holed up here for a while without any phones," Fisher answered. "And you don't know how big this thing has blown up. Fortunately, since the pilot dropped my name when he radioed LAX, I received a call and was able to get a head start over here. We need to go over what we are going to say before—"

A heads-up knock came from the door. It then opened from the outside.

A striking though severe-looking woman stepped in. Like Fisher, she was dressed in a suit, though without the tie. She was almost as tall as Hanson and about ten years older, her hair gray. She had an East Coast blue blood air about her.

Fisher stood up when she walked in. Hanson found himself doing the same.

"Who's she?" Hanson whispered to Fisher.

Fisher's face was grim when he answered.

"Homeland."

Chapter 31

The woman strode deeper into the room, her piercing gray eyes sweeping over the three of them. They rested on Hanson, and a smile broke out on her face as she held out her hand. "Mr. Hanson? My name is Evelyn Watkins. Well done up there."

Relieved, Hanson shook her hand. She turned toward the others. "Samantha Ramsell and Special Agent Daniel Fisher. It's a pleasure to meet you also."

Hanson was feeling more comfortable around this woman already. But he noticed that Samantha and Fisher still looked wary.

"You arrived quickly, Agent Watkins," Samantha said. "Did you drive up from the Los Angeles office?"

"Yes," Watkins replied. "When my superiors realized how urgent the situation was, they sent me here immediately."

"Urgent?" Hanson asked, confused.

Watkin's head tilted, and she looked at him quizzically.

"They've been stuck in here the whole time," Fisher explained.

She nodded her head in understanding. She walked over to the television and switched it on. News anchor Doug Morgan appeared on the screen. Behind him, a video of large jets lined up on airport runways was playing.

Watkins muted the television and turned to Hanson. "The FFA, as they did in 9/11, has issued a ground stop command. All domestic planes in the air are to land at their destination, but no planes may depart. International flights are being diverted to Canada and Mexico. The nation is now on Imminent Alert threat level."

"I had no idea," Hanson said, stunned.

"It's clear from what the terrorist said there are more Muslim extremists like him out there," Watkins continued. "Until we are sure there is no further threat, all air travel over America is grounded."

Video of Hanson punching the copilot appeared on the screen.

"How did that get out so fast?" Hanson asked, his heart sinking to his stomach as he viewed himself on national television.

"From the web. Passengers downloaded multiple files before the plane landed. At the moment, you're trending on the internet. My cyber unit informs me you are even breaking records."

Jesus Christ, thought Hanson. All his life he had been trying to blend in, to be invisible. That was now over.

"Clackamas law enforcement is obviously much more interested in you now," Watkins continued. "But they've been instructed that Homeland is spearheading the investigation. That's why I'm here. Did the terrorist say anything to you down in that plane's hold?"

Hanson stared at the screen. Below the copilot's image was a tagline: *Who was Richard Ganesh?*

Now Hanson understood why the thug had stayed on the plane and made a big show of being a Muslim terrorist. Thugs were masters at deception. This whole thing was a diversion to throw law enforcement off their scent.

Time to fix that.

"He said 'Glory to Kali,'" Hanson answered.

"Pardon?"

"Ganesh wasn't a Muslim terrorist out of Pakistan, Miss Watkins," Hanson replied. "He was an Indian thug. And I don't mean a more brutish terrorist, but—"

"He's some sort of leftover from the thuggee cult from 1830s India," she finished for him.

Everyone else's mouths opened a bit in surprise. "You've heard of them?" Samantha asked.

"There was a paper written back in the mid-eighties titled: *'Fear and Trembling: Terrorism in Three Religious Traditions,'*" Watkins answered. "It dealt with the added power that religious terrorists had over secular terrorists. The focus was on Muslim assassins, Jewish zealots, and Hindu thugs."

"I never knew such a paper existed," Hanson said.

"It's not required reading, but I found it interesting," Watkins replied. "Sleeman's campaign against the thugs is one of the few success stories on combatting religious terrorism."

"That report was written over thirty years ago," Hanson said as he shook his head. "And the facts on thuggee have evolved since then. Thugs weren't a religious terrorist group; they were simply bandits in it for the money."

"So I've heard," she replied. "When I saw Agent Fisher's name brought up, I called the Agent in Charge at the Portland office. At my request, he handed over Fisher's report on you. I am aware of all of your theories."

"Then you must realize that these guys are borrowing a page from Sleeman's playbook," Hanson said.

"I don't follow."

"The approvers," Hanson explained. "They're like your criminal informants. These guys gave Sleeman all his information.

"At first, they wouldn't confess. Then Sleeman came up with the idea of pitting the different factions against each other. Hindus versus Muslims. Lower caste versus higher caste. In the end, he couldn't stop the thugs from talking."

"And you feel the same is happening now?" Watkins asked.

"Yes, but now it's Christians pitted against Muslims," Hanson continued. "That's what this whole thing must be about, to distract you from hunting them."

"And that's what you think?" Watkins said.

"Yes."

"Then let me tell you what I know," she continued. "When Ganesh's name came up, Homeland was in his house in Richmond, Virginia within an hour. We found a secret room with a Koran. His car in the Atlanta airport parking lot had a prayer rug in it. The fibers from the rug match fibers found on the floor of the hidden room. Ganesh secretly prayed there daily."

"That could be for show," Samantha said.

"If it was a ruse, then he was dedicated to it. We also found his cell phone in his car's glove box, and the NSA has studied it. Ganesh had received a call in the middle of the night and drove straight for Atlanta. The NSA has also looked into and forwarded me all of Ganesh's conversations from the past several months on it."

"They have that capability?" Samantha asked.

"They do," Watkins said with a tight smile. Hanson noted that now her expression lacked any warmth.

"Ganesh had a handler," Watkins continued. "We couldn't pin down who that was. Different burner phones were being used for each call. We also found a laptop in the secret room. For the past two years, it's been used to visit extremist and bomb-making sites."

"What about his family?" Fisher asked.

"They're cooperating. His wife was the source for the cell phone's passcode. From what we can tell, she and their son don't know anything. On the outside, Ganesh was a practicing Hindu. He has an idol—"

"*Murti*," Hanson interjected.

"What?"

"Never mind," Hanson replied, sighing. "How did they get him on the plane?"

"What makes you think he wasn't already assigned to that plane?" Watkins asked, her eyes narrowing.

"Because they're after us," Samantha answered as she took off her scarf and stood next to Hanson. She pointed at the rings around both of their necks. "Haven't you wondered about these?"

Watkins stared at the bruises but didn't answer.

"If you've read Fisher's reports, then you know that we have been trailing thugs for over a week now," Samantha continued.

"I concede that you have been on to something," Watkins replied. "The murder in Oregon and this Vankatesan in New York. He's disappeared."

"So, you believe us?" Hanson asked, relieved.

Watkins shook her head. "No. I think you've stumbled onto something else. The dead cow could be part of an attack on our food chain. Maybe a poisoning gone bad, and the cow died prematurely. The terrorists mutilated it to make it look like a satanic thing."

"What about the thug-like attempts at strangling?" Hanson asked.

"A sign that our laws work, and keep guns out of foreign terrorist's hands," Watkins said. "They use knives and trucks now. Strangling is not out of the question."

Hanson, Fisher, and Samantha stood in stunned silence.

"Listen, look at it from where I am standing," Watkins continued. "I have all of this proof of Muslim extremism and dozens of cameras showing Ganesh spouting Muslim rhetoric with a bomb in hand. All you have is a dead cow, rings around your necks, and Hanson's word that once they were all alone without cameras in the hold, Ganesh changed his tune to worshipping a Hindu Goddess of Death and not Allah."

"She's not a Goddess of death—" Hanson muttered.

"You didn't answer Hanson's question about Ganesh," Fisher interjected. "Was he originally assigned to that plane?"

"No, and that is one of the main reasons we are on such high alert. Somehow, they hacked Avian's computer system and switched him in. Homeland's cybercrime unit is looking into that."

"What about the original copilot?" Hanson asked worriedly.

"We don't know. Last I heard, the FBI were tracking his phone movements," Watkins answered. She stood up. "Now, I've heard all that I have needed to hear. You all must be exhausted—"

Hanson moved forward and put a hand on her arm.

"Please, you need to listen to us," he said. "Because from what we've seen this past week, I think this crisis is larger than you think, Agent Watkins. You need to understand that two centuries ago, a group of men invented the perfect murder. And despite what everyone thinks, they haven't stopped; killing not only because they think it's necessary, but also for the belief that death by their hands is their divine right."

"A centuries-old Hindu death cult, Mr. Hanson? You expect me to believe that?"

"At least look into it. We can't let the Muslim community take the blame for this."

"We're past that, Mr. Hanson," Watkins said. "Representative Charles Conyngham, the Chairman of Homeland Security Subcommittee on Counterterrorism and Intelligence, is planning on pushing through legislation this week to shut down our borders to Muslim immigration and deporting any family that has any hint of extremism related to it."

Samantha spoke up next to him. "Conyngham? Some say he's preparing for the next presidential election cycle by taking a hard stance on Islam."

"He's a visionary," Watkins added.

"Agent Watkins, you can't let this happen," Hanson said desperately. "It's history happening all over again."

"How so?" Watkins asked.

"To combat thuggee, the East India Company came up with series of draconian laws to control them. Men were being rounded up on only hearsay. Some were held indefinitely without trial. If someone was convicted of thuggee, then it stood to reason that male relatives must also be thugs since it was thought hereditary. They were rounded up also."

"It stopped thuggee."

"The laws broadened. Thirty years later, the Criminal Tribes Act was passed. The British went after everybody. If someone within a village was convicted of theft, the whole village was tainted. All men had to report in weekly."

"They almost took down a plane today, Mr. Hanson. What the British did back then sounds like good ideas for what we're dealing with now."

Hanson was incensed. "Then I'm not going to let it happen. You say I'm trending right now? Wait till everyone hears what I have to say about thugs—"

"It's against the law to impersonate a federal officer," Watkins said quietly.

Hanson felt his blood turn cold.

"You can't hold impersonating me against him," Fisher said as he stepped closer. "He didn't do it for any gain."

Watkins whirled on Fisher. "Careful, Agent," she said. "I already have the go-ahead from the Secretary. I'm to head up the National Joint Terrorism Task Force to deal with this problem. I have the TSA looking into how the bomb got on the plane. Our cyber unit will be looking into Avian's computer system. And since I feel there is a related threat to the food chain, I am contemplating assigning the FBI's Portland office to look into that."

Fisher took a step back. "You can't."

"I will," she replied. "Homeland can't compel the FBI to do anything, but I'm sure the president will strongly suggest to all of our superiors that we all show that we are cooperating."

Hanson made to step even closer to her, but Fisher put a hand on his shoulder.

"We won't give you any trouble, I'll keep an eye on them," Fisher said.

Hanson tried to break free of Fisher's grip, but Fisher squeezed even harder.

"Right, Steve?" Fisher said.

Hanson took a step back.

"You most likely already know I have an appointment in L.A.," Fisher added. "I would like to keep it."

"Acceptable," Watkins said. "I know it has to do with your thug theory. It won't pan out for you. I just want you near a large media market when Hanson finally wises up."

Watkin's phone buzzed. She gave a small grunt of satisfaction as she read the text. She looked back up at Hanson.

"And you have a choice to make, Steve Hanson," she continued. "You need to let go of this delusion. I do think that you fell into something, but you have been looking at fringe conspiracies for far too long and didn't see it for what it was. This nation doesn't need a pseudo-science hack right now—"

She unmuted the television.

"It needs a hero," Watkins finished as she let herself out.

Hanson turned to the television. Doug Morgan was back on.

"—though the crew and passengers of Avian 951 are on the ground safe, there are still many repercussions to be felt," Morgan said. "We go now to right here in New York with Senior National Correspondent Jennifer Steel."

Hanson glanced over at Samantha. If Steel's image bothered her, she didn't show it.

Jennifer Steel's face filled the screen. She was standing outside in the dark and was lit by the film crew's lights. Hanson could faintly detect another source of illumination flickering across her features. People were scurrying in the background.

"Thank you, Doug. I'm standing here in one of New York's predominant Muslim districts, where a local anti-Islamic group have taken things into their own hands."

The camera panned around and revealed the source of the flickering light.

It was a fire. At first, the camera was too tight on the scene, but then it pulled out and pointed upward to display a minaret standing above the flames as they licked higher. Next to him, Samantha gasped at what they were all witnessing.

A mosque was burning.

Chapter 32

Hidden Hills neighborhood, Los Angeles, 10:51 PDT

"We're almost there," Fisher announced.

They had left Edwards within an hour of Watkin's dismissal, collecting their belongings before loading into Fisher's government-issued SUV. After passing through a phalanx of journalists at the base's gate, Hanson and Samantha had spent the next two hours on their phones reassuring their family and friends.

Hanson glanced out of his back seat window. Well-lit mansions drifted by.

Cresswell's neighborhood. They had looked him up online and discovered he was a real estate tycoon and that he lived here. Any more information was scant.

Fisher pulled up to a gate and pressed the intercom's button.

A male voice responded. "Identify yourself."

"Special Agent Daniel Fisher," Fisher replied as he held up his ID to the nearby camera. "I have an appointment."

The gate rolled sideways.

"He's expecting us this late?" Hanson asked as he looked at his watch.

"Yes," Fisher answered. "When you informed me that you were coming to L.A. to somehow corner him, I decided to make things easier and arranged a meeting for tomorrow. Though, after the plane incident, I called him back and pushed up the timetable."

"Does your boss know what you are doing?" Samantha asked.

"I talked to him while you were gathering your luggage," Fisher answered. "He's angry about Watkin's threats. He wants me to follow through with Cresswell."

"He believes us," Hanson said.

"No, he has his doubts, but he trusts me," Fisher clarified. "And he remembered your help last year. If it weren't for that, I think this investigation would have never gotten off the ground."

Hanson saw that Samantha had a question on her lips, but Fisher's glare put a stop to that.

They came to a stop near the main doors of the Victorian-style mansion. Six large columns rose thirty feet above them, and stone tiger statues guarded each side of the stone steps.

The doors were of heavy oak and eight feet high. There was a doorbell, and each door had a large brass tiger head with a heavy ring clenched in its jaws. Hanson went right for the knockers.

"I've always wanted to do this," he said as he banged on them.

Fisher shook his head. "You don't get out much, do you?"

The door swung open. A balding man who looked like he just stepped off the set of *Downton Abbey* stood there.

"Agent Fisher, Mr. Cresswell is ready for you," the butler said.

Inside, all three of them took in the strange scene before them.

The mansion was decorated as if it was an old English hunting lodge. The mounted heads of animals from all over the world adorned most of the walls. Indian art and tapestries covered the rest. A large elephant gun hung above the mantel of a giant fireplace. Near the sweeping staircase was a large painting of an English officer in a red uniform. A curved scabbard with a saber was strapped to his belt.

It was noticeably cooler in the building, and Samantha and Hanson shivered a bit. Fisher was less bothered due to his wearing of a suit.

The butler led them to a more modern media room. A woman interviewing Avian 951's pilot, Captain Delgado, was playing on the television.

An old man, well into his eighties, stepped into the room. Wispy white hair covered his head, and age spots dotted his wrinkled face. He was wearing a thick red robe, though his thin legs were bare down to his red slippers. He was almost as tall as Hanson, and his blue eyes still looked sharp and wary. Other men were gathering in the room, surrounding them—Cresswell's staff. Hanson's pulse quickened. He could tell from their stances that they were armed.

"Order your men to back off, Cresswell. I'm going to reach for my ID," Fisher said as he stepped forward.

"Badges can be faked," Cresswell replied, his voice firm. "How do I know this isn't some last-minute thug trick to silence me once and for all?"

Samantha stepped out from behind Fisher. "Mr. Cresswell, perhaps if you—"

"A woman," Cresswell whispered, the expression on his face softening a bit. "Thugs don't use women."

Samantha pressed on. "Perhaps if you look at your television."

Cresswell turned around in time to see Hanson punching Ganesh.

"You're the one who threw the terrorist off of the plane," Cresswell said as he turned back toward Hanson.

"He wasn't a terrorist," Hanson revealed as he lifted his chin to expose the welt around his neck.

"Bloody hell!" Cresswell exclaimed.

After Cresswell dismissed his men, he sat and listened as Hanson and Samantha related everything that had happened to them since meeting at the Tully dairy farm. Cresswell was attentive as they spoke, and his face showed no disbelief. After they finished their tale, he left to retrieve some things from his vault.

Hanson moved to the painting of the Englishman. It drew his sight to a curved saber mounted nearby.

"And what's this?" Samantha asked as she joined him.

"It's a Pattern 1796 light Cavalry saber," Hanson answered with awe in his voice. "It's one of the finest blades ever mass-produced for combat. Hanson's hand stretched toward the bright, chrome-like finish of the hilt.

"The hilt was plated in silver to protect it from India's humidity," Cresswell said as he walked down the grand stairway toward them. A three-ring binder was clutched in his right hand. He stood before the blade also. "Do you like it?"

"It's beautiful," Hanson answered.

"It's central to this whole business," Cresswell stated as he set everything down on a table. "It belonged to Captain William Cresswell of the Thuggee Suppression Department." He nodded toward the wall. Everyone looked up at the painting.

"He was murdered by thugs," Cresswell added.

"Only one EIC official was killed by thugs during the whole campaign, a Lieutenant Maunsell," Hanson said. "History doesn't mention any other Englishman dying at the hands of thugs."

"The thugs disguised his death," Cresswell explained. "Captain William Cresswell is listed as missing at sea."

"And you think something else happened?" Samantha asked.

"Yes," Cresswell answered, "It was 1841. There was a rumor that a few low caste thug leftovers were operating south of Cattuck, the Goulahs. Captain Cresswell and a small detachment of sepoys were sent to investigate. But once down there, he found much more."

"How do you know this?" Fisher asked.

"After news of Captain Cresswell perishing reached his family, an Indian leatherworker approached the estate, claiming he had a message. Unfortunately, he was sent away by the valet who met him at the door. The next morning, this case and the saber were found left on the doorstep. The untouchable was never seen again."

"So, though Captain Cresswell was lost at sea, the sword made its way home?" Samantha noted.

"There was more. The blade was damaged. As if it had been used in a duel," Cresswell added.

"How do thugs fit in?" Fisher asked.

Hanson frowned at the impatient FBI agent. Cresswell was talking about sword duels. Hanson could discuss that all night.

"Twenty years ago, I sent the blade out to have it sharpened," Cresswell answered. "I also decided to replace the lining inside its case, and when I peeled that back, I found these."

Cresswell opened the binder. Inside were several pages of yellowed paper protected in plastic sleeves.

"Though I believe thugs killed him in the end, my ancestor outwitted them by smuggling a report out."

"Report?" Samantha asked as she reached for the binder.

"The Suppression Department produced reams of paperwork," Hanson explained. "The bulk of *Ramaseeana* is reports. They all followed a formula of officials riding into town, approvers pointing out suspects, property being recovered, and the murder victims located and tallied."

"Read it," Cresswell said as he looked at Samantha.

"*To Superintendent William H. Sleeman,*" she began. "*Sir, it is with honor that I write this message for you and great pleasure that I can answer your questions that you must have about t'hug activity in the Cattuck region and the town of Gurnah.*"

"Long-winded back then," Fisher observed.

"It wasn't Twitter," Hanson replied. "All of their correspondence started like that. Predictable."

"*Today, we killed over thirty t'hugs in armed combat,*" she continued.

"Bloody hell!" Hanson exclaimed.

Today we killed over thirty t'hugs in armed combat, and I write this report in fear that I may not make it out of Gurnah alive.

The day's events started in the late afternoon as we approached Gurnah from the west. We had left the main road north and circled around, meaning to arrive unannounced by cutting through the area's shmashana. While still in the forest, we heard a cry of fear ahead of us. When we cleared the trees, we found three t'hugs strangling a man on the charnel grounds.

Samantha looked up from the report, a questioning look on her face.

"*Shmashana* is the open-air crematoria, Miss Ramsell," Cresswell answered. "This area was usually bordered by the charnel grounds, where people who had no family were left on the ground to decompose."

"That sounds...messy," Fisher said.

"A Hindu's soul could linger if the body remained whole," Cresswell continued, shrugging. "Fire, scavengers, and the weather helped in speeding up the dissolution of the body."

"While we Christians worked hard to keep our bodies intact, for the day when our souls would rejoin our bodies for the Resurrection during Last Judgment," Hanson added. "Coffins were lined with lead to further preserve the body."

Cresswell looked impressed. "Interesting. Did you learn that studying religion?"

Hanson started to nod his head but then thought better of it.

"I wrote an article on vampires," he mumbled.

Fisher rolled his eyes. Samantha continued reading. The report in her hands was several pages long, so everyone sat at the table and made themselves comfortable.

My sepoys shot and killed the t'hugs as we entered the charnel grounds. The corpses of a thousand dead surrounded us. We turned our attention to the man still living.

The t'hug victim's name was Debun, a chamar traveling north. His ailing father had passed away earlier on the road. The old man's cloth-wrapped body was nearby.

Debun explained that he had made his way to the charnel grounds on his own. As he passed the building where the Dom caste lived, the keepers of the sacred flames for cremations, three men had come hurrying out. They offered to help and led Debun away to the clearing's edge, where they attacked him. Only Providence and our arrival spared him from death.

I had my approver, Chidoo, examine the t'hugs. They were not the Goulahs we were looking for.

As we let Debun observe last rites for his father, Lt. Malcolm noted that it was lucky that we had heard Debun yell. Debun informed us that the cry for help had come from the Dom's building.

I had my men fix bayonets, and we made our way to the cremation area. Debun followed, keeping close to our small supply train in the formation's rear.

The sun was low at this point; the area was deep in shadow. My sepoys kept their composure, but the superstitious drovers and bishti water carriers were shaking with fear, for they believed that ghosts, spirits, and even Kali herself made their home on the cremation grounds.

We approached the building, a single-story affair of mud bricks and a thick thatched roof that peaked fifteen feet higher. It stretched back fifty feet into the forest. The front was a covered patio, where wood was stacked to keep dry for pyres in the rainy season. Only one door seemed to exist.

Our alertness saved us. Several dozen Indians armed with kukris rushed us from the forest, all shouting the same battle cry.

"Kali khilaya jan cahi'e!"

Kali must be fed.

We met them with bullets.

My sepoys proved themselves and dropped ten t'hugs with their initial volley. Lt. Malcolm killed two more with pistols.

I charged forward on my horse. Several of them tried to take me down in old-fashioned t'hug style by attempting to lasso me. More tried to pull me down with their hands. My saber put an end to that.

The sepoys were dispatching the remainder as I made my way to the building's door. A t'hug leaped up from behind a woodpile. I shot him with my pistol and made my way inside.

Words can't describe the horror I discovered, but I shall try.

We had found their temple. A garish idol of Kali, both beautiful and terrible, loomed over a bloody altar.

The entire building was one room, and black tapestries covered the walls. Only candles provided dim illumination.

Pews filled the front half. Near those was the altar, flanked by a lectern of gold and lapis, on which rested a large tome.

Kali dominated my attention first.

She stood ten feet tall and was crafted of wood. Her form was painted a dark blue. Her face was one of rage, with the eyes blazing red, as were her lips and the long tongue that hung out between ivory white fangs. Her hair was black and unbridled. Her chest was bare, and around her waist was a girdle of tiger skin.

Her four arms were each holding a weapon. The upper pair had tulwars; their tips almost touched each other above her head. Her lower right hand held a khadga. The lower left hand held a rumal.

Hanging from the elbows of the upper arms were two of the largest diamonds I had ever seen. Maybe they had come from the Kollur Mine, famous for colossal gems such as the Pitt Diamond or the Mountain of Light. These diamonds were the size of a dove's egg and were in the shape of a drop of water.

I turned my gaze to the altar and to the source of the pitiful cry of despair we had all heard earlier.

It was a boy, sacrificed in the style as put down in the Rudhiradhyaya, that bloody chapter of the Calica Purana.

The sight was dreadful, and I tremble now as I write this. The boy had been decapitated, though the blade responsible was nowhere present. His blood still ran freely into grooves carved into the wooden surface, which channeled it to golden vases at the corners.

Bundles of ghee-soaked wood were stacked under the altar also. The clarified butter is usually used to make the funeral pyres burn hotter.

I said a prayer as I covered the boy's body with a nearby shroud. Lt. Malcolm appeared at the door and announced that the t'hugs were dead. I ordered him to have the sepoys stand at the ready and watch the door.

I went to the book. It was a splendid tome bound in leather, trimmed with gold and encrusted with rubies and emeralds. As I suspected, the page it was opened to read like a copy of the Rudhiradhyaya, as translated by Blaquiere several decades ago. But there are some glaring irregularities I must take time to point out.

The book is bound in leather; the pages vellum, or calfskin. It is also scribed in English and not Sanskrit.

The contents differed also. Animal sacrifice is not mentioned, as in Blaquiere's rendition. I also recalled that human sacrifices, properly prepared, were to appease Kali for a thousand years. This tome has it at only a decade.

I looked further on in the book, expecting more Puranas. Instead, I was surprised to find chapters with more familiar headings.

Genesis, Numbers, Exodus.

I glanced at Genesis. It spoke of Kali's battle with Raktabija. Numbers was an account of their victims.

Exodus was more chilling. It described how the t'hugs planned to leave India for England. It listed ships and ports to be used.

My blood ran cold. I couldn't let that happen.

I removed a page from the book. My original intent was to send you a message by rider with the page to alert you as fast as possible. At the same time, my men and I would return more slowly with everything else, but what happened next changed all of that.

More t'hugs attacked my detachment, moving in from the rear. Malcolm left to assist. I would have joined him, but movement at the back of the room caught my eye.

A large door behind a tapestry opened, and men in white and yellow robes entered the room. A man bearing a tulwar led them.

I rushed back into the temple, my saber in my hand, demanding to know their intent. The t'hug's leader informed me that they "were saving the world". Though, at the moment, I reasoned that didn't include me, for he came at me with his tulwar. I parried his cut with my saber, our curved blades an equal match.

We dueled, and I watched with frustration as the other t'hugs used the time to remove the blood-filled vases, book, and the idol itself. They carried all out the back door.

There was blood on his blade—the sacrifice. The tulwar seemed hungry for more, but my swordplay caused him to lose ground.

I almost had him, but he knocked a candle into the altar. Flames instantly shot up as high as the roof from the ghee-soaked wood. The tapestries must also have been treated with the clarified butter for the fire to spread to them.

A flaming beam crashed down and separated us. I could only watch as the t'hug made his escape.

I barely made it out, the whole building becoming a pyre, the t'hugs wiping out any evidence of their temple. Outside, it was now night, and the t'hugs were retreating. Two of my men, Pitambar and Gopal, lay dead.

Over thirty dead t'hugs lay about us, each one most likely having a son, uncle, or father back in Gurnah. Malcolm and I reasoned that the whole town would be against us.

We made for the fort, taking Pitambar and Gopal with us. Fortunately, it was less than a coss away. It lay on the south side of Gurnah. The whole town was astir, the men massing in the streets. The soldiers of the Madras 54th let us inside before the gathering mob could work themselves into a dangerous frenzy.

Captain Chancellor met us. I was hoping for a Company man, but I could tell he was a British regular. As long as England wasn't still sending us lunatics out of Bedlam, I reasoned I could make do with him.

Our position was still precarious. Most of Chancellor's men were on patrol near Vizagapatam, the area's port city. They wouldn't be back until the next morning. I had him expel all his Indian staff from the fort and wake the rest of his men so that my sepoys could sleep in shifts.

I have spent the night writing this report. Outside, dawn is near, and I just heard the call of a large owl to my left, followed by an answering call to my right. A favorable omen t'hugs call thakur.

They believe their Goddess is on their side. I pray our God is stronger. T'hugs watch us on all fronts. I plan to have the chamar carry this message to my family in

Calcutta, where I hope it makes its way to you. When the reinforcements arrive, I will search the city. If I survive, I hope to deliver a complete report to you in person.
Believe me, my dear Sir, very truly and faithfully yours,

Captain William Cresswell

Chapter 34

The room was quiet as everyone digested what Samantha had just read out loud. Hanson stared at the sword on the wall, his mind in the past as he imagined the two men dueling as the thug temple burned around them.

The butler glided into the room and nodded in Cresswell's direction.

"Your rooms are prepared," Cresswell announced.

"We don't mean to impose—" Fisher began.

"I insist," Cresswell said. "For twenty years, I have been waiting for someone to believe me. Please, stay."

Samantha rose from her chair. "Thank you, Mr. Cresswell."

"Henry."

"Henry. Thank you. I'm going to take you up on that. It's been a long day."

The men all stood as Wilfred led her away and up the stairs. She paused at the halfway point to turn around and look back at Hanson. He didn't notice as he was already excitedly talking to Cresswell.

"That letter was interesting. But what prompted you to go to the FBI and claim that they were here in the United States?" Hanson asked.

Cresswell led them back to the media room, where the news was still on. A high school yearbook photo of Hanson was being displayed. The goofy one, with the caption "Most Likely Not to Get Married" underneath it.

"God damn it," Hanson swore.

There was a laptop on the coffee table. Cresswell changed the television's input and then transmitted what was on the computer to the big screen.

It was a map of the United States. Red dots were pinned on almost every state on the eastern seaboard, except for Maine. The pins stretched west only a short way. The abrupt end of them formed a curved boundary that started at Chicago and arced through Indianapolis, Atlanta, and finally stopping in Tallahassee. Many of the larger cities in this zone had multiple pins.

Hanson realized that Cresswell was doing what Sleeman had done. He was mapping the thug's *beles*. Hanson ran a finger over the screen as he traced the curved outline made by the red dots.

"What do you see?" Fisher asked.

"Something about this pattern seems familiar," Hanson said. He pulled a flash drive from his pocket. "Mr. Cresswell, there's a file on this titled 'Locations.' Could you have the list of places on that file inputted on this map?"

"Yes," Cresswell answered as he held up the flash drive to study it. "What do these locations represent?"

"Cattle mutilations, over the past four decades," Hanson answered. "Is this map why you went to the FBI?"

"Yes," Cresswell answered. He approached the screen also. "Sleeman was crushing thuggee in India, but that was because of the heavy-handed laws they were passing. The thugs my ancestor faced were based near a major port, so I wondered if the thugs had somehow fled India to a place less restrictive.

"I realize they could have gone anywhere, but I began my search here in the United States. I used my considerable resources and began investigating the one thing the thug's always left behind—missing persons.

"Two thousand people a year disappear in the United States. But in my search for thugs, I set myself a higher standard of criteria, such as focusing on adults traveling from home. The numbers I came up with were astonishing.

"In my mind I felt that I had guessed right. This pattern was proof of that. I went to the FBI with my findings."

"These people could be disappearing for any number of reasons," Fisher observed.

"For a while, when the FBI rejected me, and my faith in this endeavor wavered, I had the same thoughts, Agent Fisher," the old man replied. "But then, a few years ago, I again felt I was on to something when the types of disappearances I was tracking almost doubled."

"Why would they double?" Fisher asked.

The old man didn't answer immediately. He glanced at Hanson instead.

"Your skeptic blogger should know the answer to this riddle," Cresswell replied.

Hanson thought about it. What happened a few years ago that would influence the thugs—

Holy crap.

"COVID," Hanson answered. Cresswell smiled grimly and nodded.

Fisher was looking back and forth between the two of them. "Okay, would someone clue me in?"

"In one of their later interviews, a thug noted that since thuggee was being destroyed by the Company, there was a noticeable rise in war, famine, and plague," Hanson answered.

"The prisoner was stating that it was the thug's murdering that kept Kali's bloodlust at bay, Agent Fisher," Cresswell continued. "Without thugs placating her, she will destroy us all."

Hanson pointed at Oregon on the map. "Your escalation in disappearances wasn't the only result of the coronavirus. A few years ago, out of nowhere, there was a definite increase in cattle mutilations in eastern Oregon. The thugs were ramping up their young *kuthowas,* training them to butcher the corpses created by the *bhurtotes.*"

"And thus, stave off the pandemic," Cresswell finished. He turned away from them. "Let me show you something else."

He led them back to the three-ring binder. There was a final page in it, and Cresswell removed it from the plastic sheath and laid it carefully on the table.

Hanson and Fisher studied it. It looked like it came from an old book, and the words on its face seemed to gracefully flow across it, each letter painstakingly crafted.

"Is that real gold?" Fisher asked.

The first letter on the page was a huge A. Gold leaf surrounded it, which was in turn bordered by indigo blue whorls.

"Yes, it's illuminated script," Hanson answered. "This is the page that your ancestor cut out?"

"Yes," Cresswell replied. "It's made from vellum. Calfskin. Something no thug would deal with. But, as Hanson has observed, these thugs that we are dealing with are not above gutting a cow."

"I can also see why the FBI refused to pursue your theories," Hanson said. "This page, this artifact of ancient Hindu religion, is written in English. That's like presenting an ancient Greek vase with 500 BC stamped on the bottom of it."

"Despite my map, the FBI wouldn't have anything to do with me when I showed them this," Cresswell confessed.

"Captain Cresswell's report mentioned that this part of the book read like a chapter out of the Calica Purana," Fisher asked. "What's a Purana?"

"Holy texts," Cresswell answered. "The Brahmins memorized the Vedas, four holy books that have been orally passed down for thousands of years. For everyone else, though, there are the eighteen major Puranas to study."

"What makes this one special?" Fisher asked.

"What Captain Cresswell was talking about is a small section of the Purana known as the Sanguinary Chapter. The Blood Chapter. In it, the God Shiva informs his sons on how to keep Kali happy," Hanson answered. He leaned over and read off the first lines.

An oblation of blood which has been rendered pure by holy texts is equal to ambrosia. The head and flesh also afford much delight to the Goddess."

Hanson could see that Fisher still looked puzzled.

"It's a 'how to' guide for human sacrifice," Hanson explained.

Chapter 35

"They had human sacrifices back then?" Fisher asked.

"Not during Captain Cresswell's time. It had been outlawed by Hindu religious leaders for quite a while," Hanson answered.

"But they still had instructions for it?"

"Hindu is the oldest active major religion," Hanson replied. "In ancient times, all religions practiced some sort of blood sacrifice."

"And the thugs were part of that?"

"Historically, no," Hanson answered. "But the British believed so two centuries ago. In their fear and ignorance of the culture surrounding them, they dreamed up a nightmarish view of Indian religion. A vision that included the thugs as vicious murderers who regularly sacrificed to fiendish gods in their dark temples. And, as I said before, I think an ancestor of Vankatesan took this British's fictional view of thuggee and made it a reality."

Hanson bent over the sheet again.

"Cresswell's report was right. Animals are missing. I remember reading that sacrificing a rhino pleased the Goddess for five hundred years," Hanson said.

"So according to the man in the painting, around 1840, he stumbled upon a modified sacrifice to Kali, one that was to keep her content for only a decade. Why shorten a sacrifice's effectiveness?" Fisher asked. "Keeping Kali appeased for centuries by killing an animal sounds like an easier alternative to murdering someone once a week."

"Because they can't stop. It's in their blood to kill," Cresswell spat.

"That can't be it. The propensity to murder isn't inherited," Fisher responded.

"Study of their skulls show that they were inclined to murder," Cresswell shot back.

Their host's prejudices were showing, and Hanson realized he needed to defuse the situation.

"Cresswell is half right," Hanson said. "They can't stop. Strangling is their gift from Kali, and it is part of the process for them to receive material rewards for serving her."

The old man's face relaxed a bit as he considered this. Fisher's glare softened also, and the FBI agent brought up another issue. "Why did they go to England first?"

Now it was Hanson's turn to frown. Fisher was asking some tough questions. He paused a moment as he recalled his research into thuggee a few years back.

"After decades of dealing with British officials, maybe England just felt familiar to the thugs at that point. So, they fled overseas, where they could gain some needed breathing room."

"And after their decade of respite was up, they took up strangling again in 1850's London," Fisher finished, guessing the rest. "But why come to America?"

Hanson threw up his hands. "Jesus, Fisher, how should I know?" Hanson replied. He then put on his best mocking voice of the FBI agent. "What does a thug eat for breakfast?"

"I don't sound like that," Fisher replied, his eyes narrowing. "But you're right. We don't have enough to guess all their motivations. What should we focus on next?"

"We need to find their base of operations," Hanson answered.

"That could be anywhere," Fisher said. "An old warehouse, office building—"

"It's a temple, as it was back then," Cresswell interjected.

"I agree," Hanson said. "But hidden away. I've been sifting through Hindu temple locations this past day—"

Cresswell was already at his laptop. A new map of the United States with different pins all over it flashed up on the screen.

"I've been searching for two decades, Mr. Hanson, eliminating temples by sending my employees to vet each one personally. But unfortunately, I've found nothing."

Hanson could feel the weight of crushing defeat. Suddenly, he felt exhausted.

"I think I will also take you up on your offer," Hanson said.

Cresswell nodded toward Wilfred, who led Hanson up the stairs. They passed old paintings and more recent photographs. Some of them showed images of a younger Cresswell with a woman and son.

Hanson was shown to an opulent bedroom furnished with fine furniture. A thick rug covered the dark, exotic wood floor, and a vast fireplace dominated a wall.

It was also decorated with more mounted animal heads. A male lion was directly over the unlit fireplace. A female lion was off to the side. An antelope was near the door to the walk-in closet. Finally, the head of what Hanson guessed was a gnu was directly over a king-sized bed.

His computer bag was already in the room.

"I noticed that you didn't have any luggage," Wilfred said. "If you wish, you may place your clothes in the laundry chute in the closet. We will have them washed by morning."

"Wow," Hanson said. "Thanks."

Wilfred left. Hanson explored the room a bit as he peeled off his clothes. He placed them in the chute and watched them slide away. He turned toward the bathroom. A shower sounded good. With the heat and the force of the wind in the Osprey's cargo hold, it felt like a week's worth of grit had been sandblasted onto him.

The shower was as large as his entire bathroom back home, encased in glass with gold trim, the floor natural stone tiles. Water came from the front, back, and above, its temperature shown on a LED display. He set everything for maximum comfort.

As usual, he spent the first tenth of his shower cleaning up and the final nine-tenths thinking. Something about Cresswell's report nagged at him, as if an answer were there. So as the hot water washed over him, he let his thoughts drift.

Captain Cresswell had discovered thugs making a sacrifice to facilitate their escape from India. The sacrifice was one of blood and was to Kali.

Kali.

Hanson pictured the thug's version of the Goddess. Looming over her worshippers with a wicked smile as they prepared their sacrifice.

Captain Cresswell was closing in on the temple, stepping over hundreds of bodies in various states of decay. Making his way past the ashes of spent funeral pyres, closing in.

Cresswell.

Captain Cresswell's British military uniform morphed into a red robe. India became L.A., and old maps mounted on walls turned into television screens. Current Cresswell searched for thugs and their home base by focusing on the missing, people whose last whereabouts formed an arc through the eastern United States. Was the old man on to something? Vankatesan lived on the East Coast in New York.

New York.

That fired off recent memories of meeting Samantha's ex-boyfriend. Carbonaux and his smarmy smile crowded into Hanson's mind. But remembering all that also made him think of his father's death.

Death.

Glittering high-rises at night dissolved into the wet and gray hillsides of Astoria during the day. His father's funeral. The feeling of loss as he sat on a pew next to his mother. She was dressed in black, a handkerchief clutched in her hand. A cross was on the wall ahead of him, and somber music from an organ filled the room. Hanson remembered being sad but also confused. He had asked his mother why they were at church on a Saturday.

His mother had put her arm around him. There were tears in her eyes when she answered.

"We're not at church."

Back then, he had wondered at that. It certainly felt like it. Someplace holy and close to God. Later, he realized that his mother had been trying to explain that they were at a funeral home chapel.

Funeral.

Cresswell's report had mentioned the Indians in his group being nervous while at the area's funeral grounds, the *shmashana,* for they believed that spirits, and Kali herself, roamed nearby. They were afraid because the *shmashana* was her home.

Hanson's eyes snapped open as hot water coursed over him, his fingertips wrinkled from the long shower. He smiled as his mind translated his last thought.

The cremation grounds are her home.

Chapter 36

Hanson studied himself in the mirror as he dried off. Though he felt refreshed after cleaning up, his body still looked, and felt, battered. A large, dark-yellowish bruise covered his chest and back from where he bounced off the walls and ceiling of the airliner's hold. The ring around his neck blazed a bright red.

He sighed as he wrapped the towel around his waist. He felt weary. The older he got, the longer it took for the bruises to fade. He also shivered a bit. Though it was nearly ninety degrees outside during the day, it was chilly in the manor.

A small hallway and the walk-in closet were right off the bathroom door. Hanson ducked into the closet, eager to find some clothes and head back out to tell the others about his theory on the thug's location.

The closet held several robes. Another idea began to form. Maybe he would run his theories by Samantha first. It felt like a reasonable pretense to knock on her door. His mind raced on what he would say when she opened—

Out in his bedroom, the gas fireplace snapped on. He wondered how high the flames were set on it, so he glanced out of the closet.

Samantha was standing there. She had just flipped a switch near the mantel.

"I hope you don't mind," she said as she stepped in front of the fire-place. "I let myself in while you were showering."

Though the lights were dimmed, he could see that she was wearing a short silk robe with a floral design. She had the robe's belt tight around her slim waist so that robe accentuated her figure rather than hide it. Her long legs were smooth in the firelight, and her blonde hair was already dry after her shower. She had let it down, so now her hair tumbled down to her shoulders and rested easily over the silk. The fire blazed at her back, while above her, the mounted head of the male lion held its eternal roaring visage.

Weariness flew out the door as Hanson walked toward her.

"I don't mind at all. I'm glad you're here."

"I was worried about you," she said as she glanced away. Suddenly, she was the shy one. "I can't imagine what happened in that cargo hold."

She turned back toward him and studied the black and yellow bruising on his chest. She reached out and traced them, the light brushing of her fingers feeling electric on his skin.

"Does it hurt?"

"No." A lie, but he sure as hell wasn't going to admit it.

Her gaze shifted to his left shoulder. A tattoo of a steamroller was there. It had the letters USMC on its side, and an eagle was driving it.

"Marine tattoo?"

He took a half step closer as he shifted the shoulder toward her.

"Yes. I got it after Kuwait. It's a long story."

A short but jagged scar was directly below the tattoo. Samantha ran her fingers over the old wound. Goose bumps raised the hairs on his arm around it.

"Did this come from Kuwait also?"

It was a direct question, and he couldn't lie to her.

"Bigfoot," he answered after a short pause.

That raised her eyebrows, but she didn't pursue that train of thought. She was focused on the here and now.

She turned to the small blue tattoo on his right shoulder.

"And this one?"

"That's a twenty-sided die. It's used in gaming."

A small smile played across her lips as she gave him the 'such a nerd' look and head shake. But she took a half step forward as she did so.

"So, twenty is a good number?" she asked.

"The best." Her cleavage was distracting. "Rolling a natural twenty always means success at whatever you are attempting."

"So why tattoo it on your shoulder?"

"It's my good luck charm," he admitted. "Whenever I, or someone else, touches my natural twenty tattoo, I always succeed at whatever I am attempting to do with my right arm."

"I've noticed you rubbing your shoulder several times, like back at the thug's *bele*."

"I needed that punch to count. I've been thinking about it a lot lately. It's like the thugs' omens—a belief to summon up confidence. But I use it sparingly," he continued as he held up his right hand and gazed at it. "I don't want to wear out the—"

He would have kept on talking, but she interrupted him by reaching up and touching the tattoo.

Surprised by that move, Hanson's head swiveled as he looked back and forth between his hand and her face. She was inches from him now and staring into his eyes. He got her message.

The time for talk was over.

He moved his right hand up to the back of her head and slid it up under her hair, shivering a bit as it tickled the back of his hand and arm. He then gently tilted her head so that her lips would meet his as he bent down. He kissed her, her lips warm and soft against his. Her tongue quickly darted in, tasting sweet.

They held their kiss as Hanson's right hand now drifted down to the knot on her robe's belt. With a tug, it came undone, and the robe parted. The same hand moved up the curve of her back and up to the robe's collar, and he slid the robe off her shoulders.

The silk robe pooled at her feet, and he opened his eyes a fraction for a peek. She looked fantastic; her soft curves hinted at in the shadows cast by the fire. He pulled her in closer so that her breasts pressed against him.

Both were breathing heavier, but he still didn't rush it, though he could feel her hands pulling on the knot on his towel. It fell beside her robe.

They kissed again, tongues dancing around each other, both enjoying the warmth from the fireplace on their bodies in the room's chill. They then stumbled over each other as they made their way to the bed and settled into the cool sheets.

Her hands ran over him, and he could feel her smile behind her kisses as she found him ready. She tried to move him into position on top of her, but he kept on his side. It had been a while, and he wanted a little foreplay to stretch the moment.

He ran his hand up her hair, positioning it so that it splashed over the silk pillows, allowing him to smell its fragrance while he kissed her on the neck. His hands continued to trace the outline of her nakedness, searching for the feel of her curves and the softness of her breasts. His right hand then drifted downward again, and it settled between her legs as he explored all of her.

He hoped his long sexual hiatus wasn't evident by fumbling around. But maybe he was doing something right, for suddenly, her left hand blindly sought out his right arm. It found his elbow and moved up his bicep until it located his shoulder. She began to slap the tattoo frantically, her body tensing and arching next to him as she did so.

She soon relaxed and released her grip on his shoulder.

"Well, whaddya know," she murmured.

He moved on top of her. He was a little clumsy about that at first, but soon their bodies synced into a natural rhythm. They stayed that way for only a moment, for she took control and rolled them over on the huge bed so that she was astride him.

He looked up at her. Her hair was like a golden curtain now, framing her face and neck as she bent close over him. His hand traced her jawline and down along her neck. He would have gone further, but he paused at the bruise that was still there. Without silk scarfs or shirt collars to hide it, it now stood out prominently. Fascinated, his fingers followed the wound's outline. He realized then that he and Samantha had a unique, and powerful, shared experience. They were the only two people in the world to have survived a thug attack.

He looked up at her face and saw she was doing the same thing he had just done. Her eyes were focused on his neck, her hand tracing his bruise, a look of concern on her face. When she looked back up at him, he could tell she had just reached the same conclusion that he had.

She pulled him close, moving frantically against him, kissing furiously.

When she eased up once more, he rolled them over so that he was back on top. He settled down lower on her, his arms under her back. She gripped him tighter also as her mouth found his again, and soon it was his movements that were more frantic as he reached his peak. She held him tightly as his body slowly coasted to a stop.

Exhausted, he rolled next to her, and she laid her head on his chest. He relaxed there, breathing in her perfume, their mutual warmth fighting the room's chill.

She turned a bit so that she could take in the room. The lion above the lit fireplace stared back.

"Back in that pasture, did you ever think we would ever end up together like this?"

"Well, I was hoping so, though I will admit..." Hanson cast his gaze to the mounted herbivore above them. "The gnu is unexpected."

"That's a gnu?" she asked as she looked up.

"Yeah, who knew?"

"Stop," she said as she thumped him on the chest and laughed. Both were feeling much more relaxed with each other. Her eyes searched the rest of the room, and they noted the male lion's head and the female lion near the antelope.

"Do you think Cresswell's forefathers bagged these with that elephant gun downstairs?"

"Likely. The two lions as trophies. Maybe the others for their meat."

She looked over at the antelope.

"Really? I wonder what they tasted like."

"You hunted when you were younger. Didn't you try any venison?"

"No. I couldn't bring myself to do it."

"You should have. I hear it's as good as gnu."

She laughed some more, though she nudged him in the ribs for the bad pun. He groaned in pain.

"Sorry, sorry," she said, kissing a bruise on his chest to make up for it.

He rolled over to put his arm around her waist and pull her close. She entwined her legs with his and touched the tattoo on his shoulder.

"Now I'm a believer," she said as her head settled on his bicep. "God, Steve, I wish we could stay in this room for a few days. It's been a week since I felt this safe. If we could only find these god damn thugs and end it."

"Well then, I have some good news," his smile broadened at the use of "news." "I was just coming over to tell you before you distracted me."

"What?"

"I know where they are."

Chapter 37

Thursday, 7:35 a.m. PDT

"They're hiding in a columbarium," Hanson announced as he bit down on some bacon.

Wilfred had set a brunch for everyone. Cresswell was out of his robes and dressed in slacks with a brown smoking jacket. Fisher was back in his suit and tie. Hanson was wearing his same clothes also, but they had been cleaned and pressed. They felt better than ever before. Hanson wondered what Wilfred's secret was.

"What's a columbarium?" Fisher asked.

"It's like a mausoleum, but for ashes," Hanson explained. He paused to dish up some eggs Benedict. "Instead of all that space for storing a coffin in a wall, think of niches, or small shelves, to hold the urns of the dearly departed."

"Cremation grounds—" Cresswell began.

"Are her home," Hanson finished. "Captain Cresswell's men were spooked because they thought that Kali was near." Hanson waved an egg-covered fork at the painting. "He found their place of worship at the town's *shmashana.*"

"I always thought of the building as a temple," Cresswell admitted as he shook his head.

"But it wasn't," Samantha said. "It was as a structure used by the Dom caste. Like a funeral home."

She was wearing jeans and a white silk blouse Wilfred had found. Hanson couldn't keep his eyes off her.

"So now you think the thugs are co-opting a funeral home somewhere?" Fisher asked.

"Look, Henry here has eliminated all of the Hindu temples in the United States. But I still feel that they would want to use some sort of holy site. Funeral homes are sometimes surrounded by cemeteries—"

"Which are consecrated grounds," Cresswell finished.

"And a funeral home would also answer the pressing question of why no bodies have been found," Hanson continued.

"The crematoriums," Fisher guessed. "But what about the *gobba* they made for you and Samantha?"

"Though they train for it, I'm guessing that the use of *gobbas* is rare," Hanson answered. "I think they only dispose of corpses 'in the field' in case of emergencies."

Fisher paused a moment to chew on a slice of orange and dwell on what Hanson just revealed.

"They're moving the bodies in plain sight with mortuary vans," Fisher finally added. "They forge the documents they need at the funeral home itself."

"And in the middle of the night, they fire up the furnaces," Samantha finished.

Cresswell appeared excited for a moment, but then his shoulders sagged.

"Even if you are right, there must be a huge number of funeral homes across the US," he said. "The Hindu temples took me twenty years. How are we going to find the right one?"

"I have an idea about that also," Hanson revealed with a grin. "Do you have a ruler? Or maybe a cloth measuring tape used in sewing?"

Cresswell nodded toward Wilfred. The butler quietly backed out of the room.

Hanson led them to the television. A news program was running a video of two men in garish armor swinging padded foam rubber swords at each other. It took Hanson a moment to realize the news segment was of him at a past LARPing event. He snatched up the remote and tried to adjust the input selection. Right before the screen changed, the television showed the larger man swinging his padded weapon and knocking Hanson's helmet off.

"Nice outfit," Fisher said with a smirk.

"Save it," Hanson growled as he turned several shades of red.

"It's been like that all morning," Cresswell said. "The networks are all asking: 'Who is Steve Hanson?' And, for that matter, they are also wondering at Miss Ramsell's role in all of this. All sorts of people are stepping forward to answer those questions."

"We need to get ahead of this," Samantha said. "I'll work on a press release to give some background on Steve. I will also mention that he will soon come forward once the authorities have finished their investigations. That should pacify the masses a bit, and people should also conclude that I'm there following the story."

"Speaking of concluding, how do we find them?" Fisher asked.

"Henry, were you able to get my data on your *bele* location map?" Hanson asked.

"An employee of mine spent a few hours last night setting it up," Cresswell answered as he pressed a few keys on his laptop.

The map of the United States flashed up. Red pins blanketed the eastern seaboard.

"The thugs' victims," Hanson announced.

Cresswell punched another key. Blue pins, less numerous than the red ones, appeared. Their border formed a faint crescent across the Midwest, starting in Arizona and sweeping up north through Colorado, Wyoming, Nebraska, and Iowa. Beyond them, more pins stretched west, though these thinned out as they approached the coast.

"The cows," Hanson added.

Everyone's heads swiveled back and forth as they studied the two groups of pins.

"What do we know about where the thugs of India hunted," Hanson prodded.

"Away from their home base, so as not to draw attention to where they lived," Cresswell answered.

"Right," Hanson replied. "This map shows where the thugs operate. Now, look at it to determine where they don't."

They were all still looking back and forth. Then, as one, they paused in the middle and looked slightly downward.

"Texas," Samantha said.

"It's as if the two sets of pins are shaped like satellite dishes focused on Texas," Fisher continued.

Wilfred walked back into the room and handed Hanson a roll of cloth measuring tape. Hanson let all six feet of it spool out.

"The borders of thug activity are shaped like arcs, segments of circles that share a common center," Hanson explained. He held the tape stretched out in front of him, his right hand over Texas, while the left moved back and forth over the blue dots. Satisfied, he switched hands, this time his left hand over Texas as his right followed the border formed by the red dots. He looked back over his shoulder.

"Henry, could you zoom in on where my left hand is?"

The states grew larger. More detail, such as roads, and the names of cities, were formed. Soon, only Texas remained on the screen. Hanson moved his hands away. All of them looked at where his left hand had been.

"The thugs are in Dallas," Samantha said.

"Ganesh lived in Virginia. Vankatesan, New York," Fisher noted.

"My guess is that thugs are everywhere in the country. But when it's their turn to kill a victim for Kali, they all travel to Dallas and start from there," Hanson said.

"They must have to do it during their vacations," Samantha added. "That's why the red dots thin out around Vermont. Maine is too far to drive their mortuary van back and forth on a typical week away from work."

"Why not hunt for human victims in the west?" Fisher asked.

"So that no one would relate cattle mutilation with people disappearing," Hanson answered. "That would focus too much attention on the crime. They messed up in Oregon, and now we have them on the run."

"So, now all we have to do is look up funeral homes online," Samantha said.

"Hold off on that," Fisher said. "I have a feeling that Watkins is monitoring all communications from this place. She's going to be suspicious when we start looking up information on Dallas, Texas."

"I wouldn't worry," Cresswell replied smugly. "I've always felt that thugs have been spying on me. I own the property behind me through a shell company, and I have fiber optics routed through a shed over there. My landlines are not on anyone's radar."

"That helps," Fisher said. "But we should give Watkins something to chew on. Samantha, could you transmit that press release over your phone? Watkins will be following that."

Samantha nodded. She walked over to Hanson and gave him a light kiss.

"Anything more I should know?" she asked.

"I think you found out everything last night," Hanson answered.

She left the room smiling.

Fisher was also grinning.

"What?" Hanson said defensively.

"It took you long enough to figure out that she was interested in you," Fisher said, "Your classmates had it right when they said you would never marry."

Hanson sighed and shrugged his shoulders a bit. "It's a process."

He turned to Cresswell, who already had funeral home results up on the screen. There were several dozen to look over in the Dallas-Fort Worth metro area. The three men spent the next several hours looking them over and discussing the merits of each one.

Hanson's stomach was growling, and he thought about calling a break for lunch, but Creswell called up a page they had looked at earlier. Tranquil Groves, an All-Faiths Funeral Home.

"You said the cattle mutilations started up in the seventies?" Cresswell asked as he turned toward Hanson.

"Yes."

Cresswell clicked on a tab marked "About Us". A description of the funeral home popped up.

"This one was struggling back then. An investment firm from England stepped in and bought the original owners out. The firm sank in even more money modifying the place."

"Maybe they were just looking after their investment," Fisher said.

"It was the seventies; the oil embargo was happening. World economies were tanking," Cresswell replied, a scowl on his face as he remembered. "Few people were throwing cash around during those times."

"I think we just answered Fisher's question of why they came to America," Hanson said. "Back in India, the British put a lot of effort into finding the hidden wealth of the thugs they captured. I bet our thugs were sitting on a large reserve of cash."

"It was a good time to invest in property if one was cash rich," Cresswell noted. "Maybe they needed to expand, and they jumped at the chance."

Hanson pointed at the screen. "Hit the tab marked 'History.'"

Old newspaper stories popped up, the gist of which was locals being outraged that the care of their departed loved ones was now in the hands of foreigners. Those clippings were followed by an article touting all the improvements the new owners would be making.

The remodeling was outlined with a couple of diagrams. The first depicted the original building, a combination funeral home, mausoleum, and columbarium. Underneath the building was a catacomb-like series of rooms that held generations of urns and caskets.

The following diagram showed the then proposed structure. The lower rooms were to be closed. Sprawling wings were to be added above ground, complete with windows and skylights to make things bright and sunny. The lower room urns and coffins would be moved there. The crematorium was to be expanded. Additional acres for the cemetery had also been purchased, and groves of trees were to be planted.

"That's it," Hanson said. "Their hidden temple is in those old, lower rooms."

Samantha walked back in.

"The press release is finished. The news blog I contribute to was more than eager for it."

"We think we found them," Hanson announced.

She viewed the screen.

"What does this place look like now?" she asked.

A few clicks brought them to Google Maps. A building in a sea of green filled the screen.

"My God, that place is huge. That's a funeral home?" Samantha asked.

"I guess they do things big in Texas," Hanson replied.

Cresswell stood up. "It's almost lunchtime. Let me find Wilfred. Miss Ramsell, if you will excuse me."

After Cresswell left, Samantha turned to Hanson.

"So now Fisher calls the FBI, and they search the building," she said.

"We've discussed that, and for several reasons, we don't think that's going to work," Hanson replied. "The thugs have been operating there undetected for decades. They must have someone high up in the law enforcement ranks running interference for them."

"If we call, this thug might warn the others," Fisher added.

"And what's the other reason?" Samantha asked.

"Watkins has everyone chasing a threat that doesn't exist, and we're on her shit list. No one is going to act on what we have now," Hanson answered.

"Then what do we do?" she asked.

"We go over there ourselves and find undeniable proof that thugs exist and bring it to the FBI at a national level," Hanson continued. "That way Watkins can't stop us from bringing in a large force from outside the Dallas area to overwhelm the thugs."

"Going into a thug stronghold doesn't sound like my idea of fun," Samantha said. "I wish there was another way."

"So do I," Hanson replied as he turned back toward the screen to regard the building depicted there. "But with every law enforcement agency searching for Muslim terrorists, we're all that is left. Like it or not, we're the new Thuggee Suppression Department."

Part Three

KALI

Chapter 38

Saturday, 4:05 p.m. CDT, South of Dallas, Texas

Vankatesan stepped out of the white SUV and onto the graveled driveway of the cattle ranch. Rolling green hills with gleaming white fences surrounded him. A brick mansion rose from the well-cared-for landscape.

A grizzled man approached. He wore a white hat and a checkered collared shirt with snaps on the chest pockets. His jeans and boots were well worn. The cowboy look was punctuated by a gun belt and holster, complete with a silver-plated six-shooter. On his other hip was a tooled leather sheath containing a large Bowie knife.

Vankatesan was wearing a tailored suit and expensive Italian shoes, and his ruby cufflinks flashed in the hot Texas sun. The two men regarded each other.

"*Aule bhae ram ram,*" the cowboy greeted.

"Peace to thee, friend," Vankatesan replied.

The cowboy grinned and strode forward to give Vankatesan a bear hug.

"Hey, pardner, how are you holding up?" Chancellor asked with a slight southern drawl.

"About as well as expected, Abe. How is your family?"

"They're fine. Luke's busy at the temple as we speak. Kate's inside whipping up a rancher's sized dinner for you."

Vankatesan gave the other man a closer look. Abraham "Slick" Chancellor was well into his sixties and looked it. Gray stubble covered his creased, weather-worn face, the hair under his hat cropped short. He was built thin and wiry and still stood ramrod straight. A well-regarded lawman in the area, he was also known for his easy-going nature and accuracy with the revolver strapped to his hip.

"Dinner sounds great, Abe, but we should talk somewhere private first."

Chancellor nodded and led him to the ranch's old bunkhouse. It had been converted into an office.

At the moment, the building was empty. Chancellor strode toward the back, took a gold-colored plastic card out of his wallet and held it up to a blank spot on the back wall.

A secret door slid open, and both men went through it and took the steps down to Chancellor's secret sanctum.

It was a small room. The walls to their sides were concealed behind yellow and white curtains. The curtain at the back was parted to reveal a chest-high niche. A two-foot-high statue of Kali rested on it.

It was meticulously crafted, the porcelain body fired to a deep blue. The two tulwars and the khadga were tiny replicas made of silver. The lower left hand held a small gold loop to represent a *rumal*. The eyes were rubies and the teeth ivory. Two small diamonds hung off the elbows of the upper arms.

It was Chancellor's *murti*, designed and blessed by Vankatesan's ancestor, Pranev, almost two centuries ago. Once they had reached England, Pranev had commissioned their construction, and a statue had been created for each member of the *Sath Zut*. Pranev himself had performed the Hindu rite of *Prana Pratishtha* to invite and establish Kali's life energy in each *murti*. The statues had been passed from father to son for generations.

Vankatesan joined Chancellor in front of the *murti*.

"My voice is filled with your praise, Kali," Chancellor said.

"And may everything that has breath praise you, Kali," Vankatesan finished, using the phrase laid down by his ancestor during one of his visions decades ago.

Chancellor took out a small, pen-like device from a pocket and held it up to his other hand. He pressed a button, and a needle darted out, lancing the tip of a finger. A small bead of blood formed. He carefully leaned toward the statue to deposit the drop on the statue's protruding tongue.

Vankatesan nodded his approval. It was a ritual observed weekly by all members of the *Sath Zut*.

Kali must be fed.

Both men stood there for a moment as Chancellor rubbed his finger with an alcohol wipe.

"She thirsts for blood, Tanvir."

Weariness swept over Vankatesan, and he ran a hand through his hair.

"I know, if Kali had her will, she would kill every human being on earth in one day. Blood is her food."

"We are standing on the edge. Where did we go wrong?" Chancellor asked.

In answer, Vankatesan turned back to the one wall that wasn't covered in tapestries. The stairs leading up were on its left side. A large television was mounted on the right. He reached to a small table for the remote and turned it on.

As expected, an image of Hanson's and Ramsell's faces popped up on the screen. Every channel that carried news followed the story twenty-four hours a day. For what felt like the hundredth time, Vankatesan watched Hanson punch Ganesh as Ramsell sprang forward to open a nearby trap door.

"We didn't kill them when we had the chance," Vankatesan answered.

The image on the screen changed to reveal a page from a yellow note pad. On it was a crude map of Death Valley. That image changed to a studio shot of a reporter interviewing one of the stars from the old *Myth-Busters* series.

"He's been resourceful," Chancellor said.

"He's been lucky," Vankatesan snarled. "Do we know where Hanson is?"

"Word in the law enforcement community is that they are both holed up in Los Angeles."

"Cresswell," Vankatesan spat. "*Bae hojana*, why haven't they gone public?"

"Though Hanson stopped Ganesh from destroying the plane, our plan still worked. Homeland is focused on Muslim extremists."

That was a break, thought Vankatesan. He switched over to more pleasant topics.

"What of the victims we will be presenting to Kali during the *chutaw*?"

"We already have them. Fortunately, Kali already had most of them chosen and lined up for the next couple of weeks. So, we just made our move on them early, drugging them instead of killing them outright, and brought them cross-country to the temple."

Drugging. It was a thug tactic of old. Back then, it was *Datura*, the stupefying poison from the seeds of the thorn apple. Thugs then killed their helpless victims.

Chancellor adjusted the television and then transmitted files from his phone.

The screen showed images of people lying in beds as they recovered from the effects of more modern drugs. Vankatesan pointed at one of them.

"And this one?"

"Captured earlier today."

"Well done, Chancellor. This chosen is to be prepared as laid down by Pranev's interpretation of the *Rudhiradhyaya* and thus be made a fitting sacrifice for the Goddess."

"How long will that take?"

"Several days, and that's with Dasgupta's and Zhang's help," Vankatesan answered as he studied the image. "When is the vote on Muslim immigration going down in Congress?"

"Tuesday."

"Excellent. We're on track for the sacrifice to occur on Monday. When the dust settles, the government will have one more thing to blame on the Muslims."

"What of the sacrifice?" Chancellor asked as he glanced toward the screen. "Are you up for it? It's going to be different from the *rumal*."

"The Christians took the heads of thugs back in the day," Vankatesan answered as his eyes flashed in anger. "It's only right that I take one of theirs."

"And Hanson. Ramsell?"

"Once Kali is appeased for the next decade, I too will go into hiding. Time will be on my side, Chancellor. It could be weeks, months, or years from now. But when the moment is right, I will strike, and they won't see me coming."

Vankatesan turned back to the statue.

"A gift for you, Kali."

Chapter 39

Sunday, 11:30 a.m. CDT, Dallas, Texas

Hanson had to admit, for a place of death, Tranquil Groves Memorial Cemetery was beautiful.

Even though it was late September, everything was golf course green. Small ponds and trees dotted the landscape. Fountains gurgled in open patio areas. Paths gracefully curved and wound throughout white gravestones. Flowers filled the roundabouts, and all the roads looked recently paved. The columbarium, a colossal square structure of gray stone in the cemetery's center, rose four stories high. The stone columns that fronted it were spaced at regular intervals.

Three-story-tall wings added to the building's length. This part of the building was younger, and their stonework, and columns, matched the older edifice. Skylights were inset on the pitched roofs. Overall, the structure almost stretched the length of two football fields east to west.

"Check out the stained glass," Samantha said in a hushed voice.

A wing also stretched south from the building and toward the cemetery's entrance. But, instead of being squared off at the end, it came together at an angle, like the prow of a ship.

It was part of the original structure. The lower half of the prow was stone, in which were mounted massive copper-sheathed doors.

A stained-glass window covered the upper half all the way up to its peak. The website had noted with pride that it was the largest stained-glass window in Texas, the work of a noted European artist. It looked worthy of an old cathedral.

In the center of the main structure, a bell tower loomed 150 feet over the landscape.

"Should we park down by the entrance?" Samantha asked.

The main lot was thirty feet from the front doors. Large reflecting pools with elegant fountains flanked the pavement on the east and west sides and partially on the north. One had to take a small stone bridge to the main doors.

"There might be cameras," Hanson answered. "Let's park on one of these side lanes and approach on foot."

He found a location to pull into, and they exited the black Range Rover that Cresswell had provided. Hanson put on a cowboy hat as he got out.

It completed his attire. He was wearing Wrangler jeans held up by a belt with a large silver and turquoise buckle. On his feet were dark leather cowboy boots. His checkered shirt had pearl snaps instead of buttons. To hide the ring around his neck, the collar was secured with a bolo tie that matched the belt buckle. Finally, he slid on some oversized aviator-style sunglasses.

"Giddyap," he said with a wide grin.

"You've said that a dozen times already," Samantha groaned.

She was wearing a wig of short, black hair. She also had on Wrangler jeans and boots. Her blouse was a blue-and-white checkered affair, accented with a red Western bandana around her neck. Sunglasses concealed her eyes. She slung the strap of an enormous denim bag over her shoulder.

"It's the hat," he replied.

"Hanson—"

"Okay, got it. No more cowboy."

They meandered through the park-like setting. Everything was well kept, and the monument-style headstones were grander closer to the main building. Most were adorned with angels.

The noon sun was beating down on them. Seeking respite, the two of them entered a nearby grove of trees.

A path curved through it. Near the center were a bench and pedestal-style drinking fountain. Both had brass plates affixed to them.

It was comfortable in the shade. Hanson studied the trees more closely. The leaves were long, thin, and dark green. With a feeling of apprehension, he brought out his phone.

"In loving memory of our son, Roger Tanner. We will miss you," Samantha announced.

"What?" Hanson asked distractedly. Images were loading on his screen.

"The bench and fountain are memorial items, donated by grieving families," Samantha explained. "It's so pretty here. I'm having a hard time believing thugs are behind this place."

"They are," Hanson said grimly as he looked over his shoulder.

"What makes you so convinced?"

"These trees are mangos."

"So?"

"Back in India, mango groves were common. The primitive roads wound through hot, open country, much like Texas.

"Local leaders, looking for good karma, I guess, would dig wells for water and plant mangos for shade along these roads. They wanted travelers to think well of them even after they had long passed away."

Samantha glanced at the brass plaques. "What does this have to do with thugs?"

"These park-like groves were favorite campgrounds for travelers. For thugs, they were *beles*."

"These campgrounds must have been quite crowded. How did the thugs pull off killing in them?"

"If another encampment were nearby, the thugs would strike up a song, singing and beating drums loudly while the *bhurtotes* did their business. Another ruse would be to pretend livestock had escaped.

Then, while the other campers watched with amusement as animals were being rounded up, victims were quietly strangled in their tents."

"And no one figured this out?"

"Sleeman did. He began mapping these mango grove *beles*. So did his man in Oudh, Captain James Paton, who designed what he called the 'Thug Road Book.' Sepoys were posted at high-volume *beles*."

Samantha looked warily at the ground. "There must have been a lot of bodies."

"There were. Remember Feringeea? Feringeea told Sleeman such fantastic stories that Sleeman commanded him to prove it. So Feringeea did.

"The thug revealed that over a dozen bodies were buried outside the town of Selohda. Sleeman was familiar with the nearby camp area.

"Getting out of the hot city would be a relief, so Sleeman's wife asked to come along. With a detachment of sepoys, they arrived at nightfall. Tents were pitched so that they could rest until morning to start their grisly work of finding Feringeea's victims."

Samantha was looking at the grave markers all around them.

"Wasn't it apparent? Over a dozen bodies?"

"No. Remember, thugs were masters of making the corpses disappear. So, when Sleeman stood outside his tent in the morning sun, he still doubted the veracity of Feringeea's claims.

"But the thug studied the landmarks and pointed out the spots. They started digging. Soon the sepoys had the bodies of several victims exhumed."

"Feringeea had said there were more. Where were the rest?"

"Sleeman had the same question," Hanson replied.

Realization dawned on Samantha. "No."

"Feringeea instructed Sleeman to strike down his sleeping tent. Mrs. Sleeman had to be awakened and taken to the breakfast area. The diggers went back to work, and soon the bodies of four Ganges water carriers and a woman were exhumed. The Sleemans had spent the night sleeping over a mass grave."

"What did Mrs. Sleeman have to say about that?"

"That though she was unaware of the bodies, her soul must have been conscious of it, for her sleep was filled with the most horrid dreams."

They both walked to the edge of the mango grove, where the sun beat down on them once more.

Hanson studied the massive building looming nearby. "The thugs are here. Let's pay a visit to their Temple of Doom."

Chapter 40

Unlike the movie, no lava-filled chasms barred their way. Air conditioning and pleasant music greeted them instead.

Glittering crystal chandeliers hung from the ceiling, and rose-colored marble sheathed the floor. Elegant statues guarded the walls.

Hanson and Samantha walked farther in, both mindful of the dozens of mourners present for funerals.

At the far end of the arcade were two sweeping staircases with thick marble balustrades, both curving up to a central landing. They flanked a large fifteen-foot-wide doorway closed off with an accordion-style partition. At the base of the stairs was a large circle of white marble that offset the rest of the floor. In its center, a casket rested on a gurney skirted with black velvet. Spotlights on the ceiling projected an American flag pattern on the white marble.

The walls here had light wood paneling with paintings mounted on them. Signs designed to aid the recently bereaved navigate the room were posted. A reader board on a silver pedestal announced the day's funeral events.

Offices were on Hanson's and Samantha's left. Next to those was a large, carpeted space appointed with elegant furniture arranged as an inviting living room. A fireplace with flickering flames dominated the area's far corner.

A counter with flower-filled vases was nearby. A receptionist behind one of them looked up and nodded in their direction. "May I help you," she asked with practiced sympathy in her voice.

Hanson touched the brim of his hat and gave a short nod.

"Ma'am."

Samantha stood on the toe of his boot.

"I mean, hello. Yes, you can help us. We are here to, umm—," Hanson paused; he hadn't really thought this part out. "Inquire about your services."

The receptionist brought out a small notepad. "I'm sorry for your loss. Who passed away?"

Now Hanson was really flustered. He blurted out the first thing that came to mind. "Uncle Owen and Aunt Beru."

"Two? Was there an accident?"

"Fiery car wreck," Hanson answered lamely.

"My condolences. Let me find you a funeral director," the receptionist replied. She stood up and exited the area through a door behind her.

Samantha spun toward Hanson. "Really, Steve, Uncle Owen?"

"Maybe she's too young to have seen the original *Star Wars* movie," Hanson replied.

"You know, people say that men think about sex every seven seconds."

Hanson opened his mouth to respond.

"I know, I know. You're going to tell me that's another untruth. I'm just bringing it up because I'm guessing that every seven seconds, you're thinking of some nerd thing."

"That's not true. I was thinking about sex last night," he said defensively.

"I remember," she replied as she tipped up his hat a little to kiss him. "Just let me do the talking."

The receptionist returned with a slightly older woman with short blonde hair and wearing a blue dress. Her name tag announced her as Annette, Funeral Director.

"Annette? Thanks so much for meeting us," Samantha greeted as she placed a driver's license card on the counter. "My name is Vicki Longridge."

Hanson held his breath. The license had been supplied by Cresswell to help them check into hotels for their long drive and stay in Texas. He hoped it held up here also.

"I'm sorry for your loss," Annette said. She picked up the card. "California? Are you the surviving next of kin?"

"Yes. I'm named in their will for handling their last arrangements."

Annette returned the card. "Thank you for choosing us. I will be helping you design the Final Celebration for your aunt and uncle. Would you like to join me in our lounge for the arrangement conference?"

"Actually, no. My husband, Jethro—"

"Ma'am," Hanson interjected.

"And I are originally from Austin, but we now live in L.A.," Samantha continued. "And, as you can imagine, the airports are a mess right now. I'm hoping that you would give us a tour and show us some of the facility's features."

"Of course, Mrs. Longridge. Follow me," Annette replied as she led them back into the hall.

"You've already experienced our Italian marble and artwork," Annette said, "It's part of the original structure, built over a century ago."

She pointed back toward the carpeted area. "And as you can see, we have added more modern amenities to help you in your planning. We can do everything here. We have several staterooms and parlors for more intimate gatherings. Beyond the office are our own floral department, the showroom for our line of caskets, and our catering kitchen. All legal planning can be done in our offices."

"What styles of interments can you accommodate?" Samantha asked.

"Our staff can handle the burial requirements of all faiths," Annette answered. "And we have our own crematorium."

They approached the casket in the middle of the room. It was a display for the burial container itself, a 16-gauge steel affair called the Aegis, designed to protect its contents for eternity. Hanson almost whistled aloud when he read the price.

Annette noticed him looking.

"Bodies can lie in repose here, for a small fee," she said.

"What's behind the folding door over there?" Hanson asked.

"The hallway to our attached garage, widened so that the pallbearers can comfortably navigate the casket to any one of our hearses."

They approached the east wall. Five doors, spread twenty feet apart, were inset. Annette held up a copper-colored card to a small panel on the wall. A lock clicked, and she opened the door.

"This is our largest room, the Oak Remembrance Chapel," Annette announced.

It was a five-hundred-person auditorium lined with comfortable padded chairs. The room sloped gently down to a stage.

As advertised, it was paneled in oak. Brass sconces and inset lights in the ceiling illuminated the room. On the wall behind the stage, nine sizeable flat-screen televisions were stacked in a 3x3 pattern to form one huge rectangular screen.

On the left side of the stage was an organ. The right had a door and window. Hanson couldn't see into the room because the window's curtains were closed.

"What's in there?" he asked.

"That's the Oak Visitation Room," Annette answered. "Where the bereaved family can spend some quiet time. It has its own bathroom and back door so that we can cater to them if they wish during the funeral."

"Uncle Owen would have wanted us to be comfortable, sweetie," Hanson said with a smile directed at Samantha.

She frowned and turned to the back wall.

"How does this work?" she asked Annette.

Hanson could see the reason for her curiosity. Of the five doors to the room, the middle one didn't open to an aisle. Instead, it led to a glass-enclosed control room. Inside, several mounted video cameras could be seen.

"We've had many celebrities and prominent members of society interred here," Annette replied proudly. "Sometimes, even the Oak Room can't handle the crowd, so we broadcast the service for people to view from home."

Samantha looked interested. "I would like to see how that works."

Annette led them back outside and opened the center door. They all crowded into the booth.

A small video engineering panel and chair next were on the left side of the room. Two cameras on tripods were on the right.

"Who carries the signal?" Samantha asked.

"Perry University, they have their own channel and broadcast news curriculum," Annette answered. "For a low price, all we have to do is throw a switch."

"Thanks, Annette," Samantha said, "Do you mind if we take some time to ourselves and look over the grounds?"

"Of course," Annette said. She handed over a brochure. "This has a map and explains our services."

Annette left them in the main hall.

"She can't be a thug," Samantha said.

"I'm guessing most people here are truly funeral home employees," Hanson replied. "I think the only thugs would be in upper management and the men that do the actual maintenance around here."

Hanson looked at the map and led them on. Away from the central lobby, they entered a labyrinth of hallways and small rooms with floor-to-ceiling niches.

The niches were small lockable cupboards with glass windows so that one could see the contents. Most niches had one to six urns inside. A small plate on each one had them labeled so they could be cross-indexed.

They were surrounded by the ashes of thousands of the dead.

One of the niches had a fresh bouquet of flowers. Hanson plucked it out of its holding ring.

"Steve!"

"I know, I'm sorry," Hanson replied guiltily. "We need it though."

They took a staircase down to the lowest level.

"Spooky down here," Samantha noted.

"This is where they sealed off the old catacombs forty years ago. I'm betting there's a secret door nearby."

A security camera was posted above them.

"Act normal," Hanson advised.

They stopped in front of a niche wall. Hanson placed the flowers in front of an niche that was about chest high on the wall. He wiped away an imaginary tear.

"I miss them," he said loudly.

As Hanson continued his show of grieving, Samantha reached into her bag and pulled out a small camera.

Another item provided by Cresswell. It had enough storage for hours and could also download its contents through Bluetooth. She placed the camera in the flowers so that it pointed at the stairwell.

"Let's explore the rest of the place," Hanson said. "We will swing back later to download what it has recorded."

Chapter 41

Hanson and Samantha walked upstairs and followed an outer hallway on the backside of the building. Daylight streamed in from the narrow windows.

"This natural light is a nice feature," Samantha observed.

Hanson grunted, a frown on his face.

"What?" she asked.

"They're more like a castle's arrow slits," he answered. "Defenders could shoot out without exposing themselves. The outer stone walls here are two feet thick. The exit doors are steel reinforced. This place is built like a fortress."

They walked up and down the newer wings till they found the crematorium. It had a viewing area into the furnace room. Hanson wondered how many illicit bodies had disappeared in there.

They made their way back to the main hall and let themselves through the vinyl accordion doors.

A wide hallway stretched away from them. Paintings hung on dark wood-paneled walls. Expensive crystal vases with fresh flowers rested on narrow side tables.

The hall opened into an oversized garage. The room's large outer doors were open on the east and west side.

Three vehicles were parked inside, two black hearses and a white van. One hearse was traditional in style, the other a modified Hummer for military funerals. The van had a logo painted on its side. *Tranquil Groves Funeral Home.* The image of a leafy tree flanked the words on the right.

"That's how they move the bodies," Samantha said.

"In plain sight," Hanson added.

They took an access door and passed by a musty-smelling storeroom that held artificial turf and shovels. Once back in the main hall, they took the grand staircase up. On the next level, they froze, both awestruck.

"What do they call this room in the brochure?" Hanson asked in a hushed voice.

"One Step Closer to Heaven," Samantha answered.

The ceiling of the upper level of the grand hall stretched cathedral-like forty feet above him, heavy beams arching to support the roof. Elegant crystal chandeliers hung from the rafters.

It had a dark marble floor to offset the elaborate white crypts that dominated the room, most of which were large rectangular marble blocks topped with a monument statuary. Some were carved with bas-relief details honoring God and heaven. The room had a wide central path. Hanson and Samantha used it to walk down the room's length to the stained-glass window at the far end.

It stretched from floor to ceiling. The sunlight that streamed through the lead-lined panes cast a myriad of colors across the white marble at its base.

The artfully arranged glass depicted heaven—pearly gates atop white clouds on a blue sky. God and Jesus were holding out their hands in invitation. Angels soared above the entire scene.

Hanson stood in front of it and gaped upward. He glanced left and right to make sure no one was looking his way. Satisfied, he then took off his sunglasses so that he could appreciate its beauty.

"I've never stood before one this large before," he admitted.

"It's considered priceless, a national treasure," Samantha replied.

They lingered by the window, captivated by its beauty.

"Is there anything more on this level?" Hanson asked, his eyes blinking.

"Yes, something I think you'll find just as interesting," she answered.

They walked toward the center of the building. Samantha led them to the right through a small doorway that put them in a carpeted hall. Elaborate niches covered the walls, the trim plated in silver.

The hall continued for thirty feet and opened into a nexus. This room was round, with three more open doorways at each compass point. The whole area was covered with black marble, and the domed ceiling was entirely of stained glass. Artificial light kept it illuminated like a huge Tiffany lamp.

There were no niches in this room; the walls were purposefully kept bare to highlight the two statues within it.

Immediately to Hanson's right was a twenty-foot-high white marble statue of Jesus. He was kneeling, the marble below him carved to look like a hillside. His left hand held an upright shepherd's crook slightly behind him, while his right hand was outstretched to reach several feet into the room. His open palm was about level with Hanson's midriff. The marbled fingers were partially worn away since thousands of passing visitors had paused to touch it over the years. Hanson couldn't resist the temptation himself, and he reached out to let his fingers slide over the smooth marble.

Another twenty-foot-tall marble statue was on the other side of the room, directly across from Jesus. This one was of a woman, who was also kneeling. She possessed four arms, the left two extended back to grasp a trident as Jesus held his crook. Her two right arms were outstretched also, leaving one hand at the same level as Jesus's, the second chest high. They showed the same wear from people touching them as they passed by.

She was clothed in a sari and had a garland of skulls around her neck. An expression of motherly concern had been carved onto her face.

"Is that—" Samantha began.

"Kali," Hanson finished as he walked over to the statue. He read the brass plate beneath it. She, and the figure of Jesus, were original artworks commissioned by Tranquil Groves four decades ago, designed to mirror each other. Hindu and Christianity. Part of the complex's all faith appeal.

"I wasn't sure," Samantha continued. "I was expecting something more sinister-looking, such as a snarling fanged demon of death and destruction to guard the Hindu underworld."

"No one can blame you," Hanson replied as he looked up at Kali's face. "Much of how we view Kali today came from the reports published by the men of the East India Company. People back in England couldn't get enough of the stories of a Goddess of murder and death. *Confessions of a Thug*, published in 1839, was a hugely popular book in England. Other Victorian thriller novels followed. Kali, the blood-soaked demon, was cemented in Western minds. Some of that prejudice colors how we view her to this day."

"What was she, then?"

"First of all, she's not the caretaker of the underworld. That's Yama. You spend a little time with him until you are reincarnated. If you were a good person, it's a pleasant stay. If you were bad, his punishments would rival our view of hell. Kali's statue is here because the cremation grounds are her home."

"Spooky."

"True. But she represents the energy of destruction, and ultimately, renewal. Dissolution through fire happens at the cremation grounds. So, it's only natural you find her here."

"She's armed to the teeth."

"To combat evil. Think of her as someone you would want on your side in a fight."

"They sacrificed to her."

"Deep in the past, all cultures did. Or showed no mercy to their enemies in the name of God."

Hanson looked back at Jesus.

"But now, a testament later, everything is a bit more mellowed out. It's the same with Kali. Over time, she has become more of a maternal Goddess, a benign deity that looks after you."

Hanson turned back to Kali, and he touched her upper palm. "She reaches out with one hand to protect you," he said quietly.

His hand drifted down to brush the other one. "And with the other, she grants you a boon, a gift."

Hanson paused as he stood in front of the statue, lost in thought. "To face Kali on the cremation grounds is to face your own fears," he finished.

Samantha stood close to him.

"And what is it you fear, Steve?"

Hanson struggled for a moment as he contemplated the most difficult thing for anyone to confront. The truth about themselves. He looked up at Kali's face regarding him.

"That someday, I will find myself old and alone, like Cresswell back in L.A., chasing shadows that no one else believes in."

She put a hand on his chest. "I don't think that will ever happen to you, no matter how hard you try to isolate yourself," she said. "In the end, I think you will find yourself surrounded by those who love you."

A grin back on his face, Hanson was about to respond when a family of four walked in. Instead, he slipped his sunglasses back on, and they retreated through the north passage.

It led to a stairwell that included roof access. They took the stairs down to the main level and made their way to the lobby area. Tired from their exploring, they settled into some chairs near the fireplace.

"We have a little time. I think I will work on my Vankatesan message," Hanson announced as he fished his new phone out of his pocket. On their drive through Texas, Hanson had begun preparing a video montage of thug omens.

Samantha's eyebrows came together a bit with concern. "Are you sure it won't rile him up too much?"

"No, these images should just make him apprehensive. Though he's on the run, I'm sure he still monitors his social media accounts—"

Next to him, Samantha tensed up and she put a hand on his arm. "Speak of the devil," she whispered, "Vankatesan's here."

Hanson's heart started pounding. "Is he alone?"

"No, that knife guy from the university, Blackbourne, is with him. They're studying one of the emergency exit doors."

Hanson resisted the impulse to turn around and forced himself to look forward and rely on Samantha.

"Now they're heading for the secret door stairwell."

"Let's give them a few minutes head start," Hanson replied.

They waited ten minutes before making their own way back to the stairwell. Once they were close to the camera, they downloaded the video from a safe distance. Then, they retreated outside to the mango grove.

Hanson played the last ten minutes of the video.

Three minutes in, two men approached. Blackbourne held up a gold-colored card to the wall itself.

A door opened.

Inside, a dimly lit corridor could be seen. Both men entered. At the last moment, as if to make sure no one was watching, Vankatesan turned around and revealed his face to the camera.

The door closed behind the thugs.

"What now?" Samantha asked.

"We get Fisher over here," Hanson replied, relief painted on his face. "We have them."

Chapter 42

Sunday, 7:05 p.m. CDT, Tranquil Groves

"We have them," the *bykureea* announced.

Vankatesan leaned in closer to the scout to look over his shoulder. "Show me."

The *bykureea* tapped a few keys. A video of Hanson removing his sunglasses and looking upward filled the computer screen. The thug scout froze the image there.

"Where was this?" Vankatesan asked.

"Upstairs, in front of the stained-glass window," the young man answered. Vankatesan remembered his name was Shen. Vankatesan had been his guru a few years back and had helped the boy strangle his first victim for Kali.

Shen kept on explaining. "When you asked us to start watching out for the *tikhur* a few hours ago as a precaution, I decided to check all of our video from the past twenty-four hours. Kali picked him out just a few minutes ago."

"And this is the first time She spotted him, deep in the heart of our stronghold?"

"He kept his face hidden by that hat and sunglasses most of the time."

Vankatesan frowned as he studied Hanson's cowboy disguise. A woman with black hair and ridiculously large sunglasses was standing next to him. Ramsell.

"What did they do while they were here?" he asked.

The room the two men were in was the thug's main computer center. Cool air flowed through multiple vents, and large screens covered the walls above several workstations. The *bykureea* transferred what he had in front of him to a wall monitor and played a sped-up video montage. Vankatesan watched with growing alarm as Hanson and Ramsell explored the funeral home.

Blackbourne strode into the room with something in his hand. "This was found across from the stairwell door," Blackbourne announced as he held up a small camera.

Blackbourne passed it over to Shen, who began studying it. Vankatesan walked to the other side of the room and motioned Blackbourne over.

"They know where we are," Vankatesan said.

"What can we do?" Blackbourne replied with frustration in his voice. "We can't just cut and run. Preparing the sacrifice for final immolation will take one more day. What's the use—" Blackbourne lowered his voice. "Of all of that wealth if Kali destroys the world around us?"

"The sacrifice will go as planned. Kali must be appeased for the next decade," Vankatesan answered.

"Hanson could be heading back here with police in tow right now," Blackbourne hissed.

"Unlikely," Vankatesan replied. "Chancellor would alert us. I think Hanson and Ramsell still have little to show for their efforts. However, just to be safe, we should move up our timeline. Is everyone here?"

"Everyone is in town. They are ready to arrive at the temple tomorrow morning."

"Send out a message. Tell everyone we have witnessed a *thibaoo*, a good omen. Have them all come in now."

"Shouldn't we have five hundred pairs of eyes out there looking for Hanson?"

"No, we all have much to do. And even if Hanson convinces the local authorities to come after us, we can hold this place until the time for the final sacrifice has arrived."

"What of Hanson? He's so close. He deserves to die."

"We will rely on Chancellor to find him. We may still get our chance," Vankatesan replied grimly.

* * *

8:50 p.m., Texas Longhorn Hotel, Dallas, Texas

"When can you get here?" Hanson asked. He had Fisher on a video chat program on his phone. Samantha was leaning over his shoulder so that Fisher could see them both.

"Timing is going to be everything—" Fisher began.

"I realize you had to stay behind so that Watkins would think that all of us were still there," Hanson interjected. "But we need you here now!"

"I can't head over tonight. The moment I buy a ticket—"

"Watkins will know about it," Samantha finished.

"Correct," Fisher said. "However, if I time my flight right, I think I can get around that. This whole terrorist thing is escalating out of control. Muslim demonstrators and counterdemonstrators are set to march all over the country. The largest protest is set to happen in Times Square late tomorrow afternoon, in time for the national news broadcast on the East coast."

"Watkins will be distracted," Hanson guessed.

"And she won't be able to react to me traveling," Fisher continued. "I will drop in at Dallas unannounced and show the local police the Vankatesan video. Fortunately for us, Watkins did make him a person of interest."

"What about the thug's mole here in Dallas?" Hanson asked.

"I'll keep my eye out for him," Fisher said. "As I said, timing is everything. If I move too soon, Watkins shuts me down."

"And if you move too late, people die in these demonstrations," Hanson finished.

"Now, if this works, how do we expose thuggee and get the message out?" Fisher asked.

"Tomorrow morning, I'm going to pay a visit to a local news affiliate," Samantha answered. "When you show up and arrest Vankatesan, it will be on the news. I know some people back in New York. With the promise of Hanson finally giving interviews, we'll make sure it goes national. Easy."

"Easy," Hanson echoed with an enthusiastic nod.

Chapter 43

Monday, 11:54 a.m. CDT, Texas Longhorn Hotel

"Easy," Hanson sighed glumly as he shook his head.

His image in the mirror shook its head also. Hanson was practicing his speech for the news cameras. Samantha had gone over with him what to say the previous night.

"Just tell them facts, as you told me."

"But millions will be watching. It's like something from one of my nightmares."

"Is it that bad?"

"I have anxiety nightmares. My worst one is that I am speaking in front of a crowd, and I've lost my pants. The entire world can see my naked ass."

"It won't be like that, Steve. And anyway, it's a nice ass," Samantha reassured him. "Now, let's work on your speech a bit more—"

Hanson squared his shoulders and focused on the mirror again.

"We are surrounded by thugs," he announced as he dug into his pants pockets and pulled forth his thumb drive and the measuring tape from Cresswell's place. "And I can prove it."

His shoulders sagged as he sighed again and stuffed the items into his pocket. He needed more coaching from Samantha when she returned. At the moment, she was making a lunch run while in disguise. He gave up on practicing in front of the mirror and instead checked once again to make sure their belongings were ready for when they left the hotel.

Their bags were lined up on the bed. Next to those were the weapons they had brought. Hanson picked up the saber and thought back to his conversation with Cresswell. Right before they had left L.A., the old man had taken Hanson aside. Several items had been laid out on a table.

"We're only going there to scout the place," Hanson said as he studied the weapons arrayed in front of him.

"They're thugs. You need to be ready for anything," Cresswell replied.

The first items were a shotgun and a stun baton. The baton looked like it could drop a bull. The shotgun was a Mossberg home security model with an 18.5-inch barrel and foregrip.

Next was the .505 elephant gun from the mantel. Hanson picked up one of the cartridges for it.

It was almost four inches long, and the rounded bullet that topped it was massive.

"That will put anything down," Cresswell said.

Hanson returned the round and picked up the next item on the table, the saber. He held it up reverently. It was lighter than he had expected. Hanson examined the front end. The blade thickened near the point.

"That made the front end heavier, giving more power to slashing attacks," Cresswell explained.

"Which the British favored," Hanson added. "And the French hated."

"Too much carnage in the sword's wake," Cresswell acknowledged. "The French preferred the thrust, which led to cleaner kills."

Hanson slid the sword back into its scabbard. "I'll make sure it gets back to you."

Cresswell held up his hands. "Please, the sword is yours."

Hanson was stunned by the generosity. "This must be an heirloom. What of your family?"

"There is none," Cresswell said with a shake of his head. He was quiet for a moment, his eyes distant. "My wife died of cancer, my son in a car accident. When I pass on, my staff will be taken care of, but most of this will go back to India, where it belongs. India endures, Hanson. It's the Cresswell line that is coming to an end."

Unsure of what to say, Hanson stood there and listened.

"But before that happens, promise me this," Cresswell said as he stared at Hanson intensely. "The thugs' tulwar is still out there. It is an evil thing. See to it that it is destroyed."

Hanson felt the weight of the saber in his hands.

"I'll make sure it happens," he promised.

"Good," Cresswell said. "Now, let's see about finding clothes for you and Miss Ramsell—"

Hanson's mind drifted back to the present as he placed the saber next to the shotgun. The elephant gun was deemed too unwieldy to lug around in the open, so it remained in the back of the Range Rover. Satisfied with the state of their gear, his mind wandered back to his upcoming television interview. For the tenth time this morning, he second-guessed the light brown shirt he was wearing. He wondered if he should change it.

A familiar voice on the television distracted him. Jennifer Steel was on location at Times Square. Her network was located less than a block away from the landmark, so she was taping her segment in front of her headquarters. Like the other buildings that surrounded the famous intersection, her station had its own mammoth-sized screen. It depicted Steel in giant-like proportions.

The camera panned south to display where Broadway and 7th Avenue came together. Demonstrators and counterdemonstrators were massed there.

"City officials are predicting this event to be larger than pre-COVID era New Year's Eve celebrations," Steel intoned.

The camera zoomed in on a line of police officers.

"Right now, the police have the Muslim crowds and counterdemonstrators separated. The planned Muslim march down Broadway, to where the 'Keep America Free of Terrorists' group is waiting, is to officially begin in a few hours."

The camera shifted back to Steel.

"Will a thin blue line of ten thousand be enough to stop the expected bloodshed?"

Hanson didn't think so. The web was exploding with conspiracy theories of terrorist cells infiltrating American neighborhoods. He suspected that the thugs, the masters of deception, had a presence on the web and were spreading lies. So though President Hayes had called for calm last night on live television, no one seemed to be listening to her. Americans fed up with immigration policies were descending on New York in droves.

Hanson switched the channel to a local news broadcast to check if Dallas had its own demonstration problems.

An image of a male reporter standing in front of the metal bars of a locked gate appeared on his screen. Beyond the gate, Hanson's heart skipped a beat as he recognized the building in the background.

Tranquil Groves.

"—In an unusual bit of news, officials at Tranquil Groves have reported a gas leak in the pipeline leading to their crematorium. So, as a precaution, they are not letting anyone within the cemetery walls."

The young man, with microphone in hand, stood to the side so that the camera could zoom in on the empty parking lot.

"The spokesperson for Tranquil Groves noted that four funerals would be affected today. To make up for this terrible inconvenience, those four funerals will be held tomorrow at no cost to the bereaved families, saving them—"

My God, Hanson thought as he muted the television and pulled out his phone.

Did the thugs detect me and Samantha yesterday? Are they going to pull out during the riots?

He dialed Samantha, and he could hear it begin to ring on her end.

Someone knocked at the room's door.

"Housekeeping," a woman's voice announced.

Hanson looked warily at the door. It was early for housekeeping, and on the doorknob was an introvert's favorite sign.

Do Not Disturb.

Wishing he had taken the time to put on his Bluetooth headset, he pinched the phone between his head and shoulder as he grabbed the shotgun and carefully made his way to the door. Samantha's voice reached his ear, but it was from her messaging service. Frowning, Hanson waited for her recorded greeting to cycle through so that he could leave an update. But, as usual, cradling a cell phone on one's shoulder was an exercise in futility, and his phone fell to the ground as his face neared the peephole. The phone's screen went dark as it lost the call, and Hanson cursed as he reflexively bent over to pick it up.

Above him, the upper half of the door exploded with a shattering roar.

Chapter 44

It was a shotgun blast through the door at head level. With a yelp, Hanson stumbled sideways into the bathroom, his ears ringing from the noise.

Two more blasts followed, one where the door chain was located and one near the knob. Someone was trying to weaken the door's integrity.

Hanson ducked into the shower stall.

The door smashed open, and Blackbourne, his head covered with a baseball cap, charged into the hotel room, a short-barreled shotgun held at the ready.

Hanson moved out of the bathroom and stood directly behind the thug, who was staring at the floor.

Most likely wondering why there wasn't a corpse on the ground.

"I'm armed," Hanson shouted. "Drop—"

The thug whirled and brought his weapon to bear, but he was nowhere near fast enough. Hanson had his shotgun up and ready.

His weapon roared as he shot Blackbourne in the face.

The thug's hat flew off as his head snapped back. Blackbourne collapsed backward and bounced off the bed and onto the carpeted floor. A cell phone, its screen still glowing, tumbled out of the breast pocket of the thin windbreaker he was wearing.

Hanson dove on the phone.

Blackbourne must have just used it to play the prerecorded woman's voice at his door, so the power-saving time-out feature hadn't kicked in yet. And most phones automatically locked a few seconds *after* a phone put itself to sleep.

Hanson had an unlocked thug phone.

It was on an audio playback program. Hanson closed that page and revealed a messaging app also in use. It contained a short string of texts.

Though curious, Hanson looked away from them for a moment and carefully glanced out his ruined doorway. The corridor was empty. Satisfied that no more thugs were nearby, he picked up his own phone from the floor, pocketed it, and turned his attention back to the thug phone and read what was there.

Unknown: *Traffic cameras found them.*

Blackbourne: *Where?*

Unknown: *The Longhorn. I checked further. Room 115.*

Blackbourne: *Can you reach them?*

Unknown: *Can't leave the Evan's building. Too busy monitoring situation.*

Blackbourne: *I will do it. Ceremonies have begun. Others can't be spared.*

Unknown: *Kali be with you.*

There was a half-hour break in the messaging, then one last update from Blackbourne.

Here now. Bring the tobacco.

That was it for messages. He and Samantha had checked out places they might need to visit, so Hanson knew that the Evan's building meant police headquarters.

Unknown was the cop on the inside.

Hanson typed out one last message for the police mole.

Hanson dead. No sign of Ramsell.

Whoever the cop was, he didn't take long to respond.

Unknown: *I will keep an eye out for her. You should return and secure the temple.*

Secure the temple for what? Hanson thought. He switched to settings and turned off the phone's automatic lock feature. He then checked to see what other applications Blackbourne had up and running.

A map appeared on the screen. It had a blue line that showed the best route between the hotel and Tranquil Groves.

Hanson tapped the phone icon. No calls on the logs. The phone was a burner, its entire usage life being less than an hour. He carefully put it away and looked over the body.

After Hanson's shotgun blast, Blackbourne's face was an unrecognizable and gut-wrenching mess. Hanson's head swam a bit. He wished he could unsee that. He searched Blackbourne's clothes, taking care to not get any gore on himself.

Blackbourne had a fob for a Mercedes in his front pants pocket; a back pocket contained a wallet. Hanson flipped through it. It held high-end credit cards, a New Hampshire driver's license, and some photographs. The pictures were of Blackbourne's wife, son, and daughter. The children were both grown, and one photo showed the daughter presenting her father with a grandson. Blackbourne was beaming. Hanson wondered when the boys were introduced to the concept of thuggee.

Blackbourne had a short and stubby flashlight clipped to his belt. Hanson removed it and attached it to his own belt. Blackbourne had it for a reason.

The jacket's breast pocket revealed two more objects. The first was the gold-colored key card that Blackbourne had used to open the secret door yesterday.

Thug card. Don't leave home without it.

The second item was a small piece of paper folded in half. The front cover had an image of flowers in soft focus. A short phrase printed with graceful letters was at the top.

In Remembrance…

A funeral program. Hanson flipped it open. This one wasn't for an interment ceremony. It was an itinerary for what was truly happening at Tranquil Groves. The thugs were using the form because they most likely had so many of them lying around.

Hanson read it.

Using the Oak Room, access from the main lobby
Today's Agenda
We Remember Pravnev's Wisdom
Chutaw
Numbers: A look back
Tuponee
Bhera
Immolation

Pravnev. Vankatesan had mentioned him. An ancestor of his and the thug who had started it all. The thugs treated him as some sort of prophet.

Chutaw. The division of the spoils. They were splitting up all their money.

He wasn't sure about the *Numbers* thing. But he recognized *Tuponee.* A thug ceremony that involved their sacred sugar, goor.

He read the next word, *Bhera,* which was "four" in *Ramasee.*

Four what? The last word held the answer.

Immolation.

Sacrifice.

There were four sacrificial victims. The thugs weren't simply evacuating Tranquil Groves. They were planning on going through their blood sacrifice ritual and disappear for the next decade, as they did in India nearly two centuries ago.

Sirens sounded in the distance.

Hanson looked up with a start. The police would almost here. He considered the wreckage of the room around him. Given time, with Fisher's help, he could explain all of this to the police. He looked back at the program in his hands.

Bhera.

Whoever these four people were, they didn't have that sort of time.

Hanson scooped up the wallet, phone, and Mercedes keys. He pulled off Blackbourne's windbreaker and put it and the baseball cap on. He then turned to his laptop bag on the bed and pulled out the small headset paired with his phone.

Outside, the sirens howled louder.

The saber's gleaming hilt caught his eye. He couldn't leave Cresswell's prized possession behind. Hanson placed the scabbard with its sword on his back, its strap across his chest. He then snatched up the shotgun and baton and dashed out of the hotel room.

He went for a fire exit door and stepped out onto a back alleyway. He could hear tires squealing from the building's front parking lot. With his heart pounding in his chest, Hanson sprinted away from the hotel as he held the shotgun held close to his side.

He needed to get out of the area. Samantha had the Range Rover. He reached into his bag and pulled out Blackbourne's car fob and pressed the "unlock door" button.

At the end of the alley, a white sedan chirped. Hanson entered it and tossed his gear onto the passenger seat. He fished out his phone and put on the headset paired to it and quick-dialed Samantha.

"Change of plans," Hanson announced when she answered.

Chapter 45

Hanson filled her in on what had happened as he pulled into traffic.

"Steer clear of the hotel. The police are soon going to have the Range Rover's license and description from the hotel desk," Hanson added.

"Do you want to meet me at the news affiliate?"

"No. I have to get inside Tranquil Groves."

"Steve!"

"They have four sacrifices for Kali inside with them," Hanson explained as he glanced at himself in the mirror. "I think I can pass as Blackbourne from a distance."

"Any idea on how many thugs are in there?"

"They're using the Oak Room. Hundreds, I guess."

"I still think you should wait for Fisher!"

"He's still in the air, and we can't reach him. I don't think the thugs are going to keep Kali waiting," Hanson answered.

"Steve…please, be careful."

Hanson could tell from her voice that she meant that. It surprised him a bit on how good that felt—to have someone who really cared about you.

"You too," he replied. "I'll let you know when I get there."

There was a phone clip on the dash. Hanson attached the thug's cell to it and called up the navigation program so that he could use Blackbourne's map to backtrack to Tranquil Groves.

* * *

Samantha had a map of her own displaying the local news affiliate location on the Range Rover's dash screen. She worried about Hanson as she drove.

Hundreds of thugs.

She thought about what else he said.

In the Oak Room.

"Find Perry University," she spoke aloud.

The Range Rover's main screen map shifted, and it displayed a location and the best route. A voice from the vehicle's speakers announced that it would take her fifteen minutes to get there.

She did it in eight. Her tires squealed as she pulled onto a pleasant-looking campus composed of stately buildings of brick and tall columns. Sidewalks wound through well-manicured lawns. Samantha located the journalism building and pulled into its lot.

She ran inside and found a map posted on the wall. Samantha glanced at it and then made her way upstairs. She located a door with an unlit ON THE AIR sign above it and let herself in.

The room's setup was familiar, and a wave of nostalgia washed over her. Several desks were close to the door with computers on them. Deeper into the room was the production area, which had a large console with multiple monitors. A window separated the workspace from the studio itself, where she could see a news desk for two people to sit at. A green backdrop for the weather segment was off to the right.

A group of a half dozen students were standing in front of the monitors. One screen showed what was being broadcasted on the station's channel—a recording of an earlier student council meeting.

Routine. Except for the engineer responsible for the broadcast currently on the air, that wasn't the screen commanding the group's attention. Samantha saw that the other three monitors had cell phone recordings from Flight 951 running on them. Video of Hanson and herself desperately trying to save the plane. The students were pointing at the screens and arguing about which sequences they wanted to run.

Samantha shut the door behind her, and everyone in the room turned to regard her. A young but serious-looking black woman stepped forward. A name tag clipped to her shirt identified her as a production manager named Tina.

"Excuse me, but you shouldn't be in here," Tina said.

"I apologize," Samantha replied as she smiled and pointed at the monitors with her and Hanson on them. "But I have a major news story—"

"Lady, a lot of people tell us that every day," the young woman countered. She gestured to a large whiteboard to the side. "But as you can see, we already have plenty to work with."

Samantha glanced at the board. It had a list of the day's events. The kids were allocating their news van to cover the Muslim demonstration in town.

"Now, I don't know who you think you are, but you should leave," Tina continued as she crossed her arms. The other kids were forming a line behind their leader.

Samantha spent a moment thinking that these kids were a bit slow on the uptake, but then it dawned on her that she was still in disguise. With a rueful smile to herself, she took off her sunglasses and wig. She shook out her blonde hair and let it fall over her shoulders. Six jaws dropped and six pairs of eyes widened. One guy did double-takes as he looked at her and the monitors behind him.

"My name is Samantha Ramsell, and I need your help—" she began.

* * *

Hanson rechecked the screen to make sure he had it right.

The navigation app hadn't led him straight to Tranquil Groves. It had instead placed him at a warehouse fifty yards from the cemetery's outer east wall. Hanson had circled the building's chain-linked outer perimeter before finally parking in view of the gate, which was a section of fence that rolled to the side. A large yellow "Caution" sign was posted on it. He studied the building on his left, the map in front of him, and the cemetery in the distance on his right. Blackbourne's navigation app only made sense if one more thing was factored in.

A tunnel. That would help explain how the thugs could move in and out of Tranquil Groves without being seen. Regular traffic at the warehouse would mask their comings and goings.

The warehouse itself was a sprawling, unassuming building with few windows. Loading docks with large doors girdled it.

It was also quiet. In the past five minutes, Hanson hadn't seen a soul inside the perimeter.

He glanced at the gate again. A metal post with a yellow box was placed on the left side. The box had a keypad and a slot.

Hanson reached up and rubbed the gold card in his jacket pocket. His ticket in.

He hesitated though as he stared at the chain links and the aptly worded caution sign. To him, it wasn't just a gate.

It was the point of no return.

Hanson picked up his phone and dialed a familiar number. She answered on the first ring.

"Dad!"

"Hi, sweetie, I'm just calling to see how you are doing," Hanson said.

"I'm fine. But we're all going crazy; the whole world is going crazy because no one has heard from you."

"I know, the Homeland agents are keeping a lid on me. It's almost over though. Once they complete their investigation, I'll be free to talk. But right now, that's not important. I just want to hear what you've been up to."

She obliged, and she gushed about the press surrounding the house and her social media spinning out of control. Hanson put her on speaker and closed his eyes so that that the sound of her voice washed over him as images of her growing up played through his memory.

She kept talking, and his mind drifted back further to a day when it had been him who spoke. Carrying on about everyday things, not realizing how close to the end his father was.

Hanson opened his eyes and stared at the gate. Time. So little of it, and so much to say. At that moment, he understood his father more than he had ever before.

"When will you be home, Dad?" El finished.

"Soon," he answered. "I just wanted to call and tell you that I love you."

"I love you too, Dad."

"And Elanor—" Hanson paused as he searched for the right words.

"Yes, Dad?"

"Be good for your mother."

"I will," she replied cheerfully. "Bye, Dad."

"Goodbye, sweetheart."

Hanson tapped the button that hung up the phone. Without her voice, it seemed unnaturally quiet in the car. Then he put the Mercedes into drive and approached the gate. No one challenged him. He slid the gold card into the slot. A green light snapped on, and he heard the squeak of oil craving pulleys as the gate slid open.

"You have reached your destination," the thug phone announced.

Hanson retrieved the card and drove in.

Chapter 46

Hanson kept his right hand on the shotgun as he drove through the lot. No one emerged from the main warehouse to challenge him.

He pulled up to a garage door that was large enough for a semi. As the gate, it had a yellow box with a keypad—but no card slot.

As Hanson pondered the keypad, the door started to open on its own.

He brought up the shotgun as his heart pounded in his chest. For a wild moment, he imagined thugs pouring forth and reaching into the car to pull him out and hold him down as a *rumal* was wrapped around his neck.

Fortunately, only quiet darkness waited for him.

Hanson took a few deep breaths and glanced at the gold card. It had an RFID chip built in. The active reader in the yellow box had detected it in the car.

He eased into the building, and the garage door rumbled down behind him. Hanson looked over the main floor as his eyes adjusted to the dim light.

Instead of wares loaded on pallets, the building was filled with hundreds of carefully parked vehicles. Judging by their license plates, it appeared that most of the lower forty-eight states were represented.

Hanson weaved around them as he drove toward an office area was in the building's northwest corner. He pulled into an empty space near the door. Still, no one challenged him.

But cameras were still an issue. Hanson realized that he had to act like he knew what he was doing if he wished to pass himself off as Blackbourne to any observers. He quickly got out of the car, pausing only long enough to sling the sword over his shoulder, hang the baton at his belt, and grab the shotgun. He then walked straight for the office door and let himself in without breaking his stride.

The place was empty. Though welcome, the lack of security was beginning to unnerve him. It didn't make any sense.

The desks had computers, in-and-out boxes, and large calendars with notations scribbled on them. The walls held rows of clipboards.

One panel was bare. Hanson walked to it and rubbed his right shoulder for luck. He then held the gold card over its surface and swept it up and down.

A five-foot section of the wall moved inward six inches with a quiet *snick*. It then rolled to the left to reveal an elevator door and a stairwell.

Hanson rode the elevator down. It opened into a large room with sterile white walls and fluorescent lighting. Thick gray paint covered the cement floor. Across from the elevator the cavernous mouth of the tunnel yawned open, and it stretched into darkness. Cool air issued from it.

To the right were eight posts with thick power cords running out of them. Parked in front of one of the pillars was a small green vehicle. Hanson recognized it as a Gator, a small utility flatbed. It was parked haphazardly, as if someone had been in a rush to get somewhere.

Blackbourne, on his way to kill him.

Hanson powered it up and flipped on its lights as he entered the tunnel.

The underground road was lit by bulbs in protective cages. Even with that, it was dark down here. Hanson could see why Blackbourne carried a flashlight.

It was a spooky drive. Hanson was keenly aware that he was driving under the cemetery, and that corpse-filled caskets were suspended in the earth above his head. His mind entertained the possibility of a cave-in of coffins trapping him with their grisly contents.

After what felt like forever, the tunnel brightened. It opened into a room that was a mirror of what was below the warehouse, only it had seven Gators parked and plugged in. An eighth bay was empty. Hanson pulled into it and got out. There was a stairwell door and elevator set in the far wall, and he made his way toward that. As he neared it, a blinking light grabbed his attention. Something was attached to the wall near the elevator button panel.

A bomb.

It was a brick of C4. A complex array of wires shrouded the explosive, some of which were connected to a bulb with mercury pooled inside of it. More wires were connected to a motion detector that was pointed toward the parking area.

Hanson froze. The motion detector's LED was blinking in acknowledgment of his presence, but his approach hadn't set it off. With a small measure of relief, he reasoned it wasn't armed yet.

But it was trapped. Hanson recalled the text message on the thug phone. *Secure the temple.* Blackbourne must have had two jobs when he left Tranquil Groves. One was to kill him. The other to rig this bomb so that it would explode if anyone used the elevator or stairwell.

But only after Blackbourne had returned. He had meant himself to be the last person to use the tunnel.

Hanson held his breath as he entered the elevator. He heard something click from within the bomb's housing. It was armed.

No going back now. When he had the chance, he would call Samantha. She would have to warn Fisher about the bomb. Hanson didn't want any first responders walking into this trap.

The ride was faster than the one at the warehouse. He had gone up only a short way, so he was still underground. The doors opened, and Hanson darted out of the elevator, shotgun up, hoping to take anyone present by surprise.

The small landing was empty. In the far-left corner was a hallway. A large, beige-colored door at least eight feet tall and half as wide loomed in front of him. To Hanson, the door's size and shape were familiar. He opened it and found what he had expected.

A computer server room.

The hum of equipment and air conditioners filled the area. The room held four rows of server racks. The setup was larger than the one he looked after back at Cosgroves, and their equipment was the latest and best that money could buy. Hanson found himself feeling a little envious.

He made sure no thugs were lurking in the area's dark corners before he advanced into the next half of the room.

Dozens of large monitors were affixed to the walls in here. Smaller screens rested on the counter in front of keyboards. Hanson counted five stations, each one cluttered with an assortment of papers and pens for jotting down notes.

Though no one was in the room, all the monitors were on, and each one displayed the same screen saver.

It was a black background with a woman's face slowly bouncing off the screen's four sides. There was no outline or hair depicted, only her features. Her eyes were red and half-lidded in a menacing glare, and they roved back and forth as if searching the room. The barest hint of a nose could be detected. From a fanged open mouth, a long red tongue writhed.

Unnerved by the leering faces, Hanson crept into the room. The face directly in front of him froze in place, and its eyes locked on him.

"Hello, Mr. Blackbourne," a woman's voice greeted from a nearby speaker.

Startled, Hanson looked behind him to see if anyone else had heard the sound. He was alone, but he now noticed something on the end of each server rack as he glanced back.

Yellowing pieces of paper with writing. The thugs had assigned computer terms to each rack, labels to keep the equipment organized. Hanson read through them.

Kernal. Algorithm. Library. Internet. Each was followed by the short phrase "version two" in smaller font size.

The capitalization of each word was not lost on Hanson. The thug ITs had cobbled together their own acronym for the computer system they had created. Hanson turned back to regard the face gazing at him from the computer screen.

KALI 2.0.

Chapter 47

"May I help you, Mr. Blackbourne?" Kali repeated. Her voice was coming out of a small black cylinder that had a red ring of light pulsing at the top. Several RFID active sensor pads were placed about the room. That was how the computer system knew he was present. The card also acted like a password.

Hanson sat down at a terminal and tapped the space bar. Kali's face was replaced by the computer's desktop screen, a pleasant image of a river winding through the countryside. The Ganges? A dozen icons filled the monitor's left side.

Hanson looked over his shoulder, paranoid that someone was sneaking up on him with a *rumal* in hand. No one was there. Hanson's shoulders sagged as he relaxed a bit. Being on constant alert against a thug sneak attack was wearing him down.

Time to fix that.

"Kali, display a map of the building and underground chambers," Hanson commanded.

"Understood."

Damn, her face might be spooky, but her voice was seductive. It was an alluring combination of power with a sultry sexiness that somehow seized at his brain. He found it soothing, and he felt like he could listen to it all day.

His reverie was interrupted as a three-dimensional map flashed up on the screen. It depicted the upper mausoleum in blue, the thuggee lower levels a pale silver. Some rooms were outlined in gold. The underground complex was more extensive than he had imagined. But getting the place's layout wasn't his primary concern.

"Kali, display the locations of everyone present."

"Understood."

Small rectangles popped up on the screen. Almost all were silver in color, though a few were gold. It was what he had hoped for.

The rectangles represented the pass cards. Hanson found his, a solitary gold marker in the computer room at the edge of the map. That was a relief—no one was sneaking up on him. Three other gold cards were in a room a level above labeled as the "Vault." Another gold marker was several levels below the vault in a vast room marked "Temple." Two more were upstairs in the building proper, in the Oak Room.

Along with hundreds of silver cards.

That explained why he hadn't seen anyone since arriving. All the rank-and-file thugs were located inside of Tranquil Grove's largest funeral parlor to participate in the day's events.

Most of them. Hanson noted that four silvers were roaming the halls upstairs. One more was even positioned up in the bell tower.

"Kali, show me the camera feed from the room labeled as "Vault" on monitor four."

"There are no surveillance cameras in inner sanctum areas."

Hanson frowned. He would have liked to see what was going on in there. He glanced at the map again. Both the Vault and Temple were outlined in gold, as were a network of hallways. Hanson guessed that only someone with a gold card could access those areas.

"Kali, show me the Oak Room."

The screen next to him shifted to reveal the Oak Room. It was as Hanson remembered it.

Except now, every seat had a thug in it. Some were even standing against the walls. Roughly two-fifths of them were Indian. Another two-fifths were Caucasian. The remaining were Chinese.

All were men. The threshold for age seemed to be eighteen; otherwise, the thugs came in all ages, shapes, and sizes. Some were old enough to be using canes and walkers. All were dressed casually, though they did share one common feature of attire. *Rumals*, be it scarf or necktie, were draped back around their necks and over their shoulders.

Two men worked the crowd. They were dressed in yellow and white robes, their *rumals* tied like sashes around their waists.

The stage was different also. A large, wooden altar rested in its center. The huge display screen was turned on, and a slideshow was playing on it. Some of the thugs were pointing at what they were viewing while others laughed and clapped. Hanson focused on what had them all excited.

His blood turned to ice.

The slideshow was a parade of thug victims. The images repeatedly showed the same location—a large chamber tiled like a high school locker room. Drains were on the floor, and a lone shower head on a hose was clipped to the wall. In between the drains was a stainless-steel dais. It was over ten feet in diameter and one foot high.

On top of the metal platform were thugs holding up their mutilated victims much in the same style that hunters did when taking photographs of their kills.

And that wasn't the worst of it.

Hanson also noted that some of the kills had been documented in a "before and after" style. The before photographs were of three thugs holding down live victims of Kali. Terror could be seen on the victims' faces, who were as varied as the thugs themselves.

Then the "after" photos cycled through.

The victims were now dead, and their eyes had been gouged out. The limbs were broken at the joints, and the bellies were slit open. Entrails oozed out and onto the dais. The heads had to be held up by the center thug as he showed off his trophy.

Hanson realized this was the "Numbers" part of the afternoon, an accounting of all the victims they had taken for Kali.

He could see the passage of time in the photos. Some were scans of Polaroids from several decades ago. The more recent were digital.

Judging by the *bhurtote's* ages, only the first kills were displayed in the before-and-after style. Subsequent kills were performed outside the building, the corpses being displayed for their photo op before being taken to the cremation chamber.

"Kali, is there a file labeled 'Numbers'?"

"Yes."

"Copy it to my desktop."

"Working."

A new icon appeared on the monitor, and Hanson opened it. It was a file of JPEGs. A number in the corner listed how many individual victims were depicted.

Five thousand four hundred nineteen. Well over what Hanson expected.

The file had three groupings. First was an archive of deceased thugs, who they were, and their murdering achievements. Next were the rank-and-file thugs that were still alive, a little over five hundred individuals.

The third group was only seven men. The gold-card-carrying thugs. Their file had a title.

Sath Zut.

The legendary seven great families that had founded thuggee after their expulsion out of Delhi. Pravnev must have patterned his upper management team after them.

There were folders inside the *Sath Zut* file, and they were arranged by name.

Blackbourne.

Scratch that one, Hanson thought with satisfaction.

Chancellor. That name was familiar. It was mentioned in Cresswell's letter. Chancellor was the commander of the Madras base in the village of Gurnah.

Captain Cresswell never had a chance.

Other names followed. Dasgupta, Liang, Mukherjee, Vankatesan, and Zhang.

Hanson clicked on the Vankatesan folder. Several rows of thumbnails appeared. On the monitor with the map, a gold icon began pulsing.

Vankatesan was in the vault.

Hanson turned back to the thumbnails and browsed through them. They all showed Vankatesan holding up the faces of eyeless corpses.

The last image showed a young Vankatesan propping up the head of his first kill as he smiled broadly. Hanson then understood why there were over five thousand kills in the photo files instead of two thousand.

Some thugs enjoyed killing to the point that they did it for pleasure, knowing that Kali would forgive their murders.

Numbed by the scenes of death, Hanson turned away. Needing some sort of distraction, his eyes settled on a sheaf of papers covered with dollar symbols. He began to read them.

It was a spreadsheet, a hard copy for the *chutaw*, or division of the loot. The papers were a list of all the thugs and the money they were to receive before everyone went their separate ways.

Hanson flipped through the pages. They revealed a simple formula— the more kills a thug had, the greater the reward. Hanson amended his earlier conclusion. Some of the thugs weren't just murdering for sport— they were killing for the money.

The total was tabulated on the last page. Hanson whistled aloud when he read it.

Thuggee incorporated was worth over ten billion.

"Kali, show me the money."

"Bank account access is currently open and thus blocked by terminal six."

Hanson's eyes darted around the room, and his hand went for the shotgun. He half expected to find a thug nearby at a keyboard.

"Kali, show me the location of terminal six."

On the map monitor the gold marker in the temple began pulsing.

Someone had a workstation down there.

"Kali, show me the records on how money was distributed in the past."

A spreadsheet appeared on the screen. It revealed that every thug was set up to appear as if they had a trust fund through an inheritance.

How did they maintain that ruse?

"Kali, show me a list of all thug members. Arrange by vocations."

A new form appeared on the screen. Computer programmers headed the list at more than one hundred thugs.

The second was financials. Thugs held key spots in banks, Wall Street, and even the IRS. That's how they hid the money. Thugs were positioned to keep their cache secret.

Hanson scanned the list for a specific job title and location.

What he was looking for wound up being one of the *Sath Zuts*. Abraham Chancellor, Sheriff of forty years in the Dallas-Fort Worth area.

Gotcha.

Hanson pulled the thumb drive out of his pocket and plugged it in. He spent the next few minutes dragging as many files as he could into the device. One other file stood out. *Khomusna.* It contained information on thuggee contingency plans. Hanson's heart chilled. They were prepared to melt down a nuclear power plant if need be.

He finished up by saving business information from Tranquil Groves itself and then retrieved the flash drive. Downloading the thug's files had taken some time, and he glanced at the monitor's bottom right corner.

It read 12:44 p.m. Fisher should be landing anytime now.

He looked at the time again. Something was wrong. Usually, the date was displayed directly below the time. However, on this monitor, the date had been replaced by a countdown timer. It read 4:15:52.

4:15:51.

4:15:50.

"Kali, what is the purpose of the countdown timer displayed?"

"That is time left until structure immolation."

"As in sacrifice?"

"No, that is the primary definition of the word. In this case, it is the secondary definition, to destroy by fire."

"How will this be achieved?"

Dots appeared on the map. They were lightly scattered throughout the main structure, more densely packed in the inner core area. There were several dozen in all. One dot was in the computer room next to his icon.

Hanson searched, and he found what he was looking for under a desk.

Another C4 bomb. Though it was different than the one on the elevator. It had a battery-powered router attached to it and did not possess a mercury switch.

"Jesus fucking Christ," Hanson muttered.

Cresswell's report had noted that Pravnev had burned his temple to the ground to cover his tracks. The same thing was happening now. Only the thugs weren't taking any chances with the massive stone building they were hiding in.

At the stroke of five, they planned on blowing up Tranquil Groves to kingdom come.

Chapter 48

Samantha held up her phone so that everyone in the news studio was included in the video conference.

"We're up and running over here," she announced. "The engineering crew is ready to receive the transmission from the Oak Room and relay it to New York."

Six heads nodded enthusiastically behind her.

Hanson grinned. "Good. Just don't announce your intentions until the last minute though. Watkins might send local agents to shut you down."

"Steve, when Fisher arrives at police headquarters, he's going to need something to convince them. Can you make it to the control room and enable the feed to our console?"

"I don't have to," Hanson answered. "To protect themselves against any accidents, they locked out the Oak Room control station and routed it to a master terminal in their temple. I don't have to deal with five hundred thugs. There's only one down there."

"Good. What else have you found?"

Hanson gave a rundown of what he had discovered. As he was talking about the thugs' money holdings, Diego, the news crews engineer, spoke up.

"Ten billion? How did they get so much money?" he asked.

"I've been looking into that," Hanson answered. "They had a lot of wealth to begin with from traditional thugging back in India. In England, they maintained an opium-smuggling triad up until World War II. After that, they switched to counterfeiting and real estate fraud, though those were the lean years. The thugs didn't really hit their stride again until the invention of the internet."

"So, you're saying—" Samantha began.

"They're hackers," Hanson finished.

"Like coding experts?" Tina asked.

"No, they're thugs, deceivers," Hanson explained. "Hollywood has hacking wrong. Everyone thinks it's some kid at a keyboard, saying things like 'What we need is in a Pentagon computer!' Then she types away for three seconds and yells 'I'm in!'"

Behind Samantha, all six kids nodded again.

"But hacking isn't like that. It's really the use of deception to trick information out of someone, like an email saying you've come into some money, but first send your bank account information so that you can receive it. Or click on the 'attachment.'"

"I've heard of that," Samantha added. "Hackers have been using these tricks for decades. They call it social engineering."

"With thugs, it's been called inveigling for the past three centuries," Hanson continued. "And it looks like they're experiencing a golden age right now. They're stealing hundreds of millions from third-world banks. They have people in software security firms planting flaws like the 'Heartbleed' bug into basic systems and exploiting them. They extort money on a national level with their ransomware programs, such as that computer attack on the gas pipeline. They have hundreds of connections deep in the dark web, where they use cryptocurrency to deal in illicit transactions, such as selling credit card numbers."

Hanson glanced to another screen at his side and spoke at it.

"Kali, save file marked as *Lopee Hona*," he commanded.

The thug's computer system answered with a sultry "Understood."

"Thanks, Kali," Hanson responded politely.

Samantha frowned. "Do you two need to get a room? Why did the thugs make the computer's voice so sexy?"

"Sexy? Really? I...umm...didn't notice."

Hanson's face was beet red on her screen as he shifted around in his chair. Samantha rolled her eyes and changed the subject to keep him focused.

"What's *Lopee Hona?*" she asked.

"I just saved their secret links to websites on the dark web," Hanson answered, appearing glad to be talking about something else. "*Lopee Hona* means 'to conceal.' I'm putting everything I can find here on my thumb drive."

"Is hacking and record keeping all that Kali does?" Samantha asked.

"No, she's also programmed with a robust search engine," Hanson answered. "It's designed to take a person's name and find everything it can about them. Then, with thugs in key positions across the states, it can access bank, police, DMV, even IRS databases. It then links up with information for sale on the dark web and uses the password-breaking programs offered there."

"Why do they want someone's background information?"

"It's part of their victim selection process. There's two ways to go about it. The first is straightforward. Some thugs collect their kills by preying on the fringe of society, such as homeless people who won't be missed.

"But other thugs like a challenge. The whole inveigling thing with *sothas*. They look for victims on the internet and lure them into traps. Kali helps vet and choose them. Thugs who murder this way earn a higher percentage of the *chutaw*."

Samantha touched the wound around her neck as she remembered that night in the rain.

Kali has chosen her, Hanson! She belongs to us now.

"The FBI is going to have a field day with that computer," she said.

"They're not going to have a chance," Hanson revealed as he tilted his camera. Samantha's heart sank to her stomach as a brick of C4 filled the screen. The kids behind her murmured in shock and dismay.

"They're going to destroy their temple," Hanson continued. "The entire building is set to explode in a little over four hours."

"Steve, we have a saying here in the newsroom. You should've led with that!"

"Sorry."

"Can you stop it?"

"No, the program controlling it is password protected."

"What are you going to do next?"

"I'm going to get that camera feed for you. You just make sure Fisher shows up with the police. When the thugs realize that they are surrounded in a building set to explode, they will all give up and release their sacrificial hostages."

"Promise me you're coming out of there also," Samantha said as she gazed straight into the camera.

Hanson looked like he wanted to respond, but she could see his eyes trace an outline around her head. The six students looking eagerly on. Audiences weren't his thing. Instead, he gave her a small smile and tapped his earpiece to hang up the phone.

Chapter 49

Hat back on and shotgun in hand, Hanson explored the level he was on. He soon found himself in a kitchen area with several nearby dorm rooms.

One hall had six doors that were heavier and had locks. A cart parked near them had canisters of nitrous oxide and anesthetic gas. Some pill bottles were resting on it also. Hanson investigated the rooms. All had beds with straps on them, though they were empty and made up.

Hanson guessed the sacrificial victims had been held down here, sedated with the nearby drugs to control them. But now, these unfortunates were most likely being kept closer to the Oak Room in anticipation of the day's events.

He moved away and soon came upon a large, carpeted foyer. More paintings of old India adorned the space. It was paneled in sandalwood, which gave the room a fragrant smell. Multiple hallways led off from the room.

An elevator was nearby, and it had an RFID panel next to it. Near that was a large yellow door. Hanson had memorized key points on the building's map, so he knew what was behind the door before he opened it.

The *bele.*

The cold, tiled room depicted in the slideshow. A chamber of horrors designed to sluice away any gore left behind after the murder and ritual desecration of the corpses by thug initiates.

The room was more extensive than he expected. It was twenty feet wide but stretched almost seventy feet long.

It had two daises. One was near the door, the other at the far end of the room. Both stainless-steel platforms had hoses with water nozzles nearby. Several dozen jugs of bleach rested on shelves.

All the thugs' first kills were recorded here. Hanson reflected on that. Murder, in a state known for swift capital punishment. Was that the reason for their success at secrecy? Even if a thug felt regret, he wouldn't escape death himself for turning in his fellow thugs. Religion, and the fear of execution, was the glue that bound thugs together and kept them silent.

The room had a subtle smell of death and decay. Hanson backed out of it.

He moved back to the elevator door. The panel next to it was framed in real gold. Only the *Sath Zut* could open these doors.

Hanson waved his card and entered.

The car had doors on each end, each one having its own button.

The one closest to him was labeled "Vault," the opposite, "Temple."

It was time to give Vankatesan a surprise. Hanson rode the car up, the Mossberg held at the ready.

Another foyer awaited him. It also had hallways running off it—secret passages for the *Sath Zut's* use only.

The walls here were plated in silver. On them, a bas-relief of Kali in her battle with Raktabija was depicted. The pictorial narrative encircled the entire room. The final scene was of her handing two *rumals* to her recently created thugs. That segment was on the immense vault door itself, which was sheathed in gold and had semiprecious stones inset. Hanson gaped at the sheer wealth in the room.

His open-mouthed awe changed to a frown when he noticed a lack of RFID panels. Locks that looked like they required massive keys were placed below gold knobs. Hanson imagined Vankatesan and the other two thugs inside, pocketing gold and jewels for themselves.

They would have to wait.

Hanson stepped back into the elevator and pressed the button for the temple. He felt himself dropping down to the lowest level yet.

The elevator opened to a large, rectangular room with a towering, cathedral-like ceiling forty feet high. Four columns covered with dark tapestries stood near each corner. The floor and walls were sheathed with black, gold-veined marble.

A large, ebony conference table dominated the back half of the room. Seven top-grain leather executive chairs with gold nail-head trim were pulled up to it. A skull and several books rested on the table's dark surface.

The front half of the room looked like a temporary command center. A large, half-circular desk had been recently placed there. Six monitors, positioned in a two by three configuration, were resting on it. A keyboard and mouse were on the desk also, as was a small laptop, its screen dark. Sitting at the desk was a man who looked to be in his late thirties. He sported a thick beard and was wearing black-rimmed glasses.

The elevator's door was placed at the halfway point of a long wall, and it put Hanson slightly behind the thug at the desk, who was intent on the monitors in front of him. Though, since he had heard the elevator door open, he was slowly turning in his chair.

"How was it, Blackbourne? Did Hanson say anything—"

Hanson was on him before he could finish, the baton crackling as he applied it. The thug's body tensed and rocked on the chair.

"I told him he missed," Hanson answered as the thug slumped over.

A *rumal* rested on the desk next to a gold plate that held a small round wafer. Hanson grabbed it and tied the man's hands behind him in the chair. He then stretched the thug's feet under the chair so that he could tie them together with the *rumal's* other end. Satisfied that the guy was going nowhere, Hanson checked his prisoner's pockets, where he discovered a wallet and phone. A Texas driver's license listed him as

Luke Chancellor, and he possessed a gold card. Hanson rolled the chair with the unconscious man away from the console and replaced it with a fancier one from the conference table. He made himself comfortable as he studied the thug's desk arrangement.

The four monitors on the right were set to act as one large screen. It showed the stage of the funeral home's main auditorium. The murderous slide show was still playing for an enthusiastic audience.

He looked at the top left monitor. It was in a split-screen mode. Twelve different images were being supplied from multiple security cameras. Each small frame changed every 10 seconds. Hanson observed them for about a minute, noting that the images returned to the original feeds after four cycles. They had about fifty cameras watching the place, and for the first time, Hanson could see who was on guard duty.

It was the squad from Portland. Ravi, Todd, Bryce, and the nameless Indian who had the pickaxe could be seen roaming the halls. Kim was upstairs in the bell tower. He was hunkered down behind the tower's crenellations, catching some shade as he rubbed his lower jaw, which looked wired shut. On another screen, Ravi had two blackened eyes and a bandage across the bridge of his nose. Todd's right arm was in a sling. Not being allowed in the auditorium must have been some sort of punishment for them.

All were armed. Ravi and Kim had semiautomatic rifles with them. The others, since Hanson had damaged or removed hands, had pistols holstered at their sides. All had earbuds and were intent on their smartphones. Though they were being punished, they were allowed to watch the spectacle while on duty.

The final computer monitor had several windows opened. One displayed the control interface for the Oak Room's video booth. The last window depicted the slideshow itself. What the thugs were watching was being sent from here.

Satisfied that no more thugs were approaching, Hanson stood to remove Blackbourne's hat and jacket as he took better stock of the room.

The temple's front wall had a large, Indian-style archway at its center. A curtain of red velvet hung behind it. Above the arch was a thick ribbon of gold that formed the outline of a giant pickaxe. Several spotlights were focused on it. The entire piece of artwork was over twenty feet tall from top to bottom. Hanson figured it must have taken a million dollars' worth of the precious metal it contained to create it.

Its positioning reminded Hanson of how a cross would be displayed in a church.

He turned away and strode past the desk to explore the far side of the chamber. At the back wall, behind the conference table, was another dais, though this one was made of copper. The *Sath Zut* had their own *bele*, a place where their heirs apparent could commit their first murders.

Like father, like son.

He approached the conference table. In front of each chair was a large, ornate book. Hanson picked up one of them.

Thug bibles. Each of the seven families had its own volume.

At the end of the table was one other publication, a battered copy of the *Ramaseeana*.

Hanson turned back to the book in his hand. The familiar names of Old Testament books leaped out at him as he thumbed through it. Genesis, Exodus, and Numbers. Other sections were labeled with proper names as the first chapters of the New Testament, though the apostles listed were much different.

Feringeea. Rumzan. Futteh Khan. Berham.

Thugs with hundreds of murders to their names, now considered saints. Hanson flipped to Berham.

It read as fanciful conversations between the king of the thugs and Pravnev. Pravnev came across as a prophet of Kali, explaining that her discontent with mankind was growing. Only thugs following the one true path could avert her world-destroying wrath.

Hanson returned to the front half of the book. Revelation. Here Pravnev prophesized the end of the world unless the thugs escaped persecution in India and took the fight to the followers of the Abrahamic God in England.

Bot-timer's voice snapped him back to the present.

"Four hours," his phone announced.

Hanson had downloaded the app earlier and had used it to sync his phone's timer to the self-destruct countdown he discovered upstairs. At this point, the bot was alerting him every half hour.

He turned his attention to the skull.

It was yellow with age and missing its lower jaw. It rested on a small, gold pedestal, the top of which was cushioned with black velvet.

There was writing across the skull's forehead in black ink.

Vankatesan (HT 122/J36)

The name of the man the skull belonged to and its catalog number. Hanson was familiar with the skull's identifying markings, as he had read an article about it during his thug research. It had come from an extensive museum collection, though this one had belonged to a smaller subset. It thus had one more word written on it to set it apart from other skulls in the display it had come from.

THUG

One of Vankatesan's forefathers had been part of the Edinburgh collection. Phrenology, or the study of skulls to explain behavior, was all the rage back at the turn of the nineteenth century. Dr. Henry Spry, a member of the Bengal Medical Service, had witnessed the hanging of several thugs. Afterward, he secretly collected their heads and sent them to Great Britain for analysis. His hope was to find the variances in the skull's cavity that led thugs to kill.

The men in Edinburgh hadn't found anything conclusive, and the battle of nature vs. nurture raged on.

Hanson wondered how it came to rest here. Most likely, with all the money they had at their disposal, the thugs had simply bribed someone during their Great Britain years, and the skull disappeared from history.

Hanson glanced at the thug in the chair. He was just beginning to stir.

Looking that direction brought the archway back to Hanson's attention. In front of the red curtain was a braided gold-colored pull cord. Hanson walked over to it and pulled the line downward. The curtain smoothly parted to reveal what he expected.

It was a large statue that loomed above him. She looked like something dreamt up out of a colonial nightmare, a demonic goddess, both beautiful and terrible.

Despite himself, Hanson said her name out loud.

"Kali."

"Must be fed," the thug behind him finished.

Chapter 50

"Not if I can help it," Hanson replied as he turned back toward the thug.

"You are only one man."

"Maybe I came in here with an army of police officers in tow."

"I would have been aware of that."

"Because of your father, Abraham Chancellor? Who I guess is hanging out at police headquarters at this moment."

The smug look on young Chancellor's face fell a bit.

"Yes, I know about him," Hanson continued. "And he won't escape either. There's going to be a whole lot of suppressing going down soon."

"This place is impregnable."

"And also set to explode. I've counted two bombs in this room alone. I'm betting you guys break records on giving yourselves up when the police cut off your escape."

The thug went quiet at that, and Hanson turned back to study the statue. Traditional *murtis* depicted her as a light blue, voluptuous woman, her tongue hanging out a bit in regret and embarrassment.

Here she was envisioned as British colonizers had imagined her. Lithe, and with a darker skin tone. Her slender upper arms held two tulwars above her head. Her lower right hand grasped the curved blade of a khadga, the left a yellow *rumal*. The breasts were bare, though partially hidden by her unbridled black hair. She wore a tiger skin as a short skirt, her right leg bent at the knee since her right foot rested on a rock. A delicate ivory necklace of small skulls circled her neck. Her snarling, fanged mouth, long red tongue, and half-lidded eyes gave her face the visage of predatory triumph. A ruby bindi, representing Kali's third eye, decorated her forehead.

She was made of porcelain, her skin fired to a glossy dark blue. The statue was obviously a newer model, created to replace the wooden statue that Captain Cresswell had discovered back in the nineteenth century. The eyes and mouth of the improved Kali appeared as if they could be illuminated. Hanson looked behind her. The statue was wired, as was the alcove she was in.

Hanson glanced up. It was more than that. The small space that she occupied was really the bottom of a shaft that stretched into the darkness above him. Red plastic, which could be lit from behind, sheathed it. Kali's platform was a lift, designed so that she could ascend to the location where the sacrifice was to be held—the Oak Room.

Hanson backed out of the alcove and looked up at Kali's arms to study the one feature that truly stood out with the statue.

The diamonds.

They were huge, the size of small eggs. They were shaped like a drop of water, and they hung from Kali's upper elbows. Each were held in place by platinum pendants that delicately outlined their shape. They glittered in the light of the room. Hanson stared at them, transfixed.

"We call them *The Sweat of Kali*, Hanson," Chancellor explained from behind him. "Have you not seen anything more beautiful? Both are flawless, white diamonds. The right measures 102.3 carats, the left 101.97."

"Where did they come from?"

"Three centuries ago, Kali placed her mark on a jewel carrier. The omens were perfect that day, and a Vankatesan strangled him. These two jewels were the only items on the man's body. A gift, from her!"

"The diamonds have been recut and polished since then," Chancellor continued. "They have been privately appraised at over twenty million dollars each."

A lot of bling, Hanson thought as he tore his eyes from the diamonds. He returned to the desk to study the video controls. They looked complicated. As he reached for his phone to call Samantha for some help, his gaze rested on the timer on the screen's lower corner.

2:45:14.

2:45:13

Hanson sat up straighter in his chair with alarm. He called up the Bot-timer app on his phone.

3:45:03

"Something wrong?" Chancellor asked.

"I'm off by an hour," Hanson muttered, confused.

"Understandable," Chancellor replied with contempt in his voice. "This must be a lot for a recluse such as yourself, hiding behind the same four walls day after day—"

"Shut up," Hanson snapped.

"It's easy to picture you being overwhelmed, making mistakes—"

"I said shut up!" Hanson snarled as he spun in his chair and brandished the baton.

The thug smiled and shrugged his shoulders.

Hanson took a few moments to adjust the time on his cell.

"Two hours forty-three minutes," Bot-timer announced.

"You're running out of time," Chancellor noted.

"I won't need it," Hanson retorted. "My guy is arriving at the police station at any moment. And when the police get here, how are you going to stop them? With *rumals*? I've only counted five guns in this place."

"You think so?" Chancellor sneered. "We spent the night moving our weapons to the ground level, just in case."

"What weapons?" Hanson asked as his heart turned cold. *That didn't sound good.*

Chancellor glanced toward the elevator.

There was the outline of another door next to it. Hanson walked over. It had no knob, but it opened with a simple push.

The room beyond was an armory. Empty shelves lined the walls, and racks took up the center. The shelves were labeled. The C4 had been stored here. On a table at the far end of the room rested a laptop computer and cell phone. It was the same setup that Ganesh had used. The computer bombs were manufactured here and not at the homes of the supposed terrorists, as Watkins had thought.

A laminated card was next to the computer with instructions on how to use it. The thugs made their bombs user-friendly.

There was a large, almost empty gun rack in the middle of the room. Three rifles, and a carelessly forgotten box of ammo on the floor, let Hanson know what had been stored here.

AR-15s.

High-powered semi-automatic rifles. Their magazines held thirty rounds. The thugs must have spent years amassing everything. And now they were cached somewhere upstairs.

Hanson rejoined Chancellor in the temple, checking his bonds yet again before settling back down at the desk.

He took a picture of the video control screen and sent it to Samantha, along with the message: "Which button?"

That done, Hanson's attention turned to the laptop sitting off to one side. Though it was powered on, its screen was dark. He reached for it.

"What was that message you sent?" Chancellor asked worriedly.

"We're going to steal your video feed in the Oak Room and transmit it to the police station."

Hanson's phone chimed. The image that he had sent had returned to him, the difference being one of the buttons was circled in red. Hanson grabbed the mouse and moved the cursor so that he could left click the button.

Two words appeared in the upper right corner.

On Air.

Now it was up to Samantha and Fisher.

Hanson placed his phone back on the desk, resting it next to the gold plate that contained a small, white disk. It looked like a sacramental wafer; the kind given out in church.

Curious, Hanson picked it up and nibbled on it. It was sweet, as if it were made of pure sugar.

Goor.

The sacrificial food of the thugs, to be consumed during the *tuponee*. Feringeea himself had noted that to taste the *goor* was to be a thug for life.

Pravnev must have changed it to wafer form to get his former Christian allies to accept it all those years ago.

Hanson spat it out and wiped his tongue with his hands. A bottle of water was nearby. He grabbed that and took a long drink.

"Too late," Chancellor said, his lips curled up in a smirk.

"Five-second rule," Hanson replied as he ran his forearm across his face.

"Doesn't apply to *goor*," Chancellor continued. "No other occupation will satisfy you now, Hanson. Even if you live a thousand years, thuggee will still call out to you."

Hanson didn't respond. He took another drink.

"I will be your guru, Hanson," Chancellor said as he gazed at the statue beyond Hanson. "*Oh Kali, Kunkali, Bhudkalee. Oh Kali, Mahakali, Dallas Walee!*"

Alarmed, Hanson spat out the water he was drinking in a spray. Then he grabbed up the baton as he stood up.

"Stop it!" Hanson yelled. "Don't say the words!"

"It's already done," the thug replied with a leer. "And when you bound me, you had your hands on my *rumal*, which had the thug classic knot, the *Goor Ghat*, tied into it. So, you're one of us now, Hanson."

Hanson switched on the prod and gave the thug a few shocks. Chancellor quivered for a few moments before he slumped in his chair.

"We'll see about that," Hanson said.

He returned to the desk to continue his hunt for incriminating evidence to save for Fisher.

"Join us," Chancellor groaned behind him.

Jesus, these guys never stop talking, Hanson thought as he turned halfway around.

He stopped.

This was the second time that the thug had distracted him away from the desk since he had arrived. There was something nearby that the thug didn't want him to see.

The only thing that remained was the laptop, its screen dark.

Hanson rubbed a finger across the mouse pad.

The screen flickered as the computer awoke from its sleep mode. It was on a website, but that was obscured by another panel with a message on it.

Your session will time out in 22 seconds. Press any key to continue.

Hanson tapped the space bar. The panel disappeared, and the page behind it was revealed.

It was a website for an offshore bank. An untraceable financial stronghold where the thugs had consolidated their wealth for the upcoming *chutaw*. The spreadsheet he had studied upstairs was a hard-copy of the information he was now viewing on the screen.

Hanson leaned closer and squinted at the monitor. Something was wrong.

The accounts for the rank-and-file thugs were cleared out. Where there once had been millions of dollars were now zeros. Five hundred thugs were now bankrupt.

But not the *Sath Zut*. Their accounts were swollen with what had been taken from the others. Numbers that ranged in the billions.

Now everything that he had experienced this afternoon made sense. Why they had spared only one man to kill him. Why all the thugs were placed in one room to the detriment of security. The difference between the countdown timer upstairs and the *Sath Zut's* timer in the temple.

Hanson slowly spun around in his chair and faced the thug now glaring at him.

"*Bhans lena,*" Hanson said.

Chapter 51

"It's a double-cross," Hanson continued.

Chancellor didn't respond.

"*Bhans lena,* to defraud other thugs during the division of the loot," Hanson elaborated. "While all the rank-and-file thugs are upstairs celebrating their supposed newfound wealth, the *Sath Zut* are sneaking out the back door right before the bombs go off a full hour ahead of time."

Chancellor's chair now shook as he strained against his bonds.

"Because why be millionaires when you could be billionaires—"

"Enough!" Chancellor shouted. "Hanson, Blackbourne is dead. Change his name to yours. All his money could belong to you. If you turn it in as evidence, the government will keep it."

Now it was Hanson's turn to remain quiet.

"Over one billion dollars, Hanson. Think of what you could do with that."

"I have. Five thousand dead by your hands," Hanson replied as he turned back to the laptop. "A lot of families could use that money."

He followed Chancellor's advice and changed Blackbourne's name to his. He entered more relevant information when the program prompted him to.

Then, since the page had been set up for this very purpose, he clicked on the thugs' boxes that showed their billions and simply dragged the thugs' wealth into his account.

In less than a minute, Hanson's net worth grew to ten billion.

He attached his flash drive to the laptop and transferred as much information as he could pertaining to the account, including how to access it. There was an option to change the password.

The website required a complicated one, at least ten characters long. A capital letter, number, and symbol had to be part of it.

Without hesitating, Hanson typed in something he could easily remember and then confirmed it in the second box.

The thugs were now locked out from their loot.

"Those Fortune 500 guys were right," Hanson said as he held up the flash drive up in front of Chancellor. "The first billion is the hardest."

"As Kali is my witness, you will die for this, Hanson."

"And throw me into your crematorium? I don't think so."

"Crematorium?" Chancellor asked, his eyebrows knitted in confusion.

"We've figured it out," Hanson explained. "You thugs dispose of all the bodies here."

The thug appeared thoughtful for a moment.

"You're only half right, Hanson," Chancellor whispered as his gaze shifted to over Hanson's left shoulder.

Hanson jumped up and spun around.

No one was sneaking up on him. But his gaze was drawn to where the thug had glanced at.

"The cremation grounds are Kali's home," the thug continued behind him. "But she is voracious god, Hanson. Did you think that we would offer her only ashes?"

The only thing within the thug's view was a support column that stretched from floor to ceiling. Hanson slowly walked over to it.

Chancellor kept on talking. "Blood is her food. And though she may not consume it right away, we have saved it for her."

The heavy, dark tapestries girdling the column were more than that. They were curtains. There was a seam in the middle of them, where they could be separated. His heart pounding with trepidation, Hanson reached for it.

"We saved all of it, Hanson—"

He parted the curtain.

The gray, eyeless face of a corpse stared back at him, its mouth open in a silent scream. Hanson was so close to it he could count the fillings in its teeth. With a gasp of fear and revulsion, he stumbled back.

Chancellor shouted out a command.

"*Gobba Kanthuna!*"

The words briefly registered with Hanson. *Gobba*, for grave. *Kanthuna*. The bodies, prepared for internment.

The column was thirty feet high, as was its match sixty feet to Hanson's left. Both had three sets of ten-foot-tall black curtains, and as in a theater, they parted.

Hanson reeled from the sight.

The columns were made of acrylic glass and rose like huge, clear pipes from the floor. Ten feet in diameter, they reminded Hanson of the tubes that people could walk through at huge aquariums. Though these weren't filled with gawking tourists.

They held corpses.

He had been wrong. The thugs weren't cremating the murder victims to destroy the evidence of their crimes. Instead, they were doing as they had when the British had discovered thuggee. They were tossing the bodies down wells.

There were thousands of corpses present. They were preserved in some sort of embalming fluid and showed little decay, though Hanson could tell the passage of time with them. The decades-old corpses at the bottom were a dark gray. That lightened halfway up the tube, with the bodies at the top retaining their original hues.

All had their bellies ripped open. Internal organs shared space with faces twisted in eternal torment.

He stumbled back, trying to get away from the ghastly sight. The desk stopped him, and he sagged against it.

"The work of decades, Hanson," the thug explained with awe in his voice.

"Close it," Hanson begged.

"I can't," Chancellor replied. "The opening of the curtains is part of a ceremony. They only close when a body has been added to a well."

Hanson looked to the elevator as he did measurements in his head. The tubes corresponded to the stainless-steel daises upstairs. The stainless-steel platforms were also covers for the death pits.

Hanson moved back around the desk.

"We can't be stopped, Hanson. We've been doing this for centuries."

Hanson glanced at the screen that showed cheering thugs.

"Thuggee will be born again. Vankatesan will make sure of that."

Hanson faced the thug, his face grim.

"I don't think so. Let's show him by sending a message."

Hanson gave the thug another series of shocks. He then rummaged in the desk and found some paper and a marker.

Chancellor remained motionless in his chair. Hanson fished out the measuring tape he had in his pocket and formed a loop with a slip knot. He placed it around the thug's head like a headband and pulled it tight.

Satisfied with that, he found some scissors and cut Chancellor's *rumal* in half. His hands and feet were still bound, but now Hanson could drag him out of his chair and lay him out on the ground. He wrote out a message and placed it next to the thug's head.

Hanson took a photograph with his cell phone camera.

Pleased with the result, Hanson crafted an email that he would later send to Vankatesan. At his feet, the thug began to stir and strain against his bonds. Hanson went back to the desk and returned with the shotgun in hand.

"What are you going to do with me?" Chancellor groaned.

Hanson paused. He couldn't kill the man in cold blood. They were both near the large conference table. Hanson examined the sides of the room, searching for a closet with heavy doors. Except for the armory, there was nothing else that fit the bill. He skirted along the rim of the room's copper-covered *gobba* as he explored the very back of the room in hope of finding something there. Nothing. He thought about the cell-like dorms upstairs.

"I'm going to take you—"

"Gobba khom!" the thug yelled.

Powered by hydraulic rams, the copper hatch sprang open. It slammed into Hanson and knocked the shotgun out of his hands.

The cover was voice-activated, like the curtains—*Khom,* the thug word for door.

With a shout, the thug had opened a pit reserved for the dead.

Hanson was standing on the very edge of it, his arm aching from the lid's impact. An inset spotlight above the pit had turned on to illuminate what was below. He instinctively looked down. He wished he hadn't.

It was the same as the columns, a scene out of a nightmare. The bodies were about fifteen feet below him, decay held back by a thin layer of formaldehyde—a charnel pit of eyeless, eviscerated victims with broken limbs that held impossible poses. Internal organs blanketed half of them.

As horrific as the view was, the smell was even worse. It hit Hanson like a physical thing. Putrefaction laced with choking chemicals. It filled the room and chased oxygen away. He felt lightheaded, and he swayed at the edge as his legs almost buckled under him.

He caught movement out of the corner of his eye. Chancellor was free of his bonds and was rushing at him, a knife in his hand, the measuring tape still around his head like a headband. Hanson stumbled along the edge as he backed up and cast about for the shotgun. The thug followed him, slashing.

Chancellor was a *kurthow,* his knife most likely hidden in his boot. He had waited for the right moment to use it.

Hanson tried to move away from the pit. Chancellor blocked him with jabs with his blade.

Chancellor was being conservative with the knife. Hanson counted several times in which he could have stabbed him. The thug wasn't trying to kill him.

He was trying to herd him into the pit.

The banking password. Ten billion dollars would be lost if Hanson died. But that money could be recovered when he begged for his life amongst the corpses he was trapped with.

The thug whirled and slashed. His spinning motion caused the tail end of the measuring tape to flutter toward Hanson.

Hanson grabbed it and jerked down. The tape, still wrapped around the thug's head, slid down over his eyes. Blinded, Chancellor clawed at it and pulled it down to his neck.

Hanson used the moment to knock the blade away. It gashed his arm as it fell into the pit, lost in the viscera below.

Chancellor's eyes followed the knife's plunge. Hanson again took advantage and hit him with a quick punch. The thug leaned back over the pit, his arms windmilling as he teetered on the edge.

Hanson braced himself as he held the measuring tape firmly.

The noose, still tied in a slip knot, tightened. Chancellor's hands flew to his neck as he tried to relieve the choking pressure.

The two men remained close to each other as they maintained their precarious balance. Chancellor was teetering at the pit's edge, his body leaning over empty space. Hanson's grip on the tape kept him from falling in.

The thug forced some more fingers under the strangling tape.

"Don't let me fall," the thug gasped.

"Give me a reason."

"We are only Kali's instruments—"

"Careful asshole," Hanson replied as he glanced at the tape in his hands. He let some of it slide through his fingers. "Your life is literally measured in inches right now." He grunted at the shift in equilibrium and braced himself more.

The thug gasped again as he strained for breath.

"We...I don't know how not to kill," he wheezed desperately, his eyes pleading. "All of my life, my father taught me to keep the world safe by feeding Kali. It's all I know."

"You regret killing innocents then?"

The thug nodded as much as he could without jeopardizing his balance. "I was forced into this life."

Hanson began to reply, but he noticed the thug's eyes focus on something to the side.

Hanson risked a glance over.

The slide show on the monitors was coming to an end. Luke Chancellor had saved his murdering career for the grand finale.

Hanson watched as the images cycled through. The photographs had been taken at the copper-lidded *bele* they were currently standing at the edge of. Chancellor had an easy smile on his face as he displayed his victims.

He also had a lot of them, nearly twenty. They were all Hispanic. The border was close by, and Hanson guessed that he hunted there.

"Please, it's all I know," the thug repeated.

The before and after sequence came up. The victim was a young woman with short, dark hair. In her teens. A child. She must have been struggling desperately, for two other thugs were forcing her arms behind her as a young and beardless Chancellor held her head. One hand gripped her hair painfully tight while the other was cupped under the chin and pinching her cheeks so that he could point her face toward the camera. It caused her lips to pucker up like a fish. He was pursing his lips also to mock her. Stark terror was in her eyes. His eyes were bright with merriment.

"Hanson, you can't blame me..."

The after picture came up. Her face was slack in death. There was no fear in her eyes, for they were gone. Gory ruins.

Chancellor's eyes still had the same merriment.

Hanson's face slowly turned back to the thug.

"Please, it's all I know," Chancellor whispered.

"You don't have to explain it to me," Hanson replied. He nodded toward the pit at his feet. "Explain it to them."

The thug's eyes flicked downward.

"They're waiting for you," Hanson finished.

He let go and watched the tape's numbers slip through his fingers.

With a wail of despair, the thug fell.

He splashed down in the center on his back, his weight causing him to sink in. The bodies around him slid into the depression he made and partially covered him. Though Hanson knew it was impossible, it appeared as if the dead were moving on their own volition, slithering through their own entrails to take the thug under the surface with them.

The copper lid started to close, triggered by a motion-control sensor near the lid's hinge.

Chancellor was screaming down below.

"Hanson, don't leave me down here. When the door closes, reactivate it. It's *Gobba khom!*"

The lid reached the halfway point. Hanson's mouth opened to speak, but he heard a noise behind him, and he turned instead.

The curtains were closing also, the criteria for recloaking the dead met. On the monitor, Chancellor held the head of the murdered girl. In the pit, he was still screaming.

"Hanson, for the love of—"

The lid closed.

Alone in the silence, Hanson remained where he was standing, his eyes on the screen as the girl's face faded away.

Chapter 52

Perry University, 1:40 p.m. CDT

"And that's what Hanson has told me so far. Any trouble on your end?" Samantha asked.

"No, there wasn't anyone from Homeland waiting at DFW to intercept me," Fisher answered with relief in his voice. "As I guessed, we're moving too fast for Watkins. I'm a few minutes from the Jack Evans building now."

"We'll start broadcasting what's coming out of the funeral home in a few minutes then." She gave him the channel.

"Good. With that, I should have local law enforcement mobilized and on-site."

"I'll be waiting for you there."

"You're not staying at the station?"

"The kids have it handled. I'm going to join their news van and broadcast from outside Tranquil Groves. If we want to stop the demonstrations in New York, the world needs to see what you're doing there."

Fisher didn't immediately respond. Samantha could tell he wasn't too keen on the idea of the press broadcasting live from an active situation.

"Okay, just be careful. Can you see what's happening on Hanson's end?"

She glanced at a screen that displayed a sweeping view of the Oak Room. A Chinese man in a yellow-and-white robe was giving a speech. A second man in robes was moving through the crowd, handing out what looked like communal wafers. Everyone was nibbling on them.

"They're having some sort of communion."

"The *tuponee*," Fisher said. "We're running out of time." He hung up the phone.

Samantha dialed up Hanson.

"How are you doing?" she asked worriedly when he answered.

"I'm fine; nobody even knows I'm here. But there have been some changes."

She could tell something significant had happened. Hanson sounded subdued.

He explained to her the double-cross and the loss of an hour.

"My God, they're destroying the building at four?"

"Yes."

"Fisher is almost at the police station."

"Could you update him for me?"

"I will. Where are you now?"

"In their temple. I'm looking at their bible right now. I was curious as to the fate of Captain Cresswell."

"Any idea as to what happened to him?"

She heard a thump as if a large book were being moved around. "I'm checking *Numbers*; it lists all the victims of Kali and the thugs who took their lives." There was a pause. "Isaac Chancellor," Hanson continued. "It was the commander's son, only sixteen at the time, who killed Captain Cresswell."

"That list must go back nearly two hundred years. How big is it?"

"Extensive. We should consider ourselves lucky." The sound of pages turning filled the phone. "Our names should have been right here, at the end. Instead, it's—"

The phone went silent.

Samantha, thinking the line was disconnected, spoke urgently into the phone.

"Steve?"

"Tom Sanford," he said.

"Who?"

"Tom Sanford is the last name on the list," Hanson answered. "He was the original copilot for Avian flight 951."

Now it was Samantha's turn to go quiet.

"With all that has been going on, I haven't stopped to think what happened to him," Hanson continued.

"Steve—"

"Thugs say that they don't choose their victims, that it's Kali that determines their destiny and puts that mark on their foreheads. Only this time, she didn't—"

"Steve—"

"I did," he finished. She could hear the anguish in his voice. "When I bought those plane tickets, I sealed that man's fate."

"Steve, it wasn't you. They killed him, not you. And if you hadn't set out to stop them, there would be more names in their bible."

"That's little comfort to his family...wait a minute, something's happening."

Samantha saw it also. The *tuponee* was over, and now the thugs were all craning their necks as they looked back over their shoulders. Something must have come through the room's main doors. After a few moments, what they were looking at came into her view.

The sacrifices.

Four people were being led down each aisle of the auditorium. The thugs, who were now standing, cheered.

The victim near the left wall was a Hispanic woman in her mid-thirties, her hair dark and cut short. And though her hands were secured behind her, she still stood ramrod straight. To Samantha, she looked military, and it took three thugs to drag her down the aisle.

Next row over was a short, thin Indian man in his fifties. He sported thinning hair and glasses. He looked frightened as the thugs yelled. Only two thugs were required to lead him in.

The third aisle was a tall, athletic-looking black man in his twenties. His head was clean-shaven, and he stood head and shoulders over the half dozen thugs surrounding him.

The fourth was a Caucasian woman. She looked to be the oldest of the group, and she had tight, curly dirty blonde hair. She had to be carried in by one thug as her thin arms dangled loosely. The other thugs pointed at her and jeered.

All four wore loose white shirts with pale yellow pants and slippers.

They were all led to the stage and forced to sit on the chairs provided. The unconscious woman was laid out on the floor. The others looked around the room nervously.

Hanson's voice came back over her phone. The anguish was gone. She could detect anger now. Resolve.

"No more."

"Steve, there's too many of them. You need to get out of there and let Fisher and the police do their job."

"I'm leaving, but I'm taking the sacrifices with me. No one gets left behind. These thugs have killed too many and hijacked Kali for far too long. Thuggee ends now."

The two robed *Sath Zuts* were out working the crowd again as they handed out tickets to their fellow thugs. Other thugs were parading the sacrifices, leading each one in front of the altar so that camera B could display their faces on the big screen.

"How are you going to do it?"

"There's a secret door nearby, one that only *Sath Zuts* with high-level security cards can open. All I have to do is snatch and grab the sacrifices and get back through the door, and the low-level thugs won't be able to follow me."

She looked at the two robed men.

"But won't the two *Sath Zuts* open the door for them?"

"No. There's too much evidence in here of their betrayal. Vankatesan and the other can't risk it. Billions are at stake. Their fellow thugs will tear them apart if they find out.

"But the key cards they're holding are a problem," Hanson continued. "I can't have a low-end thug showing initiative and taking a card to give chase. I need both of those *Sath Zuts* on the stage when I break in so that I can collect their cards for myself."

"Anything I can do to help?" Samantha asked.

Hanson paused. After all their time together these past few weeks, Samantha could tell he was thinking, coming up with one of his plans. And even though she was now used to his way of doing things, what he said next still took her by surprise.

"Yeah, ask your news crew if they do the weather over there."

Chapter 53

Jack Evans Building, 1:52 p.m. CDT

Fisher entered the bright, glass-enclosed lobby of Dallas Police Headquarters and strode over to the officer at the receptionist counter.

"I'm here to join Assistant Special Agent in Charge Paul Hopperton," Fisher announced as he displayed his badge and identification.

"He's upstairs," the desk officer replied.

Fisher wasn't surprised. Hopperton most likely had just passed through himself minutes ago. Fisher's Special Agent in Charge in Portland had just called the SAC in the Dallas office to let him know that Special Agent Dan Fisher (yes, that Dan Fisher, the one mentioned on Flight 951) was arriving with vital information for the day's events. Hopperton's job was to pave the way for him.

The officer gave Fisher a visitor's badge and directions. Fisher took the stairs up to the next level. His phone trilled halfway up.

"Samantha? Is everything okay over there?" he asked.

"Fisher, it's worse. Hanson says Tranquil Groves is set to blow up at four."

Tires squealed in the background. She was already on the road.

"That's two hours from now," Fisher replied with alarm. "How did Hanson get that wrong?"

"It's a double-cross. He just found out," Samantha shouted over the howl of car horns blaring. "But he has a plan—"

Fisher groaned. Things were about to go sideways.

"First, remember that law enforcement mole, Chancellor?"

"I do. Taking him out of the equation will the first thing I do when I find him."

"Hanson had thought the same, but he's changed his mind. Now he says to keep your enemies close," Samantha continued. "The mole will be giving the thugs information when he can. You need to feed him—"

"Misinformation," Fisher guessed, "I need to deceive the deceiver. Anything else?"

"The thugs think that Hanson is dead. Keep it that way. And they are heavily armed. Oh, and Hanson says he needs a helicopter in the air."

"I'll have everyone there in thirty minutes," Fisher replied. "Now, tell me what Hanson is doing during all of this."

She did. His eyes widened and his shoulders sagged as she talked.

"My God, Samantha, you can't be serious."

"Fisher, those four people in there. He's all they have—"

He straightened back up. She was right. "I understand. Let him know I'll be there with help as soon as possible."

He ran down the hall to the main operations room and burst in.

Due to the upcoming Muslim demonstrations, it was a zoo inside. The room was packed with Dallas deputy chiefs, SWAT officers, sheriffs, and every other law enforcement commander Dallas had to offer. They all seemed to be circled around a trio of men in the middle of the room. From his online research, Fisher recognized one of them as the chief of police. The other was Hopperton himself, a tall black man in a suit like Fisher's, only more expensive. The third was an old guy wearing a cowboy hat. Hopperton turned slightly and gave Fisher a slight head nod.

Fisher made his way over to them but stopped halfway over. The trio, upon seeing him, had parted to reveal the true center of the room.

Watkins.

She was dressed in the same outfit he had seen before, a suit with no tie. Looking both casual and yet more official than any of the men in the room. She had a predatory smile on her face as she addressed him.

"Special Agent Fisher, I've been waiting for you."

* * *

Perry University

"Put it up now," Tina commanded.

Diego flipped a switch. On the wall, the monitor that displayed the school council meeting changed. It now held video of the thugs parading their soon-to-be sacrifices.

They were going through a raffle process. Hanson had reasoned that the subsequent three kills were bonuses, each one worth a million dollars to the thug selected to strangle them. Entertainment before the main event—the blood sacrifice to appease Kali for a decade.

"We're broadcasting," Diego said.

To all three people watching right now, Tina thought. Unfortunately, student council meetings didn't garner high ratings.

But that would soon change. Samantha had provided an internet address to connect with one of the major networks in New York. Diego was transmitting what they had. Someone on the other end just had to pick it up.

Behind her, the door burst open.

Charlotte Shields, her school advisor, stormed in. An imposing, gray-haired woman in her fifties, Miss Shields wore a blue polyester dress and thick, steel-rimmed glasses. She had a look of anger and dismay on her face.

Tina groaned. When she had earlier thought that only three people were watching, she had forgotten that one of them was Shields.

"Tina, what the hell is going on?" Shields demanded as she glared around the room. "You know you can't go off the day's schedule."

A policy strictly enforced since a technician had streamed porn late at night while he had the room alone.

"Miss Shields, it's not what you think," Tina said as she gestured at the screen. "Samantha Ramsell was just here. This has to do with the terrorist attack on Flight 951—"

Shields shook her head, her face reddening. "Really? Samantha Ramsell? Tina, change it back. As of right now, you're suspended. And if you don't change it, you're done here, permanently."

Tina wavered. She had worked hard to get into this school and had earned a scholarship to afford it. Without that, she wouldn't be able to get into another worthwhile school.

But Samantha had told her that this was important. That no matter what, the truth had to come out. Tina crossed her arms and stood in front of the console.

"I'm not changing it back."

Fury was on Shields's face.

"Fine, you're done here!" she yelled as she lunged for the controls.

* * *

Jack Evans Building

"How did you—" Fisher began.

"Get here ahead of you?" Watkins finished as she stepped forward. "Ever since this began, I've had a Gulfstream with my name on it. So, when my people told me you had purchased a plane ticket for Dallas, I made my way here."

"And I'm glad you did, your input has been most insightful," the police chief said. He was a tall blond man with a craggy face. His name tag read Dresden.

The tag on the cowboy next to him read Chancellor.

Thug.

"I'm glad you're all here, actually," Fisher lied as he turned to Watkins. "I have new information. The terrorists—"

"Careful, Agent Fisher," Watkins hissed. "Your career is on the line."

Fisher glanced at Hopperton. The Dallas ASAC looked as if he wanted to intervene, but his frustrated expression let Fisher know that his hands were tied. Watkins had a lot more power than he had realized.

"You told us a bit about Agent Fisher, but how does this Hanson fella fit into all of this?" Chancellor interrupted with a slight drawl.

"Though we appreciate what Steve Hanson did on Avian 951, his past as a conspiracy theorist has been problematic," Watkins answered. "And, despite the overwhelming evidence, Hanson has convinced Agent Fisher here that we are not dealing with a subcontinent Muslim cell."

"What are we dealing with, then?" Chancellor asked.

"Yes, Agent Fisher, tell them," Watkins added.

Fisher swore inwardly. They were both giving him enough rope to hang himself.

But he was out of time.

"It's a domestic terrorist cell," Fisher explained. "A religious cult born out of ancient India that has made its way to America. The attack on Avian 951 was just a distraction so that all of us here would be too busy chasing after Islamic extremists while they make their escape."

"Indians?" Hopperton asked dubiously. "You mean like Hindus, not Muslims?"

"No, I mean—" Fisher hesitated as he realized he was losing his one ally in the room. "I mean thugs."

All the men present appeared confused. Watkins placed her hand on her chest.

"Maybe this will help," she said. "Cover your heart, Indie. Cover your heart."

"Those guys? From the movie?" Dresden asked.

"You can't be serious," Hopperton added.

"I am," Fisher answered. "Hanson told me that they're here."

"And where is Hanson," Watkins asked.

"I don't know. He hasn't answered my calls these past few hours," Fisher lied.

A fleeting smile crossed Chancellor's face.

Watkins, however, remained grim.

"It was your job to keep watch over him, Agent Fisher," she said. "Not to come here with your fabrications."

"I'm not lying, and I can prove it," Fisher retorted.

A nearby wall held a large television tuned to a local news channel. Fisher grabbed the nearby remote and held it up.

"They've been right here under your noses," he said as he selected the channel that Samantha had provided. "And now—"

The screen flickered.

"I give you the true terrorists of Avian 951," he finished. He turned so that he could see Watkins's expression.

She, and everyone else, stared blankly over his shoulder.

"Is this a joke?" Hopperton asked.

Fisher glanced back. On the screen weren't five hundred thugs, as Samantha had described.

It was seven college kids lined up at a table.

"What is this?" Chancellor asked.

"I think it's a student council meeting," Dresden answered. "It's on the local university channel."

"No," Fisher said weakly, his shoulders slumped.

"It's over, Fisher," Watkins said as she took the remote from his hand. "Let me show you what's really happening here."

The station changed to a network channel. National News Correspondent Jennifer Steel filled the screen. Behind her, an angry mob crowded Times Square.

"It's clear that Muslim extremists are behind the recent hijacking, and a massive protest clash is about to erupt in New York because of that," she said as she faced the men near her. "I should be there directing our resources. Unfortunately, I find myself here—quelling baseless allegations of a long-dead cult being responsible instead."

She put the remote back down on the table.

"We stand on the eve of one of the most important votes in US history, one that will ensure our safety for generations," she continued. "However, Fisher, Hanson, and Ramsell disagree with that. They think they can derail the vote if false information were to get out and create the smallest shadow of a doubt. This would be enough to influence the few key votes still undecided."

Fisher remained quiet as he stared at the television.

"Agent Hopperton? You're the ASAC for the Dallas area?" Watkins asked.

Hopperton, who looked both defeated and embarrassed, nodded.

"You know what to do," Watkins finished.

Hopperton turned toward Fisher.

"Special Agent Fisher, I'm sorry, but the president has us all working together on this serious matter. I need you to surrender your gun and badge, please."

With a sigh, Fisher took out his badge and placed it on the table. He then removed his Glock and rested that next to the badge. Police officers crowded around him.

"Take him out of here," Watkins snarled.

Fisher snatched up the remote as three policemen grabbed him and dragged him back.

"You have to listen to me," Fisher shouted. He pointed the remote and thumbed the button labeled "Last." Someone tried to deflect his aim.

Jennifer Steel remained on the screen. Too many bodies were between the remote and the television.

Watkins watched with a smug expression as Fisher was dragged away.

He glanced up. A round mirror for corners was suspended above. Fisher pointed the remote at it and pressed the button.

Someone grabbed it out of his hands.

"You have to listen to me!" he shouted again as he struggled. More hands locked on him, subduing him. Then he was out in the hallway and being dragged toward the elevators.

A radio crackled—Dresden's voice came through.

"Let him go. Have him come back in here."

They released him and lined up behind him silently. Confused for a moment, Fisher glared back at them. Then he dashed back into operations.

Inside, he found the room quiet, and everyone was facing the television. The old cowboy had a worried expression on his face. Watkins appeared furious.

"What am I looking at?" the police chief asked.

The television now showed a packed auditorium. Hundreds of men were cheering as four people on stage were being paraded. A vase that looked like it was made of pure gold made its way around the room as men were dropped tickets into it. Two men in yellow-and-white robes were pacing up and down the aisles with microphones in hand.

"You're looking at the last surviving vestiges of thuggee, a doomsday cult dedicated to murder to satisfy their blood craving Goddess," Fisher answered. "Before the day is out, those four people are to be sacrificed. And they're only minutes away from this room, at Tranquil Groves Cemetery."

"This is a lie," Watkins spat. "A trick."

An officer stepped forward. "Sir, I think he's telling the truth. Remember when that senator passed away a few years ago? I recognize the room. It's Tranquil Grove's largest funeral parlor. They have cameras set up in there."

"It could be just a funeral then—" Dresden mused.

Another officer spoke up from the control side of the room. "Captain, there's been a situation all day at Tranquil Groves. A gas leak. We have a traffic camera outside of their gates."

On the main screen to the control room's side, an image of the mausoleum's parking lot appeared.

Empty.

The heads of everyone swiveled back and forth between the two monitors.

"Thugs, you say?" Dresden asked.

"Dresden, think about what you are doing," Watkins warned.

It didn't take Dresden long at all to think about it. "Escort Agent Watkins out of here," he commanded.

She didn't give them the chance. Instead, she strode out of the room, her face red with rage. The door slammed behind her.

Hopperton handed back Fisher's gun and badge. "Sorry, Special Agent Fisher."

Fisher took them back, feeling whole again.

"What now, Agent Fisher?" Dresden asked. Behind the police chief, Chancellor's face was neutral.

Fisher ignored the thug and pointed to the television. "For the past four decades, the most prolific serial killers in history have been hiding in your backyard. Terrorists responsible for the recent airline attack. Men prepared to murder four innocents before the day is finished."

Anger was smoldering in everyone's eyes around him.

"You ask me what now? I'm reminded of a quote from the men who first fought thuggee. 'Mercy to such wretches would be an extreme cruelty to mankind. They must be met in their own ways.'"

"Whoever those men were, they sound like Texans to me," Dresden replied.

Chapter 54

Tranquil Groves, 2:04 p.m. CDT

Samantha rammed the cemetery's main gate. The wrought-iron panels were flung to the side with a shriek of tearing metal as her SUV careened into the center of the graveyard's main turnaround, where she crushed flowers underneath her tires. The white news van from the university followed her path of destruction and parked next to her.

A young Japanese man jumped out and looked nervously at the damage.

"Will we get in trouble for that?" Nick Miyamoto asked.

"Mangled roses are the least of our worries," Samantha replied as she reached over and dragged the kid towards her. She had to keep the vehicles between them and the main building. What she was asking of this young man was dangerous.

"It's going to be like a war zone soon," she explained. "Place the camera so that it overlooks the hood of my rig but keep the SUV's cab between yourself and the mausoleum, especially that tower."

Miyamoto went to work. Soon, he had the recording equipment and a monitor set up.

"Is this going to work?" he asked as he viewed the scene through his camera.

"Yes," Samantha answered. "What year are you, Nick?"

"Junior."

"Time for a lesson then. And this is the truth for any career. When it comes to success, it's not just what you know."

She pulled up her contact list on her phone.

"It's who you know."

* * *

National Evening News Studio, New York, 3:19 p.m., EDT

"Forty-one minutes," someone called out.

Sophie Gould barely heard it. The studio was a near madhouse as the deadline for the day's main news broadcast neared. She pushed up her glasses to help her focus.

"Jameson!" a voice bellowed.

Doug Morgan strode into the room, a cell phone pressed to his ear and a tablet in his opposite hand. Andrew Jameson, the man in charge of the broadcast, joined the venerable news anchor. Morgan handed him the tablet as he continued to talk excitedly into his phone.

Sophie thought about how they would be missed. But unfortunately, change was inevitable. She wasn't looking forward to the new era. She glanced back at her screens.

Jennifer Steel dominated most of them. However, Sophie knew that Carbonaux was close by, dictating instructions to her earpiece as he stayed in control of everything that she did.

Micromanaging everyone was a philosophy that also extended to the studio area. She had been at the receiving end of his condescending suggestions numerous times. Others had told her Steel treated her makeup and lighting crew the same way. How she looked was more important to her than the news itself. The two were a toxic combination.

Morgan and Jameson, along with every other upper-level manager in the building, approached her workstation. It was an unprecedented circumstance, and Sophie pushed up her glasses again as her anxiety rose.

"Sophie, there's a feed coming in from Texas. Can you call it up?" Morgan asked as his eyes scanned her wall of monitors.

She turned her attention back to the computer screen immediately in front of her. Feeds were coming in from all over the world. She searched for the Texas connection as Jameson and Morgan continued their dialogue.

"What is this all about?" Jameson asked.

"I have Samantha Ramsell on the phone right now," Morgan answered excitedly. "She's telling me she has the true terrorists responsible for Avian 951 holed up in a funeral parlor."

"And this?" Jameson asked as he held up the tablet.

"She sent background information on the terrorists to my email account," Morgan answered. He turned his attention to the phone. "It's coming up now, Samantha."

Excitement was coursing through everyone at hand, and Sophie knew why. Ever since the plane incident, Samantha Ramsell had been tied to Steve Hanson, and everyone wanted to get to him through her. But despite her numerous contacts with the New York media powerhouses, no one had heard from her except for the blog *Left Unsaid*. With the protests occurring right outside on Times Square, the day was already big. But now, with Samantha on the line, this day was going to be twice as huge.

A large monitor showed Congressman Charles Conyngham waiting for his upcoming interview. She replaced that with the video coming in from Texas.

Samantha's image filled the screen. She was wearing a white-and-blue blouse with a red bandana tied around her neck. Headstones were lined up on a well-kept cemetery directly behind her, and a colossal mausoleum dominated the far background. The sun was still up, and the sky was blue. On the adjacent monitor, it was overcast, and the tall buildings of downtown deepened the shadows further. The neon of Times Square, and Jennifer Steel, dominated that screen.

Steel was clearly doing what she usually did between takes, complaining about her lighting. Samantha was having problems of her own. A slight wind had kicked up, and her loose hair was blowing in her face. For a few moments, she looked like she was casting about for a hair tie.

"Do you want some time for hair and makeup?" a voice said from behind the camera.

"No, too many lives are at stake," Samantha answered. Everyone in the studio watched as she quickly formed a ponytail, gathered her hair behind her in a bun, and jammed a pencil in to keep it in place. With her hair up, Sophie noticed an earpiece.

"Samantha, we can see you," Morgan said.

"Thank God," she said as she looked up. "Listen, you have to convince Andrew to switch to me now. I have the real—"

"Andrew is right here. He can hear you."

She appeared relieved at that. "Andrew, I sent some notes to Doug. Homeland has it wrong; the real terrorists are here behind me."

Jameson leaned into the phone Morgan was holding up. "I'm reading it now, Samantha. What you have here is mostly background on something called…thuggee?"

"Yes, they're the men behind all of this."

"Like the guys in that Harrison Ford movie—"

"The same, but different," she replied. "Please, you must put me on. You can't let what's happening in New York follow through."

"Samantha, can you bring Steve Hanson to the camera?" Morgan asked.

She went quiet for a moment.

"No, he's busy at the moment."

There was a general murmur in the room.

No Hanson, no news segment from Dallas.

"Samantha, we are all aware of your reputation. You were even in line for the anchor chair, but you have to understand our plight here," Jameson said.

Samantha darted forward to the camera and disappeared. The camera shook a bit.

"What is she doing?" someone asked.

"I think she's showing the cameraman how to do his job," someone else observed dryly.

Now everyone studied the differences between the two broadcasts themselves. One showed the tension-filled bustle of Times Square, which seemed poised to explode like a powder keg.

Texas was a different story. A sun-drenched cemetery that was aptly devoid of the living. All that was missing was the chirping of crickets.

Samantha reappeared in front of the camera. "Doug, please," she pleaded as she looked straight at them.

Everyone in the studio turned to Morgan, including Jameson. They knew Jameson trusted Morgan's gut feeling when it came to the news. Though Sophie thought that in this case, the situation was a no-brainer.

Morgan was still for a moment as he stared at both monitors. "We're going with Samantha," he finally announced.

Everyone had stunned looks on their faces.

"You heard him," Jameson shouted. "We have a news broadcast to put on. Move it!"

The room exploded into action. Sophie turned back to her station, shaking her head, thinking the same thing as everyone else in the room. Jameson and Morgan were almost retired anyway, so they weren't hurting their careers.

But they were destroying their legacy.

* * *

Tranquil Groves, inside, 2:24 p.m. CDT

Hanson slowly opened the heavy steel door.

He was leaving the *Sath Zut's* core area. He had spent the past half hour preparing, avoiding the patrolling guards as he did so. At the bell tower, he had primed and left the thug computer bomb in the belfry. Later, in a storeroom, he had picked up a roll of artificial turf. When he returned to the temple, he loaded the remaining box of bullets into the magazines of the AR-15s that had been left behind and partially filled a third magazine as a spare. Having a second rifle ready was critical to his plan. Amongst the paperwork on Chancellor's desk had been a list of the four people to be sacrificed. The Hispanic woman was an army major. To the thugs, she represented a favorite target of old, a sepoy. To Hanson, she was someone who would be useful with a weapon in her hands.

Hanson crept out. He was in the service hall behind the Oak Visitation Room. He left the steel-reinforced door open.

Immediately in front of him were two other doors. The left led to a private bathroom for mourning families, and the right led to the visitation room itself. The hall stretched farther, toward the building's kitchens.

Hanson eased himself into the visitation room, aware that less than thirty feet away, behind the door that led out to the auditorium, were five hundred thugs.

He could hear them cheering as their raffle process wound down. For every sacrifice, they were choosing a team of one strangler and four handlers. Each *bhurtote* was to receive a bonus of a million dollars, the *shumseeas* a half million. Everyone was excited about the money and the deaths that were soon to follow.

Little did they realize that the entire spectacle was a distraction while the *Sath Zut* transferred that money, and billions more, into their accounts.

The carpeted visitation room was furnished with comfortable couches, easy chairs, and a coffee table. A television was mounted on the wall near the window.

Hanson carefully laid down the gear he had been carrying onto the couches—two AR-15s, the artificial turf, and one of the cell phones. He kept the saber strapped to his back.

One of the walls had a bulletin board. It had been placed there to display sympathy cards.

Hanson took a handful of pushpins and unrolled the artificial turf. He tacked it up on the back wall, close to the hall door.

It gave him a green screen. It was part of a special effect process officially known as chromakey, a backdrop that allowed broadcast engineers to superimpose any background behind their subjects. News programs used them to display weather maps.

Hanson grabbed another handful of pins and turned to the front wall. He had downloaded a video messaging app on the thug phone he had out. He carefully arranged the pins around it so that it was now mounted on the wall at eye level. Satisfied with the arrangement, Hanson started the video-streaming program. In a few moments, he could see himself standing in front of the green backdrop.

He tapped on his earpiece and then dialed up a number on his own phone.

"Diego here."

Hanson glanced at the small screen on the wall.

"Can you see me?" Hanson whispered.

"Yes."

Hanson could hear pounding coming through Diego's connection.

"Everything okay over there?" Hanson asked.

"Our student adviser almost shut us down," Diego answered. "We had to throw her out. The others are holding the door. The bad news is that she's told us that we are all expelled. The good news, though, is that New York is picking up our broadcast."

"Good. On the way from Los Angeles, I had put together a film clip. Do you have that video file Samantha provided?"

Hanson continued to prepare himself as he talked. He leaned the two rifles by the main door. He then turned on the television, muted it, and then switched it to the college station. With relief, he saw that Samantha was in position outside.

"I pulled it off her phone, and I've already looked at it. But I have to admit, Mr. Hanson, it doesn't make any sense."

"That's because you're not a thug," Hanson explained.

* * *

New York, 3:33 p.m., EDT

If it was controlled chaos before, it was pandemonium now.

Sophie was frantically preparing for the upcoming broadcast. They were going to start their program nearly a half-hour before schedule. Nearby, Morgan was studying a monitor at his anchor desk.

"Samantha, we're almost ready. Can you give us an idea of what's going to happen over there?"

Samantha was looking beyond the camera. Over the speakers, everyone in the room could hear sirens approaching.

"Doug, do you remember the Alamo?"

Sophie was confused. Samantha was in Texas. Was this a rhetorical question?

"Yes," Morgan replied.

On the monitor, the peaceful scene changed. Police cars raced by Samantha's position. Dozens of them. They fanned out behind her on the roads lacing the cemetery.

And they kept coming. Dozens became over a hundred. Sophie guessed that every department in the Dallas area had sent something to the cemetery.

When they reached their positions, officers jumped out. Most held rifles, which they pointed at the mausoleum as they took cover behind the cemetery's monuments.

"It's going to be something like that," Samantha finished.

Chapter 55

Dallas Police Mobile Command Center, 2:39 p.m. CDT

Chancellor's hand traced the outline of his second phone in his pocket. He needed to warn his fellow thugs that they had been discovered, but so far, he hadn't had the chance. The Oregon FBI agent was sticking to him like glue, excited about his role in the day's events.

"This command truck is huge!" Fisher exclaimed.

They were in the vehicle's conference area, a small beige room with four chairs surrounding a semicircular table. Large monitors that displayed the local news broadcasts were on the walls. If it weren't for the gentle rocking motion, one would think they were in a building.

Agent Hopperton and Dresden were also present, cell phones in hand as they directed their forces. All the men had body armor on. Fisher's and Hopperton's also had dark blue windbreakers with FBI printed on the back in large yellow letters.

"Hey, who are you calling next?" Fisher asked excitedly.

"The fire department," Chancellor answered, his eyebrows knitting together in annoyance. "We need their help evacuating the immediate area before those bombs go off."

Besides revealing the video feed from inside Tranquil Groves, Agent

Fisher had also warned everyone about the explosives set to go off at four o'clock.

Chancellor needed to know the extent of the damage Hanson had wreaked before Blackbourne killed him.

"Has Hanson passed on anything else to you?"

"We briefly talked a few hours ago. He hasn't answered my more recent calls," Fisher answered with a frown. "He and Samantha were inside that place yesterday. Hanson does IT work back in Portland. He was able to configure a back door into their video system. So that's how we're getting this feed now."

"How did he find out about the bombs?"

"He had a video camera hidden in a stairwell. He caught one of their leaders discussing them."

Chancellor swore to himself. Vankatesan should have been more careful. Hanson had even known the correct time for when the bombs were due to go off.

"Hey, that's us on the news," Fisher announced as he waved a finger at the monitor.

Their camper-sized command center could be seen pulling up to the right side of Ramsell.

"We can't have the press inside an active crime scene," Dresden said.

"Sir, as I've been explaining to your man Chancellor here, she's the reason we have eyes inside," Fisher replied as he stood up. "Without her, we're blind."

The police chief didn't look pleased with that bit of news. "All right, she stays. But she's your responsibility, Agent Fisher. Make sure she doesn't poke her head too far out if any shooting starts."

The back door to the room opened, and sunlight and warm air streamed in. Chancellor could see that Ramsell's remote broadcasting unit only twenty feet away. Fisher jumped out and went to her.

Chancellor stepped outside also and put on his cowboy hat. He reached into his pocket and brought out the second cell phone. With Fisher out of his hair for the moment, it was time to warn the others.

* * *

The Vault, 2:47 p.m. CDT

Vankatesan held up the tulwar in front of him to admire it. Even in the dim candlelight, it glowed with a bright sheen from the sandalwood oil he had coated on it yesterday.

The sword had been in his family for over three centuries. The blade curved from its sharpened point to a cross guard stylized in the shape of two tiger's paws. The grip was wrapped in leather, which was capped off in the end with a pommel in the form of a tiger's head. This was plated in gold, and the eyes were rubies.

The only thing that marred the perfection of the sword were dents on the blade and dried blood near the hilt. Pravnev had let them remain —a reminder to all thugs of the threats that constantly surround them. And on how demanding their Goddess could be.

Vankatesan laid the sword down on a table covered with red velvet. Four gold vases, also polished with sandalwood oil, stood near it. These vessels had been recently blessed to receive the blood soon to flow into them.

Chaplets of flowers rested nearby also, as did a gold bowl containing a fine sandalwood powder. After his fellow thugs finished their strangulations upstairs, the statue of Kali was to ascend for the final, true sacrifice. The chosen victim, drugged so as not to struggle on the altar, would then be covered with the flowers and sprinkled with the remaining sandalwood dust—the final steps to ensure that the blood would turn to ambrosia.

And pacify great Kali for a decade.

Vankatesan turned his gaze to the large room. It was directly under the main auditorium upstairs. Large slabs of basalt had been used to line the walls. Bas-relief artwork had been then carved into the rock, images of Kali, and thugs killing in her name.

Dasgupta approached him. As Zhang and Vankatesan himself, he was dressed in a long, flowing robe of white-and-yellow silk. Each had their personal *rumals* tied around the waist. Dasgupta was holding out his phone.

"It's Chancellor," Dasgupta announced, his eyes wide and panic in his voice. "We're surrounded by the police."

Fury crossed Vankatesan's face.

"This must be Ramsell's doing. How did she convince them?"

"She and Hanson somehow hacked our computers. Our cameras upstairs are actually broadcasting to the outside," Dasgupta answered.

Vankatesan stood there, stunned.

"As planned, Luke and Blackbourne have already gone dark and are at the rendezvous point to secure our transport," Zhang said as he turned toward the doors. "Should I go downstairs and turn the broadcast off?"

Vankatesan held up his hand. "No, wait," he commanded. "Since the authorities are watching, let's give them a show. We'll make it look like we're going down fighting."

A smile chased away the worry on Zhang's face. "They'll find the main tunnel soon enough, but the second tunnel is much harder to find. When they observe our fellow thugs perish in the explosion, they won't even think about looking for us for a long time."

When rebuilding the mausoleum, an old prohibition tunnel had been discovered. The *Sath Zut* had immediately concealed it, and its existence was known only to them. Vankatesan brought out his own phone.

"Dasgupta, let Chancellor know what we're planning. I'll contact Muhkerjee upstairs and tell him put on one last inveigling for the world to witness."

* * *

2:50 p.m., CDT

"Samantha!" Fisher yelled.

Samantha turned toward him. "Fisher! Thank God."

He reached her. Some kid had a camera pointed at them.

"Are we on the air right now?" he asked worriedly.

"No, but we cut in a few minutes," she answered. "Is the mole here?"

"Yes, it's the cowboy behind me...don't look at him!" Fisher answered as Samantha craned her neck for a better look. "The guy's been on the force since the seventies. He's an institution around here. It took all I had to make sure he didn't have a chance to warn his fellow thugs."

"He's on his phone. He must be texting them."

"It's too late now," Fisher replied. "We have them surrounded."

She opened her mouth to ask something else but instead put a hand to her earpiece. She shooed him away.

"Thuggee is about to go live," she explained.

Times Square, 3:52 p.m., EDT

"Ask him if he's worried that the other side's armed," Carbonaux instructed.

He watched with satisfaction as Steel repeated the question to the man dressed in camouflage next to her. Carbonaux's microphone was connected directly to her earpiece, and he continued to use that bridge to tell her what he wanted her to say on-air as the situation around them escalated.

They were standing right outside their own studio. Anti-Muslim protesters crowded the area, most of them dressed in pseudomilitary garb or decorated in red, white, and blue. Carbonaux could see anger on most of their faces, and he had also seen a few guns protruding out of poorly concealed holsters.

He smiled to himself. He was ending his tenure as a field producer with a bang. This clash was going to be the news story of the year.

But he still had to jazz it up a bit. The events on Flight 951 were proving to be a tough act to follow, and lately there was even talk of Samantha returning to New York. Everyone at work had been enthralled at seeing her in action on the plane, and her written piece about Hanson was the most popular article on the web.

Carbonaux scowled as the self-proclaimed skeptic's face intruded his thoughts. A few days ago, Hanson had stood in his kitchen and bragged about being part of a big story.

And he hadn't believed it.

Samantha must be laughing at him now.

Avian 951 was still on everyone's minds. Carbonaux needed to draw attention back to his achievements.

Some gunfire would help.

"Tell him you talked to the Muslim group earlier today. Tell him they're looking for revenge for their mosque burning down," Carbonaux whispered.

Steel nodded slightly. He didn't have to be close to see that. She was displayed on the massive jumbotron above their heads. He watched a giant-sized Steel push her microphone in front of the guy's face.

"Then we'll show them who this country really belongs to," the man snarled as his beard bristled. He and the group he was with surged forward. The Muslim crowd behind the line of police also broke free of their barricades and rushed ahead.

Carbonaux kept his eyes on the big screen. History, in the making.

History done his way.

The image above changed—a dark background with huge letters in bright red appeared.

BREAKING NEWS!

No shit, Carbonaux thought with a frown. What was happening here was already being broadcasted. It was redundant to cut away from it just to announce it.

The show's masthead appeared on the screen—*The Nightly News with Doug Morgan*. To the right was a graphic of a spinning globe, and the station's theme music trumpeted out onto the street. Someone had turned up the volume on the outside speakers.

Morgan was horning in on his moment of glory. Carbonaux shook his head. He was looking forward to the day that guy, and Jameson, were gone.

Morgan's face flashed into view. "Good evening," he greeted. "I'm Doug Morgan, with breaking news—"

"Get ready, Jennifer. They're going to cut back to you any moment."

Steel turned her back to the surging crowd as she faced her camera.

"Moments ago, we just received word of a massive confrontation—" Morgan continued.

"Get ready…" Carbonaux commanded his cameraman.

"In Dallas, Texas, where guest correspondent Samantha Ramsell is standing by," Morgan finished.

"What the hell?" Carbonaux shouted.

"What the hell?" Steel repeated, her hand to her ear.

The jumbotron changed from the studio's mute lighting to an exterior scene in bright sunlight. So bright that the screen's LEDs illuminated Times Square. Sensing the sudden shift, everyone in the crowd stopped and looked up.

The massive screen displayed Samantha standing in front of a cemetery. Police cars with flashing lights surrounded a huge building. Cops with pistols and rifles in their hands were hunkered down behind monuments and gravestones. A caption at the bottom of the screen read: "Samantha Ramsell, live from Dallas, Texas."

"Thank you, Doug. I'm reporting from Tranquil Groves Cemetery, where authorities have surrounded the domestic terrorists responsible for the attempted bombing of Avian Flight 951."

The camera stayed with Samantha, but Morgan's voice returned.

"Samantha, can you explain to us how this all came about?"

"Yes, Doug, I've been working an exposé on a long-hidden cult called thuggee, which had been recently discovered by someone we have all come to know, Steve Hanson."

"Thuggee. Now, you're talking about a cult known for strangling its victims. A cult that was destroyed nearly two hundred years ago in India."

Carbonaux watched with frustration as everyone on the street held up their phone to look up thuggee.

"Yes, Doug. But despite what everyone thinks, they have survived, and they've been secretly killing thousands by strangulation for a murderous religion dreamed up by the men originally tasked to destroy the thugs."

"And the attack on Avian 951?"

"Were not the actions of Muslim extremists. It was the work of the cult trying to silence Hanson and myself."

"And the whole world fell for this deception?"

"The world can't be blamed. The men behind all of this have been doing it for hundreds of years. They are known as the thugs. A word whose very meaning is 'deceive.'"

"Samantha, we have a second feed being sent from your location. Can you describe to us what we are about to show?"

"I can, Doug."

The jumbotron changed once again. Now Carbonaux was viewing some sort of auditorium filled with hundreds of men. Two of them were dressed in robes as they worked the crowd. A handful more were gathered around a Hispanic woman on stage. She was struggling against them as they forced her up from her chair. On the room's front wall, six large televisions made up one giant screen. It displayed the magnified image of the wooden altar resting in the middle of it all.

"To keep the Goddess Kali from devouring the world, these men have been strangling a victim once a week, and even twice a week during COVID, to placate her. Today, three stranglings, and a beheading to follow, are designed to appease Kali for the next decade so that the thugs can once again vanish into history to regroup."

On the street, people were now looking up "Kali" on their phones. Carbonaux was losing his audience.

"Would someone please start shooting someone," he grumbled as he looked around him.

On the screen, four men dragged the woman toward the altar. She was struggling so hard that each of them had to take an appendage and lift her up. They stretched her out spread-eagle fashion as they carried her. Samantha's narration continued.

"In their secret language, the men holding her are known as *shumseeas*, the handlers. They keep the victim immobile."

They laid her on the altar and maintained their grips on her. The primary camera was too distant to show details, but camera B was now zoomed directly on her, and she was now magnified on the room's big screen. Everyone watching could see the anger on her face turn to terror.

The men in the auditorium shouted and raised their fists.

A fifth thug approached the altar. He was a balding, middle-aged man who looked like he would be more at home behind a desk. He had a length of cloth in his hands, which he held up to the screaming crowd. He then got up on the altar himself and straddled the woman's back.

"The scarf is called the *rumal*, a divine gift from their Goddess. The man astride her is the *bhurtote*, the strangler," Samantha explained quietly.

A murmur of horror rippled through the entire crowd at Times Square as the man slowly draped the *rumal* in front of the woman's face.

Morgan's voice broke in.

"My God, the police, they're too late."

The *rumal* wrapped around the woman's neck.

Morgan, desperate. "We're going to have to cut away—wait, what's this?"

Something was happening on the stage. The video of the woman's face wavered, and then changed. Carbonaux, and the entire crowd in Times Square, gasped out in surprise when they recognized the person now depicted on the auditorium's front wall.

Steve Hanson.

It was a simple head and shoulders shot, and he occupied the middle of the screen. He was wearing a light brown shirt, and he had a sword strapped to his back. A glaring, red welt encircled his neck. His eyes stared straight into the camera.

Due to some sort of special effect, his background was a video of owls perched on tree branches. It appeared as if they were looming over his shoulders as they preened and flapped their wings.

"I wouldn't do that," Hanson announced with a grim smile on his face. "The omens aren't right."

Chapter 56

Outside Tranquil Groves, 2:57 p.m., CDT

Fisher crowded Samantha a bit to the side as he looked at her monitor. He watched with relief as the *bhurtote* removed his *rumal* from the woman's neck and twisted around to gape at Hanson behind him.

"I know what you're thinking," Hanson continued as the owls flanking him were replaced by rabbits hopping across a green lawn.

"Hanson, still alive."

Jackals fighting over a kill appeared.

"It gets worse."

Partridges came next, a clip showing them scurry for cover in dried brush. In the Oak Room itself, Fisher noted that all the thug's initial expressions of surprise were now replaced by looks of rage. They were also taking their *rumals* into their hands and twisting them.

"This video you're viewing isn't closed-circuit anymore; it's being broadcast live to the outside."

Now the thugs had looks of dismay. On the big screen was a cartoon of the Easter Bunny hopping around and tossing colored eggs.

"So that means that now the world not only knows what you are—"

Mr. Owl taking three licks of a Tootsie Pop cycled through.

"Who you are—"

Bugs Bunny eating a carrot.

"But most importantly, where you are. And right now, where you are is being surrounded by every law enforcement officer Dallas has to offer."

Now panic was on the thug's faces. A robed Indian was slowly walking down the aisles and mounting the stage. The other robed man remained with the crowd.

"So, I'm giving you all one chance."

From the *Partridge Family* opening credits, a line of brightly colored cartoon partridges walked left to right behind Hanson.

"Stand down. Release your hostages. Surrender and leave this place. The first ten of you out the door will to be approvers. If you don't do this," Hanson paused a moment, "I will personally rain down death and destruction on all of you."

An image of Bruce Willis from the movie *The Jackal* appeared. The auditorium erupted in uproar as Hanson stared impassively from his screen. The Indian on the stage was holding up his hands as he tried to calm them down.

"Hanson has no authority to negotiate with these guys." Dresden yelled from the mobile command center. "What the hell does he think he's doing?"

"Sir, no one here knows more about thugs than Hanson," Fisher yelled back. "If anyone can figure out a way to make the thugs give themselves up, it's him."

Again, Dresden didn't look happy about what he was hearing.

"Where the hell is he, anyway?" Dresden asked as he turned back to the monitor he was sharing with Hopperton and Chancellor.

"He's broadcasting from the university's studio," Fisher lied.

"Well then, we had better hope they listen to him, or else I'm going to treat this as an active shooter situation and take the place before they kill that hostage."

"Sir, you can't do that. Tranquil Groves is built like a fortress. They'll cut you down."

"Then what do you suggest we do?" Dresden yelled.

"Have your men hold their positions and wait for the signal. Then, they just need to lay down continuous suppression fire on the building." Fisher answered. "You just need to suppress the thugs."

"And what the hell is the signal?"

Fisher glanced at the small door at the back of the stage.

"You'll know it when you see it."

* * *

Mukherjee held his hands up and placed a serene look on his face. His fellow thugs were near riot. He needed to calm them down.

'Make it look like we are going down fighting' Vankatesan's text had stated. For the young *Sath Zut*, that was all the instruction that he needed.

He raised his hands higher, and the sleeves of his robe hung off his elbows.

"Thuggee has been here before!" he roared.

In the auditorium, his fellow thugs quieted. The ones on stage remained with their captives and kept them secure. Mukherjee stared into the camera.

"Nearly two hundred years ago, the Suppression Department had most of us captured. But even as they languished their cells, Kali's gifts to us were still apparent. Her wisdom poured forth and was given voice by thug prisoners to be recorded by our captors. Do you remember what they said?"

"Kali will never forsake us if we do not neglect her," the crowd roared back.

"Do you think the institution formed by Kali, the Goddess, can be suppressed by the hand of man?"

"It cannot!" the thugs yelled.

Mukherjee smiled. But the crowd murmured to each other and pointed to over his shoulder. He looked back.

Though Hanson had been silent, the video behind him was still playing. The animals were gone. In their place, on Hanson's right side, was the title card for the movie *The Omen*. The title itself was in red letters, and the "O" had the numbers 666 inside of it. The silhouette of a boy casting a shadow in the shape of a wolf stood under the O.

On Hanson's left side was a still photo of young Damien himself. But he had animated it so that the head was shaking to the negative while Mukherjee spoke.

Frowning, Mukherjee turned back to the crowd. "They say that their God is the creator and that He is displeased with us," Mukherjee continued. "But if He is all-powerful, why has He allowed us to exist for so long? Their God has appointed blood for Her food, saying *khoon tu kao!* Feed thou upon blood! What can She do? It is His will. And did not God make us thugs? It is our fate. So, we do not fear their God."

More thugs pointed at the wall behind him. Mukherjee glanced over his shoulder. The title card for *Damien: Omen II* was up now. A teenage boy with a crow on his shoulder was shaking his head.

Hanson was mocking them all. Fortunately, Liang was approaching, and he had his phone up as he read a text. Vankatesan, or Chancellor, must have sent a message. Mukherjee hoped it was good news.

"Hanson wants us to surrender, as we did in days of old," Mukherjee continued. "But we know our fate if that were to happen. Death waits for us there. So today, we fight as thugs. We fight as the children of Kali. And if we should fall, realize that we will all know the embrace of the Mother!"

It should have been a rousing speech, and his fellow thugs should have thought that fighting to the end was to be just an act. Instead, the thugs in the room appeared uncertain. Knowing what to expect, Mukherjee once again looked behind him.

Omen III: The Final Conflict was up. A young and sinister-appearing Sam Neill was shaking his head.

"Is that your final answer?" Hanson asked.

Liang made the stage, and he stopped beside Mukherjee. "We stand together, Hanson," the Chinese thug answered as he put away his phone. "Though we have labeled you *tikhur*, we are not worried. You are miles away from us in some studio, and the police will not be able to take this place in time. Kali will still have her feast today."

Behind Hanson, the video changed back to two owls, one behind each shoulder. Then, that image divided and became four owls.

"So be it," Hanson replied. "But when your fellow thugs are dying all around you, and this building is coming down around your ears, I want all of you to remember one thing."

Mukherjee only paid half attention to Hanson's bluff as he signaled to the *bhurtote* to recommence the strangulation of the woman. He watched as the *rumal* was wrapped around her throat, and he felt that familiar thrill as she began struggling.

He turned back to the screen as an afterthought. Hundreds of owls now filled the background behind Hanson.

"And what is it I should remember, Hanson?" Mukherjee sneered.

Hanson didn't reply. Instead, he darted forward and out of the camera's view. Only the owls remained on the screen.

Then the door to the small visitation room burst open, and somehow Hanson was standing right there, less than ten feet away. He now had one of their AR-15's slung over his shoulder and next to his sword. Mukherjee's breath caught in his throat when he realized that a second AR-15 was in Hanson's hands, and it was pointed at his chest.

"I warned you..." Hanson answered.

3:01 p.m., CDT

Hanson opened fire.

It wasn't random, indiscriminate shooting. The room held five hundred thugs, and he had only thirty bullets in the rifle's magazine, so he had to be selective. It was a quote from a long-dead thug that determined Hanson's first target.

The thug's interrogator had asked how much time it took to strangle a man. The thug had brought up his hands to snap his fingers. *"It is the work of an instant,"* the thug had answered. He then wagged another finger at the scribe recording his confession.

"You are long in writing it."

That phrase flashed through Hanson's mind as he shot the *bhurtote* first.

The bullet entered the man's chest from the side and tore through his heart, killing him instantly. The force of the bullet's impact knocked his lifeless body off the woman on the altar.

Hanson targeted the *shumseeas* next; two quick shots, center mass. The two men holding the woman's hands crumpled to the ground.

Over their initial shock, the two *Sath Zuts* were now leaping forward, their hands outstretched. Hanson swung his rifle around and shot the Chinese thug and the mouthy Indian in the chest at point-blank range. The bullets exploded out of the men's backs and found secondary targets in the crowd behind them.

In his peripheral vision, Hanson could see the woman, her hands free, twist around and onto her back. The two remaining *shumseeas* were still holding her ankles. She sat up and hit one of the thugs with a quick jab to the throat. He released her foot as he sagged to his knees. Then, since one of her legs were free, she kicked out a bone-crunching blow to the other's jaw. He stumbled back.

Hanson wasn't surprised at her taking control of the situation. He had read her name and occupation earlier on a list back in the control room.

Isabella Romero-Hernandez, U.S. Army.

"Major!" Hanson shouted. She looked toward him.

"You want this?" Hanson continued as he tossed his rifle toward her.

She caught it, and in one fluid motion, she brought it up and pointed it straight at Hanson's head.

"Down, Marine!" she shouted.

Hanson heard her rifle roar as he ducked. A body hit the floor behind him. He had overlooked a thug standing on the far side of the stage.

Hernandez continued shooting; her attention focused on the thugs around the other prisoners. Hanson unslung his second rifle from over his shoulder and joined her. Thugs dropped dead around them. With frightened yells, the two male prisoners both rolled off their chairs and took cover. In a few short moments, the stage itself was clear. Hanson and Hernandez swung back and faced the auditorium.

"There's too many of them!" she yelled.

She was right—they were surrounded. Even if the weapons were on full auto, the entire crowd could rush forward and overwhelm them with sheer numbers. Hanson's plan should have been doomed to failure.

But these were thugs.

Easily the most craven villains in all of history. Men who only killed if the odds were overwhelmingly in their favor and they had complete surprise. And if a freaking rabbit had hopped across the road at the right time.

Hanson wasn't expecting any heroics.

They didn't disappoint. To a man, the thugs, as they screamed in surprise and fear, turned and fled. The younger and stronger ones tossed the older and weaker to the ground and scrambled over them as they crowded into the aisles.

These guys weren't going to be a problem.

But then the guards appeared at the auditorium's main doors.

The Portland squad was still out there, and they had weapons. Hanson spotted Bryce and Todd bringing up their rifles to bear.

The fleeing thugs crashed into them as a surging tidal wave and swept them back out of the room. Todd howled in frustration.

"What the hell?" Hernandez shouted, not believing what she was seeing.

"Major, cover me!" Hanson yelled. "I'm freeing the others." He moved forward and grabbed a knife off a dead thug. He then bent over the two men who were bound with plastic ties.

Hanson knew who they were also. "Jerry, hold up your hands," he commanded.

Jerry, a college football player, complied. Hanson moved to the next man, a retail clerk from Boston named Kushal.

As he worked, Hanson could hear Hernandez take an occasional shot. Though they weren't being rushed en masse, some of the thugs stuck at the back of the pack were turning back around in desperation.

Hanson moved over to the unconscious woman on the ground. Susan, from Philadelphia, unemployed. He guessed she was to be the final sacrifice, and the thugs had kept her drugged so that she wouldn't struggle on the altar when they cut off her head.

Hanson looked up. It was utter chaos. Half the thugs were out, while the other half were still fighting and screaming for the exits.

"What's exactly is going on here?" Hernandez shouted over the uproar.

"The usual, Major, the Marines saving the army's butt."

She shook her head, but he could see a slight smile on her face. "I mean, who are these guys?"

"They're a doomsday cult. Your deaths were meant to stave off Armageddon."

Bot-timer: "Fifty-five minutes."

"And now, we're leaving," Hanson announced as he gestured behind him. "Out this door and all the way back. Take a left in the hallway." Hanson pointed at the ground. "Jerry, I need you to take her with you."

The kid scooped up Susan. Then, he and Kushal rushed through the door.

"Hanson!" yelled Hernandez.

Hanson spun back around. She was still facing the crowd but now had her rifle pointed a bit higher.

Panicked thugs still blocked the exits, but the door to the control room must have been clear. Hanson could see that it was open, and a half dozen thugs had flooded into the small area.

The glass to the control room shattered as they opened fire on the stage.

Bullets flew all around them and pierced the stage's wood floor and walls. The large screen behind them, which now had the images of hundreds of owls, splintered and went dark.

Hanson and Hernandez both ducked behind the altar and shot back.

Both hit a target. Six thugs became four, and the remaining ones dropped down behind the control room's console. For a moment, Hanson thought he recognized one of them.

Ravi.

More thugs piled into the control room, shooting as they came in. Hanson and Hernandez dropped them also.

"I'm out," she announced as she crouched behind the altar.

"This is our last magazine, twenty bullets," Hanson replied as he handed it to her.

She switched out her magazines.

"You have five shots left. What are you going to do? Wave that sword at them?"

"Twenty-five bullets, and one former Marine, that should be

enough," Hanson said with a grin. Then a thought occurred to him. "How did you know I was in the Marines, anyway?"

"Are you kidding? Before these guys grabbed me, you were on the news twenty-four hours a day. I know which grade school you attended. Captain Grey, right?"

"Jesus Christ," Hanson sighed. Even if he survived this, his life was going to be a living nightmare.

"Hanson, the room is almost empty. When those doors clear, their gunmen can come at us from five different angles."

"It's now or never," Hanson replied. "Cover me; I need to get key cards off those two robed guys over there."

Hernandez poured bullets into the control booth as Hanson dashed over and searched the two dead men's robes. He found the cards in chest pockets.

"Major, go!" Hanson shouted.

His turn to cover her. He fired his last five bullets as she ran by.

The last of the fleeing thugs exited the room, and thug gunmen filled the doorways.

Hanson sprinted for the back door as a hail of bullets howled passed by him. Hernandez was there, returning fire.

"Go!" he yelled as he grabbed her arm. "These walls won't stop those rounds."

They made the back hallway, and Hanson guided them left. The open door to the building's secure core stood only thirty feet away. Kushal and Jerry, who was still carrying Susan, waited inside.

"Run!" Hanson yelled as he gave Hernandez the bum's rush to hurry her along. Bullets were now erupting from the wall on their left and lodging into the wall on their right. The destruction gained on them as they sprinted for the door.

They just made it. Both dove through as bullets ricocheted off the steel portal. Kushal pulled it shut, and it locked with a satisfying click.

Hanson and Hernandez remained on the ground, panting.

"You're Steve Hanson," Kushal and Jerry said together.

Hanson held up a hand. "Later," he wheezed. "Right now, we need to get out of here."

"Can they follow us in here?" Hernandez asked as she glanced at the door.

"No," Hanson answered as he stood. He held up the gold cards. "They can't get in without these. Only their leadership can get in here."

"Do you have all of them?" Kushal asked.

"No. There are three card-carrying cultists in here with us," Hanson admitted. "So, stay alert."

"Won't they let the rest of them in to hunt us down?" Jerry asked.

"I don't think so. There's a double-cross going on, and billions of dollars are at stake. If the rank and file get in here and find out, they'll tear their leaders apart."

"So now what? The police have this place surrounded. Do we hunker down in here and wait?" Hernandez asked.

Bot-timer: "Fifty minutes."

"Who was that?" Kushal asked as his eyes searched the room.

"This place is rigged to blow up in less than an hour," Hanson explained as he walked a short way down the hallway to a door. "We can't stay."

"But there are hundreds of them, and they're armed. They'll cut us down if we try to make it out of here," Hernandez argued. "And I'm down to seven bullets, and all you have is a sword. How are we getting out of here?"

Hanson opened the door. Behind it was a stairwell with steps going up.

"By taking the route they won't expect."

* * *

"They're in the inner sanctum," a thug shouted from the stage.

Ravi, still in the control room, shook his head in frustration as he tried to understand what had just happened.

"Has anyone called Vankatesan to open the doors?" Ravi asked Jason, who was at his side.

"He's not answering," Jason replied as he put his phone away.

Ravi wasn't surprised. Vankatesan was most likely focused on his own important task. He and Jason retreated to Tranquil Grove's main reception area and stood next to the display casket.

The sound of continuous gunfire filled the halls. When Hanson had broken into the auditorium, the police surrounding them had begun shooting. The thugs had raided their weapons caches and taken their posts by the narrow windows to fire back.

"What do we do? Jason asked. He had to raise his voice above the din.

"Is the main tunnel guarded like I commanded?" Ravi asked.

"Yes, I posted the most faithful there. Hanson, or any weak-hearted thug, won't escape that way," Jason answered.

"Good. Chancellor has been sending me texts. He said to keep everyone on ground level. Even though every exit door is chained and padlocked, we need to have every one of them guarded. The police may try to breach one of them."

Jason rushed off. Ravi turned away to look for a window he could shoot from.

It brought the sweeping staircase into his view. He froze to stare at the steps that went up. It was the *sotha* in him that made him pause, his talent for getting into the heads of his victims. So far, Hanson had outmaneuvered them at every turn by reacting in unconventional ways.

Two young thugs rushed by with AR-15's in their hands.

Ravi pointed at them. "You two, follow me."

Ignoring Chancellor's command of keeping every thug on the ground floor, Ravi raced up the stairs. He knew his prey, and he wanted Hanson for himself.

Chapter 58

3:13 p.m., EDT

"We're secure in here," Vankatesan stated as he glanced over at the locked doors to the vault.

"Then should we chance it and let everyone else into the sanctum areas to hunt them down?" Liang asked.

Vankatesan thought about it. It was risky, but Hanson couldn't be allowed to escape. He was about to answer in the affirmative when his and Dasgupta's phones both chimed.

Vankatesan's notification was an email on his university account, a message that contained a photograph of the temporary computer desk in the temple below. On the desk's monitors was his university bio photo enlarged to enormous dimensions. Next to that, in an equally large font, was a message.

THUGS HATE HIM.
SEE HOW THIS SATH ZUT
AND OTHERS LIKE HIM KEPT
ALL OF THE BILLIONS FOR
THEMSELVES.

Vankatesan showed what was on his phone to the others.

"We can't let anyone in now. They'll kill us when we leave our secure area and make our way to our escape tunnel," Liang said, his eyes wide.

Dasgupta held up his own phone. "My message is from Chancellor. He's asking about Luke."

All three men remained quiet for a moment.

"Luke and Blackbourne must be dead," Liang guessed. "How do we tell—"

"We don't," Vankatesan interjected.

"But Abe—"

"Doesn't need to know, yet," Vankatesan snarled. "It's just us now. If we want to get out of here alive, we need him at the top of his game. If he finds out Luke is dead, he may crack."

"What do we do then?"

Vankatesan glanced at the monitor. With the auditorium empty, the news station had switched to the exterior view. Samantha Ramsell was on the screen. Beyond her, the police could be seen pouring bullets into the mausoleum.

"Send Abe a text. Tell him his son stopped by on his way out of here. Since we were all going to go 'dark' and leave our phones behind to stop any accidental tracking, Abe will accept this."

The others nodded.

"As for us, we will finish what we have begun," Vankatesan continued. He walked to the back of the room to where a video camera mounted on a tripod waited. "Except, instead of broadcasting our work to the others upstairs as we originally intended, we will televise it to the world."

"Is that possible?" Dasgupta asked.

"This camera is wired to the same feeds as the ones in the auditorium," Vankatesan answered.

"But why do it?" Liang asked.

"I want everyone to know that in the end, Hanson ultimately failed to stop us," Vankatesan answered as he looked toward the front of the room.

"And that Kali feasted on her blood offering."

* * *

3:16 p.m.

"Clear," Hanson announced.

He stepped out from the hidden staircase and onto the carpeted hallway of the upper-class niches. Silver urns rested behind small panes of glass. The distant sound of gunfire could be heard throughout the building.

"Where to next, Hanson?" Hernandez asked.

Hanson pointed down the hall. "Over there is a staircase with roof access. We're going up all the way," he answered. He pulled out his cell phone.

"Who are you calling?"

"Our ride."

Fisher answered on the first ring.

"Where are you?" Fisher asked. Hanson could hear more gunfire in the background. It sounded like a battle zone.

"We're on the upper level. So have that chopper on standby."

"The helicopter is in the air, but the thugs have a man on the tower. They won't come close as long as he is up there."

"I'll take care of that when the time comes. Is the mole nearby?"

"Yes. He's watching me now."

"Good. Convince him that we're coming out the east exit door."

"Understood."

Hanson hung up and turned to the others.

"Let's go."

They half-ran down the hall. Hernandez led the way since she was armed. They entered the All-Faiths room, its multi-colored dome ceiling still glowing. As before, the statue of Jesus was near their entrance. Hernandez, out of reflex, paused and made the sign of the cross as she stood in front of the figure.

"In the name of the Father, and of the Son, and of the Holy Spirit—"

"Amen," Hanson interrupted. "Let's go, Major."

Jerry, carrying Susan, had already hustled on by. Hanson increased his speed to catch up to them.

He detected movement to his left. Hanson turned, and his heart sank.

Pickaxe.

The thug was coming down the west hallway and was only thirty feet away. He had a Glock in his hand, held down by his side.

Caught in the open, Jerry froze.

"Move," Hanson shouted as he leaped forward and pushed Jerry in the back. The kid, along with Susan, stumbled on, and he curled his body to protect her as he fell to the floor behind the safety of the marble statue of Kali.

Hanson had planned to follow them, but that didn't happen. Jerry's and Susan's combined mass had been too much, and Hanson instead bounced back to stand directly in front of the armed thug.

There was no hesitation on the pickaxe's part. Instead, the thug's look of surprise turned to elation as he brought up his pistol and fired. The gun roared as the first shot targeted Hanson's stomach, the second his chest. The Glock continued its upward sweep to lock on his head.

Hernandez's AR-15 barked behind Hanson, and its bullet sent the Indian spinning, his last shot going wide. The nameless thug collapsed to the ground, dead.

Too late.

Hanson stood in the middle of the room, his left hand over his abdomen, his right over his chest as he panted in rapid, shallow breaths.

"Hanson, are you okay?" Hernandez yelled.

Hanson didn't answer. He remained where he was, his arms wrapped around him.

"Are you hit?" she clarified as she stood closer to him and looked him over.

Hanson, not feeling any pain, gently removed his hands from his body. They weren't covered in blood. Which was impossible—he had seen how the thug's pistol had lined up with his body. There was no way he could have missed.

Then he noticed Kali's hands.

The statue's two outstretched hands were in ruins, and chunks of marble littered the ground below them.

They had deflected the bullets.

With her upper right hand, she offers protection…

Hanson ran over to the thug's body and claimed the Glock for himself.

And with the lower, she offers boons, gifts…

Hernandez was studying Kali.

"The statue blocked the bullets. It's a miracle, thank God," she observed as she once again turned toward Jesus and made the sign of the cross.

Hanson also paused in front of Kali and looked up at her face. Was there a bit more of a smile there? A look of understanding? Hanson was surprised at himself. What was he hoping to see?

The marble face was unchanged.

"Don't forget to thank Kali," Hanson said as he ejected the pistol's magazine to study it. Fifteen bullets left. He slammed the magazine back home and racked a bullet into the chamber as he gave the statue one final look.

"Jesus has only one right hand. Come on."

Hanson led them the short distance to the next stairwell and took the stairs up. They stopped at the locked doors to the roof.

Bot-timer: "Forty minutes."

"Won't these guys by expecting this possibility," Hernandez asked.

"No, they have a man on the tower. Right now, they're thinking there's no way a helicopter can get close."

"They would be right. So how are you going to get him out of there?"

Hanson brought out another thug phone and powered it on.

"I have an app for that."

* * *

4:21 p.m., EDT, the Nightly News control room

"I'm sorry, but your son's not here," Samantha replied to the woman standing near her.

"Samantha, how are you so sure that none of the prisoners are local?" Morgan broke in.

Sophie was wondering the same thing. During the past few minutes, the police had escorted a man up to Samantha. He had been worried that his brother, who had gone missing a day ago, was amongst the prisoners. Samantha had not seemed surprised when the man realized his brother wasn't there.

And now a woman, a brunette in her early thirties, had just approached also. Everyone in the studio could see that she was extremely distraught. She had just told Samantha that her seven-year-old son had recently disappeared also.

"Your son's not here," Samantha repeated as the police officer accompanying the woman moved her to the side and behind the protection of the large SUV parked there. Samantha turned back toward her camera.

"The thugs don't hunt close to home," Samantha answered. "So as not to draw suspicion to their base of operations."

"Hunt, so they're predators."

"Serial killers. All of those men in there have several murders to their name."

"Then I must ask you, Samantha, how is Hanson going to get them out? There must be hundreds of those thugs in there, and a huge gun battle is raging behind you. Hanson is only one man. What chance does he have?"

"He has a good chance, Doug," she answered. "Even though they greatly outnumber him, the thugs fear him. They even have a name for someone like Hanson in their own language. They call him *tikhur*."

"*Tikhur*? What's that?" Morgan asked.

In the background, the mausoleum's tower exploded with a shattering roar. Sophie could see police officers closer to the structure duck behind the monuments they were using for cover. The officers on the outer perimeter also reflexively hunched down with looks of surprise and shock on their faces.

Samantha was the only one present who didn't look surprised, and she didn't flinch in the slightest.

"A man dangerous to thugs," she answered.

* * *

3:24 p.m., CDT

"Go, go, go!" Hanson yelled.

Though there had been some distance between them and the explosion, the sound and force of it had still been overwhelming. The civilians were shaky on their feet as Hanson used a gold card to open the outer door. Bright sunlight and hot outside air greeted them. Hernandez led as he pushed the others out.

They were on the roof of the north side of the building. It was part of the newer addition, and Hanson guessed that the hearse garage was below them. A light layer of gravel covered the roof, and air conditioning units hummed close by.

The central and older part of the mausoleum loomed over them to the south. It had a rooftop stairway egress structure like the one they had just come out of. That, along with the pall of smoke rising from where the bell tower had stood, blocked the low-lying sun and gave welcoming shade on the hot roof.

Hernandez blinked in the light. The sound of gunfire echoed from the cemetery below them.

Bot-timer: "Thirty-five minutes."

"You know, they had us drugged most of the time and in these damned pajamas. Where are we?" she asked.

"Texas. Dallas," Hanson answered. "Come on, let's move away from the edge and closer to this taller structure. That will give the helicopter some room to land." He looked to the north. "It should be—"

"Marine!" Hernandez yelled as she pushed him roughly to the ground.

Hanson reflexively put out his hands to break his fall, and the Glock flew from his grip. He landed on the rooftop, and hot gravel chewed into his palms.

A shot, louder than the background battle below, rang out.

Hernandez's upper right arm exploded in a red mist. She screamed as she spun and fell to the ground. Her AR-15 landed near her.

Hanson looked up.

Ravi and two other thugs were positioning themselves above them. They were in the narrow space between the older building's egress structure and waist-high parapet.

Hanson had no idea where the Glock had gone. He instead scrambled toward Hernandez, his feet trying to get traction in the loose gravel. Out of the corner of his eye, he could see Jerry sprint with Susan for the cover of an air conditioning unit.

"Major!" Hanson yelled.

She didn't respond. Her rifle was ten feet away from him.

Bullets were kicking up the gravel in small spurts as the thugs began shooting at him.

The thugs were lousy shots, but one of them was going to find its mark. Hanson's body tensed for the expected impacts.

Another gun went off, this one sounding different from the rifles above.

The Glock.

Kushal had scooped it up and was now shooting, screaming in desperation as he fired off shots as fast as he could squeeze the trigger. Bullets flew wildly, and most were way off the mark. Kushal was just as bad of a shot as the thugs.

But his shooting had the desired effect. The thugs dropped for cover behind the stone parapet.

Kushal kept firing until the Glock's hammer clicked impotently as it snapped forward.

With smiles on their faces, the thugs rose back up, shooting as they did so.

Hanson was waiting for them.

He had used the precious moments Kushal had provided to grab Hernandez's AR-15. He swung the rifle's barrel upward.

"Six shots left," Hernandez moaned.

Bullets poured into the ground where Hanson had been moments before. The thugs, seeing that he had moved, tried to adjust.

Hanson shot the left thug in the shoulder, and his rifle fell away. Hanson put the second bullet into the man's chest.

Ravi was already ducking down. Hanson wasn't surprised. The *sotha* was smart. Hanson fired but only gouged the brick wall behind where Ravi had just been.

The third thug was still shooting, and a bullet whizzed by Hanson's ear. Hanson put a slug in his right arm, the next between the eyes. The thug sagged down, a blood-spray pattern on the wall marking where his head had been.

Hernandez whispered weakly behind him. "One."

Hanson kept his rifle pointed upward.

"Jerry, leave Sue back there. You and Kushal get up here and get Hernandez behind some cover," Hanson commanded, his eyes not leaving the rooftop.

"Hanson!" Ravi shouted from above.

Hanson didn't answer. He remained still, his eyes moving left and right.

"Hanson, can you hear me?"

He had only one bullet left. Ravi had several rifles and magazines to choose from.

"Always the quiet one, aren't you, Hanson? You know, you were a mystery to us in the beginning. Kali couldn't find anything substantial on you."

Ravi had the high ground. Hanson cleared his head. He needed to think as the thug above him.

"But I figured you out. An introvert. After that, you made sense to me. I still remember that night back in Portland, Hanson. Inveigling you. You were like a child, lost in the woods."

Hanson pictured Ravi above him, his back to the parapet as he held his rifle, bodies to his right and left. He had to move over those.

"How long had it been since you had been with a woman, Hanson? You looked so desperate in that bar."

Did I look desperate? Hanson blinked and frowned, the end of his rifle lowering a bit. Asshole. Ravi was getting into his head. Hanson had to get into his. Which way would the thug move?

"At least tell me that you fucked her, Hanson! That way, I'll know that I'm the greatest *sotha* that ever lived," Ravi yelled as he laughed out loud.

Ravi was right-handed. It would be easier for him to crab over to his left as he held his rifle.

"No answer? I expected that. I know you. You can imagine my amusement when you bragged of your elk trophies. Hanson, the great white hunter!"

Hanson knelt down.

"For it was true when I told you I didn't hunt wild game. I hunt a higher game. Mankind! So, while you pit your cunning against the instincts of an animal, I must subdue the suspicions and fears of intelligent men and women."

Ravi would want space and freedom of movement as he stood up. Hanson tracked his aim a little to the left of the egress structure above. Behind him, he could hear the helicopter closing in.

"I cannot describe my joy to you, of seeing suspicion change to friendship, and friendship, trust. And after that, the moment when my soft *rumal* completes the hunt."

Hanson lifted the end of his rifle an inch higher.

"But maybe it's better this way. With bullets. Both of us hunting the most dangerous game there is. Now, one of us will know the satisfaction of seeing the other man's face—"

Hanson's finger tightened on the trigger.

"As he dies!" Ravi shrieked as he stood up and brought his rifle to bear.

Hanson didn't even have to adjust. Ravi's chest was already in his line of sight. Hanson put his last bullet through the thug's heart. Ravi soundlessly collapsed back behind the parapet and out of sight.

"True that," Hanson muttered.

He dropped the rifle. A blue-and-white helicopter was almost on top of them, the words "Dallas Police" across its top. Hanson could barely hear his phone above the roar of the rotors.

Bot-timer: "Thirty minutes."

Hanson smiled to himself. They were going to make it. Jerry and Kushal had Hernandez between them. Hanson moved to the air unit where Susan was and picked her up. He took a moment to study her up close.

She had needle tracks on her thin, bony arms. Her face looked haggard and withdrawn, like the last image of a photo sequence showing the ravages of drug use. Hanson realized then that she was what thugs considered a soft target, a homeless person who wouldn't be missed.

Hanson carried her over to the others. Jerry had Hernandez in his arms while Kushal was applying pressure to her shoulder. The major's face was a mask of pain.

It looked bad; the bullet had blasted its way through bone. They were going to have to fly directly to a hospital.

Hanson huddled next to them as the helicopter settled nearby and kicked up gravel and dust.

"And just what were you doing back there, Major?" Hanson yelled.

She smiled weakly. "You know, the usual. The army saving the Marine's butt—"

"Indeed," Hanson replied. The doors to the helicopter opened, and the pilot waved them in as his eyes scanned the nearby rooftop.

"Time to go," Hanson yelled. He watched as the others struggled to get Hernandez inside. The grit in the air was thick. Hanson looked down at the woman he was carrying and shielded her face with his hand.

Her eyes were open.

She had a desperate look on her face. Hanson could see her mouth moving also, but her voice was coming out in a light rasp. He couldn't understand what she was saying.

Her hand reached out and grabbed his collar and dragged him closer. Her mouth was still moving, and her eyes were pleading.

She looked like she wanted to tell him something...

* * *

3:34 p.m., CDT

"What's taking them so long?" Samantha asked.

She had watched the police helicopter come in low from the north and drop behind Tranquil Groves's older central structure. Even though the gunfire hadn't abated, the police were careful not to send any bullets toward the rooftop.

"They have a lot of people to load…look, there," Fisher replied at her side.

The helicopter could be seen rising. Fisher's phone trilled.

"Hanson?" Fisher answered. Samantha spent an agonizing moment waiting for an update as Fisher stood there listening. Then, finally, a grin spread across his face.

"They're all out!" Fisher yelled.

Samantha took a moment to compose herself, then she turned back to the camera.

"The hostage crisis is over, Doug. Only the thugs remain in the building," she announced.

"We see the helicopter. This is an amazing turn of events," Morgan replied.

Fisher was still talking on his phone nearby. "One of them is hurt; they're going to the hospital first," he announced.

"Samantha, do we know who was hurt?" Morgan asked.

Samantha wanted that answer also. Hanson was on the phone, but had he been wounded?

Samantha looked over at Fisher, hoping he would take a moment to look at the camera. Instead, he was looking up at the helicopter.

"I see you," Fisher said, "Which hospital are you going to?"

Fisher appeared busy. Samantha frowned. She was going to have to get to him later. She turned back to her camera. Behind it, she saw that Nick was on his cell.

"Miss Ramsell," Nick said, "It's Diego. He says he has a camera feed coming in from a guy named Vankatesan. Diego says you really need to see it."

Samantha couldn't keep the shock off her face.

"Samantha, who is Vankatesan?" Morgan asked.

"The leader of the thugs and the architect behind all of this," Samantha answered. She nodded at Nick.

"Tell Diego to put him on," she commanded.

Samantha looked to the monitor near her. Its screen flickered, and Vankatesan's face filled the whole of it. He had a quiet, benign look on his face.

"Hello, Miss Ramsell," Vankatesan greeted.

What she was seeing was being broadcasted to the world. Samantha couldn't keep the contempt out of her voice.

"And here we have Tanvir Vankatesan. Deceiver. Murderer. Thug."

Vankatesan put a hurt look on his face. "You cut me to the quick, Miss Ramsell. And here I am, to offer you a boon."

"You're turning yourself in?" Samantha asked.

"No, I have something that all reporters crave. I am here to give you a scoop."

Vankatesan stepped away to reveal what was behind him.

"My God," Morgan said in Samantha's earpiece.

It was an altar carved out of stone. Evil, leering faces were inscribed on it. Grooves were cut onto its top. These led like gutters to the slab's four corners, where gold vases waited.

On the altar was a boy dressed in yellow-and-white clothing. He had chestnut-colored hair and appeared to be around seven years old. Flowers that were covered in fine dust were draped over him. A medical face mask, connected to a canister, covered his mouth and nose. Some sort of anesthetic gas was keeping the boy sedated.

Next to Samantha, the woman who had been looking for her lost child moaned in despair.

Samantha was stunned. Hanson had been wrong. She had been wrong. There weren't four sacrifices.

There was a fifth.

"Speechless, Miss Ramsell?" Vankatesan asked. He was back in the picture, and he stood next to a lectern. It had a huge, jeweled encrusted book on it. He opened it to a page marked with a silk ribbon.

"Then I will tell your television audience what you have omitted,"

Vankatesan continued as he turned to his book. In the background, two more robed men approached the altar, a Chinese man at the feet, an Indian at the head. Samantha recognized the Indian as Dasgupta. His arm was still in a sling.

Outside, the gunfire was intensifying, as if the thugs knew that they had to defend their leaders in their final act. Dresden was yelling into his radio as he tried to figure out a way to get inside. Fisher was staring at the receding helicopter as he talked into his phone. Samantha could hear him describing the situation to Hanson.

"They should know that in reality, we are saving the world," Vankatesan continued. He studied the book in front of him for a moment, then reached over to a nearby table and picked up a scabbard with a sword in it.

Samantha could see it was curved, like Cresswell's saber. Vankatesan held it out in front of him as his other hand pressed a button on the lectern.

The darkened archway on the back wall lit up in a lurid red, and it cast its light into the room. The camera had to take a moment to adjust.

Vankatesan took a step toward the altar.

"Kali, Kali!" he shouted.

The nearby policeman was holding the mother back, who was desperately trying to get at the monitor. Samantha looked up at Nick. "Give me that phone," she yelled.

Nick handed it to her.

"Diego, listen carefully. If he goes through with this, I want you to cut off the feed."

Diego sounded confused on the phone. "But Miss Ramsell, you told us that getting out the truth was—"

"Diego, this is different. This is a child—a mother's son. There are too many perverted people out there, and I won't have this cycling forever on the internet. I'm going to try to talk him out of it. But if I fail, I want you to cut the feed at the source. Not one digital byte leaves that building, do you understand?"

"Yes, ma'am," Diego answered.

Samantha turned to the mother.

"What is your son's name?" Samantha asked.

"Ryan," the woman answered.

Samantha turned back to her monitor. Vankatesan was a few steps closer to the altar.

"Devi Bajrefwari Lawha Dandayai, Namah!" he shouted.

He was near the boy now. The scabbard was in his left hand. With his right, he pulled the sword out about six inches. Samantha could see him run his thumb along the broadside of the blade.

Samantha guessed that there was some sort of oil on the sword, and now some of it was on the thug's hand. Vankatesan reached out and smeared it onto the boy's throat.

"Tanvir!" Samantha shouted into her mike.

The thug stepped back to his camera.

"My apologies, Miss Ramsell. I should translate for your audience. I was simply calling on the Goddess. Hail, Kali! Goddess of thunder. Hail, iron-sceptered Goddess!"

He pressed another button. A rumbling could be heard in the background.

"Tanvir. Professor. The boy, his name is Ryan."

Vankatesan was unmoved.

"I know. His name will be written in our book in a place of honor."

"Then think of your family. They're watching this. Think about what they—"

"It is for them that I do this!" Vankatesan yelled, his face twisted in anger. "Look around you, Ramsell! Famine. War. The pandemic. Do you think it was simply masks that stopped COVID? Her growing displeasure was evident, and for a moment, the entire world teetered on the edge of destruction! It was only through the tireless work of thuggee that her plague was stopped! In the end, my family, and all of you, will understand that!"

Vankatesan strode away from the monitor and came to a stop ten feet from the altar.

"Kali, Kali!" he shouted.

The other two men reached out. One took hold of the boy's ankles.

The other removed the gas mask, pulled the boy's arms above his head, and held on to his wrists.

Outside, the police were redoubling their efforts. However, a hail-storm of bullets still issued out of the mausoleum and kept them at bay. Fisher was yelling into his phone.

Samantha glanced up at the sky. The helicopter was a speck now, but was it turning around?

"O horrid-toothed Goddess. Eat! Cut! Destroy all that is malignant!" shouted Vankatesan.

The thug then drew his blade. He held it, and the scabbard, above him so that they formed a half-circle above his head.

Kali arrived.

It was her swords that first ascended into view—two curved blades held aloft, mirroring Vankatesan.

"Tanvir, please!" Samantha shouted. She held up her hand, ready to give the signal to cut the feed.

"Cut with this sword!" the thug screamed.

Kali rose higher, a black silhouette against the red backdrop. Her lower left hand held a *rumal*. In her lower right, some weird blade that Hanson had called a khadga. Despite the shaft's glaring red light, Samantha could see something glitter on each of Kali's upper elbows.

The diamonds. The sweat of Kali.

Still, the statue rose. The eyes and mouth glowed red, and her hungry gaze was locked on the boy.

"Bind! Bind! Seize! Seize! Drink blood!"

The statue now came level with the room. Ten feet high, it loomed over the thugs in the room.

"Salutations, to Kali!"

Panting with excitement, Vankatesan turned back to the camera and stepped to the lectern one more time.

"The boy's blood is as ambrosia. It will satisfy Kali for the decade to come!"

He pressed the last button. Stage lights mounted on the ceiling turned on and illuminated Kali in all her glory for the whole world to view.

Samantha, and everyone around her, could see that her skin was a dark blue, and her unbridled hair was as black as midnight. An ivory skull necklace was around her neck. Her chest was bare, and her long, snaking tongue protruded from her mouth. Narrow spotlights must have been focused near her elbows, for now the diamonds shone with a scintillating brilliance.

But for all of that, that wasn't the detail that held everyone's attention.

Clinging to the front of the statue was a man.

They couldn't tell who he was, for his face was hidden in the statue's hair. And with the lights on, everyone now realized that the statue was not complete. The lower right arm was broken off between the elbow and shoulder. The arm itself was gripped between the man's legs.

The khadga was in his hand, and he was leaning out with it, matching his arm to where hers had been, completing the illusion that the statue was whole as it had risen in silhouette.

He was in a precarious position as he leaned out. His other hand was clutching the statue's neck, trying to hold on as he had to keep adjusting his grasp on the statue's polished surface.

Samantha, and everyone else nearby, gaped at their monitors.

The other two thugs hadn't noticed yet. Instead, they were looking to their leader. Vankatesan, for his part, was turning back around as he placed the scabbard on the table as he brought his sword above his head.

"History repeats itself, Ramsell. Once again, those who oppose us are too late..." Vankatesan let the last part trail off as he looked upon Kali in surprise.

From the statue came the sound of a loud sneeze. Kali's hair dispersed from the man's face to reveal him.

"Yeah...about that," said Hanson.

Chapter 59

Earlier...

She looked like she wanted to tell him something...

"A boy," Susan whispered.

Hanson thought he had misheard her, and he shook his head at her in confusion.

"Do you have the boy?" she asked as she twisted in his arms to study the crowd by the helicopter.

"There was no boy," Hanson replied. "Kushal, Jerry. Was there a boy with you?"

"They had us drugged most of the time," Jerry yelled back.

"We didn't see anyone else," Kushal added.

She still had a hold of Hanson's collar. "They didn't drug me. They thought that they didn't need to. They didn't think I was awake."

"What did you see?" Hanson prodded.

"My door was open. They carried a child into the room across from me. They were careful with him. They said he was special."

"We have to go now!" the pilot yelled.

Hanson bore Susan to the chopper and handed her off.

"There's one more person in there," Hanson yelled at the pilot. "I'm going back for him. It's important that you radio everyone that you got all of us. Do you understand?"

The pilot looked confused for a moment, but when he saw Hanson step back from the chopper, he nodded.

Hanson turned and ran for the roof's exit door. He felt the wind pick up at his back as the helicopter rose off the mausoleum.

Bot-timer: "Twenty-five minutes."

Hanson put on his earpiece and dialed up Fisher.

"Hanson?" Fisher answered.

"Fisher, the most important thing right now is that you pretend I'm on that chopper," Hanson said as he raced down the hall.

"They're all out!" Fisher yelled on the other end.

Hanson sprinted by Kali and Jesus.

"I was wrong about the number of sacrifices. Vankatesan has one more special victim, a kid, in here with him. I'm going back for him. I would have taken the major with me, but she took a bad hit on the roof. The chopper is going straight for a hospital."

"One of them is hurt; they're going to the hospital first," Fisher said.

Hanson made the end of the hall and waved his card. The whole panel, urn niches and all, swung open. Hanson jumped into the stairwell.

"I see you," Fisher said as he continued his ruse. "Which hospital are you going to?"

"I think everything is going down in a room called the vault," Hanson explained as he ran down the stairs. "It's sealed shut, but I can access it by climbing up an elevator shaft."

"Vankatesan's on the television screen," Fisher said.

"Understood," Hanson replied. He raced down the hall until he came to a door. He slowly opened it and found himself in the foyer outside the vault.

"I see the boy," Fisher continued.

Hanson's shoulders sagged. Though Vankatesan was only feet away at this point, the vault doors were secured. He was going to have to take the long way.

Hanson moved to the elevator, and both waved his card and pressed the button furiously. He hopped in when the doors slid open.

"Vankatesan just flipped a switch. The archway behind him is lit up in red," Fisher reported.

Hanson paced in the elevator as he willed it to go faster. The doors opened, and Hanson dashed into the main temple.

A red light from behind the statue now illuminated the room. Kali was a dark silhouette.

Fisher's voice came over the earpiece. "There are three men in the room. The boy is on an altar. Vankatesan has a sword."

"I have a shotgun," Hanson replied. He had traded it for an AR-15 and had left it in the armory. He made his way to that room's door.

A rumbling noise from behind stopped him. He turned.

Kali was rising.

Hanson aborted his retrieving of the shotgun and sprinted for the statue. It was already two feet off the ground.

He passed the corpse columns.

Four feet.

Hanson jumped up and grasped her left leg. Most of his body was on the platform with the statue, but his legs hung free as the lift rose. The top of the arch was close now, and he had a wild fear of being sheared in half.

He desperately pulled with his arms and tucked his legs in. The interior wall of the shaft brushed the bottom of his feet.

"I'm with the statue," Hanson wheezed as he stood up. "If I hide in her shadow, I think I can surprise them."

"The other thugs have the boy's feet and hands. Vankatesan is making a speech."

Hanson looked up. There was an opening forty feet above him, and he could hear voices coming out of it.

Three to one odds. He needed another weapon. His gaze settled on the khadga.

It reminded him of one of his throwing axes. Kali had one foot up on a rock. Hanson clambered up and stood on her bent leg to reach for it.

It wouldn't give, so he yanked on it harder.

Her lower right arm snapped off.

"Jesus Christ, can't anything be easy," Hanson muttered.

"What was that?" Fisher asked.

Hanson ignored him. With the arm in his hands, he had a better grip on the khadga. He twisted it free.

But even if he did successfully hide, the statue was now glaringly incomplete. The thugs above would know something was amiss as soon as they saw her.

Grasping the khadga in his right hand, Hanson stretched out and lined up his arm where Kali's had been. It was too far. He needed to hold onto something.

He shifted the broken arm to between his legs and clamped it between them. His left hand now free, he reached out and clutched at the back of the statue's neck.

His clothes were dark, but he was afraid his face would still stand out. Hanson took a moment to drape Kali's hair in front of him. The wig was musty, and he had to resist the urge to sneeze.

Bot-timer: "Twenty minutes."

He was ten feet from the entrance now. Hanson stretched out with the khadga in hand. He realized he had it backward, so he spun it around like a tennis racket at the last moment as Vankatesan's booming voice washed over him.

Kali, and Hanson, rose into view.

Through Kali's hair, Hanson could see that the three thugs present were staring right at him.

The mind sees what it wants to see...the mind sees what it wants to see...

The thugs didn't react to him, and the statue rose the last few feet before coming to a stop. Vankatesan was in the back of the room, near a lectern. He turned away to speak at a video camera. He then pressed a button.

Stage lights snapped on. On the statue Hanson felt exposed. Vankatesan was turning back toward Kali.

"History repeats itself, Ramsell. Once again, those who oppose us are too late..." Vankatesan's look of triumph turned to one of confusion.

The tickling in his nose was too much. Hanson let loose a violent sneeze that cleared the hair from his face. Below him, all three thugs stared, dumbfounded.

"Yeah…about that," said Hanson.

He released his hold of Kali, grabbed the broken arm with his left hand, and leaped off the statue. As he fell, he threw the khadga at the thug holding the boy's hands.

It took one lazy turn as it flew. Then its curved edge cleaved into the man's skull. The thug's head snapped back as he crumpled to the ground.

Vankatesan's look of dismay now turned to anger, and he took several steps forward, his tulwar raised high. A Chinese man was at the boy's feet, and he was reaching for a knife.

"Need a hand?" Hanson yelled as he threw the statue's arm at Vankatesan. The thug instinctively tried to back up as he swatted at the appendage. He tripped on his robes and fell.

Hanson twisted toward the man at the boy's feet, his right hand going over his left shoulder as he reached for the hilt of the saber. He drew it as he rushed the *kurthow* lunging at him, and he brought the blade down on the thug's knife-hand. His sword sliced through fingers and knocked the knife free. With a cry of pain, the thug clutched his ruined hand to his chest.

Hanson ran him through with the saber.

The thug's body fell away from him. Hanson pulled the saber out and spun to his right to place himself between the boy and Vankatesan.

The thug had risen from the floor and had taken a few steps toward the altar. But when he saw Hanson waiting there, he stopped, a wary look on his face.

Realizing that Vankatesan was all that was left and that he didn't have a gun, Hanson relaxed a bit and stood up from his defensive crouch.

Vankatesan did the same.

"Looks like someone's god has abandoned him," Hanson taunted.

Vankatesan's eyes swept over the carnage surrounding the altar. Then the thug looked up at the statue of Kali. The scowl that had been pinching his face was replaced with an unnerving smile.

"Actually, Hanson, She is still with me. She has even answered my prayers."

Hanson's sword lowered a bit. "What the hell do you mean by that?"

"I prayed, Hanson. I prayed that before all of this was over that somehow, She would deliver you to me," Vankatesan answered as he held up a hand to Kali and then toward him. "And here you are."

"You're kidding, right?" Hanson replied incredulously, "Look all around you, Vankatesan. Your fellow *Sath Zut* are dead, everything you built is in ruins, and you think that is a good thing?"

Vankatesan gave a slight shrug. "She works in mysterious ways."

Hanson shook his head. "It's over. Let the boy go and command your thugs upstairs to give themselves up. There's no use letting them all die. They'll get a fair trial—"

"You mean like Sleeman gave us?" Vankatesan snarled. "Thousands, Hanson. Thousands of men were found guilty in frontier courts with the slimmest of evidence. How many thugs had a fair trial? And how many innocent men fell into the Company's trap?"

Hanson remained silent.

"No, Hanson—" Vankatesan began as he paced back to the table. He laid his sword and scabbard upon it. Then the thug carefully removed the *rumal* around his waist.

"There will be no giving up today."

* * *

"What are they doing?" Morgan asked.

Samantha barely heard him as gunfire was still raging all around her. Outside of the cemetery's walls, truck sirens wailed as firefighters worked to clear the neighboring households.

She was focused on her monitor. Vankatesan had lain his *rumal* on a table. In the background, Hanson removed his earpiece and placed it on the altar behind him.

Though he was responding to Morgan in the studio, Jameson's voice still came faintly to Samantha. "I think they're getting ready to duel."

Vankatesan removed his yellow-and-white robe next. He still was still wearing pale-yellow pants of silk, but he was naked from the waist up. To Samantha's dismay, she saw that Vankatesan was built like an Olympic athlete. Muscle rippled on the thug's lean body as he picked up his sword.

"Touch your shoulder Hanson," she whispered.

* * *

Bot-timer: "Fifteen minutes."

Hanson watched Vankatesan drop his robe on the table. Christ, the thug looked like he worked out several hours a day. Hanson took off the scabbard that had been slung over his shoulder. He kept his shirt on.

Vankatesan reached for a nearby gold bowl with his free hand. It held some sort of paste, and he used his thumb to scoop a small bit of it out and wipe it across his forehead.

"Millions dead by thuggee, Hanson," Vankatesan continued. "That's the lie that history has been focused on all of these past decades. The West has conveniently forgotten that millions of Indians died of famine during the Company's rule—"

"Enough, I get it, thug. Terrible mistakes were made while the Company was running things. Everyone realizes that now," Hanson replied as he took a few steps forward himself, his saber held out in front of him. He had recognized what Vankatesan had smeared across his forehead. Sandalwood paste. A small ritual that brought Vankatesan closer to his God—and kindled both courage and confidence.

Hanson's left hand began to rise toward his right shoulder. He had his own good luck charm. He paused halfway, though, as a taunt to keep Vankatesan off-balance came to mind.

"But you have to admit," Hanson continued as he spread his arms wide. "When the Company decided to wipe out thuggee, and then stencil the word 'THUG' on your great granddaddy's skull, they got that part right."

With a scream of rage, Vankatesan was on him.

* * *

Outside

"Samantha!" Fisher yelled.

She ignored him. Terror gripped her heart as Vankatesan charged Hanson and brought his sword crashing down. Hanson barely brought his own blade up to block it. Now Vankatesan was only a few feet from Hanson, savagely hacking at him.

"Samantha!" Fisher yelled again.

She glanced up. Fisher was back at the command vehicle's big screen. Throughout the cemetery, the police continued to trade gunfire with the thugs.

"Samantha, can he do this?" Fisher shouted as he gestured toward the screen.

She shook her head a bit and shrugged her shoulders. She wasn't sure.

A look of concern crossed Fisher's face. "Are you hit?"

That puzzled her. What was Fisher talking about?

Then she realized that she was holding her right shoulder.

* * *

The Vault

Vankatesan was coming at him like a berserker as he swung his tulwar with both hands clasped around the hilt. Hanson had parried the first blow one-handed, but the thug had almost knocked his sword out of his grasp. Hanson had to reinforce his grip with his left hand.

Vankatesan's strength was enhanced by adrenaline-fueled rage, and his blows were bone-jarring. Hanson continued to parry them, but soon realized that parry was too delicate of a term. He was now simply blocking the thug's slashing attacks, both swords ringing loudly as they beat against each other. Vankatesan's assault had him off balance, and Hanson couldn't get his feet set.

He was also being driven back toward the altar, where the boy still lay.

Hanson felt a desperate need to rub his right shoulder to even the odds but feared letting go of his sword for even just a moment.

He was forced back another step, and he felt something hard and unyielding against his heel.

The altar.

Vankatesan swung his blade horizontally. Hanson blocked it but had to twist and lose ground. He found himself at the boy's side, near his waist.

Vankatesan was at the boy's head. The thug took a moment to look down at the oil-smeared neck, and his evil smile let Hanson guess what he was going to do next.

Vankatesan took a step back and swung the tulwar in a downward stroke.

Hanson had no choice. He released his left hand's hold on the saber's hilt and stretched out in a desperate attempt to parry the blow.

The thug changed his sword's trajectory and slashed it across Hanson's exposed chest instead.

Agony seared Hanson's senses, and he shrieked in pain as the tulwar tore into him, slicing through his shirt, skin, and the muscle beneath. He collapsed against the altar, his sword arm dropping to his side.

Vankatesan brought up his blade to sweep through Hanson's neck.

And stopped. A look of religious ecstasy crossed the thug's face.

"Kali khilaya jan cahi'e!" he shouted as he backed up a few steps and pointed his sword toward the statue.

Hanson didn't react. The pain from his wound was excruciating, and he labored for breath. Next to him, the boy stirred.

"Kali khilaya jan cahi'e!" Vankatesan shouted again, this time at the camera. He was also panting as his exertions caught up to him. Then, remembering his audience, he switched back to English.

"Kali must be fed," the thug gasped at the camera. He turned back toward Hanson and pointed his sword to a point beyond him. Wearily, Hanson looked to the statue.

The thug's sword had slung his blood toward the alcove. Some of it now dripped down Kali's face and rolled down her tongue.

"She delights in your blood, Hanson," Vankatesan announced

triumphantly. The thug was now pacing back and forth as he stared at the statue in awe.

Hanson stood back up, wobbling as he did so. Too soon. He sagged back against the altar as the room spun. The wound across his chest hurt like hell, but it wasn't debilitating. He just needed more time to catch his breath.

"It was all a lie," Hanson gasped out.

Vankatesan continued pacing, but he cocked his head questioningly.

"You have to have seen it, Vankatesan," Hanson continued, his words coming out haltingly as he struggled to regain his breath. "History is being rewritten as we speak. All those things the approvers said, it was all bullshit."

The thug didn't reply. He, too, was trying to get his second wind.

Hanson's head was clearing, and his strength was returning. He was even able to bring his blade up warily every time Vankatesan moved closer to him, only to gratefully let it sag back down when the thug paced away.

"Your religion was based on a lie," Hanson continued. "That was prompted by the fearful imaginations of a man who didn't understand what he was seeing."

"The same can be said of all religions," Vankatesan sneered. "But still, my faith sustains me." He then gestured toward Hanson.

"But you're the self-proclaimed skeptic. It's you everyone must be wondering about. Have you, somewhere between looking for lake monsters or UFOs, gone searching for shipwrecks on Turkish mountains—"

Hanson didn't respond.

"Or have you pointed a telescope at the night sky, where you searched for nebula where a star once shown in the east?"

Still, Hanson remained quiet, but now he was standing, and his saber was up at his side.

"Yes, I can see I hit a nerve," Vankatesan continued. "Nonbelievers surround us, Hanson. Every day they offer up 'proof' that there are no gods, that all religions are a sham. So, what I wonder is—"

The thug bent down at the knees as he prepared to spring forward.

"Here at the end, what do you believe, Steve Hanson?"

Hanson was also bent down at the knees, and his left hand was massaging his right shoulder.

"Let me show you, thug."

Vankatesan once again charged forward.

This time, Hanson met him halfway.

The thug brought his tulwar up for a sweeping two-handed blow. Hanson, his feet under him in a proper stance, quickly lunged forward, and the point of his saber stretched for Vankatesan's chest.

Vankatesan aborted his move and swatted at Hanson's saber in a clumsy attempt at a parry. He was forced to back up as he did so.

Away from the altar.

Behind him, Hanson heard the boy yawn.

Hanson pursued Vankatesan, his feet moving in small, quick steps as he maintained an easy balance. Ahead of him, Vankatesan wound up for one of his haymakers.

Hanson feinted, which forced Vankatesan to again protect himself. The thug's parry missed, and Hanson quickly followed up with his actual attack, a lunging cut along the thug's right arm.

A look of pain crossed his opponent's face, and Hanson allowed himself a smile of satisfaction. Now, this fight was going his way.

Though it still wasn't easy. He was using a saber instead of a foil. Its balance made dueling with it difficult. He also couldn't move his upper body as freely as he wanted. He could feel the wound on his chest painfully tearing every time he thrust.

Vankatesan changed tact. Though his stance was all wrong, he tried a stabbing lunge himself.

Hanson parried it and then followed with a quick riposte that slashed the thug's left arm.

Vankatesan backed up a few more steps. It brought him close to one of the room's candelabras. Hanson swept his saber across the top of it, the blade collecting and slinging the hot wax onto Vankatesan's bare chest. The thug gasped in pain and looked at Hanson in surprise.

"All's fair," Hanson grunted as he lunged again. That attack resulted in a cut along the thug's side.

Vankatesan was panting for breath. His body glistened in sweat, and his curly hair clung to his forehead in wet ringlets. His eyes betrayed his fear.

Hanson didn't let up, and the saber rang as it blocked the tulwar. It felt lighter in his hands now, as if the blade wanted to settle an old score.

Defiance replaced fear on the thug's face.

"You may kill me, Hanson," Vankatesan gasped. "But you will not win. The boy is prepared. Be it the razor's edge of a sword or fire, Kali will have him."

Hanson didn't reply, but he stepped closer as he swung the saber.

"And I do not fear death," Vankatesan continued. "I have lived my life as Kali has ordained. Paradise awaits me, Hanson. This, I am sure. What can you be sure of?"

Hanson feinted.

"All I know right now is that if you have your paradise, then there must be a hell," Hanson growled. The thug reacted to his deceptive attack, and his blade thrust to Hanson's left.

"And whatever hell is—" Hanson's left arm snapped forward, and his hand darted under Vankatesan's extended tulwar. He grabbed the thug's right hand behind the guard and held it, and the tulwar, close. The maneuver gave Hanson the opening he needed. He plunged his saber into Vankatesan's chest, and two feet of bloodied steel burst out of the thug's back.

"You're already there," Hanson finished as Vankatesan's body slumped to the floor.

* * *

Outside

Chancellor kept his face impassive as Vankatesan fell to the ground, for he knew that he was being watched. The Portland agent thought he had been clever, but Chancellor was aware that Fisher knew he was a thug.

It explained the lies Fisher had been telling all afternoon about Hanson's movements. And soon Fisher would make a move on him.

Unless he was proactive.

Hopperton shouted orders nearby. With word that bombs were going off soon, everyone was pulling back to the outer perimeter. Chancellor walked over to him.

"Unbelievable," Hopperton said.

"Yes, Hanson did it, again," Chancellor forced himself to say.

"Not that," Hopperton replied. "I'm talking about the fact that these terrorists have been hiding under our noses this whole time."

"I've been making a few calls to the Jack Evans building," Chancellor said. "These thugs could not have done this without inside help. I think someone in my department is one of them."

"Do you know who it is?"

"I have some theories, and I should know for sure in a few minutes," Chancellor replied as he held up his phone. "So right now, I don't trust anybody on the Dallas police force, and I need your help."

"Sure thing, Slick. You've always been there for me. What can I do?"

"Position all of your men evenly throughout the perimeter. If Hanson gets out with that child, our thug may make a move on them. I need your agents in place so that they can react quickly to the threat."

"Done," Hopperton said as he brought up his own phone to his ear.

"Thanks, pardner. I knew I could count on you," Chancellor said.

* * *

Fisher kept one eye on Chancellor and one on Hanson.

The thug was talking to Hopperton. Hanson was bent over the boy on the altar.

Fisher thought about making a move against Chancellor now. However, with Hanson still trapped inside, he decided that he may still need the thug in play, so he dialed Hanson's number instead. On the monitor, Hanson put his earpiece back on.

"The boy's all right; he's waking up," Hanson said. "I think they kept him sedated with some sort of gas. It kept his body purer for the sacrifice."

Fisher glanced to his left. Both Samantha and the boy's mother were staring at their own monitor, relief on their faces.

"I know, we can see you both," Fisher said.

He saw Hanson give a start and then glance over his shoulder.

"You saw all of that—" Hanson began.

"We'll talk about it later," Fisher replied. "Right now, you need to get out of there."

Hanson was slinging his sword and scabbard over his shoulder again. He grimaced in pain as the strap rubbed against his chest. His shirt was soaked in blood.

A lot of blood.

"There are a couple of things I need to do first," Hanson replied.

He picked up the boy and carried him to the alcove, where he placed him at the Kali's feet. He then moved behind the camera for a moment. When Hanson came back on screen, he had a C-4 bomb in his hands, which he put on the altar. He then placed Vankatesan's sword on top of it.

Bot-timer: "Ten minutes."

"Hanson, you have less than ten minutes left," Fisher said into his phone.

Hanson was now standing in front of the camera.

"I know," he replied. "I think the *Sath Zut* had their own way out. I'm going to find it." Hanson then looked straight into the lens.

"See you in nine," he finished as he reached up and turned the camera off.

Chapter 60

The Vault, 3:50 p.m.

Vankatesan's lectern was equipped like a stage manager's prompt corner. Hanson found and toggled a switch labeled "Descend." Kali began to sink, and he ran to the statue and hopped on.

The boy was fully awake, and he was standing up, though his eyes were glassy, and his jaw slack.

"My legs feel funny," the kid announced. Then he giggled.

The statue continued its descent, and the walls bathed them in red light.

Bot-timer: "Nine minutes."

The app was going off every minute now.

"Who was that?" the kid asked.

"My phone," Hanson answered.

"That lady is naked."

"I know."

"That's nasty. My mom is going to be mad that you let me see naked ladies."

Hanson had to admit that sounded bad.

"Then close your eyes, he instructed.

The kid did so, and he slapped his hand over his eyes also for good measure. Over the earpiece, Fisher spoke up.

"Hanson, you need to hurry," he advised.

"I am. I'm just stuck on the world's slowest elevator," Hanson replied.

"Who are you talking to?" the kid asked.

"Someone on the phone," Hanson answered. "Now, quiet, this is important."

The boy responded to that by clapping his other hand across his mouth.

"Do you know where that secret tunnel is?" Fisher asked.

"No, that was a bluff," Hanson answered. "Tell the police to focus their fire on the front doors of the building."

"Hanson, I think their outside thug is on to me."

"That's fine. Keep him guessing. It's a double fake. I'm going out the back garage doors instead. There are no windows in there, so the area should be clear."

Bot-timer: "Eight minutes."

"Who was that?" Fisher said.

"Whobh bah dhat?" the kid echoed through his hand as he looked blindly around him.

Hanson rolled his eyes and hung up the phone.

The rest of the ride was painfully slow. When they neared the bottom, he picked up the boy and jumped off even though the lift still had a few feet to go. Hanson gasped in pain as he ran as fast as he could across the temple floor. They entered the armory.

He set the boy down, wobbling a bit as he did so. The white shirt that the thugs had provided for the boy was covered in Hanson's blood.

"The naked lady is gone. You can open your eyes now," Hanson said.

"It's bhark ind vere!"

"Hands…" Hanson prompted.

The kid removed his hands from his face.

The Mossberg was on the table, where he had left it. Hanson picked it up.

"Can I have this?" the kid said behind him.

Hanson turned around. The boy had the last AR-15 in his hands. He was waving it around and pointing it at everything in the room, including Hanson.

"Pew…pew…pew…"

Hanson grabbed it out of the kid's hands and put it back on the table.

"Let's go, Jonny Quest."

They took the elevator up. Hanson tucked the boy in a corner while he stood ready with the shotgun. He hoped there weren't any thugs between them and the exit. The boy had already seen enough.

The foyer was empty.

Bot-timer: "Seven minutes."

"Who was that?"

Hanson took the kid by the hand and made his way down the hall to his left.

* * *

Tranquil Groves main reception area, 3:54 p.m.

"Everyone to me!" Jason shouted.

The gunfire surrounding him was a continuous roar, and the whole room was filled with a smoky haze and smelled of gunpowder. Small cardboard boxes that once held ammunition were scattered on the ground. Though the thugs had stockpiled an enormous reserve of bullets, they were running out.

Bryce stood next to Jason. Since Jason's arm was in a sling, and Bryce was missing a hand, neither of them could use rifles. So instead, they had both taken on the role of commanding the building's defenses.

"Everyone, listen up," Bryce added.

The gunfire abated and heads turned their way.

"Chancellor just texted me," Jason yelled. "The police are going to focus on the main front door, so Slick thinks that Hanson's going for an emergency exit instead! He must pass through here on his way up from the temple. So, I want everyone to make their way here. No matter what, Hanson doesn't get through!"

From throughout the building, thugs converged on him.

* * *

3:55 p.m.

Hanson burst into the garage; his shotgun held out at the ready.

The long room was empty, and only the same two hearses that he had seen earlier were parked in it. Hanson swept through the area, just to make sure no thugs were hiding. The muffled sound of gunfire could be heard from the long hall that stretched to the funeral parlor's main reception area.

Hanson relaxed a bit and went hunting for the controls that opened the garage doors. He stopped in dismay when he approached one of the exits.

The garage doors weren't lightweight fiberglass. Instead, they were made of steel. On each side of them were three eyelets for placing a padlock. Six padlocks secured each door.

Bot-timer: "Four minutes."

"Who was that?" the kid asked.

And that wasn't half of it. On the ground in front of each door were three concrete pylons—bollards that had been screwed into place. Each one had a large, hexagon-shaped stud on top where a massive wrench could be used to tighten them down.

Hanson ran to one of them in desperation and wrapped his arms around it as he tried to twist it off. His blood smeared on the post, and he grunted from the exertion.

"Dude, do you even lift?" the kid asked. Then he laughed.

Hanson looked wildly around the room. They were sealed in.

There were doors set in the interior wall. Closets. Hanson went to one. If he could find the wrench and remove a few bollards, he might be able to ram the doors.

It turned out to be a storeroom for caskets. Large shelves held several dozen.

Bot-timer: "Three minutes."

"Who was that?" the kid said again.

Hanson dialed up Fisher.

"Hanson, you're cutting it close!" Fisher shouted into Hanson's earpiece.

"Change of plans. The garage is sealed," Hanson replied. An Aegis casket was on a lower shelf. Hanson rolled a gurney near it to load it up. "I'm coming out the front for real."

"The front door?"

"Something like that. Maintain your fire till the last moment."

Hanson hung up and wheeled the casket into the garage. He pulled up to the converted Hummer and opened the back. With a pained grunt, he shoved the casket in.

He rolled the gurney back into the storeroom and selected a second Aegis casket. He moved it to the hearse and crammed it in next to the other one.

Bot-timer: "Two minutes."

Hanson opened the passenger door and pushed the kid in. Then he dashed one last time into the storeroom. He threw caskets open and grabbed as many pillows as he could. He carried these to the hearse's front passenger side, where the boy already had his seatbelt on. Hanson stuffed the pillows all around him.

"These are soft," the kid said as he stroked them.

"They should be. They're designed to keep you comfortable for all of eternity," Hanson muttered. He hoped they would be enough. The hearse had airbags, but he wasn't sure if the kid was heavy enough to engage them.

Hanson ran to the driver's side and leaped in. He tossed the shotgun and the saber on the back seat. He then turned to the dashboard.

No keys.

Bot-timer: "One minute."

Hanson jumped back out and went to a nearby pegboard. Two sets of keys hung there. He grabbed them both.

"Fifty seconds."

Hanson slid back in. Tried the first set. They didn't fit.

"Maybe you should try the other key," the kid suggested.

"Forty seconds."

Second set. The hearse started up, and Hanson slammed it into reverse.

"Hang on," he ordered as he floored it. The boy clutched his pillow tighter.

The tires squealed as the hearse lurched backward. Hanson cranked the wheel hard and aimed for the hallway.

The hearse shot into it. Fortunately, the hall was large enough to comfortably accommodate the vehicle. But despite that, the passenger side of the Hummer still ground into the wall, shearing off the mirror and crashing through the small tables that held flowers in Baccarat vases.

"We're going backward," the kid said as he looked out the window. Then he glanced at Hanson, his eyes wide and awe in his voice. "In time!"

"Thirty seconds."

"Who was that?" Hanson and the kid said together.

"Ha, jinx," the boy added.

The Hummer crashed through the folding partition that separated the hall from the main room. In his remaining side mirror, Hanson could see that the entire area was filled with thugs. Most of them were set up at the narrow windows, their AR-15s pointed outward. However, a large group were in the center of the room, positioned to watch all possible egress points.

Hanson spotted Todd and Bryce. He briefly wondered what their real names were.

Then the hearse slammed into the demo casket. Hanson stomped on the brakes as the Hummer's back window shattered.

The casket launched from its gurney and tumbled across the marble floor. It took a few bounces before it smashed into the two Portland thugs. Their crushed and lifeless bodies were tossed to the side as the casket plowed into a dozen more thugs.

The hearse came to a stop in the center of the room.

"Ten seconds."

Hanson put the hearse in drive and floored it.

"Nine."

He couldn't continue down the hall. A gauntlet of thugs would pour high-powered bullets into the hearse's side, slaughtering him and the boy.

"Eight."

He had to keep the back of the hearse to the thugs. Hanson angled for the stairs and hit the first step. With a bone-jarring lurch, the hearse began to climb.

"Seven."

Below them, the thugs opened fire, and they filled the back of the hearse with a hail of bullets that punched through both glass and metal.

"Six."

The Aegis caskets lived up to their name as they absorbed the brunt of the thug's attack. Hanson's driver's side window exploded, and a bullet creased his shoulder. He yelled in pain.

"It's an earthquake," the kid observed as he calmly gazed around him.

"Five."

They made the top. Crypts surrounded them, and the Hummer careened into one and cracked it open. A casket tipped out of it.

"Sorry," Hanson muttered.

"Four."

He lined up in the center path and accelerated. Ahead, the stained-glass window shone vividly as sunlight poured though the images of Jesus and God standing before the entrance to heaven. Hanson was a bit surprised that it was still whole. The police must have been doing their best to avoid damaging it. Hanson could sympathize.

It was a national treasure.

"Three."

Hanson reached for and buckled his seat belt.

"Two."

The entire window filled Hanson's vision. Jesus stood in front of him, and he looked down at him with an enigmatic expression. Hanson hoped it was forgiveness.

"Jesus!" the kid yelled as he pointed.

Hanson put his right arm across the boy's chest.

"One."

The hearse punched through the Pearly Gates.

Time slowed for Hanson. A million glass shards surrounded him in a cloud of rainbow hues as the hearse sailed into the outside air, thirty feet off the ground. The shards spun leisurely, and they caught the sun's rays in dazzling brilliance.

Bot-timer: "We have lift-off!"

Tranquil Groves exploded.

Hanson saw it in his mirror. The edges of the mausoleum seemed to blur for a moment as the outer structural explosives went off. Then, a fraction of a second later, the primary charges followed.

The massive stone building erupted in a titanic roar.

Hanson looked forward. The hearse was dropping fast. He had hoped to reach the cemetery's water feature for a softer landing, but a cement path was rushing up at him instead. His arm still across the boy's chest, Hanson braced for impact.

From behind them, the pressure wave hit.

* * *

The blast knocked Samantha and the woman next to her down. Debris rained all around them.

The police fared a little bit better because they were hunkered down behind monuments or their vehicles. The two women had been a bit more in the open as they watched for any sign that Hanson and the boy had made it out.

Dazed, she stood back up and turned toward where the mausoleum once stood.

A vast cloud of smoke and dust hung there instead. For a moment, it looked like it was going to engulf them, but it stopped. Then, slowly, the dust began to drift away from them in the slight breeze.

"Did they make it?" the mother asked with tears in her eyes.

"I don't know—" Samantha began.

She strained to see through the cloud. The gunfire had stopped, and except for the chatter of some radios, it was quiet in the cemetery.

As the cloud thinned, a shape began to form out in the parking lot. It was a hearse lying on its side, its undercarriage exposed toward the crowd. The driver's side door had been ripped off, and it lay on the ground next to it. Except for one wheel slowly turning, there was no other movement.

In her ear, Morgan's voice. "Samantha? Did they make it?"

She remembered that she was still on the air. And most likely, millions still watched. "They had to have, Doug," she answered. "After all that has happened, it wouldn't be fair."

Morgan remained quiet on his end. The wheel on the hearse stopped spinning.

"It wouldn't be fair," Samantha whispered.

The dust cloud drifted farther back. The hearse rested there, alone.

Then a head popped up from inside the vehicle.

Hanson.

He looked hurt, and he struggled to lever himself up into a sitting position on top of the vehicle. Then, for a moment, he rested there as he studied the area around him.

The radio chatter subsided. A hush descended on the cemetery.

Then Hanson reached down, and with an effort, he hauled something up. It was Ryan, clutching a pillow and waving furiously.

The whole cemetery erupted into a cheer.

"My God, have you seen anything like this!" Morgan shouted in her ear.

Next to her, the boy's mother broke away and sprinted for the hearse.

"Samantha, the world wants to know. Is it over? Is this truly the end of the thugs?" Morgan asked.

Samantha looked to her side. Fisher was nearby, but his back was to her. He was facing toward the Dallas police chief and the cowboy standing near him.

"No, Doug, there's one more thing to take care of."

* * *

Chancellor made his way to Dresden. The police chief still looked a bit stunned by the shock wave that had just rolled over them.

"We did it," Dresden said.

Chancellor clapped a hand on the chief's shoulder. "Well done, John. Not a hostage killed." Chancellor paused for a moment. "Your father would have been proud."

The thug could see the appreciation in the other man's eyes.

"But we have one more task ahead of us," Chancellor continued. "I've been making some calls. These thugs couldn't have eluded us all these years without some help. I think I've found their inside man."

Dresden's eyes hardened. "Who is it?"

"I don't know exactly," Chancellor answered. "All I know is that it's an FBI agent."

Dresden craned his neck and looked around. Chancellor knew what he was seeing. Blue jackets with "FBI' printed on their backs were scattered throughout the area.

"One of them may still make a move on the boy," Chancellor warned.

"What do we do?" Dresden asked.

"For now, disarm and take all of them," Chancellor answered. "But for God's sake, don't kill any of them."

"There's so many of them."

"We still outnumber them," Chancellor said with a smile. "It's been my experience that three to one odds are more than enough."

Dresden nodded and brought his radio to his face. He paused. "What about Fisher?"

"He's definitely not their inside man," Chancellor replied. "But take him too. He may interfere when all of this goes down."

Chancellor watched as Dresden made the call. Behind him, he could sense Fisher closing in on him.

Then chaos broke out.

Throughout the entire perimeter, Dallas police officers turned their guns on the FBI agents. They screamed at them to give up their weapons. Instead, the FBI agents brought up their own firearms and refused.

Chancellor watched with satisfaction as policemen drew their weapons on Fisher. The Oregon agent looked surprised. He tried to move forward, but the Dallas officers blocked him. Fisher then began shouting in their direction, but his voice was lost in the din.

Out on the cemetery, Chancellor noted that the boy's mother was closing on the hearse.

"What about them? Someone needs to secure Hanson and the boy," Dresden asked.

"Let me do it. You have your hands full here," Chancellor answered as he gave Dresden a paternal smile.

"Thanks, Slick, for everything."

"Think nothin' of it," the thug replied. He adjusted his hat and turned away from the chaos growing around him as he walked toward the ruined hearse.

Chapter 61

Hanson sagged to the ground.

It was the blood loss. Though the pressure wave had carried the hearse farther and enabled it to plunge into and skip across the cemetery's decorative pond, the landing had still been rough. The airbag had blasted into his chest, and the sideways wrenching motion of the tumbling vehicle had ripped the gash across his chest wider.

The bleeding was significant, and the deflated airbag was now dyed a bright red. Fortunately, the boy was unfazed by the ride. As Hanson rested in the soft grass, the kid stood up.

"That's my mom!" the boy yelled.

Hanson glanced over. A woman had reached them, and she kneeled to hold her son.

"Ryan," she sobbed.

The kid looked behind him at the smoldering ruins that had once been Tranquil Groves Columbarium. "I didn't do that," Ryan said, his eyes wide.

The woman laughed at that, and she stroked the boy's hair. She turned to Hanson. "Thank you."

Talking felt like an effort. Hanson simply grinned and nodded his head. To his side, a man in a cowboy hat was walking toward them.

Seeing that everything was going to be okay, Hanson relaxed and settled himself down on the grass.

His phone vibrated in his pocket.

Hanson frowned. His earpiece was gone, so he fished out his phone from his pants pocket. It was covered with blood.

Yelling came through the phone's speaker—multiple men screaming, "Drop your gun!"

"Fisher?" Hanson asked.

"Hanson?! Hanson, the thug has turned everyone against me. He's coming your way!"

Hanson tried to stand, but the world spun around him, and he stumbled back down. The woman next to him looked at him questioningly.

"How?" Hanson asked.

"The guy's a legend around here. They call him Slick, and he has everyone eating out of his hand!" Fisher yelled. Hanson listened as Fisher shouted at someone near him. "Don't shoot. I'm just using my phone!"

Hanson didn't have the shotgun or the sword. Both were somewhere in the hearse. He turned toward the mother. "That man walking toward us, he's one of them," Hanson said. "He's coming for your boy."

Confusion and fear crossed her face.

"Keep the hearse between you and him," Hanson instructed. "Run!"

She scooped up her son and began running.

"Mom, ice cream's that way!" Ryan yelled as he pointed over her shoulder.

Hanson turned back to his phone, his fingers flying over the screen. "Fisher, I found this guy's son inside. I even have a photo, and I'm sending it to you!"

"Understood!" Fisher answered.

"Just have the cops keep their eye on me," Hanson continued, his head swimming as he uploaded the photo. "I have a plan. I'll stall the thug, and I'll try to draw his fire if I have to."

"Hanson, talk around here is that this guy can shoot the head off of a rattlesnake at a hundred feet away!"

Hanson hit send on his phone messaging app.

"I didn't say it was a good plan," he muttered.

* * *

Samantha watched with alarm as police officers and FBI agents screamed and pointed their weapons at each other.

"Agent Fisher, what's happening!" she yelled.

Fisher had his back to her. Four police officers had their guns drawn on him. In his right hand, his weapon was out also. He had his phone held in his left.

"It's Chancellor. He's turned everyone against me!"

Fisher was looking at his phone as if waiting for a text or something. More cops joined the four on Fisher. He was being surrounded. Samantha looked toward the hearse. The thug was closing in on Hanson.

"Dan, hurry! He's going to kill them!"

"I know!" Fisher yelled as he waved his gun to keep the police at bay.

* * *

Chancellor walked toward the wrecked hearse. Behind him, he could sense the hostility and confusion as the police confronted the dozens of FBI agents present. That situation wasn't going to resolve itself soon.

The mother picked up her child and ran away. For a moment, he was concerned, but then he realized they weren't going anywhere. He reached down and felt the hilt of the large knife strapped onto his belt on his left side. Though it wasn't a weapon as pleasing as the tulwar was to Kali, it would do. He just had to make sure the boy was facing the correct direction when he took his life.

Correction. When Kali took the boy's life. He was but her instrument.

He didn't have any illusions about surviving the next few minutes. As soon as he sacrificed the boy, snipers posted on the perimeter would kill him. But Chancellor didn't mind. He was going to die in his true home, close to his Goddess, and with his son well taken care of. It was more than any old thug could ask for from Kali.

His eyes rested on Hanson struggling to stay conscious on the ground. Chancellor's right hand lowered and released the holster clip on his six-shooter.

Well, maybe he could ask his God for one more small boon…

* * *

Since Hanson was on his hands and knees, it was the thug's leather boots that first came into his view. He wearily looked up.

"Let me guess. Everyone calls you the 'Cowboy and the Indian' when you and Vankatesan get together," Hanson observed as he let his head hang back down.

Chancellor laughed—a harsh, barking sound. "True, and I always wished I had a dollar for every time that I heard it."

Then the thug paused, as if a new thought occurred to him. "But I guess I do, thanks to you. With everyone gone, billions of dollars are mine now."

Hanson let him ramble. For every second that he talked, the mother and her child were moving farther away.

"My ancestor took the King's shilling two centuries ago and sailed to India," Chancellor continued as he stood near Hanson, his arms resting easily at his sides. "Twenty shillings, now ten billion. Quite the investment. My family's reward for killing in Kali's name!"

"That's not how She works, Slick," Hanson snarled. "Everyone is so worked up on how the British propagated this idea of a blood-soaked Goddess, they forget that it was the thugs that brought up these lies in the first place!"

"They were not lies! The men that said these things, they're our saints! Feringheea, Alayar—"

"Were liars! I bet you have seen it yourself. Their boasts of the number of men that they killed aren't holding up to scrutiny, and thus are decreasing as time wears on. The myth of individual thugs killing nearly a thousand victims each—"

"Actually, there is one who reached a thousand."

It was the way Chancellor said it. His tone. Hanson looked up into his face and at his malevolent smile.

"That's right, Hanson," Chancellor continued. "One thousand and four, to be exact. When they search my home, they'll find evidence of my work. Futteh Khan, Ramzan, even the king of thugs, Behram, can't hold a candle to me. I'll be remembered as the greatest thug that ever lived!"

Hanson's head again dropped back down. The green grass below him was now painted in red.

"How?"

"The border. Thousands go missing in Mexico every year, Hanson. No one cares."

"Impossible."

"There's a thug who is a pilot that flies young thugs and me out there. You didn't think it was all cows, did you? Sure, we get their feet wet with that, but I have been making pilgrimages to the Mexican border for the past four decades, where I show the boys how to do it for real. We wipe out whole groups at a time. There's a canyon down there filled with more *gobbas* than you can count. Just like the old days. The kids love it."

"Gloat all you want. It's over now."

"Not quite," Chancellor replied. "The boy still needs to die, and I'm afraid your FBI friend won't be able to convince the police to stop me. I've been deceiving everyone here for forty years. My word is God to them!"

"The boy got away."

"No, Hanson, he's right over there. The bridge over our pond collapsed. The boy and his mother are trapped, and they're hiding behind the hearse. I think I'll just mosey on over there and..." he patted the hilt of his knife. "Save the world."

"The police will kill you when you do that."

"I know. But my son will live on. A powerful billionaire, carrying on the Chancellor name. What more could a father ask for?"

Hanson looked behind him. The thug was right. Ryan and his mother were huddled behind the hearse.

Time to play his last card.

"Speaking of junior, have you heard from him lately?"

Now it was Hanson's tone that gave Chancellor pause. The thug looked at him suspiciously.

"I didn't think so," Hanson continued. "Reception must suck in the bottom of those wells of yours, those charnel pits."

"You lie," Chancellor hissed.

Hanson tossed his phone out at Chancellor's feet. The thug reached down and picked it up. A picture filled its screen, and he studied it.

It was the photograph Hanson had taken down in the temple. Luke, as he lay on the ground with the measuring tape wrapped around his head. A caption was printed out next to the thug's head.

Skull size 22 inches. Must be a thug.

"Vankatesan said Luke made it out!"

"Vankatesan lied to you, Slick. Most likely so you wouldn't lose it out here."

"Only thugs know how to open those doors."

"*Gobba khom,*" Hanson whispered.

Chancellor stood there speechless.

"But hey, there's a bright side to all of this," Hanson continued as a grin spread across his face. "Now, you can tell everyone that at least he died *well.*"

Hanson watched as the expressions on the thug's face quickly went through the stages of grief. Denial. Pain. Rage. Hanson recalled that there were more phases, conditions like depression, and acceptance. But at the moment, those didn't matter.

Chancellor had stopped at rage.

* * *

Fisher's phone chimed as Hanson's JPEG file loaded.

"Dresden!" Fisher yelled. "I need you to see this."

The police chief barely heard him. He was dealing with Hopperton, who was bellowing in anger as he was restrained. But he turned his head at the sound of his name.

"Dresden, Chancellor's the thug!" Fisher yelled.

"Impossible. I've known him my entire life."

"You know his family, then?"

"Yes."

"Dresden, you need to see this. Now!"

Too many cops were between him and the chief, so Fisher tossed the phone.

Dresden caught it and looked at it. He spent agonizing moments fishing for his glasses in a pocket. Then he looked at it again.

"What the hell is this?"

"Do you recognize that man?" Fisher yelled.

"Yes, it's Luke Chancellor."

"Dresden, Hanson took that photo inside the building. This thug thing runs in the family. If the son is a thug, then so is the father!"

Dresden looked up at the distant form of Chancellor.

"So is the father!" Fisher shouted desperately.

Relief flooded Fisher as he watched Dresden grab the mic for his radio and gave out the order he wanted to hear.

"Snipers, acquire and target Chancellor near the hearse. Shoot on sight."

But the relief turned to despair as he heard the response he was dreading.

"Uh, sir, could you repeat that—"

* * *

"Congratulations, Hanson, you've changed my mind on saving the world," Chancellor said.

On the ground on all fours, Hanson tensed as he willed his body for one last action, a quick roll to the right. There was a headstone nearby. Maybe he could hide behind it as the cops figured out what was happening.

"Kali take you all!" the thug yelled as he drew his pistol.

Chancellor was fast on the draw, and his gun hand snapped up, the silver-plated revolver spinning on his finger, flashing in the light.

Instead of rolling, Hanson froze, mesmerized by the sight.

And then the thug wasn't there. It was as if he vanished into thin air. Both the cowboy hat and the spinning revolver hung in the air for a moment before falling to the ground.

The sound of a gunshot filled the still air of the cemetery.

* * *

Fisher turned toward it.

Everyone present turned also. They were all professional law enforcement officers, and each of them had hundreds of hours logged on gun ranges. As one, everyone turned toward where they heard the report of an unfamiliar weapon.

What they all saw was a large-bore rifle. An elephant gun. They shifted their gaze to the person wielding it.

Samantha.

She was standing in front of the Land Rover, the still-smoking rifle held out in front of her as she remained focused downrange. A part of Fisher thought for a moment that she should have been knocked over on her back from the .505's kick. But, instead, he saw a set of grooves dug into the small garden at her feet, where the rifle's recoil had driven her several feet back.

Multiple weapons swiveled in Samantha's direction.

Fisher could guess what was going through everyone's mind.

One of their own was down.

"Don't shoot. For God's sake, don't shoot!" Fisher shouted as he raced over to Samantha. He holstered his own gun and held up his badge instead.

He reached her. She was still frozen in place, her eyes on Hanson. Fisher took the rifle out of her hands. That snapped her out of it, and she looked at him. Tears were streaming down her face.

"He was going to kill him, Dan," she said.

"I know, I know."

Her legs buckled, and she leaned into him. Fisher dropped the rifle and caught her. He could sense Dallas police officers circling them.

She was sobbing now, and her body shook.

"He was going to kill him."

Special Agent Daniel Fisher gently lowered her to the ground and onto the soft bed of flowers. He used his body to shield her.

"I know."

Hanson crawled over to where Chancellor's body lay and propped himself up into a kneeling position.

The thug hadn't vanished. Instead, the bullet from the .505 had slammed into Chancellor's body armor with such force that it had knocked him ten feet over to the side. Hanson, focused on the pistol, just hadn't tracked him.

Chancellor was on his back and gasping in pain. The bullet had struck a glancing blow to the chest but hadn't penetrated the armor.

"What was that?" Chancellor groaned.

"Elephant gun. Five-oh-five. You should see the size of the slug that thing throws out. Your insides must be like pudding right now."

"Hurts," the thug wheezed.

"There's something you should know," Hanson continued as he leaned over him. "Does the name Cresswell ring a bell?"

Now a smile came to the thug's face, a rictus grin of blood-rimmed teeth. "Captain Cresswell. Young Alex's first kill back in India all those years ago."

"The elephant gun belongs to a descendant of Cresswell. So, I guess what they say is true…"

Chancellor turned his head and glared at Hanson.

"Karma really can be a bitch," Hanson finished.

"Thuggee will live on!"

"No, it won't. Like every other doomsday cult that doesn't pan out, everyone will see what a crock of shit it was when the world keeps on spinning."

Chancellor's labored breathing was coming more rapidly now, and blood frothed at his lips. His hands stretched upward to seek Hanson's neck. He couldn't reach, so he instead grabbed Hanson's collar and feebly pulled him down closer.

They were inches apart now, and Chancellor's hands weakly clutched at Hanson's throat. Hanson wearily batted them aside. "Thuggee dies with you, Slick. Tell that to Vankatesan when you see him."

Chancellor looked like he wanted to say more, but he couldn't muster the effort. Hanson watched as life left the thug's body, and he finally lay still.

Too weak to do anything else himself, Hanson rolled off the thug. The grass under him felt like a soft bed.

He looked up. He had placed himself in the shade of a monument, and a headstone reared above him. On it was a large statue of an angel. Her arms, and her wings, were spread wide as she looked down on him.

Or, instead of wings, was it an extra set of arms? He wasn't sure now —his vision was blurred around the edges. The sky behind her was an intense blue, and she just a silhouette. Hanson stared as the form above faded back and forth between angel and Goddess.

In the end, he decided it didn't matter. Either way, she was now reaching for him, beckoning. His strength gone and the world fading from his view, Hanson closed his eyes and wondered what waited for him on the other side.

Chapter 62

The A-Team.

Hannibal was explaining a plan to BA Baracus while Murdock and Face looked on. As usual, Murdock was all for it, but B.A. appeared skeptical.

It wasn't what Hanson expected heaven would be. Where were the cats? Still, he went with it and continued to observe the quartet do their thing. But then he slowly became aware that the gangs' usual explosive solution to their problems was now contained within a rectangular plastic frame—and that starched sheets under him were causing his back to itch.

He was lying in a hospital bed. Nearby, rhythmic beeping issued from a machine that displayed his body's major functions. Heartbeat sounded normal.

Several bags hung from a stainless-steel pole. Clear plastic hoses ran down from them, and their ends terminated with needles that pierced his arm.

He had survived.

The large television hanging from the ceiling was now running a commercial announcing that the station it was tuned to was running an *A-Team* marathon, and more action was to come.

That meant his mother was nearby.

Hanson looked to his left. She was sitting slightly behind the hospital bed as she read a magazine. Daylight eked through the cracks of the closed blinds behind her.

"Hey," Hanson croaked.

She looked up. His mother had a mask on, but she removed that so that he could see the smile on her face as she stood.

"I bet you're thirsty," she replied as she handed him a cup of water.

Hanson drank from the angled straw.

"How do you feel?" she asked.

Elica Hanson was a tall, large-boned woman with Nordic features. At seventy-two, blonde hair was now steel gray. Careworn wrinkles creased her face, though her eyes were still bright lavender.

"Not half bad," Hanson answered. He ran a hand across his hospital gown and felt a long seam of stitches across his chest. He should have been in agony. "They must be pumping me with strong pain relievers. How long was I out?"

"It's been almost twenty-four hours."

"How did you get here so fast?"

"Dan set it up. He arranged a direct flight and car for me."

"Dan? You mean Fisher?"

"Yes, Steve, he was concerned about you. I've been here since midnight."

Hanson relaxed and sank his head back into his pillow. A new thought struck him.

"A woman was shot. Is she all right?"

"It was rough for a while since the bullet fractured her humerus, but Isabella is going to be fine," his mother answered. "She's here in the same hospital, and I've already visited her. You can look in on her soon. Now, is there anything you need?"

There was, but his anxiety was kicking in. There was no way in hell he was going to use a bedpan.

"Could you help me to the bathroom over there?"

The monitor and IV stand were on wheels. Hanson made his way across the room with one hand holding the pole like a staff for support. His other hand clutched the material of his hospital gown behind him so that his ass wouldn't be exposed. A few minutes later, after his teeth were brushed and water had been splashed across his face, he felt human again.

He stepped back into the hospital room and found his mother talking to a woman wearing a white coat and carrying a stethoscope around the back of her neck. She was maskless, but she maintained her distance by remaining near the door. Again, Hanson made sure his gown's backside was secure.

The doctor was a petite Indian woman in her mid-forties. Wavy, raven-colored hair framed her tan face, and Hanson couldn't help but think of Kali when looking at her. Beautiful, without the terrible.

What he was thinking must have been clearly showing on his face, for the doctor smiled at him as her dark eyes looked him over critically.

"No, Mr. Hanson, it's not a cosmic coincidence that I've shown up in your hospital room," she said. "When I heard they were bringing you to my hospital, I pulled rank and took over your treatment."

Realizing that he had been caught staring, Hanson turned several shades of red. His mother came to his rescue.

"Dr. Basu was the one who stitched you up," his mother explained. "I told the nurses outside the door that you had just awoken."

"You wanted my case?" Hanson asked.

"Yes. Like the whole world, I watched you rescue those hostages. People in the next few days are going to be thanking you for saving them. I wanted a chance to thank you for saving her," Dr. Basu replied as she glanced toward something behind Hanson.

Hanson turned. Situated between two large cabinets was a small counter space. On it were several bouquets of flowers. Next to those, he recognized the family Bible, a large leather-bound volume that had belonged to his grandmother. It had dozens of dog-eared bookmarks sticking out of it. His mother always took it with her wherever she went.

Resting nearby was a small statue of Kali.

It was about five inches tall. Her skin was a light blue, and she was in a traditional pose—a khadga in one hand and the head of a vanquished demon in the other. A lower hand held a bowl to capture the demon's blood. Below her right foot rested Shiva, and her tongue hung out in embarrassment for doing so. The statue stood on a small platform that had several fresh flower blossoms placed on it.

"I asked Elica if it would be okay," Dr. Basu said.

It took his mom only minutes to be on a first-name basis with anybody.

"Of course, Doctor. Lord knows every bit helps," his mother said appreciatively.

Hanson approached the statue.

"Your *murti?*" he asked.

"Yes, She's been in my family for years. In my home, we think of her as both a benevolent mother and fierce protector."

"And I saved her?"

"Samantha Ramsell has been on the air quite a bit the past twenty-four hours, explaining what had happened. A lot of how the Christian world views Kali came from that period back in India when the men of the East India Company published their experiences."

"The *Ramaseeana* and *Confessions of a Thug*," Hanson noted.

"The ideas from those books still echo to this day," Basu continued. "And then this cult, these thugs, kept those concepts alive for all these years." Basu reached out to stroke the *murti's* black hair. "They forced their evil on her. But you put an end to it. So, thank you, Mr. Hanson. Thank you for releasing her from the bloody rituals of the thugs."

Hanson couldn't think of a response, so he stood there, tongue-tied. Basu reached for her stethoscope.

"And, at least, let me show my appreciation by making sure you're all patched up."

She masked up and put on some latex gloves. Then she studied his vital signs on the monitor and checked his stitches. Hanson had to undo the tie behind his neck with one hand as his other still held the gap closed behind him. Then he stood there, his chest and shoulders bare, as he kept the gown from slipping down even farther by pressing his elbows tight against his body.

"I do apologize though for the scar this is going to leave behind," Dr. Basu said, her brows knitted with concern.

"There's going to be a scar!?" Hanson replied excitedly.

Concern was now confusion. "Yes, I'm afraid there's nothing I can do about it," Basu answered.

Hanson's mother leaned in. "Doctor, you just told my son that he is going to bear the scar of a sword wound," she said as her eyes rolled a bit. "You just made his decade."

Hanson couldn't stop grinning.

"Well, in that case, it's going to be a wicked-looking scar, Mr. Hanson."

"Thanks, Doc," Hanson said.

Basu made her way to the door. "Just get some rest now. I'll tell the staff to leave you alone for a while."

His mother helped him get his gown back on. Hanson noticed her look of concern as she studied the sword wound more closely. She then turned her gaze to his left arm, where the scar from his Bigfoot encounter remained. Above that was the military tattoo from Kuwait.

"All these years, I've been trying to protect you. Overprotective, really," his mother confessed as she stared at the tattoo. "And yet, you always seem to find trouble."

Hanson remained quiet. He could tell that she was remembering a different hospital room from a day long past.

"He had so little time with you, and yet you're so much like him," she mused as she wiped away a tear running down her cheek. A thoughtful look crossed her face. "It must be the genes."

"Well, Mom, science has—"

A soft knock came from the door. Samantha, with half her face concealed behind a mask, peeked in.

"Is he still awake?"

Hanson remembered his manners. "Mom, this is—"

"Sam, my dear, come in," his mom replied as she walked toward Samantha, her arms spread wide.

Sam?

The two hugged. Hanson's head swiveled as he looked back and forth between the two women.

"Oh Steve, she and I and Fisher have been taking turns watching over you," his mother explained. "Sam and I have become good friends. I sent out a text announcing that you were awake."

Hanson noticed it then. Weariness was in the eyes of both his mother and Samantha. They've both had a long twenty-four hours. Suddenly, he felt guilty for being all rested up.

"I hope you kept my childhood stories to yourself this time," Hanson said worriedly.

"Even if she knows a few things, you can't prove they came from me, Steve," his mom replied as she winked at Samantha.

Samantha took off her mask and grinned back. "True, a reporter never reveals her sources, Elica."

His mother glanced at her phone. "Look at the time! Dan's arranged a car to take me to the airport and pick up my granddaughter."

His mother turned to him and gave him a quick peck on the cheek. "She seems nice," his mother whispered hopefully.

Hanson grinned. "I think so too."

His mother hugged and pecked Samantha on the cheek also before she left the room.

Samantha walked over to him, and she slipped her arms around his waist. "What were you and your mom discussing?"

Hanson looked thoughtfully at the door. "The usual. Nature versus nurture. How is the son shaped by the father?"

Her eyebrows shot up. "Heady stuff. Any conclusions?"

"Yeah. A mother's work is never done."

She smiled at that and then kissed him. They stood there and held their kiss for a long time.

"Are you okay?" she asked when they both came up for air. The beeping on the monitor had kicked up several notches, and he kept his hand on the pole to steady himself.

He studied her for a moment.

"Are you okay?" he asked.

A haunted look crossed her face.

"I am," she finally answered. "Taking a life, it's something I never thought I would ever do. But yesterday, I remembered what you had said —not to think of your opponent as human. At that moment, I didn't think of him as a person. I thought of him—"

"As a thug," Hanson finished.

"It helped," she said quietly.

"Well, I, for one, am glad that you did so," Hanson confessed as he kissed her again.

The door burst open, and Fisher strode in.

"Elica is on her way to the airport," Fisher announced as he pulled off his mask. "Is our boy still awake?"

Hanson disentangled himself from Samantha.

"I'm awake," he replied.

"How're you feeling?" Fisher asked.

"I'm all right," Hanson answered. "But I do have a question. Are Samantha and I okay with the law?"

Fisher held up a reassuring hand. "You two are fine. Texas has strong self-defense laws. If a person thinks that an innocent is about to be killed, lethal force can be used."

Hanson breathed out a sigh of relief.

"Just don't leave the state anytime soon though," Fisher continued. "You both still have some official interviews to go through."

"How are things on your end?" Samantha asked.

Fisher frowned. "About as well as can be expected. Even though it's clear that five hundred men were prevented from killing five innocent hostages, there are still many questions to be answered. And with a huge cloud containing the ashes of thousands of Texans drifting over Dallas, a lot of people think it could have been handled better."

Hanson could see the worry in Fisher's eyes. Much of this was going to come down on him.

"Wait a minute," Hanson said. "Ashes. I saved that. I have Tranquil Grove's files on everyone interred there, so at least that information isn't lost. Where my stuff?"

On the opposite side of the room, across from Kali, was another counter. Hanson could see the saber lying on it. He scooted over, and he also found his phone, wallet, flashlight, and thumb drive. He picked up the thumb drive and held it up triumphantly.

"What's that?" Fisher asked with some hope now in his voice.

"Would it help your situation if you were the agent that in one day solved over five thousand homicides? A list of not only the victims but details on the perpetrators themselves."

Fisher's eyebrows shot up.

"I also saved the data from their British years. How. Where. When. You'll be able to clear all of that up also."

"Interpol will be interested in that," Fisher noted.

"I saved everything, Fisher. I also found information on how they pulled off the hijacking of Avian 951 so fast," Hanson continued. "They had several emergency protocols in place, contingency plans to deflect law enforcement agencies on all levels. They could have taken down a nuclear power plant, or cause Wall Street to crash."

"Steve, what about that file marked as *Lopee Hona*? The file that means 'to conceal'?" Samantha asked.

"Their dark web connections. With this, your cyber department now has information on criminal websites that had been hiding from you all these years."

Hanson handed the flash drive to Fisher.

"There's one more thing," Hanson added. "I also had access to their bank accounts. Money that could ease the pain for a lot of people and help with the clean-up. On that drive are details on how to access their cash, ten billion dollars."

Fisher's jaw dropped a little. "I hope it's password protected," he said.

"It is," Hanson replied. "The program called for a robust one, ten characters, at least one capital letter, a number, and a symbol. I settled on the obvious. *Space:1999*."

"Your favorite sci-fi television show is the password to billions? It figures," Fisher said.

Behind him, Hanson heard Samantha whisper. "Every. Seven. Seconds."

Hanson grinned at that. "We still need to binge watch it. I have both seasons on DVD!"

Fisher was making his way to the door, acting as if Hanson was going to start the show in the next few minutes.

"Yeah…um…soon," he replied as he opened the door a bit. But then he paused.

"But I do have one last question," he said. "It's about those diamonds."

Hanson quieted down.

"Everyone saw them on the television. And when Samantha talked about the Cresswell papers on the news, she's mentioned them as well. Everyone knows you rode the lift down with them."

Hanson didn't say anything, though he fidgeted a bit.

"The police asked the boy about it. He's told them he didn't know—his eyes were closed most of the time."

"And you're wondering if I took them?" Hanson asked. "Come on, man. The place was about to explode in five minutes. I had other things on my mind."

Fisher remained by the door and stared at him. Hanson fidgeted some more.

"Okay, I had to ask. I'll see you two later." The door shut behind him.

Hanson shuffled over and peeked out. He watched Fisher enter an elevator. Satisfied that he was gone, Hanson hustled back to the counter.

"Where are my pants?" he asked.

Samantha looked at him questioningly.

"You know, the ones with all of the pockets."

"Steve, you were soaked in blood. They had to cut your clothes off you."

Hanson looked in the garbage can.

Realization was beginning to dawn on Samantha.

"Oh Steve, don't tell me—"

"Yeah," Hanson answered glumly as he picked up the flashlight and pressed the button. It remained dark.

"At least they saved your broken flashlight," she continued as she tried to lighten the mood. "What's wrong with it, the bulb?"

"No," Hanson answered as he unscrewed the cap. "It's the batteries."

He upended the flashlight tube. Two large diamonds tumbled out of it.

Samantha gasped.

"They must still be in the pants," Hanson finished with a grin.

Samantha picked them both up. Her hand moved up and down a bit.

"Haven't you ever held diamonds before?" Hanson asked.

"I have," she answered. "I've just never held any that had such...heft."

She gave them back to Hanson, and he looked them over closely.

"I couldn't tell Fisher. He'd be obligated to report them," Hanson explained.

"Where did the thugs get them?" Samantha asked.

"Wherever they came from, it's lost to antiquity," Hanson answered. He placed one of them in her right hand. Her eyebrows arched.

"A souvenir," he said. "All that remains of thuggee."

She held up the diamond up to a light and smiled. Then a worried look came across her face. "You know, all major diamonds have unique names," she said. "What do we call these?"

Hanson didn't respond.

"Maybe we could call them the Binary Stars of India," she continued.

Hanson reached out and closed her hand around the diamond.

"The Sweat of Kali," he replied.

She frowned but then shrugged. "Well, I guess beggars can't be choosers," she replied as she put hers in her pants pocket.

Hanson was placing his diamond back into the flashlight.

"I'm just glad it's all over," he said.

"You really don't know, do you?" she asked.

"Know what?"

She studied him for a moment more and then walked to the two large windows that ran from floor to ceiling. They were covered with vertical blinds. She opened the set closest to her and gave him a "come hither" look.

With a bit of trepidation, Hanson slowly walked over as he wheeled his medical equipment with one hand and kept his gown closed with the other. Finally, he joined her at the window and looked out.

Below him was a parking lot filled with news vehicles, a forest of radio masts and satellite dishes rising from them. Cameras mounted on tripods lined the sidewalks. Reporters noticed he was at the window. Cameras and phones swiveled his way.

Hanson stepped away a bit.

"Where did they all come from?"

"From all over the world," Samantha answered. "And they're all here for one purpose. To interview you."

"Me?" He couldn't keep the fear out of his voice.

"Steve, it will be all right," Samantha replied. "You've faced down the thug's Goddess of death and destruction. This can't be worse."

A thought occurred to him. "Wait a minute; I promised you an exclusive."

"I remember."

"So that means I only have to talk to you, right. You and I, all alone in a room together."

"I like the alone in a room part. The network is putting me up in a nearby hotel," she replied as she moved close to him. "Tonight, after you get out of this hospital, you could—"

"Come over and get exclusive together?" Hanson finished as his face neared hers.

They kissed, and once again, his hospital monitor went wild. Finally, they parted, and she made her way back to the door.

"Well, I've never heard 'exclusive' used as a euphemism before, but yes. I'll see you then."

The door closed and Hanson stared at it for a moment, forgetful of his surroundings. His robe parted behind him as he used both hands to wheel the monitor back to his bed.

And in the parking lot below, the world watched.

Epilogue

New York, 3 months later

"Should I put these magazines out?" Lijaun asked.

Dr. Jacob Gordon took a moment to wipe the fog from his glasses before he answered his receptionist. Outside, it was cold and crisp, and a new blanket of snow covered New York. And since decorations and lights had yet to be taken down, it still looked like Christmas.

She had a half dozen publications in hand. She handed them to him, and he looked them over. Unlike the cliché, Gordon regularly updated the magazines in his reception area. However, since the events of Dallas, Texas still dominated the news, he had to be selective of what he put out.

"No, I don't want him, or his mother, to see any of these. They could be harmful to the boy, and she may seek help elsewhere,' he answered.

A science magazine was on top of the pile. It had the headline THE DAY THE INTERNET BROKE: HOW IT HAPPENED! Below that was a fanciful illustration of smoking computer server farms across the United States. Inset was a small photo of someone's naked ass—the image grainy as if it had been taken from a distance.

Gordon's shoulders shook a bit as he snorted at the memory. Steve

Hanson had been all over the news for the entire month of October as he gave interviews to every media outlet there was. As a psychologist, Gordon could tell the man was an introvert, and all the attention was killing him. After his time in the spotlight, the rumor was Hanson had retreated to the Northwest to hole up in his home with his cats.

Gordon shuffled to a national news magazine. A photograph of Samantha Ramsell behind a news anchor's desk dominated it. A banner headline—AND THERE YOU HAVE IT—was splashed across the top.

Samantha Ramsell's catchphrase from the end of her nightly broadcasts. That was a story in of itself. A few days after the events in Dallas, a viral video began making the rounds on the web. It contained side-by-side comparisons of Ramsell and the network's heir apparent, Jennifer Steel. The contrasts of the two women had been glaring. The video had wrapped up with a clip of Ramsell not wanting to show young Ryan's impending death. That was followed by Steel shouting, "Someone start shooting someone!" to the crowd behind her. The internet's response had been overwhelming, and Samantha Ramsell was now the replacement for Doug Morgan. Steel, and her producer boyfriend, were fired in the network shakeup that followed.

Ramsell was already garnering the highest ratings ever for evening news broadcasts. Television audiences felt they could trust her. It also helped she wasn't a diva as Steel had been. So far, her only request had been that she wanted six students from a Texas University to be part of her news team.

The cover had several other headlines that spoke of the fallout from the thug incident. Homeland had mishandled the whole affair, and heads were rolling. An FBI agent from Oregon, Daniel Fisher, had helped with the case, and he was currently breaking records for solving cold murders. People were guessing that whatever he wanted to do in the future, he would be able to write his own ticket.

A small headline mentioned Conyngham's legislation being tabled. The legislator was fading into the background, his presidential bid unlikely at this point.

Gordon glanced at the next magazine cover. This one indirectly involved him.

It was an entertainment publication. On it, two women stood back-to-back, their arms crossed and serious, yet sad, expressions on their faces. One was a tall redhead, the other an Indian. Behind them, a statue of an evil-looking Kali loomed.

Camilla Blackbourne and Samaira Vankatesan, stars of the hit reality shows *Thug Wife* and *Confessions of a Thug Wife*. Both series had roughly the same format. In each episode, the wives would discuss what they were doing while their husbands were out of town. Then, by using captured data from thug computers, the producers reenacted the murders. Chilling scenes of thugs standing over the bodies of their victims while asking their wives to cook their favorite meals when they returned home were typical.

Though the ratings for both shows were astronomical, many people were outraged that the two women were profiting from murder. Moreover, they wondered how much the wives knew, and for that matter, how much did the sons know?

And that's where Gordon came in.

It was the boys who everyone was most curious about. How far along were they to becoming killers like their fathers?

History played a part in everyone's concerns. When Sleeman had captured thugs, he was left with the problem of what to do with the sons. Since he reasoned that murder was in the boys' blood, there was no hope for them. They had to be contained but productive. The School of Industry was born, where the boys toiled for most of their lives—paying for the sins of their fathers. People today were clamoring for the same thing. The boys must be contained.

Gordon put the magazine down and frowned.

Not if he could help it.

A dozen of these boys were in New York. Several hundred more were spread across the states. All were patients of psychologists to determine if they were a danger.

Gordon was convinced they weren't, and this was an opportunity that couldn't be passed up.

Though the phrenologists were wrong about skull shape, they were on the right track. Serial killers were different from the rest of society.

Most had lower resting heart rates, and low orbital cortex activity was another marker.

Gordon was excited. Members of his profession had over two hundred boys to test, boys who came from generations of murderers. Proposals were underway to have their brains mapped by MRIs to find out if anything made them unique.

And even if the boys were predisposed to killing, they could be taught *not* to kill. Nature versus nurture. These cases could put an end to the age-old question. Nobel prizes could be won.

And he was a part of it.

He looked at his watch. One of those boys was here now. He approached a door and knocked before he let himself in.

The large space he entered was designed as a child's playroom. Colorful wooden boxes held toys for various age groups. Tables with materials for drawing and painting were placed against the walls. Several comfortable chairs, and a couch, were positioned around a coffee table in the middle of the carpeted room.

At first, he didn't see his patient, a boy of fourteen years—short for his age but possessing a handsome face like his father. Then Gordon heard grunting noises from behind the couch, as if someone were struggling to breathe. He walked deeper into the room.

Jayesh Vankatesan was kneeling behind the couch with two action figures in his hands. One doll was fashionably dressed and known for his role as a mild-mannered boyfriend. The other was a soldier wearing combat fatigues. Jayesh was play-acting with them, and one toy had a small ribbon in his hands and was busy strangling the other. The noise that Gordon had heard was the boy making his own sound effects for the killing.

Jayesh looked up in surprise when he detected Gordon behind him. But instead of looking guilty at being caught at his play, he smiled instead.

"Hello Dr. Gordon, how was your Christmas?" Jayesh asked.

Gordon was thrilled. Jayesh had been a patient of his for the past ten weeks now. During that time, the boy had been polite and talkative but reticent about his father—or anything to do with thugs. This was a breakthrough. Gordon had to admit to himself that this was something he had wanted to see. He was even thinking about placing the toys in the boy's hands several weeks ago, just to see what Jayesh knew, but he realized that was wrong. Sometime back in the eighties, social workers had made that same mistake and contributed to a satanic scare.

"I had a very nice Christmas, thank you, Jayesh," Gordon replied as he sat down in a soft chair. At sixty years of age, it felt good to rest. He continued to watch his patient at play.

Though the military action figure was known for never losing a fight, the debonair doll had the upper-hand and was strangling the soldier. Gordon shook his head at himself. He had thought it was the other way around. Gordon belatedly remembered reading something about sepoys being some of the thug's favorite targets.

Satisfied that the right toy had prevailed, Jayesh put the action-figures down and sat across from Gordon.

"My holiday was just okay," the boy admitted as he looked straight at Gordon's face.

Gordon nodded in understanding. Jayesh still reeled from the trauma of seeing his father killed on television. That scene had garnered millions of viewings and was still popular on the web.

"Do you want to tell me about it?" Gordon asked.

And Jayesh did. He related his past week while Gordon sat back and took notes. Interacting with the boy was a pleasure. Gordon had other patients, children who were continually distracted by their phones or lacked basic social skills because of their screen time growing up.

These sons of thugs had grown up without phones for most of their young lives. As a result, their social skills were much more advanced than other children. A study could be made from that fact alone.

A clock on the wall showed that almost an hour had passed.

"Our time is almost up, Jayesh, is there anything else you want to share with me?"

Jayesh looked hesitant, and his eyes cast about the room. Then, when he looked back up, there was the barest hint of tears in his eyes.

"I'm lonely, Doctor," Jayesh confessed. "I haven't seen my old friends for a long time."

Gordon understood. The boys were being kept separated to limit their influence on each other. He could see the pain on Jayesh's face.

Jayesh continued. "I know you see Kyle right after me, and Lee sees that other psychologist."

The two other boys who visited his office complex, ages twelve and thirteen. The spirit of Christmas was still in the air, and Gordon made up his mind.

"I'll tell you what, Jayesh. Next week, I'll keep you around for an extra fifteen minutes and have Kyle come in a bit earlier. I'll also ask Dr. Augustus if Lee could come in early also. So, you can all meet in here for a few minutes."

The boy's face lit up. "Thank you, Doctor!"

Gordon smiled back. He was also excited. He was curious to see the boys interact in a controlled environment with him observing. With a grunt, he stood up.

"I'll check to see if your mother is here, Jayesh. Continue your play if you want."

Jayesh nodded and moved back behind the couch.

Gordon stopped at the door, finding it difficult to keep a professional detachment as he watched Jayesh. Being the Christmas season, he had gone to church, which he used to do every Sunday, but now, only twice a year.

His church visit two days ago had reminded him of his Christian upbringing, so he felt some measure of alarm as the boy resumed his thug role-playing. He liked the child, cared for him even. And though he was a man of science, he was also a Christian first. He couldn't let this other God prevail.

Gordon knelt. "Jayesh, did your father ever tell you what sin is?"

Jayesh looked up, wide-eyed, and shook his head.

Gordon was pleased that Jayesh was listening. Lately, the boy always looked at his face while he was talking to him. It was refreshing to see since distraction ruled in this day and age. "It's a great wrong, a great evil in the eyes of the Lord. And murder is amongst the greatest of those evils."

* * *

Jayesh nodded this time as he faced Dr. Gordon. He liked this man; he was always nice to him. But lately, he had to keep his expression neutral as he looked at him.

It was the mark over the doctor's brow that held Jayesh's attention. His father had always told him that if he believed, genuinely believed, in Kali, he would see that mark and understand.

Unknown to his mother, Jayesh had been to Dallas. He had tasted the goor. But he had yet to take the final step—to take a life with Kali as witness. She had been sated by the death of hundreds of Her thugs, but now Her hunger was growing once again. And since his father was dead, he realized that he would have to wait for the right moment and make arrangements on his own.

And that moment would be soon. He looked in awe at the doctor's face. His father had once shown him the Hindi word for death, and that word was now emblazoned across Gordon's forehead, each letter on fire. His fate was set. Kali had chosen him.

But the good doctor was a crafty man skilled at detecting lies. His father had told him that to gain the trust of such men, you had to reveal a little about yourself first. That was why Jayesh had played with the toys. He knew Gordon would be excited about that.

"Murder is a sin, and God punishes those who sin," Gordon continued with concern in his voice. "Do you understand?"

And now the doctor was asking him a direct question. Again, Jayesh remembered his father's advice. Couch your lies in the truth.

Jayesh put down the action figures and stood up. He smiled at the weak old man in front of him.

"I'll be all right, Doctor. I understand about God. I have no worries about Him," Jayesh answered honestly.

He turned away and grabbed a box of Legos off the shelf, their rattle masking what he whispered next.

"She'll forgive me."

Afterword

Real or imagined?

That was the question that I faced when I began writing this story. Like most people of our generation, I was first introduced to thuggee with the movie *Indiana Jones and the Temple of Doom*, which depicted them as a blood-thirsty cult that sacrificed to Kali and sought to raise their Goddess to true power. Thuggee was further ingrained in my mind a few years later when I read John Canning's anthology *50 True Tales of Terror*. In the chapter on thuggee, Canning wrote of highway robbers tricking and slaying hundreds of thousands of victims on the roads of India. Killing in the name of Kali before finally being put down by the British.

Record books estimated their victims at over a million. These numbers boggled my imagination back then, and the concept of thuggee rattled around in the back of my mind for thirty years before I decided to write a book about it. So, since it had been a while since I had investigated thuggee, I started my research by sitting down in front of my computer and looking up online what new information could be found. What I discovered took me by surprise.

Thuggee wasn't real.

I grabbed the sides of my monitor in panic when I read that. My murderous villains on which my tale hinged were a figment of someone's imagination. I had no story. In desperation, I combed through articles on the web, looking for something to hang my novel on. I discovered that historian Mike Dash had published a nonfiction book, *Thug, The True Story of India's Murderous Cult*. I purchased it and read it in a couple of days. Dash spoke of another historian, Kim A. Wagner, and his work, *Thuggee, Banditry and the British in Early Nineteenth-Century India*. I ordered up that one and read it also.

Both books were compelling and took on the theory as mentioned above—that thuggee had never existed at all. That it was entirely made up, a boogeyman conjured by frightened East India Company officials, a "colonial construct". Another theory was that it was a calculated scare tactic to help cement EIC control over India. Dash and Wagner both took closer looks at the reams of reports recorded by the British and others. They sought to read between the lines and glean what truth they could find and determine if there was indeed a form of thuggee that existed.

Their conclusion was that it did, though blood-soaked cultists were replaced by murderous bandits. Men who killed for plunder and loot, and not for the Goddess Kali. Men who murdered through deceit and strangulations, not by ripping out flaming hearts as in the movies. Thuggee, and how I viewed Sleeman and Kali, changed and evolved for me—and my story with it.

Equally fascinating was that even with the mountain of documentation from that era in India, no one still can entirely agree with what thuggee was. As I researched online, I noticed that the Wikipedia article on thuggee was evolving before my eyes as different factions sought to control it. Other online articles had various historians calling out other historians as they pointed out each other's flaws in research and conclusions.

In the end, it came down to what I believed about thuggee myself. I don't presume to know all the answers. In the broad spectrum of Sleeman's version of a thuggee infested India on one end or no thuggee at all on the other, I find myself somewhere in the center with Dash and Wagner. A place that, though it doesn't have blood sacrifices in dark temples, still has ample frightening details to write about—such as killers who pretended to be your friend and then strangle you when you least expected it. And then bury your mutilated corpse so that it would never be found.

Chilling stuff. I've saved the worst for last. Besides *Ramaseeana*, Sleeman contributed to a second book on thuggee, with the drier title *Report on the Depredations Committed by the Thug Gangs of Upper and Central India*. Published near the end of the thug campaign in 1840, in it Sleeman extolls his successes but also laments his failures. He noted that many thugs escaped his net and fled to military service with nearby Indian and Mughal rulers. He concluded that thuggee, the most secretive murderous cult in all of history, would never be entirely destroyed, writing that: "All these persons would return to their old trade, and teach it to their sons, and to the needy and dissolute of their neighborhood, and thus reorganize their gangs should our pursuit be soon relaxed."

Think about that for a moment.

I did.

Acknowledgments

I want to start by thanking my family.

Dad played a large part in how and where the story climaxed. It was a week before Memorial Weekend, and I was almost finished with my research. But I had yet to figure out where the final confrontation would be. I was leaning toward inventing a vast Hindu temple somewhere in the United States and placing the thugs in a hidden base underneath. But then mom and dad showed up for a visit, and dad, who had just done some research on some long-lost deceased relatives, expressed his desire to take a trip to a columbarium to pay his respects.

I knew columbariums focused on storing urns instead of caskets, but I had yet to visit one, so I tagged along. While dad drove, I brooded over the third act of my book. Finally, we arrived, and since we were the only visitors at the moment, we were given a key, a map to our ancestor's final resting places, and left to our own devices.

We let ourselves into a large building. Due to watching spooky movies, I was expecting dreary halls and dark shadows. Instead, I was pleasantly surprised to find the columbarium beautiful inside. The upper floors were spacious, and stained-glass windows and marble statues decorated the halls. Skylights provided bright, cheerful light. Urns with ashes of the dearly departed rested in ornate niches.

The relatives we were searching for had passed away decades ago. We consulted the map provided to us, and we realized that older generations rested in chambers on lower levels. So, we took the stairs down, and we soon found ourselves in darkened rooms with light switches in odd places.

Dad had a penlight, and he searched for our relatives amongst the hundreds of niches that held the urns. I remained in the center of the room. During the entire trip, I had been preoccupied with the final third of my story, at a loss on how to end it.

That changed.

My brain was exploding as I stood there in the dark. In just a few moments, while surrounded by the ashes of thousands, all the remaining pieces of the puzzle of the story I was working on fell into place. A cascade of ideas melding into one cohesive whole. This novel was born at that moment. What happened that day makes sense to me now, for the story is about Kali, and the cremation grounds are her home. And when I returned to my house, I jumped on my computer and began writing the story that was now trapped within my mind.

So, thanks, dad.

My brother and sister Mark and Steph have always supported me in my endeavors, as did my mother, who recently passed away. Their unquestioning faith has meant much to me.

Also in my corner is my daughter, Maggie. My pride and joy, and the reason why every day feels like Father's Day. I love you very much.

I also wish to thank everyone on social media that have been encouraging me ever since I published my first book, *UFO*. Thanks again for your attention and kind words.

Four friends have stood by me since the eighties, enduring decades of *Dungeons and Dragons* fan fiction. I thank Craig, Mac, Ron, and Tim for their support and insight into the story. Extra recognition goes to Mac. When I finished the manuscript, I sent it unedited to him (all 170,000 words of it, or more than twice the recommended length for a thriller novel). So, thanks for reading that, Mac. At least you know what Hanson eats for breakfast.

And again, special thanks to Joyce for her support and contributions to the novel. The story is peppered with her corrections and suggestions, and I, and the book, are better for it.

A lot of research went into the writing of this novel. Most of the information I found on thuggee came from several historians, and I would like to give credit where credit is due. From Mike Dash, there is *THUG, The True Story of India's Murderous Cult.* I also read several publications by Kim A. Wagner. First is his book *Thuggee, Banditry and the British in Early Nineteenth-Century India.* Wagner also has several academic papers on the subject, and I focused on: *In Unrestrained Conversation: Approvers and the Colonial Ethnography of Crime in Nineteenth-Century India, Confessions of a skull: Phrenology and Colonial Knowledge in Early Nineteenth-Century India,* and *Thugs and Assassins: New Terrorism and the Resurrection of Colonial Knowledge.*

And, of course, no book written on thuggee would be complete without consulting William Henry Sleeman's *Ramaseeana, or, a Vocabulary of the Peculiar Language Used by the Thugs.*

Kali figures prominently in the story. For more in-depth information on her, I turned to an anthology titled *Encountering KĀLĪ, In the Margins, at the Center, in the West,* edited by Rachel Fell McDermott and Jeffrey J. Kripal.

A note on Kali. To the men of the East India Company, Kali, and the worship of her, was a threat to their rule—and also a strong female presence that challenged the patriarchal sensibilities of the Victorian missionaries arriving on India's shores. To combat her, British colonizers spread misinformation about her, and these lies and exaggerations still color how the west views her today. The cover of this book was purposefully designed to reflect that: a sexualized and dangerous blood-thirsty demon set to destroy all things good.

She's not like that, and though I wrote this novel to entertain, I also hope to inform and that you, the reader, come away with little more understanding of that which we know little.

I have put together a team to assist in my self-publishing, and I would like to thank those people also. First, there is my beta-reader Amanda Nicole Ryan, whose feedback is always much appreciated. Second, for the interior layout of the book, I turned to Brady Moller at Fiverr. Like my previous novel, *UFO,* the inside of this book looks fantastic.

And third, I wanted something provocative for the cover, and I turned to the crew at Moorbooks Design. They knocked it out of the ballpark.

And finally, I have gratitude to you, reader. I hope you enjoyed the story.

About the Author

Award-winning author Matt Andrus is an enthusiast of the weird and unusual. As a child growing up in the 1970s, he was drawn to books and documentaries detailing paranormal events such as The Bermuda Triangle or creatures such as the Loch Ness Monster and Sasquatch. And though evidence to explain away these classic mysteries continues to surface, he feels that behind each one, there is still an adventure to be had. To that end, his *The Unexplained, Explained* series is designed to both inform and entertain with vivid storytelling. He currently resides in the Pacific Northwest. Visit him on Facebook, Twitter, or at his website: www.mattandrus.com to follow him or leave a book review, which is always much appreciated.

www.ingramcontent.com/pod-product-compliance
Lightning Source LLC
Chambersburg PA
CBHW061049210726
48294CB00001B/77